PENGUIN BOOKS

THE
EXILED

Sarah Daniels is a former archaeologist who escaped academia and now writes stories from her home in rural Lincolnshire. Her work has been published in various online magazines and has been nominated for Best British and Irish Flash Fiction and Best Small Fictions. *The Exiled* is her second novel, and part of an unputdownable duology.

THE
EXILED

SARAH DANIELS

PENGUIN BOOKS

PENGUIN BOOKS

UK | USA | Canada | Ireland | Australia
India | New Zealand | South Africa

Penguin Books is part of the Penguin Random House group of companies
whose addresses can be found at global.penguinrandomhouse.com.

www.penguin.co.uk
www.puffin.co.uk
www.ladybird.co.uk

Penguin
Random House
UK

First published 2023

001

Set in 10.25/15.25pt SabonLTStd
Typeset by Jouve (UK), Milton Keynes
Printed and bound in Great Britain by Clays Ltd, Elcograf S.p.A.

The authorized representative in the EEA is Penguin Random House Ireland,
Morrison Chambers, 32 Nassau Street, Dublin D02 YH68

A CIP catalogue record for this book is available from the British Library

ISBN: 978-0-241-50805-3

All correspondence to:
Penguin Books, Penguin Random House Children's
One Embassy Gardens, 8 Viaduct Gardens, London SW11 7BW

For every working-class kid –
turns out we are allowed to be authors.

PART ONE

EXILE

Midnight. Sunday 13 March 2095

The temperature is currently -2°C. I expect it to drop further before the sun rises again. Current rations provide 1,500 calories per person per day.

We are the survivors of the cruise ship *Arcadia*. I believe we number more than a thousand. We've made it through a sub-zero winter with almost no fuel and the most basic shelters.

If you're hearing this, please let me know that you're still coming.

The Coalies could attack at any moment.

We need you.

Days in the camp: 120

1

ESTHER

My face stares back from the opposite wall of the alley. Even at midnight, I can make out the white glare of my skin, the eyes scratched out. Above my picture, in block capitals, the text reads **MOST WANTED**.

When the first posters appeared in the camp, people were convinced that Janek hid surveillance cameras in the eyes. No matter how many times the Coalies replace them, they only survive a few hours. Before long, someone brings a crowbar or a shard of glass and slices through the eyes until all that's left is tattered paper and brick dust. The vandalism's a blessing in a way. It means I don't have to look myself in the face.

I blow into my hands. *Come on, Pat. I'm freezing my butt off down here.*

This alley leads away from the quayside shipyards, through the maze of warehouses and backstreets, and all the way to the other side of the camp. The red-brick buildings scrape the sky, but at ground level they're filled with abandoned dumpsters and rats. As soon as we'd caught our breath after the Landfall mission went so disastrously wrong, we started mapping out the territory. It took us weeks to feel out the edges of the place. To understand what we'd been left with.

Pat's footsteps clomp down the nearest alley, getting nearer, and the next second he comes into view. He's wearing all black and carrying a holdall across his back.

'All clear?' I say.

'Let's go a different way.' He walks past me without slowing, glancing at the poster I've been staring at for the past five minutes.

I don't move. 'Why do we need to find another way?'

'I scouted the alley for booby traps, but there's a corner at the top of one of the buildings I couldn't get a clear view of. I don't want to risk walking through it in case there's a trap hidden up where I can't see.' Pat carries on down the alley, away from the section of fence we need to get to. When he realizes I'm not following, he stops.

I fold my arms. 'Don't lie to me, Huang.'

'Like I'd dare.'

'You didn't mention not being able to see when you checked for booby traps last night. Or the night before that.'

The air crackles with frost, and Pat's breath streams out in a cloud. 'I'm telling you: I can't see well enough now. Let's go.'

I stare Pat right in his distractingly attractive face and look for signs of lying. Because he is lying. This is the path we've taken every night this week. The routine always the same: him going ahead to look for booby traps. Me hanging back in the shadows, wearing a patched augmented-reality mask to disguise myself.

I spin on my heel and make for the alleyway he's trying so desperately to keep me out of.

He grabs me by the arm, not hard enough to hurt. 'Esther.' His face pleads with me, and for a millisecond I think about obeying.

Damn you and your cute face, Patrick Huang.

'We've got a job to do. If we don't make it to the fence in time, we'll miss our window. That's the quickest route. Tell me what's up there.'

He relents. I stride along the backstreet. The shadows bleed away as we walk, and there's the familiar tumble of rats running in the darkness. At first, all I see is the same industrial architecture as always: brick-lined ground, metal fire escapes, blank doors. Everything brutal and lifeless. My breath catches when I see why Pat tried to put me off. There's a new wanted poster. It shows Nik as he was when we first met. Hair slightly too long. Cocky grin on his face. Our eyes are untouched. This time, someone has daubed a word over us in red paint, so thick it runs in lines over our faces: TRAITORS.

I bite the end of my tongue between my teeth and try not to let Pat see the flash of pain.

'They don't mean it . . .' Pat whispers.

'There are more?'

'All the way along this stretch of warehouses.'

'Let's find a different way,' I say.

Pat's new route takes us down to the edge of the water. My heart rate triples when I catch my first glimpse of the *Arcadia*. It lies exactly where it fell four months ago. Half out of the water, straddling the ocean and the dock like a leviathan. Its anchor chain – the individual links as long as my leg – hangs from a hole in the front of the hull. Each rope dangling from the rail is a reminder of someone who went into the water that day. The smell of rotting seaweed and seawater taints the air. As always, I keep my eyes away from the blackened area at the back of the ship. That's where the fire spread from the captain's office, eating up deck after deck.

The ship obliterated this section of dock when it ploughed into it. The prow sliced through the concrete, churning it up in great slabs. The rubble extends in all directions. As we pass in front of the debris, I can't block out the sounds the ship makes. The structure creaks with the movement of the water, wails echo round its metal hulk like death cries.

Pat checks me with a glance, but doesn't say anything. He knows being this close to the *Arcadia* triggers memories. *A flash of red, a body drops to the ground.*

When we finally turn a corner and the *Arcadia* slips out of view, the tension in my body lessens. We trudge uphill along an alley until we're as far from the ship and the ocean as we can go.

After I crashed the ship, people ran for their lives, but the Coalies fenced off a stretch of the coast with terrifying speed. Hundreds of us were trapped inside a finger of land less than five square miles. They didn't even seem to care what was inside the fence, as long as we couldn't escape. So we ended up with a handful of derelict industrial buildings and empty factories and a long slice of beach and sand dunes that are now covered in tents and hastily thrown-up shelters. Silas Cuinn claimed the far end of the camp. I've had no reason to enter his territory and have no intention of changing that. Silas saved me from Hadley last year, but I'm not stupid enough to think that makes us friends.

The fence surrounding the camp billows in the breeze like a sail. It's made from some sort of silky mesh that's so thin I can only see the shape of the road and the abandoned buildings on the other side. There's no way to climb it. The gaps in the mesh are too small for even the smallest fingers, and the fact that it moves around makes getting a grip on it impossible. Tonight, that might change.

Pat swings the holdall off his back and unzips it. I turn off the AR mask to ease the tension headache it brings and hug myself to keep warm while Pat gets our gear ready. It feels below freezing tonight, a fact that makes my chest tight with grief. Tomorrow, we'll check the tents and cardboard hovels of the camp to see who didn't make it. We'll carry their bodies to the sandy place we've set aside as a graveyard.

My stomach rumbles, and my mind is dragged to the mealy chocolate-style protein bar nestled in the pocket of my uniform. Not yet. Wait a couple more hours.

'Ready?' I say, looking up at the fence. I've tried climbing it. And I've tried going underneath. And I've tried cutting through, which was the worst option because damaging it brings the Coalies, and then you have to run for your life.

Pat's standing a few metres along the fence, his back to me. 'We've only got five minutes until the next Coaly patrol comes this way,' he says, walking back to me. 'Let's give it a miss.'

'No. The reinforcements might arrive any day. We've got to be ready if General Lall tells us it's time to fight.'

Pat bends down to fasten a set of pads over the tops of my

8

boots. 'Last time you said you could still feel the shock from the fence, so I've made the material thicker. It should do nothing but tingle now. And I tightened the strap around the wrist too.'

'Good. Can we get on with it?' I say.

I need something, just a tiny win against the people keeping us here. More importantly, I need to know that there are ways through this barrier when the time comes.

'You'll be complaining if you get shocked again.' He tightens the Velcro on my kneepads.

'Keep an eye out for bots while I'm climbing. And I think we might have a visitor,' I say, nodding towards the end of the buildings where a small shadow watches us.

I walk as far from the fence as I can get, tensing and releasing my hands.

'Attempt ninety-three,' Pat says. 'Remember: make contact and pull downwards so that the micro-hooks go through the mesh.'

'Got it.'

My back's pressed against the brick wall of an abandoned warehouse, so cold I can feel it leaching through my uniform. Pat arranges a wooden box halfway between me and the fence. I take a breath and hold on to the moment of stillness. I run. Pushing myself off from the crate, I hit the fence and lose all hope. It billows away from me like I'm trying to climb a bedsheet. Then my knee catches it, and I manage to grab a section with my hands, and I clamp my knees, my ankles on to it. I'm suspended halfway up, swinging.

'Yeah!' A high-pitched voice comes from the alleyway. 'We did it!'

'Go to bed, Dylan,' I call, making no attempt to mask my irritation.

'I can help. Look, I got all of these,' he yells. His footsteps echo closer in the darkness.

I twist round so that I can see him, and get a swirl of vertigo. I'm only a few metres up, but I still don't fancy the fall. Dylan wafts a bag back and forth, and I know without asking what's in it. Wanted posters printed in black, white and felony red.

'Try bringing your knee slightly up before you move away from the fence,' Pat says. I can tell he's standing with his arms crossed, like he does, and that Dylan will be copying him movement for movement.

I do as Pat says and feel the pad on my knee reattach. Dylan lets out another whoop of triumph. 'She's doing it!'

Excitement forces me upwards. By the time I reach the top, I'm panting and sweaty, but this is the highest we've managed to get and, as far as I can tell, we've not tripped the security system.

Without the haze of the fence to obscure my view, I can see further and clearer than at ground level. There's a short stretch of broken tarmac, a few knotty, leafless shrubs, then the train track and a line of saplings. Everything's bleached colourless by the thin street lights, dusty with frost. There's an abandoned trailer, tyres flattened against the ground. This territory that the Federated States has temporarily *gifted* us is a wasteland right on the edge of its capital city. It'd be poetic that this is where they've decided to keep us if it wasn't so soul-destroying. In the distance, a bus trundles along the road towards us, turning before it's close enough to make out any details. I can just see the distant twinkling lights of the first high-rise buildings of downtown. We're so close to the life of the city, I can almost touch it. I wish I could go further. Haul myself over the top and run and run.

'Next patrol will be here in two minutes,' Pat says.

'Just another second.'

I take a breath and try to drink in the details. I might not get this far out of the camp again for a while.

'You got any food?' I hear Dylan say somewhere beneath me. The kid's hungry 24-7, which isn't surprising. Eleven-year-olds should be eating three full meals a day. He's lucky if he gets anything at all.

'Will you go home to bed if I feed you?' Pat asks.

'Cross my heart,' Dylan says.

'I've got a protein bar,' I say. I take one arm off the fence and rummage in my pocket with my free hand, pulling out the foil-wrapped rectangle. I toss it. Dylan makes a clean catch, tears into the wrapper and shoves the whole thing in his mouth at once.

'Better?' I ask.

He nods. 'Better.'

'Now get lost,' Pat says to him without unfolding his arms.

'Hey, Dylan,' I shout after him.

'Yeah?'

'Thanks for tearing down all those posters.'

Dylan grins and makes finger guns at us as he jogs backwards, before turning and sprinting into the darkness.

'What's the betting he doesn't go straight home?' Pat says, half to himself.

Above my head, something catches my eye. Silvery, thin

as money spiders' silk. 'There's something else up here,' I say.

'Describe it.'

'Looks like a wire. Goes all the way along the top of the fence.' Something that thin can't be dangerous. I stretch up to it.

'Esther, don't touch –'

Before my finger even makes contact, a charge shoots through my hand, through my arm, through my head. A burst of static blinds me. Then I'm on the ground, eardrums trilling so loud my whole body vibrates.

I open my eyes to a cloud of stars. Pat's face is in front of me. His eyes are all tight with worry, and his mouth moves like he's talking, but I can't hear anything. He looks along the fence, and his face crumples in fear. Then he's pulling on my arm.

I force myself up. The smell of burning follows me, and there's pain, dull and all-encompassing. 'What happened?' I croak. My brain feels like breath on a mirror.

'What happened is you can't leave things well enough alone.' His voice is stern as he pulls me into the nearest alley.

I'm struggling under my own weight. My legs bend beneath me. Pat manoeuvres us into a doorway so that we're barely sheltered by a fire-escape staircase.

I put my head back against the wall. 'What's that smell?'

'That's the smell you make when you're set on fire.'

'I touched the wire,' I say. 'It hurt like hell.'

'That's what two thousand volts will do for you. And I *think* you triggered the alarm system. They'll be here any second. If we can get a couple of alleys away, we'll lose them. Reckon you can walk?'

I push my back into the wall and lift upwards. My legs wobble. There's a strobe of light near the fence. Dread trickles down my spine. 'Go,' I whisper.

Pat puts his finger to his lips. He shakes his head and reaches his hand behind my ear, bringing us eye to eye so that I can smell the earthy jasmine tea his mum brews on his breath. His fingers move around in my hair until he finds the flat button that activates my AR mask, and I feel the tightening ache of it round my temples, see the blue haze wash over my eyes. Now my face is disguised by the holographic image of someone else's. It's not high-tech – this model is so old it sometimes glitches off, revealing my true face, and it doesn't cope well with facial expressions. It won't help if the Coalies get near enough to look closely.

I try to make myself small, pulling my knees to my chest. Pat turns off his torch. This is the worst game of hide-and-seek ever.

We close our eyes.

I hear them coming. Boots on cobbles.

Sitting like this, not seeing, not breathing, every sound is magnified. A set of footsteps scuffs on the stony floor. I sense the light wash over us. *Please. Please.* We're a pile of blankets. We're discarded trash. The footsteps draw closer. Any second now, the beam of the torch will strafe over us again, and this time it will stop, and they'll find us. What comes after that I don't know. We'll be disappeared just like everyone the Coalies snatch from the camp.

There's a shout. The footsteps stop. My moment of relief turns to horror because that was Dylan's voice. I want to scream at him to run. I want to shout, 'No!' because everything's on its head. He shouldn't be doing this – distracting them. We're the ones who should be protecting him.

The footsteps clatter away from us.

2

MEG

Ice water splashes over the sides of the boat, soaking through my thin gloves. My skin tingles with salt and cold, and I can feel the burn of it gathering in the corners of my eyes. My hair – grimy after so long in the cells – clings to my face like seaweed. I ignore it. The only thing I can think about is reaching dry land.

'Cold out here, isn't it?' I say to the bloke driving the boat. 'Bet you're not cold in all that get-up though. Doesn't look like the water's getting through those gloves. You've got a definite style, you lot. Very gothic.'

He ignores me. I rub a layer of salt water off my face, feel the flecks of it like acid on my lips.

Hey, Seb, I'm almost home.

There's a tingle down my spine. 'Creepy old thing,' I say out loud, forcing the feeling away and keeping my eyes on the *Arcadia*. Half sunk and tilted on to its side. It could be a rock through the blue haze of dawn. Already there are gulls circling it, their nests of straggling twigs and flotsam making it even more carcass-like, and I can't help but think of rotting flesh.

'It wasn't creepy when I was a kid. It was home,' I say, half to myself.

Talking out loud seems to take the edge off the memories. My voice somehow stops me from being haunted. It's not that I'm scared of Mum and Dad's ghosts or anything. It's just sometimes I feel as if the sea's not really finished with me. Like I could still drown. The moment I saw my parents' bodies lying blueish and stiff in the morgue was the moment I agreed to help the Feds with their plan. And, in exchange, I'll be able to talk to Seb in real life, not just in my head.

'You talk too much,' the Coaly says.

'You can hear me then?'

'Shut up.'

I pinch my lips together. When it comes to the Coalies, I've learned that you keep your mouth shut.

I've not lost my marbles. But that was a long few months alone, Seb, and talking to you kept me going, didn't it? Those moments when I thought I wasn't making it out alive.

I'm going to do whatever it takes to get back to you.

We lurch over a wave, and I clamp on to the side of the boat. They gave me a life jacket before we set off and showed me how to inflate it using the plastic fob on the front. Even so, I don't fancy taking a dip.

'Get ready,' the Coaly says.

His thick-gloved hand is wrapped round the tiller. My view of the ship disappears as he manoeuvres us to face the shore. The boat slows before we hit the breakers, and when the Coaly cuts the engine we rise over quiet humps of water. It's almost peaceful in the early hours.

There are lights along the shore. Handfuls of them close to the ground at the edge of the camp, more spilling from the tall buildings close to the *Arcadia*. Can't tell from here, on account of the bad light, but I remember from the plans that the camp has tents and shacks in this middle section, and big warehouses down the city end. I should head for the warehouse end. Ask the right questions and I'll find what I'm looking for.

'This is where you get off,' the Coaly says.

What? I lean forward and peer down into the murky ocean. No bottom in sight. We're close to the shore, but there's still a wall of breaking waves between us and the beach.

'Go a bit closer, mate,' I say.

He's unflinching. Like he won't be budging a single centimetre.

'Your lot banned swimming when I was a kid. If you plonk me in the water here, I'm going to drown. And I'm guessing it'll be you who's questioned when my body washes up, won't it? Go closer.'

The Coaly's head tilts like he's thinking. He grabs me by the top of the life jacket and uses his fat fingers to pull the cord. It shushes as it balloons. He pulls me to the edge, and I scrabble, my boots skidding over the boards. I will myself to stay in the boat, fingernails tearing at the edge as he hoists me over.

Seb, I'm scared.

For a second, I'm hanging over the ocean, staring into my own pale reflection in the Coaly's visor. Then I'm tumbling, underwater, the sea shocking and ice-cold and everywhere all at once so that it feels like the universe is made of frost. Loud and silent.

I won't scream, Seb. I won't let them beat us.

I force myself to relax. I hold my breath in the dark water. The life jacket tightens round my shoulders. All I have to do is let the thing pull me up. My head breaks the surface and I splutter through streaming water. Somewhere in the distance the boat's engine is whining away from me. That Coaly left me without a backward glance.

I float on my back and breathe deep, air like ice filling my lungs, waves lifting me up and down. Then I bat my arms in the water until I'm facing the right way.

There's the *Arcadia*. There's the camp.

3

ESTHER

I wake to the sound of canvas flapping above me and sunlight seeping through the tent door. My body aches. Feels like I'm crackling when I move. I close my eyes and breathe, wanting just a few more seconds of rest.

'You're awake,' a woman says, ducking her head under the flap of the tent beyond my feet.

'Mrs Huang, I –' I start to say.

'You nothing. Lie yourself down until Patrick has had a look at you. And if I've told you once, I've told you a thousand times: it's Niamh.'

She places the tray she's carrying down on a low table by the door, then pokes her head back out. 'Patrick, your friend's awake.'

Pat appears in the doorway. He sees me and smiles. 'Having a lie-in, are we?'

'Your mother threatened me with violence if I tried to get up,' I say.

Mrs Huang pours tea from a pot, adds a spoon of something,

and places the cup in my hands. I prop myself up to take a sip. It's spicy and hot. I can feel it soothing my muscles.

'Is Dylan safe?' I say.

'He got back here about an hour after us. Spent a while running in circles to shake the Coalies off before that though,' Pat says.

'Wish that kid would listen when we tell him to go home. He shouldn't be out at night.'

'He's got no one to look after him. My mum's tried, but he's as wild as they come. It's rich coming from you anyway. How many times have I got to tell you not to touch anything that looks suspicious?'

'It won't happen again.'

'We both know it will. Because you seem to have a problem taking other people's suggestions, even when it's for your own good.'

'I had enough of taking orders on the *Arcadia*.'

'Like I'd be stupid enough to try and give you an order. Maybe take some advice once in a while.'

Mrs Huang unfolds her arms and says something in Cantonese to Pat. He replies, quietly, over his shoulder. Mrs Huang dips out of the tent.

'She's hates me,' I say.

'Hate's a strong word. She's angry at us though. She can't understand why I got out of the gang if I'm going to put myself in danger trying to find a way through the fence.'

'Maybe she has a point,' I say.

He sits down and leans forward on his elbows so that we're face to face. 'I didn't leave Cuinn's gang because I'm scared of a fight. I left because some girl persuaded me the enemy we need to be fighting is the Coalies.'

'She sounds like she's got genius-level intellect.'

He breaks into a grin. 'Oh, she does, does she?' Pat slides his hand under the blanket and takes mine. Warm and steady.

'We should be careful for a few nights. Coalies might increase their patrols after we set the alarm off again,' I say. 'I'll go north instead. Carry on mapping the fence up there.'

Pat leans away and takes a sip of tea, looking at me through the steam. 'And what am I supposed to do while you're out having fun?'

'You can mess about with whatever little project you're working on.' I look over his shoulder to where there's an upturned crate being used as a workbench, the surface cluttered with broken machinery and wires.

'Little project? I'll have you know I've got some very complicated explosive devices in the pipeline.'

'Good. Because when help arrives, we're going to need all the firepower we can get.'

'I don't want you out there alone. Skip tonight. I'll come with you tomorrow.'

'I'll be careful,' I say.

'Obey this order: drink your tea.'

'You need a haircut,' I fire back. He laughs and pulls the blanket up over my waist, tucking it in round me.

There's a yell outside.

'Stay there,' Pat says. He dashes out.

I kick the blanket off, push myself up, pause a second to check my balance, then take the three steps to the door. Pat and Mrs Huang are just outside. I blink in the sunlight, even though it's grey and overcast. Pat stretches his arm round my shoulder to hold me up, and I lean into him. It's nice to feel the warmth through his sleeve.

'Told you to stay in bed,' he says.

'Didn't want to miss the excitement.'

A group of kids are huddled round an upturned saucepan on the ground. Dylan's among them, a feverish grin on his face. He spots me and waves. From inside the saucepan, there's a sound like rain on metal, and the kids jump back, screaming and running in circles like midges. Mrs Huang laughs. The adults gathered around shout in Cantonese. Either spurring the kids on to be brave or heightening their play-terror, I'm not sure.

The pan goes quiet. Dylan creeps towards it, touching the handle gingerly with the end of his wind-bitten fingers. As soon as he tilts it up, there's a flash of metal leg under the edge, and then the sound reverberates again. Dylan drops the handle and runs off, squealing. Everybody laughs.

'Go help him,' I say to Pat, nudging him with my shoulder.

'OK, listen up!' he shouts, walking into the midst of the kids. 'First off, I don't see a single one of you with your face covered. What's the first rule of dealing with a surveillance bot?'

'Don't let it see your face!' the kids chorus.

'Good. Now, everybody grab a weapon! Whoever stuns the thing gets a lucky dip in the gummy vitamin jar!'

The kids are gone before he's even finished the sentence, grabbing bits of driftwood and long sticks, covering their faces with whatever bits of clothing they can find. One comes back waving a cricket bat in the air.

Pat kneels next to the pan. 'Remember, just one whack. We don't want to kill it because it'll send a distress signal. Just stun it. Three, two, one, go!'

He swings the pan out of the way. Underneath, the pointed metal legs of the spider surveillance bot scrabble in the sandy dirt. Its body spins, trying to record the situation for whoever's reviewing the footage. The kids don't give it a chance. Pat leaps out of the way as they try to wallop the bot. He stands back, breathing hard, and flashes me and his mum a grin. The bot has been engulfed in seconds, and a loud thunk with the baseball bat tells me someone landed a good hit.

'Someone got it. Now, what do we do once it's stunned?'

'Pull its legs off!' one of the kids shouts.

'We pull its legs off. You have to grab it right here,' Pat says, and he takes it by the edge of its body like he's holding a crab and lifts it into the air. Its legs squirm. In a flash, Pat uses his free hand to grab one of the legs, gives it a neat twist and pull, and tosses the leg on to the ground. The kids are feral with excitement.

'There's more and more of them inside the camp,' Mrs Huang says.

'And not much we can do, other than destroy any we get our hands on.'

'It's a wonder General Lall keeps letting the Coalies breach the ceasefire terms. It's almost as though she's turning a blind eye to what's going on in here.'

I look at Mrs Huang in surprise. This is the first time she's been so blunt about the rebellion. I open my mouth to reply, but she cuts me off with a wave.

'I've been meaning to have a chat with you for a few weeks

now.' She looks at me sideways, and there's no flicker of a smile on her face.

My cheeks flush. The pop of anxiety in my chest gives me a sick feeling.

'My son likes you,' she says.

'I like him too,' I say before I can stop myself. She raises an eyebrow.

Pat's twisting another leg off the bot.

'I'd rather you didn't. I'd rather he stayed half the camp away from you and the trouble you drag after you.'

'I'd never put him in danger –'

'You already do, every time you take him off trying to get out of the camp. Every time you talk to him in public when you know full well you're the most wanted seventeen-year-old in history. While we're on the subject, you put the rest of us at risk too, every time he brings you back here. That AR mask does next to nothing to disguise you, glitching the way it does. Everyone knows who you are.'

The hair on my neck prickles. I look round at the adults in the group. Some of them are glaring at me. An old woman whispers behind her hand to the person next to her. Mrs Huang's right. I'm the guilty one, and I'm putting them at risk just being here.

'Are the rumours true? Your lot are working on something again?' she says. Arms crossed. Just like Pat.

'I can't talk about it,' I say.

'I'll take that as a yes.' She gets closer to me. 'Didn't you do enough the last time?'

I swallow the lump in my throat. My mouth's drier than the sand dunes.

'Aye, at least you've got the decency to look ashamed. Do us all a favour and leave our Patrick out of it. He'll be better off without you. You can stop coming round here as well.' Mrs Huang saunters away and into a tent beyond the kids.

I want the ground to swallow me. It's all true. I'm the reason these people are here. I'm the reason so many aren't here too.

'The final step is to bury the body so that the camera can't send anything back to the Coalies,' Pat shouts to the kids.

Mrs Huang re-emerges with a bottle of gummy vitamins. 'Now, who got a good hit in?'

'Me! Me!' the kids shout. They swarm her, reaching grubby fingers into the bottle one by one.

Pat pushes his way through to grab one, then comes and hands it to me.

'Thanks,' I say, popping it into my mouth. I chew. It's strawberry, but tastes like sand in my mouth.

'You OK?'

'Sure. Look, I'm going to get back. Corp will be wondering where I am, and I don't want to put her in a bad mood.'

'I'll come too.'

'No, stay here. Looks like they could use your help finishing that thing off,' I say, nodding to where the kids have lost control of the bot, and it's spinning on the dusty ground, carving circles with its last remaining foot.

'Two ticks,' he shouts. He jogs back to the gang of kids and drops the pan back on top of the bot so that they can carry it off easily.

'Wait,' Pat says, hurrying after me. He grabs my hand and pulls me to a stop.

'See you later, OK?' I say.

'Not OK. What have you got going on that means you're trying to ditch me for the day?'

'It's not that,' I start, and even though I don't mean to, my eyes flick up to where Mrs Huang is standing.

'Did my mum say something?'

'She's just worried.'

'Can't believe she actually said something to you. I asked her – I told her – to mind her own business.' He crosses his arms and shoots a glare at his mum.

'Shhhhh, don't. I don't want to cause any problems between you.'

'Let me guess. Was it *we don't need your kind of trouble round here*?'

I take a deep breath and let it out in a shudder. 'That, and I'm leading you astray apparently.'

'For God's sake, Mother,' he mumbles.

'She's got a point, Pat. We almost got caught last night, and it wasn't the first time. My face is plastered over half the camp –'

He takes my hand, and I let him hold it between us. He runs his thumb over my knuckles. 'You don't get to decide for both of us.'

'What?'

'I'm not going to let you do the whole cutting-me-off-to-protect-me thing. It's a bit cliché, to be honest.' He pushes my hair off my face. I feel my cheeks redden.

'Your mother's watching,' I say.

He turns round to where Mrs Huang is still glaring. 'Let's get out of here.'

26

The Exiled

As we leave, Mrs Huang shouts after us.

Pat waves back at his mum and shouts something that sounds like the start of an argument.

'What did she say?' I ask.

'She told us to stay out of trouble.'

4

MEG

My legs are shaky from the walk along the wet sand, and my stomach's grumbling like an old boiler. Least my clothes have pretty much dried out. Was a stroke of luck finding this fire. When I smelt smoke, I poked my head through a door and saw it not ten steps inside this warehouse. People are sleeping and sitting round it, and I thought, *Shove this. I'm too cold to be polite.* When I crouched down next to it, nobody said nothing so I've been sitting here for a while.

Once I'd got my breath back and pulled myself out of the water after that bloody Coaly chucked me in, I made for the silhouette of the ship in the distance. First, it was just beach. Then there were lines and lines of tents. Some things that weren't even as nice as tents. Tarps held up by planks and fastened down with beach rocks. People snoring inside. Babies crying.

By the time it was fully morning, the sand had given way to gritty concrete, then some buildings that had seen better days. Now I'm in amongst the warehouses. Huge things like cliffs. Some of them don't even have windows, just brick walls that go up and up into the sky. I recognize it all from my training. Handcuffed to that chair in the bare cell, watching hour after hour of footage. Video of the ship crashing. The hull filling with water. The bodies in the water.

I stretch my fingers closer to the flames and wiggle them. An old man's pottering around, clanging pans and generally messing about. He's all wrapped up in a blanket, and every now and again he's taken by these long coughs. Sounds like he's bringing up a lung.

I make myself small, trying to look timid and unthreatening so that he doesn't throw me out.

He pushes a pan of water into the embers of the fire, all blackened like it's been used a million times. Even though it's daytime outside, it feels like twilight in here. The glow from the fire tapers off, then it's just shadows and darkness. I get the feeling the space is so big it'd make my stomach flip.

After a few minutes, the water starts pinging in the old man's pan, and he scatters in a sachet of dried milk and throws in a teabag. He stirs it with his finger – all knotted with arthritis and cracked from the cold – splashes a bit into a bowl, and hands it to me.

'Thanks,' I say. It's not much more than manky water, but it's hot, and it's better than nothing.

He slurps. His face is all saggy like he used to have more flesh on his bones, and the jowls hang in stubbly layers.

'I'm looking for someone,' I say when he's halfway through his tea.

He wipes his mouth on his sleeve. 'Lots of folk in here,' he says.

That gives me the creeps. I don't want to think about all the others that are lurking inside. Someone shushes us from a dark corner and turns over under their blanket.

The man pulls a long ribbon of paper from a box beside the fire. There's a flash of a boy's face in black and white before the man stuffs it into the bottom of the fire. He blows on it until the flame catches, and the paper crinkles to ash.

'The people on the wanted posters, what did they do?' I say.

He eyes me suspiciously. 'You ask a lot of questions. Don't take kindly to snitches in this warehouse. If that's your game, you'd better get off before we deal with you.'

Next second he's on his feet and shambling into the dark. Bloody hell. Spooked him. I don't want to spend any longer in the camp than I have to, but if everyone's as tight-lipped as this old geezer it's going to be tricky. Thought people would help me. Maybe I really am on my own.

'If someone's missing, you need to check the wall,' a voice says from the shadows, crackling with phlegm.

'What wall?'

'Wall of the missing. You know, the big thing in the Pit with all the pictures on it? Now, get lost so that we can sleep.'

'Fine,' I say. 'This place is a shithole anyway.'

5

ESTHER

By the time we get to the coastguard station, the only physical reminder of falling from the fence last night is a sensation of thinness that stretches through my muscles. Much worse is the gnawing guilt over what Pat's mum said.

I clench my fists until the nails bite into the palms. This wasn't how it was meant to be. Things were supposed to be better after we got off the *Arcadia*, but now we're all haunted by it. It sits sideways in the water, and I've tried to shake the memory of her, but the moment I rest or close my eyes, or stop moving for even a second, it all floods back.

Her face is pale with shock. Dark waves all around. Metallic smoke. We have to go . . .

I'm trying to loosen her grip, and I'm drawn to the thought of the little white envelope I keep wrapped in my spare pair of socks and stuffed into the bottom of my med bag. The two blue pills that I'd find if I opened it.

I squeeze my eyes closed, and when I open them again I force myself to scan the horizon for signs of Coalies instead of dwelling on the *Arcadia*. I've no idea if they'd come by land or ocean. Across the water, the sun is insipid through the milky morning haze. Almost the entire population of the camp lives in the southern area, where they huddle in the shelter provided by the warehouses. Corp and I live here, in this abandoned coastguard station, halfway between the buildings of the main camp and the territory that Silas Cuinn has claimed. Forced to live in isolation because it's too dangerous for us to live with the others.

Silver lining – I can barely see the ship from here. Having it loom over me was a constant reminder of what I did, so when General Lall ordered us out of the main camp I wasn't entirely sorry. At least out here there are moments when I can ease the guilt by pretending the wreck doesn't exist.

Pat kicks his boots against the bottom rung of the ladder, showering sand, and starts to climb. For a second, he disappears, then his head peeks back over the top.

'I'm fine,' I say, ignoring the hand he stretches down to help me. I instantly regret my tone.

'Esther,' he chides.

I reach to him and let him pull me up, feeling the strength and roughness of his hand.

Pat goes inside. I hear the creak-slam of the station house's front door. Even after two months here, I can't bear to call this place home. It's always the coastguard station, or just *the place*.

At the top of the ladder, I pause to listen to the soothing crash of the waves nearby. It's a strange building made of bleached planks the colour of weathered bone. The back portion of the building was built right into the sand dunes;

the front sits out over the water on stilts as thick as tree trunks. It straddles a wide ramp that leads down to the ocean – a relic that would once have launched coastguard boats in an emergency. When we arrived, some of the walls were so decayed we had to tack tarps over the gaps to make it weatherproof. It still shakes and howls with the wind.

Inside, Pat has already hung his jacket by the front door and left his boots neatly on the shoe rack, a sparse layer of sand covering the wooden floorboards. This is an equipment room, full of the old clothes that were left behind when it was abandoned. It's all so antiquated none of it can be used. Hundred-year-old jackets hang like ghosts on the walls, grey with dust and cobwebs. There's a pile of boots in one corner, an orange float attached to a rope, a first-aid kit, empty apart from the wrapper of a long-ago-used plaster.

I take the rickety stairs up and cross the landing to the kitchen-lounge-dining area. You can imagine the coastguards making their dinner up here, watching the ocean for signs of trouble out of the windows at the front. Down the corridor there's a bunk room and a shower room where the only running water is chunky and brown. There's nowhere to put a clinic, and no resources even if we did have the space, so we do rounds of the camp every day and treat patients wherever they lie.

Corp's standing by the camping stove that's our only source of heat, and the hollow smell of gas tells me she's just boiled the water. There's a cup of tea going cold on the counter next to her, and I get the feeling she's been staring out of that window a good long time.

'You decided to come back,' Corp says finally, turning. 'I take it you've been at the fence again.'

Without thinking, I stand to attention and sense Pat straighten next to me. A throwback to my time on the *Arcadia* when Corp gave the orders. I never got out of the habit.

'I ordered him to help me,' I say.

'You don't have any business ordering anyone to do anything,' Corp snaps back.

'She did not,' Pat says.

'Let me handle this,' I say.

'I don't take orders. In fact, I persuaded her to go. Esther said it was getting too dangerous after we set the alarm off last time. But I'd finished the gear I was working on, and I wanted to try it out.'

'I don't care whose idea it was. I gave you clear instructions to stay home.'

'This again,' I mutter.

'Watch your tone, cadet.'

Corp's face is rigid and, despite the fact that we're a million miles and half a year from the training room on the *Arcadia*, my heart thumps with anxiety. I could never handle being given demerits by Corp.

'Or what? You'll stop me treating people with the medical supplies the Federated States don't give us? Rescind my access to the state-of-the-art medical facility we haven't got?'

'We do what we can,' she says, smooth, quiet. Chilling. 'Trust that General Lall will tell us when it's time to take action.'

I clench my teeth and drop my eyes. Corp looks out of the window.

'Did they answer last night?' I say.

Corp sighs. Her expression softens, and I know she's going to deliver bad news. 'I tried every frequency used by the rebellion. No reply.'

Every night, I get my hopes up; every morning, my heart sinks a little deeper.

'We have to consider whether there's anyone left out there to hear the transmissions,' Pat says quietly.

Corp catches my eye. I know all three of us are thinking the same thing. What happened on the *Arcadia* changed everything. While Nik worked on rebuilding the ship's engine, his counterparts on the other stranded ships were doing the exact same. But once we started the *Arcadia*'s engine the gig was up. Pretty soon the Coalies realized if it could happen on the *Arcadia* it could happen on any of the ships still anchored along their coastline. Within months, every ship that could start its engine made a break for it. Each night, we listened to the old radio Corp had found in the coastguard station. Celebrating when ships made it to open waters. Crying on the day the radio suddenly went quiet.

If the radio is silent, it could mean all the ships are gone. Maybe they've left us behind. Maybe they're all dead. My heart breaks thinking about either.

Corp clears her throat. 'General Lall persuaded the other ships to come back for us. As soon as they arrive, we'll have enough firepower to mount a coordinated uprising. Until then, any risky behaviour threatens the course of action we've worked hard to outline.' She looks pointedly at me. 'And, if you need it spelling out, that includes breaching the fence, being caught on Coaly surveillance feeds in the Pit, or asking questions about missing family that might flag you as a wanted person.'

At the mention of looking for my family, I feel my hackles rise in rebellion. 'It's taking too long. What if the other ships don't get here in time? The Coalies could decide to attack us at any moment, and General Lall's got us here twiddling our thumbs. She should be happy we're out there, looking for ways to escape.' My voice creaks with emotion.

'Our orders are to wait. General Lall is coordinating the arrival of the reinforcements and then –'

'How long do we carry on doing nothing?'

'General Lall would have informed us of any change to the plan. We keep trying to contact the other ships. We wait for orders. Nothing's changed.'

'It's been two months.'

Corp takes a step forward and squeezes my shoulders. 'As long as there are sick people in this camp, we'll carry on treating them. Hold your nerve, cadet. Our best chance of escape is waiting for the others to get here. Understand?'

'We're losing people that we shouldn't be losing. Are you happy watching them die?'

'Take it easy,' Pat says.

I bite my tongue, and the silence thickens like soup.

Pat folds his arms. 'Esther got electrocuted.'

I snap my head round to look at him. 'Not helpful, Pat.'

'You might have concussion.'

'Did she fall?' Corp asks, then she's standing close to me again and looking too deep into my eyes.

Nobody here looks at each other too closely any more. It's too painful to see other people wasting away, too humiliating to know they see it in us too. Instead, we skim the surface. Keep each other at arm's length.

She runs her hands over my skull, presses her fingers to the cervical vertebrae at the top of my spine. 'That's just great, Esther. Because what's going to help is if there's one less medic in the camp. Pat, you're off duty for the rest of the day as punishment. Go to bed.'

He looks like he's about to argue, then shakes his head and marches out of the room. I hear him slam the door to the bunk room down the corridor.

'Go and collect our rations. And consider this an order: wait until John has left before you go to the handover site. Do not *accidentally* bump into him. Do not go to the Pit. Do not make enquiries about your parents. It will attract attention, and we can't afford for any of us to be arrested. This is your final warning, cadet. Disobey me again and I'll take your med bag and ask you to leave this facility.'

'You'll throw me out?'

'Without hesitation. You can stay in one of the warehouses with the other civilians. Perhaps you'll learn to be a little more appreciative of the things we've got.'

'Appreciative –'

'We have more than most people here.'

'And Lall is expecting us to keep this entire camp of malnourished people alive with a few multivitamins and wishful thinking. What is she doing exactly? Has she had any contact with the other ships? Because from what I've seen she's happy to sit in her warm headquarters, flying in and out on her helicopter and having endless chats with the Coalies.'

Corp takes the cup of tea from the counter and throws it in the sink. Liquid glugs down the plughole. 'The reason we're here and not in headquarters is that we're a security risk to ourselves and to the rebellion. Obviously, General Lall can't let either of us have information that we might pass to the Coalies if we're arrested. We've got to trust that she's doing everything she can to bring help.'

'I can't have this argument again. I can't keep saying we need to act. I can't keep being told to wait,' I say.

Corp's staring out of the window again. 'You're right.'

'Hang on. What?'

'I said you're right. We can't wait forever. But the general won't see us. We can't get into headquarters. Unless someone answers the broadcasts, my hands are tied.'

She walks out. Her feet thud on the stairs, and then there's the distant sound of the front door closing. Ten seconds later, her coatless figure strides away from the coastguard station, treading a line between the beach and the shallow water.

I sense Pat next to me. He knits his fingers with mine, and we watch Corp get smaller and smaller.

'I want to believe they're coming back for us,' I say.

6

MEG

By this point, I've got blisters on my blisters. I lean on a wall, and my fingernails dig into it. I pull off one of my boots and inspect the damage under my sock. There's a thick blister that jiggles when I poke it.

It's pretty miserable in this place, Seb. Worse than I expected.

It's taken me the best part of the morning, but I've walked from the waterfront to the other side of camp. I've had a good look round the warehouse my handler told me is rebellion headquarters – careful not to look suspicious, obviously. And I've asked no fewer than twenty people if they know where to find what I'm looking for. They're shut up tighter than clams. Can't decide whether the past four months has made everyone super paranoid or super loyal.

A scuttling noise comes from up the road, like feet on hard ground, then a group of kids appear. They march past in a procession, all of them raggedy and skinny. Every one of them has the kind of sharp cheekbones that come from not eating well enough, and their eyes are too deep-set in their faces. The one at the front is holding a bag in front of her, and it's wiggling like there's something alive in there.

A few paces past me there's a loud whistle, and the whole group of them swerves to the opposite edge of the street. All of them at once. They press their backs to the wall of the alley and shimmy along, looking exactly like they're trying to walk along a window ledge. Then, just as quick and at the exact same point, they jump back to the centre of the street and carry on their procession.

I lean back on the wall and watch them pass. The last one's a straggler, a kid of about ten or eleven.

'Oi, kid,' I call. He freezes with his back to the wall again. Both hands flat against the brickwork. 'What you got in the bag?'

'Cat,' he says. 'Going to the Pit so Nan Smokey can skin it for us.' He grins.

My stomach lurches. For everything I went through in those Coaly cells, I was never so desperate for food that I'd think of catching a feral cat. 'What's with the synchronized walking?'

'What?'

'Why'd you all flatten yourselves against the wall there? You playing a game?'

He looks at me like I've got two heads. Then his eyes shoot up to a place a metre or so above my head. 'It's the booby traps,' he says.

Dread drops over me like a sheet of rain. My handler warned me there'd be booby traps. They're meant to keep people's movements restricted to certain areas so that they'll be easier to round up. I got distracted by the bloody blisters on my feet and by the fact I haven't got any leads, and I forgot that I should be checking whatever streets I walk along. Craning upwards, I spot the orb of red glass attached to the wall.

Shit, Seb, this is a situation.

The kid's eyes come back to me. 'Sorry.' He jumps to safety, then jogs after his friends.

I trawl through memories of the time I spent with my handler going over plans of the camp. He said they were anti-personnel booby traps triggered by sensors when people get within range. And I've gone and walked right underneath one. How come I didn't set it off already?

I pull my coat up over my head and close my eyes. Can't stay here forever. The kids showed me where was safe, but that spot's a good few metres from here. I press myself against the wall, figuring that I might stay out of range if I'm flat to it. I inch along, the bricks scraping the back of my coat.

Right, Seb, I'm going to do it.

I jump. For a second, I reckon I've made it. Then something hits me with a thwump, and I smash into the ground. And I can feel something wrapping round my ankles. A thin rope over each ankle and at either end something that looks like a metal bar. Bitter panic coats the back of my throat.

'Don't wriggle,' a voice says. And then that kid is next to me on the ground.

'You came back,' I say breathlessly.

'Guess I'm a hero. Just stay still. Still as a statue. It's a snare trap.' He carefully unties my bootlaces like he's defusing

41

a bomb. 'Right. On three, I'm going to pull your boots off, and you whip your legs out, OK?'

I nod. He takes one boot heel in each hand. 'One. Two. Three!' The second he says three, I snatch my feet away from the lines. They suck flat against the ground like they're trying to catch me.

The kid grins. He holds my boots out to me.

'Cheers,' I say. I take the boots and stare at the kid. My heart's beating nineteen to the dozen. 'That was a close one.'

'No problem,' he says. He jogs away.

'Hey, what's your name, kid?'

'Dylan,' he shouts over his shoulder.

'You want some food?'

He freezes. Turns.

In my pockets, there's ten vacuum-packed meals. They were meant to be used as bribes, but so far no one's let me get close enough to even offer. I pull one out now and wave it in the air. Dylan watches the shiny foil package move back and forth. I toss it to him, then pull another one from my pocket. He looks like I've offered him the crown jewels.

Lured by the food, he comes back to me. I start walking away from the booby trap, following the direction the kids took. Dylan falls into step next to me and tears the top off the first silver packet. He pours cold soup into his mouth. It dribbles out of the corners and down his chin.

'How come you didn't know about the booby traps?' he says, mushing the chunky bits of soup between his teeth.

I shrug. 'I've stayed mostly in my tent. Just forgot where they were.'

'You should be more careful. There's traps everywhere

down this end of the camp. The fence is electrified too, and the Coalies patrol on a schedule so you have to be careful when they're coming round. You don't want to be trapped in a snare if they're on their way.'

He drops the empty silver package on the ground and burps. I hand him a second one and watch him tear into it.

'Lucky for me you were there. How come you know so much about everything?'

'Everyone knows where the traps are.'

At a crossroads, Dylan takes a hard left, and I let him lead me. By my reckoning, we're heading towards the Pit, the massive central warehouse that acts as the camp's market.

'No, I can tell you've got your finger on the pulse. Bet you know all the tea. Bet you know everyone. Bet you even know the rebellion.'

I shove my hands in my coat pockets as I walk. Need to be careful not to spook the kid, but he's so excitable he's willing to tell me anything.

'Course I do,' he says. 'I'm one of their best helpers.' He walks taller just talking about them.

'No way. So you know all of them? Like Nikhil Lall and Esther Crossland?'

'Not Nik really. But I know Esther and Pat. I'm always seeing them.'

Pat. That's a name I've not heard before. I make a mental note to pass it on to my handler. When the Pit comes into view, I stop and face the kid. 'Esther Crossland. Isn't she the one that crashed the ship?'

'Well, yeah, but she didn't have a choice.'

'Right. Well, I'd love to meet her.'

'Oh, you can't. She's been exiled. The Coalies are after her so she has to hide. Thanks for the food.'

'Thanks for saving me from that snare trap. I'm Meg, by the way, if you want to know whose life you saved.'

The kid beams a toothy smile at me. He sprints off into the Pit.

And I'm going to follow him like a bloodhound.

7

ESTHER

I sneak through the door marked FIRE EXIT. This is nothing more than a concrete box, the stairs reaching upwards, as cold inside as it is out. My eyes take a minute to adjust to the dark inside the warehouse fire escape. Against the opposite wall, barely three steps away, there's a big wooden crate where John usually places our supplies. I'm supposed to come once it's dark so that there's no risk of either one of us being followed. But I'm sick of waiting for our situation to change. This is purgatory. It's a living death. I need to do something because if I don't this is where our story ends.

John's not here yet. I settle down next to the box to wait. My vision's hazy and bluish from the augmented-reality mask, and it squeezes my temples like the start of a tension headache. I can't take it off though. It keeps me hidden from drones and surveillance bots, and from any real person as long as they're not looking too closely.

A little over two months ago, the first wanted posters went up. A week later, General Lall exiled us. Cut Corp and me off from everything and everyone associated with the rebellion. We were never allowed back into rebellion HQ. Enid pitched it as killing two birds with one stone: nobody spying on the rebellion would be able to turn us in, and we'd have no information to give up if we were arrested. Everybody's safe.

Nik was long gone by that point.

The door handle clunks downwards, the hinges creak, and a shaft of late-afternoon sunlight washes in. John's silhouette fills the doorway. This is Enid Hader's second in command.

'Afternoon, John,' I say.

He looks at me, gap-toothed mouth working on empty air. Then he runs.

'Dammit,' I mutter, and I'm after him. 'Just want to talk,' I shout.

John traces a path from the fire-escape door down to the sea. Over the salt-bleached sand. He's heading back towards the main camp, to General Lall's HQ. Up ahead, the first row of tents huddle against the ground, bright blue porta-potties dotted between them. I'll be able to keep track of him in the tents, but the second he gets among the maze of bigger shelters I won't be able to see him any more. Then he'll get into the proper streets between the warehouses and be gone. Once I've lost him, it'll be another twenty-four hours before I can try again. Or maybe he'll tell Enid I've been ambushing him to get info, and they'll find some other way to deliver our rations.

'Not allowed to talk to you.'

He throws the words over his shoulder so they come out stilted and breathless. He's fast, even with the leg I know was damaged in the explosion in the *Arcadia*'s market. He's getting away from me, but now we're heading for a low hummock of sand that he's going to have to run up. He slows as he reaches the top, and I launch myself at the backs of his knees, locking my arms round his legs. He shrieks and falls, and somehow we're both tumbling down the other side of the hummock, sand flying. He gets up, and I try to go after him, but the sand slips under my boots. My muscles are weak from undernourishment.

'I brought a bribe!' I shout.

John skids to a halt. He turns back to face me. 'Can't talk to you. Lall's orders.'

'You don't work for General Lall,' I say, panting.

I've got a stitch in my side and the kind of aching pain in my windpipe that comes from pushing your body too far. I rise shakily to my feet, holding one hand out, willing him not to run. I won't be able to chase him again. There's nothing left in the tank.

'Enid's orders too,' he says.

He's still protesting, but I've got his attention. I reach into my bag for the bribe I've been saving: a short cardboard tube that makes a grating rattle when you shake it.

'What is that?' he says.

His eyes are fishy-wide, with a tinge of grey film that warns of deepening cataracts. I'll get a closer look at those soon as I can. The last thing anyone needs in here is to lose their sight.

'Crisps. Still sealed.' I shake the tube so that John can hear it's full.

He makes a show of thinking, sticking the end of his tongue out of the corner of his mouth. 'You got until I've eaten them.'

'Deal,' I say, and I hold the tube out for him to take.

He drops the bag he's carrying on to the sand and plumps himself down. He peels back the silvery lid of the tube, gesturing at me with it to sit down.

'Enid will have my guts for garters,' he says, but at the same time he takes one of the pale crisps from the tube and munches it. He rolls his eyes upwards in pleasure. 'Take some,' he says.

'No, thanks.'

John's one of the few people I know who hasn't changed measurably during the hardship of winter in the camp. His thin-on-top, straggly mullet is as dirty as ever; he has the same amount of teeth as he did before the Coalies tried to clear the *Arcadia*. He doesn't even seem to have lost much weight, which should be impossible given how little there is to go around. He slaps wet lips together like he's drinking tea and stares across the waves.

'I need to talk to General Lall. It's important,' I say, launching into the same speech I give John every time I manage to pin him down.

'Well, you can't.' He takes my hand by force and places a neat pile of crisps in it. They're salty and greasy and so delicious they make me want to cry.

'It's about the other ships. We haven't heard from them in months.'

He stops munching and squints at me from the corner of his eye. 'Sorry. Can't get you in to see the general even if I wanted to,' he says.

'But you could get me a meeting with Enid, and Enid could get me in front of the general,' I say.

My fingers are throbbing from the cold. Instead of sating my hunger, the handful of crisps seems to have reminded my stomach what food is, and now it's grumbling violently. I shove my hands under my armpits and kick the sand with my heel, stamping the blood back into my rapidly solidifying toes.

John's shaking his head. I suddenly get the feeling that I'm not asking the right questions.

'Wait, is Enid in the camp?' I say.

He smiles, broad and gummy, jagged flecks of crisp crowding the corners. 'My lips is sealed, doc.'

My heart thumps. It's not unusual to see General Lall's helicopter flitting in and out, taking her to whatever diplomatic discussions she's part of on a given day. But Enid doesn't leave the camp unless there's a damn good reason.

I grab John's arm. 'Has she finally gone to get him?'

'That'd be telling.' He taps the side of his nose.

I bite down the mix of anger and hurt and joy that thinking about Nik Lall sparks in me. Just when I tell myself I've healed the wound he inflicted, he raises his ugly head again.

John's determined not to tell me about Nik, but he might talk about something else, especially now I've buttered him up with junk food.

'What's General Lall doing to get the reinforcements here? What's she doing about the food shortages? Does she think the Coalies will attack soon? Have you heard anything about my parents? Is anyone even looking for them?'

Is it my imagination, or was that a flicker of unease on John's face? I can't tell whether he's not allowed to tell me anything, or if there's nothing to tell. I haven't seen Mum and

Dad in four months. They'll be four months older. Four months greyer. Have they lost teeth? Hair? Their lives? Not knowing is the worst part. Some nights, it gets so hard that I wish for the bad news. I wish that John or Enid or even General Lall would come walking down the sand, a hard look on their face, and tell me that, in fact, my parents didn't make it off the *Arcadia*. At least it would be the end of this. At least then I could feel the rawness of grief.

Across the beach, the tide's going out, lengthening the gap between us and the ocean. The *Arcadia* is an other-worldly figure in the distance.

'When can we come back to headquarters?' I say.

John seems to waver. Then he tilts the tube and lets the final crumbs slide into his mouth.

'You and Corp can't exist. Corp on account of she's a government medic what went AWOL. And you on account of you took control of the *Arcadia* and crashed her.' He waves a hand in the direction of the ship, raising his eyebrows so that the wrinkles on his forehead deepen. 'Go home. Lay low. Don't go places you're not meant to be, nor asking questions you're not meant to be asking. In all likelihood, the Coalies think you're dead, and it's best all round if they carry on thinking it. Food rations for you lot in there.' He nods towards the plastic bag sitting on the sand next to him. It looks almost empty.

I scoop it up and push it inside my med bag, fastening the top tight. Don't want the Neath kids sneaking their hands in. By my reckoning, we're down to 1,250 calories a day. Not quite starvation rations, but not comfortable. A handful of rice, a few beans, some energy bars. If we're lucky and there's flour, Pat will make potstickers stuffed with seaweed and cook them over the fire. We'll snarf them down while the ashy bits burn our mouths. And maybe, with full bellies, we'll sleep soundly for a few hours.

'Anything good in there?' I say.

Suddenly I find I want to talk. Corp gets quieter and quieter the thinner she gets. Pat is a bright spot, distracting me from the fact that we're trapped by telling me about his next big idea to get us over the fence. But John is a connection to the real world, and I want to keep him here as long as I can. Maybe he'll let some nugget of information slip.

'You expecting Sunday dinner?' He laughs at his own joke.

I smile. 'I need Enid to get someone a job,' I say.

'Who's that then?'

'Dylan, the kid that hangs out round the Huangs' place. He's going to get himself into trouble trying to help.'

'Don't think you're in a position to be asking Enid for favours.'

'He's a good kid, and he's got a ton of energy. Just help me keep him out of prison, OK?'

'Fine. He can run errands up at HQ. Tell him to come in the morning.'

'Thanks,' I say.

The tension in my neck eases a fraction. With Dylan kept busy, he's less likely to run into any Coalies.

'There's families in Warehouse Eleven want some attention. Stop going to the Pit. You've got the essentials. I bring your food. You've got water. There's nothing you could need up there, and every time you sneak in you put yourself in danger.'

He's right: there is nothing I need. But there are things I want. To check the wall for news about my parents. To hear gossip, and ask people what's happening on the outside. To feel like life is carrying on, even though all I do is wait. At least in the Pit there's life to cling to.

John throws the empty crisp tube on to the ground. He heaves himself up, brushes the sand from his trousers, and starts off down the beach.

'Do we sit here until they subjugate us by force?' I say. 'How long does the general expect us to wait?'

John gives a tiny shrug. 'She doesn't talk about you, doesn't think about you from what I can tell. You're not even on her radar.' He turns his back and scuffs towards the main camp.

I trace my fingers up my neck until I find the control pad of the AR mask and flick it to on. The pressure in my head is instantaneous, spreading as quickly as the mask drops over my face. It's like wearing a too-tight hat. The world takes on a different hue that makes everything seem even colder.

The sun's still high enough that it picks out the landward side of the *Arcadia*. Gulls circle it like it's a whale carcass. I spent my first sixteen years trying to escape that ship. Now that the place I grew up on is gone, I feel the loss of it like a sinkhole has opened up inside me.

I face the far end of the camp where the coastguard station sits quietly against the sand dunes. Pat and Corp will be there. I can tell Corp about the people that need help in Warehouse Eleven. We can eat some meagre dinner together.

Instead, I turn for the Pit.

8

ESTHER

I lurk in the shadows at the end of a brick-walled alley. Three streets meet here, opening into a yard that's criss-crossed by flat metal rails. A relic left over from when freight wagons rolled in and out of the warehouses. The doors to the Pit are big enough to drive HGVs through.

This moment is one of terror. I have to make the decision to step out into the open, to expose myself to danger. To give up the shelter of the alleys and backstreets.

Before I can make my move, my AR mask blips. For a second, the world glitches with its real colours, and I know in the same instant my real face is visible to anyone looking. Sometimes, it just needs a refresh, but now is not the ideal moment. I pull the control screen from my pocket. An error message sits in the centre of the digiscreen. I hold the power button to reset it. Only the most cutting-edge technology here.

I'm still messing with the connection when Dylan sprints in front of the entrance to the Pit. He stops and talks to a girl

I don't know, then he's gone again, disappearing inside. The Pit is an echo of the market at home. On the *Arcadia*, the market was where you found people and food, and the kind of treats and comforts that make life brighter. There's life in the Pit too. Only harder, more desperate.

I stride forward, my face down even as my eyes are lifted and scanning for cameras.

Despite it all, my spirits are raised by coming to the Pit. Here, people take whatever they can find and turn it into something useful. It's like we're weeds growing back on the tiniest speck of soil. First, I'll find Dylan and tell him he's got a job. Then I'll go to the wall and look for traces of Mum and Dad.

On the upper storeys, the windows are devoid of light, the glass cracked or smashed. I'm looking for Coalies. I'm looking for drones. I'm looking for anyone or anything that might be a threat. Seeing nothing, I cross the yard, stepping over the rails that are like hardened arteries and dodging puddles of thick ice. The brickwork glints with frost already, and it's barely eight o'clock. Smoke pours from the open front of the Pit. It crackles in my nose and throat as I pass through the big rolling metal doors. In the weeks after Landfall, the Pit was colonized and grew into the cold heart of the camp. Whatever job this place used to have is lost to time, but the traces of it are everywhere. Doors marked with red EMERGENCY EXIT signs. Giant hooks hanging from the ceiling. Everything is hard and grey and rusted.

Inside, hawkers cluster round the fires lit inside metal bins; two dozen of them or more are dotted round the edges of the cavernous warehouse. Others have blankets laid out on the ground. Even with the fires, it's cold as the grave in here. I recognize some of the stallholders from the market on the *Arcadia*.

There used to be bread and dumplings and shellfish. Fresh fruit sometimes. And coffee. What I wouldn't give for a cup of watery coffee in the Lookout cafe instead of the awful stuff we get here. But the cafe owner drowned. And the market blew up. And there's almost nothing to eat here, no matter what you've got to trade.

The light from the lamp posts recedes the further I get into the Pit, the gloam gathering in the far corners of the building. I'm hit by the smell of roasting meat, and I close my eyes and breathe it in. Oily and charred. My stomach growls, the hunger so hollow and deep it feels like the oldest part of me. Remember, it's not what you think. There's no meat in the food deliveries from the Federated States. Whatever's cooking was caught here in the camp.

The smell's coming from a fire tended by a small-eyed woman with feathers braided into her hair, all salty and matted. She warms her hands over the flames.

'What've you got?' I say.

'Meat,' she says, and she shrugs like the exchange is too much effort for her.

My mouth waters, and I'm sick with myself. Across the top of the fire, skewered on thin sticks, are chunks of flesh. There's a foot with tufts of fur still attached. Fat hisses on the flames.

'How much?'

'One ration oil, one rice,' she says.

I nod and carry on walking towards the back of the Pit. I'm not desperate enough to eat what's being cooked here yet.

At the back is the wall of the disappeared. I don't know who started it – I suppose someone looking for the person they'd lost. Someone just like me, who still scans the faces of strangers, hoping for a miracle. The bricks are covered with pictures and descriptions of the people we haven't been able to account for. Someone's made a wreath from long blades of dark green seagrass. There are bird feathers and seashells and bits of tumbled beach stone all along the bottom of the wall. The only treasures people could find in the camp to decorate the memorial.

I start at one end, and look at each face in turn. Some are photos that must have been taken before the crash. Others are single sheets of paper with a name hastily scrawled on them. I've spent countless hours here. At the start, I imagined finding my own face on the wall. I imagined discovering that my parents had posted it, and that they were out there looking for me.

And it would be a lie to say I'd never thought about Alex. I've imagined it a thousand times. Maybe I'd bump into him in the Pit, or find him walking along the quayside. I don't know what I'd say if I did meet him. In my head, I walk away without a word. Or I run and throw my arms round him, feeling the warmth of him after so long. Or I shoot him dead on the spot.

'All right.' Dylan has appeared next to me.

I smile and turn off my AR mask for a second so he's sure it's me. 'Looking for trouble?'

'Looking for food,' he says.

'Aren't you always. I got you a job.'

'For real?'

'For real. But you have to promise you'll get better at taking orders, OK? Enid won't be pleased if you get into mischief when you're supposed to be helping.'

He hugs me. His bony arms pressing in beneath my ribs, squeezing me until I could cry. I kneel down and hug him properly.

A girl steps up to the wall, walking slowly along it, inspecting the images of the missing one by one.

Dylan sees me staring at her. 'That's Meg. You know her or something?' he says.

Before I can answer, there's a shout from outside the Pit. Then people start running.

Dylan's hand tightens round my coat.

'Go!' I hiss to him. 'Find somewhere to hide!'

Dylan speeds off into the shadows.

I run for the exit. Adrenaline is as bitter as coffee in my mouth, and my heart's beating in response. I can hear screaming, engines, dogs barking. I sprint out into the yard and skid to a halt. Lights blind me. I shield my eyes with my arm, but somehow it makes no difference.

The people who fled first are now running back towards me from the three streets. No, not running. Being herded.

They're here. The Coalies are inside the camp. I spin round, trying to find somewhere to go. The light sears my eyes. A dog snarls at the end of a lead.

The old fear rushes back, wild and uncontrollable. I see my sister May, as clear as if she's standing here with me. I hear the gunshot. I see her fall. The blood.

The world glitches, and I remember with horror that I'm wearing a disguise. If they see it malfunction, it will give me away in a millisecond. I fumble with the off switch behind my ear, and the blue haze lifts.

Their boots crunch on the floor. People crush together, covering their faces with sleeves. Trying to stay away from the gnashing teeth of the dogs.

'You're in no danger. Remain where you are.'

The tinny, metallic voice sends terror shooting through me.

9

MEG

Black uniforms. Black visors. And weapons. Deadly weapons. One of them says: 'You're in no danger. Remain where you are.' In no universe does that ever mean *you're in no danger*.

There are dogs and trucks too, and torchlight so bright it's like the sun. But I'm trying to hide a grin. Because I'm right where I need to be. Knew following that kid would pay off.

Someone makes a break for it and gets grabbed and dragged back. We're all clumped together in the yard in front of the Pit.

A Coaly opens fire. I squeeze my eyes shut and press my hands over my ears.

She's a few metres away from me, covering her eyes with her sleeve and trying to turn off her AR mask without anyone clocking her. A round of gunfire breaks through the air, and my heart jumps into my throat. I open my eyes, expecting to find a pool of blood and a human shape on the ground. Instead, there's a man cowering in front of a Coaly and a cloud of dust rising from the air. The Coaly fires again, pointing his weapon at the ground.

'On your knees,' comes a Coaly's voice. 'On your knees. You are not in danger.'

I edge closer to Esther Crossland.

One of the Coalies is sauntering towards me with the kind of confidence that comes from holding a weapon. The surety that everyone will do what you order. My hands are still clamped over my ears. He grabs me by the wrist and drags me. Then pushes me to the ground, sending pain jolting through my legs. I'm right next to her now. Close enough to touch.

Without thinking, I put my hand out to her. She looks at it for a second, then takes it and squeezes.

Gotcha.

10

ESTHER

My eyes ache in the light from the Coalies' truck. Its engine's idling, filling the yard with the stench of exhaust. One of the Coalies marches to the flatbed, pulls out a rattling bag and stands in front of me. Another one takes up position behind me. So close I should be able to smell them.

This is it. The invasion we've been afraid of since the start. They're taking our final scrap of freedom.

They line us up. And I'm surprised to find that the emotion that rises to the top isn't terror. It's not anger. It's not even hope. It's relief. I won't have to face another night so cold and hopeless it makes me want to walk into the sea.

The girl holding my hand pushes strands of hair back from her eyes and turns to look at me, and in that moment recognition hits me. Her soft brown hair needs washing, and she seems older than last time I saw her, but there's no mistaking her. This is the girl I left behind in the Lookout. The one I could have helped, but chose not to.

It feels like a lifetime since I looked into those eyes and turned my back. I had a future then, and a boyfriend. I had a sister.

Down the line, someone is weeping. I don't understand what's changed in the world of General Lall and the Coalies and the Federated States. I don't know why their ceasefire is being violated, or what negotiation has failed.

The girl's breathing is laboured after her tussle with the Coaly. I can feel the faint heat of her body. She looks sideways at me. There's a defiant glint in her eye.

'What's your name?' I whisper.

'M-Meg,' she says. Her voice trembles now, the defiant spark gone. There's a silent thrum in her fingers. She's trembling.

'I'm Esther.'

In the light from the fires, we keep hold of each other. I've seen the Coalies kill. I've seen them take people and make them disappear. When the ship was cleared, their Commander Hadley tied a noose round my neck. And I'm sure they're going to kill us now.

It's weird. I've lost so much I don't think there's anything else that can hurt me in the world. And now, instead of fear and panic, I feel the decompression of relief. There'll be no more running, no more hiding, no more anything. But, if this is the end, please make it quick.

'Name. Age. Occupation,' the Coaly barks at me.

'What?' I say.

'Name. Age. Occupation.'

I grit my teeth. 'Why?'

'Name. Age. Occupation. Or you'll get a slap.'

'Kara Franklin. Seventeen years old. Medic,' I say.

The Coaly shoves a hand into his bag and lifts something metallic out. A nasty-looking curve of steel that would fit in the palm of my hand. The Coaly holds it to his face, 'Kara Franklin. Seventeen years old. Medic.' The metal thing beeps and opens out like a mussel shell.

'What is that?' I say. Dread is rising in me now. If it's not going to be quick, it's going to be slow. 'Take your hands off me,' I snarl. My voice is aggressive and so loud I sense the people kneeling next to me snap to attention. Whoever was crying falls silent. May would be proud of me.

In this moment, kneeling on the ground, I realize hiding has been a mistake. Instead of skulking round the camp, trying to evade the Coalies, I should have taken action. I should have found a way to fight alongside the rebellion, even if it meant the Coalies knowing where I was. I should have lived the way May would have. It wasn't the Coalies that forced me into hiding. It was General Lall. I cowered and hid because of her. That ends now.

The Coaly lowers the metal shell towards my face. Two rows of spikes line the inside surface. The Coaly behind grips my head. I manage to shake it free and throw myself backwards, letting a scream of rage rip from my throat. I won't go down without a fight.

'Hold her,' one of them says.

'The admiral said no force.'

'Negative. We can't install these without force.'

More Coalies join in. More and more hands until I'm trapped. Huffing and snarling like an animal. The dogs bark and drag on their leads. Far away, I hear Meg's voice raised in protest.

Then I can't move. The metal touches my ear. It bites. Pain burns at every needle point as it slowly pierces my flesh. Blood runs in stripes from my ear and down my neck.

The Coalies release me. I sag to the ground, panting, my hands flat against the cold. Next they take hold of Meg. She yells something incoherent, and then her boots are kicking against the ground.

'Stop!' I shout. I left that girl once before. I won't ignore what's happening to her again.

I surge at the nearest Coaly. Manage to knock one off balance, but then two of them grab me by the arms and drag me away from Meg. Across the yard, between the flatbed trucks and dogs that have the people penned in. I expect them to stop and give me a kicking, but we keep going down the street that leads to the quayside. My heels scuff on the ground.

We reach the waterfront. Both of them still dragging me.

They're going to toss me into the sea.

I steel myself for the fall and the shock of icy water.

They throw me down right at the edge of the water, and they walk away. I'm left in a confused heap, as they make their way back up towards the Pit. I can hear them laughing inside their helmets, uncanny and monotone.

'You can't do this to us!' I scream. 'There's a truce! General Lall will hear about this!' I shout at their backs. Even as the words leave my mouth, I know how utterly reckless I've been. If they recognize me, they'll have one of the Federated States' most wanted traitors in their hands. And I'll face months of interrogation.

The Exiled

One of the Coalies stops dead. Then he saunters back, and crouches down in front of me. I refuse to cower. I stare at the reflection of my face in his visor.

'What makes you think Lall doesn't already know?' he says.

11

MEG

I'm standing next to Esther Crossland. She's got blood streaking from her head down to the collar of her uniform, and she's so skinny it's no wonder those Coalies didn't match her to the picture on her arrest warrant.

She's handed over some rations in exchange for a cup of oily bone broth, and now I'm leaning on the outside wall of the Pit, trying to get my thoughts in line while she stares at me. I let the broth warm my hands, let the steam defrost my face. She chews the inside corner of her mouth, nipping off fragments of flesh. Must hurt. Her eyes are orbs, the skin around them tightened and pulled back, cheeks sunken so you can see the shape of her mandible. Her hair's not been washed in a while, and it's all rough with sand and salt. She's fared even worse than me, to be honest.

The Coalies cleared out after they put these things on our ears, off to find some other poor souls to harass. I wasn't scared of them. Well, only a bit. But, if I needed to, I'd tell them who I was, and they'd check, and then they'd let me get on with it.

Imagine the luck of it, Seb. Imagine the pain, deep and delicious, of the Coalies piercing my ear with that thing and at the same time she's kneeling right next to me. She even took my hand when I offered it.

'What happened after the Lookout?' she says. 'The Coalies had you. How did you get away?'

I take a sip of broth. It smells like dog fur and oil. 'Well, I fell, and they grabbed me. Everyone else ran off, yourself included.' I pause and snatch a glimpse of her face. She winces. 'And then I was in a cell for a few days. Don't know really cos there was no sunlight to tell whether it was night or day.' I flex my fingers, remembering the feeling of the bones being snapped out of place by that big old Coaly they called Hadley. I'm not even slightly sorry that one's gone.

'Then what?' She's worrying that mouth again. Keep half expecting to see a gush of blood.

'One morning, early, the Coalies all run out of there like they're under attack, and then the whole ship's moving, and then there's an almighty bang.'

She's watching me like this is some sort of epic adventure story.

'And then the place is on its side. I can't tell which way is up, but I'm still in this cell, and I know the door's locked, even though now it's below me. It's like it's in the floor instead of the wall. And it's messing with my head, you know? Because nothing feels right. It gets worse and worse, and I know the ship's going down. That's when I hear water. So I manage to get to the door, and by now it's almost like looking straight downwards. There's a little window in the door that they use to look in when you're in the cell, and somehow it's come open and it's flapping about, so I put my face up against it, and I see that the corridor is already trickling with water.

'Now I'm thinking: this cell is on the port side of the ship, and we've gone over on our side, and now the water's coming in. But I'm trapped. And if I don't get out of here, if I don't climb, the water's going to fill it. I try the handle, obviously, but there's nothing. Then I hear someone wading through the water, and I look out and it's one of the Coalies, a woman. Her hair's all over the place, and it looks like she's been crying because her eyes are all puffy and red. The water's creeping up, and I can smell the salt of it. She's knee-deep now, walking along what used to be the wall of the corridor. Good job it's a broad one, I think, else she'd be having to swim. I shout to her. And she looks at me for a second, and she keeps going.'

'She left you?'

'Yeah, well, I was getting used to that, wasn't I?'

I see that land like a sucker punch. Esther takes my empty cup and replaces it with her untouched broth.

'So how did you get out?'

I shrug. 'She must have changed her mind because she comes back, and she unhooks the bunch of keys from her belt and holds it up to me. I stretch down through the tiny window, and I can't tell you the relief when I manage to grab hold of the keys. "Which one?" I shout, but she's already gone.'

But that Coaly didn't leave. She waited until I found the right key, dodging the door as it swung downwards into the water-filled corridor.

'Found the right key, thank God. Then let myself out.'

What really happened was that I splashed down into the corridor, and the Coaly hauled me up, and we got off the *Arcadia* together. But as soon as we set foot on dry land she handed me over to her mates, and I spent the next four months in an interrogation room. I don't tell Esther the hours I was made to look at pictures of rebels, hundreds of them, over and over. They asked me if I was one of them. If it was me that dropped the leaflets. If it was me who wanted to start the engine and crash the *Arcadia*. I told them none of it was me. But I soon realized they liked it better when they thought I was being helpful. When Esther's picture blinked on to the screen, I could say for the first time that I did recognize her, and I knew for sure she was in the Lookout when the leaflets started to drop.

Esther looks like she's going to be sick. I could almost feel sorry for her.

'Where have you been staying?' she says, clearing the emotion from her throat.

'Tent. About halfway up the beach,' I say, lying through my teeth. Few more minutes' tugging on her heartstrings and she's going to be wrapped round my finger. 'You a medic still?' I ask, nodding at the snake symbol on her uniform.

'For my sins,' she says.

'Do you get extra food and stuff?' I take a slurp of broth, watching her with big, wide eyes.

'I might be able to get you something extra. Meet me here in the morning?'

'All right,' I say.

She gives me a slight smile, and she honestly looks like

she's been broken, face all long and bony. Eyes glistening. It gives me a good feeling that I've managed to hurt her already. There's more where that came from.

She turns back to look at me from the other side of the yard. I give her a little wave, a smile of gratitude.

Can't wait to tell them I found her.

It's midnight on Monday 14 March 2095. The temperature is currently 0°C.

I need you to tell someone what's happening to us. We've been held here since the beaching of the cruise ship *Arcadia* four months ago. Federated States forces have erected a fence round much of the camp and hidden booby traps in the streets. We have no access to medical facilities. We have no legal counsel. We have no news from the world outside.

I heard a rumour that there's an infection in the camp. If it's true – please, don't let it be true – we won't survive without help.

Days in the camp: 121

Is anyone still out there?

12

ESTHER

Pat pulls my ear forward, looking at the shell-shaped cuff that's pinned there. I'm sitting on a pile of shipping pallets that are stacked against the outside wall of a warehouse. Behind us, all of the warehouses sit, blank-faced. In front of us, there's a short stretch of brick-lined quayside, and a sharp drop into the ocean. The edge is marked by a thick black chain on uprights – some half-hearted attempt at stopping people falling in. We're close enough to the makeshift tents and shelters for me to see the haze from the fires floating through the shallow morning light.

Corp's next to Pat, both of them frowning at the thing the Coalies attached to me. Last night I made a half-hearted attempt to clean around the thing before getting into bed and trying to shut the nightmare of the Coalies out of my head.

'My guess would be some sort of tracking device,' Pat says. He sprays disinfectant on my ear, and the sting's sharp enough to make me gasp. 'Sorry,' he says. He dabs at the blood with a swab.

It's the itch that's really grating on me. I can scratch round the side of it, but I can't get my finger under the edge of the metal. I tried opening it with my nails, but it's no use.

'Makes sense. Right from the start, the Coalies have said they can't give us more rations until they know how many of us are in here.'

'It's also a convenient first step if they're planning to come in here and take control,' Pat says.

A shudder runs along my spine. I have the horrible feeling that we're running out of time.

Corp's frown deepens. 'Can we get them off?' she asks.

'Hard to tell. They love their anti-personnel devices, and I wouldn't put it past them to insert a trigger in these.'

'You think General Lall really signed off on us being tagged?' I ask.

'I have no earthly idea what's going on inside General Lall's head,' Corp replies.

Corp closes the flap on her med bag, and that's the sign that the conversation's over. I won't get any more from her about General Lall. Headquarters. Anything. Apart from when I can ambush John, I get no contact with anything outside this camp. A volcano could explode a mile from here, and no one would tell me until I was knee-deep in lava.

She puts her hands on her hips. 'Dammit, Esther, you weren't meant to be in the Pit.'

'How come you've already got one?' I ask, and I point to the metal cuff clasped tightly round her earlobe, a smear of brown blood circling it.

'Don't change the subject. You disobeyed a direct order. Again.'

I watch a seagull pulling the legs from a dead crab. There's no point trying to argue. We've been through it all a thousand times. When we first got off the *Arcadia*, we talked everything through, night after night, warming our hands on the camping stove while we debated what course of action we should take. We made plans. Then I saw my own face on a wanted poster outside rebellion HQ. Somehow, the Coalies had decided I was alive, and suddenly I was on the Federated States' most-wanted list. Nik and Corp too.

'I can't keep having this conversation with you,' Corp says.

'Then don't. I don't need you telling me what to do,' I say, and it's true. Something clicked in me when I was kneeling on the ground next to Meg. I don't care what they tell me to do. The way we're being treated is wrong. I'm not putting up with it any more.

Corp paces off, stopping with her back to me, staring down. I see her shake her head before she turns to face me. 'Esther Crossland, you are relieved of duty.'

'What?'

'You heard me. You're done. You're off the team. You can stay at the house tonight, but then I want you out.'

I can't help it, but I start to laugh. It bubbles up from somewhere inside me, and it feels so strange and wonderful that I don't try to stop it.

'What's funny?' Corp says.

'Nothing, I just –' I lean on my knees, trying to get my breath through howls of laughter – 'I got fired from a job that pays nothing, with so few medical supplies we're basically applying plasters, and you're evicting me from a place with walls made of tarps.'

My eyes blur with tears, and I have to bend over until I can breathe again. When I look up and wipe my eyes, I find Corp staring at me. She breaks into a grin. The first smile I've seen from her in weeks, and it makes me want to run in circles out of pure happiness. She opens her arms, and we laugh, hugging each other and rocking back and forth.

'You know this is a pretty nice assignment. A lot of people would kill for these perks. Accommodation included, at least one square meal a day,' she says.

We start walking towards the entrance of the nearest warehouse, our arms still round each other.

'Not to mention a state-of-the-art security system courtesy of the Federated States,' I say, gesturing to somewhere in the distance where the fence stands.

Corp goes quiet. 'I just want you to be safe. We lost so many people last year. I can't face losing you too. I worked for the Coalies, remember? I was one of them for years. I know what they'll do if they catch you.'

'I know.'

There's a shout somewhere in the distance. A figure runs past us, a man wearing baggy trousers and trainers with no laces. 'Is he running away from something, or towards something?' I say.

'Don't know,' Pat says. 'But let's not wait to see if something's chasing him.'

The three of us dash after the man. When we round the corner of the warehouse, we run into a crowd. People jostle, everyone talking at once. The eerie sound of the Federated States national anthem trills thinly through the air.

Pat ducks through the throng, and I see him talking to someone, then he picks his way back to us.

'What's going on?' I ask.

'They're saying someone went missing from the camp this morning.'

'That doesn't make any sense,' Corp says.

I push through the crowd, catching snippets of sentences. *Executed. Fugitives. Wanted.* When I reach the front, I see people crowded round a new poster. But this one's different to the others. There's just a blank space that shimmers where the light touches it.

'It's a video display,' Pat says, elbowing people aside so that he's standing next to me. Corp joins us.

A woman waves her hand in front of the poster, and the national anthem starts. On the display, the Federated States flag flutters against a cloudless blue sky. The image shifts, and we're looking into a huge pillared building, all glass and polished floors.

'I've been there before,' Corp whispers. 'That's Thirtieth Street Station. What the hell . . .'

The footage zooms in on a man, a confused expression on his face. He stares at the commuters bustling around him.

'That's him!' someone shouts. 'That's the one the Coalies took in the night.'

'That's Bill,' another voice pipes up.

A feeling of dread washes over me. I find Pat's hand, and he grasps my fingers.

Now there are figures in black circling the man. The civilians scurry away, leaving him exposed, and I swear I can see him shaking.

A gunshot so loud that every single person jumps. The man crumples to the ground. Corp covers her face with her hands. My head spins. Why have they done this?

The man disappears from the display, and in his place is my face. And Nik's. Side by side and smiling. Then a voice speaks from the poster: 'The fugitives will not protect you. Report them to the Federated States today. You have the power to make things better.'

For the first time, nobody makes a sound.

I'm not wearing the mask. Everybody here can see my face. Everybody knows who I am. They all know I'm responsible for them being trapped here. And now they've been told to turn me in.

The poster fades to black. *The fugitives will not protect you.*

I feel like my chest's about to explode with all the rage building up inside me. I shake off Pat's hand and step forward out of the crowd, each pair of eyes fixed on me. I turn to face them, and I try to look at every person in turn. My teeth are clenched so tight my face aches.

There's a brick lying on the ground beneath the poster. I take it, feeling the cold, rough edges grazing the skin of my hand. Then I use all the rage I have to smash the brick into the poster. It does nothing. I scream and whack it again, as hard as I can. This time there's a tiny scratch. I throw the brick at it, then run forward and start clawing at its edges, trying to prise it from the wall. A woman joins me, and within a second there are six of us tearing at the thing. We get it off the wall and throw it down on the ground. Then people are stamping and stamping, cracks appearing in the display, pieces being torn off and tossed away.

Everybody wants a turn. They push each other aside in a frenzy, half-mad and breathless.

'This mob's getting angrier by the second. We need to leave,' Pat says.

13

ESTHER

People are still shouting fifteen minutes later and I can hear their voices alleys away. Our collective rage simmers in my chest.

Pat jogs up. 'Good news: we're all clear. No new traps in the alleys around the entrance either.'

'OK, medic, lead the way.' Corp's cuff shines steel grey against her brown skin. She looks thinner today. Her cheeks have lost their roundness, and there are dark rings under her eyes. I'll put an extra portion of protein out for dinner tonight.

Pat turns on a torch as the door swings closed behind us and we pick our way through the sleeping people and piles of rubbish. People are coughing in the murk.

'What did John say exactly?' Corp asks when we leave the first corridor and follow a path through the big loading bay that takes up most of the ground floor.

'Just that people need help in Eleven,' I say.

There are a handful of latrines for the hundreds of people who spewed from the *Arcadia* when I ran her aground. That means human waste. Lots of it. With nowhere to go, it smells like death. In the summer, this place will be thick with flies.

This is on me. This suffering is my fault.

I'm the one who needs to fix it.

'You and Pat take the first-floor offices,' says Corp. 'There were five families up there last time I checked. I'll search down here. Shout if you find anything.'

We head for the stairs at the back of the building. At the top, I push open the door into the first dank corridor.

'You think she's serious about firing you?' Pat says.

'I don't know how many more times I can disobey her without her making good on her threat to chuck me out.'

'We'll have to share my mother's tent.'

I feel myself blush, and I'm grateful it's so dark in here Pat won't be able to see. 'We?'

'If you go, I go.'

I stop in the middle of the corridor and turn to face him. He holds the torch up so that he can see my face, careful not to blind me. My cheeks are burning. I realize that we're completely alone for the first time in weeks.

Until something moves in the darkness. It brushes my leg. I squeal and leap away, holding on to Pat with both hands.

'It was a rat,' he says. Then he's looking at me again.

We're standing so close that I can feel his breath on my lips.

The moment is broken by a weak cough coming from one of the rooms along the corridor. I shake out my hands and carry on walking, trying to calm my heart rate as I go. 'Nobody should be living like this. We need to do more,' I say.

'What are you thinking?'

'Maybe we find some other way to get out of here. Things are getting worse. And what if General Lall has failed? Maybe it's time we act.'

'What if she hasn't failed? What if the reinforcements rock up tomorrow?'

'Then we'll have lost nothing. We could try the old Neath gangs.'

'You can't be serious.'

'I've heard there might be ways to get people out –'

'By going to Silas Cuinn? That's a hard no, Esther.'

'I'm not asking for your approval, Patrick. I'm asking if there's any truth in what people say. Does he smuggle people out or not?'

'No idea.'

'But you're –' I start. He stares at me, waiting for me to say it. I lick my lips. 'Look, I'm not being judgemental, but you're a Neath.'

'Nice. Thought we'd left all of that ticket-holder-versus Neath-crap behind on the *Arcadia*.' His voice is hard-edged.

'You know that's not what I mean. You can pretend all you want, but everyone knows your cousins live up in his territory.'

He crosses his arms and stares at me.

'Can you at least put out some feelers?' I say.

'I'm only going to say this once. I will not be helping you make contact with the gang leader who tried to have you murdered.'

The air crackles between us. I let out a frustrated huff. 'Let's get this over with.'

Pat strides past me, and I can feel the anger radiating from him. He struggled so hard to free himself from Silas's gang. Going to Silas for help now would be a huge risk. I'm not asking for me; I'm asking for the camp. Because it feels like we're running out of time.

Pat flashes the torch through each doorway. 'Esther.'

My heart plummets. Through one of the doorways is a small office, noticeboard still stuck to the wall, a wheely chair in the corner. I pull my scarf over my face to guard against the fishy odour that wafts from the room. The floor's slick, and the flies haven't waited for summer. There are five people laid out on rough beds. And one person-shaped thing with a plastic sheet pulled up over its head. Pat gently pulls the sheet back.

For a second, I'm flooded with relief – I don't recognize the gaunt, lifeless face. In an instant, the feeling gives way to stomach-churning guilt, and I'm once again reminded that none of this would be happening if I'd made different choices.

In the next bed, someone groans. I step closer to a woman as she turns her head to the side and vomits a trail of thin liquid. 'We're going to look after you,' I say, knowing even as the words come out of my mouth that it's not true. Platitudes are all I have to offer.

Sunken eyes. Diarrhoea. Lips crusted and cracked and white. Wrinkled skin. Dehydration. But why? Water's rationed, but no one should be dying of thirst. There's been rain. I rest my hand on her forehead.

'There's no fever,' I say.

'The others too,' Pat says. He stands and looks around.

'Let's nano her,' I say. 'See what we're dealing with. Corp!' I shout.

I take a syringe from my med bag and load a three-centimetre-long glossy pill into the needle end. These nanites will let us confirm the diagnosis within minutes.

Corp appears in the doorway. She looks at the woman without saying anything. We both know what this is.

This must be an intestinal infection, so I pull the woman's T-shirt up and press the syringe into her flesh. The nanites will go after anything that shouldn't be there and send a report before the tiny robots die. The woman's too weak to flinch when I press the trigger of the syringe and punch the nanite capsule into her gut.

'I'll be back,' I say. She closes her eyes in response.

The three of us leave the warehouse the way we came and find a spot in the fresh air outside. The buildings rise round us like cliff faces, but if I look upwards I can see a shard of clear sky. I turn the nano display on. A tiny screen's all you need for a report. A circle turns at the centre while it connects to the nanites. We watched a video of them in training. Tiny long-tailed robots. First, they break out of the capsule they were held in. When they find something foreign, a virus or bacteria or fungal spore, they grip it with their pedipalps and figure out what it is. Then they send us the info. I just injected a few thousand robots into my patient.

Corp takes a walkie-talkie from her belt. She moves away, speaking to someone on the other end. 'Do you have the results?' she says, turning to face me.

I look at the nano display in my hand. The circle disappears, and the result flashes up with a bacterium that makes me dizzy with despair. '*Vibrio cholerae*,' I say.

Corp covers her eyes with her hand. She brings the walkie-talkie back to her mouth and presses the button. It clicks.

'Go ahead,' says a voice on the other end.

Corp clears her throat before she speaks, and I can tell she's trying to keep the emotion from her voice. 'Yep. It's confirmed. We've got cholera. I need to see General Lall.'

14

ESTHER

Corp slams the door to the coastguard station and charges upstairs.

'Guessing it didn't go well,' I say.

She throws her med bag and wad of folded plastic on to the floor in the middle of the room and starts to pace. Her face is wildly intense. Pat and I share a glance.

Corp marches and turns, marches and turns. She chews the skin round her thumbnail, a habit she's picked up over the last few weeks. I never saw her so anxious when she was teaching class aboard the *Arcadia*, and back then she was living a double life as part of the rebellion. I don't like this unstable version of her.

'Did you even see her?' Pat says.

'For all of one minute. She said she'd see what she can do. Then she left.'

'Did you tell her we need drips? Did you tell her we need proper sanitation?' I say.

'I'm not an idiot,' Corp snaps.

I shut my mouth. If there's one thing growing up in the confines of the *Arcadia* taught me, it's that being trapped in a tiny space with other people can fray tempers, even when they love each other. I sit on the edge of one of the threadbare armchairs and wait for her to feel like talking. She slams around, rinsing cups and filling a pan from a bottle of water.

'Sorry,' she says finally. She leans on the sink and hunches her shoulders.

'It's OK.'

'She said she can't risk *rocking the boat*. The ceasefire is more important than demanding help apparently.'

'Did you tell her how many are going to die in here? Did you tell her there might not be any people left to help at this rate?'

Corp shakes her head. 'I can't believe this is happening.'

Her voice is so laced with desperation I want to cry. In this moment, I think I'd do anything to get the old Corp back. The hard-ass who spent hours teaching us how to fix people. The woman who got me through losing my sister.

Pat unfolds the blue sheet Corp was carrying. He spreads it out flat on the floor between the chairs. It's a digimap, shining as it powers up. The blue of its electronic sea cool and soothing. The wreck of the *Arcadia* is visible and fixed at the bottom of the map. Our camp straggling northwards from the wreckage. It shows the warehouses, the Pit, the mess of tents that pockmark the sand dunes, the no-go area that is Silas Cuinn's territory at the top edge of the plan. And now it displays something new: tiny spots of light in their hundreds. Right in the middle, hovering somewhere between the warehouses and Silas's territory, there are three pinpricks in a tiny rectangular building.

'Is that us?' I say.

'It's everyone who's been tagged so far,' Corp says. 'Enid had a pickpocket snatch one from a Coaly unit.'

'What do they do exactly?'

Corp shrugs. 'It's just as we thought. They're trackers. It's going to make it easier for the Coalies to give us the resources we need.'

'And to round us up if they ever need to,' Pat says.

A horrible thought occurs to me. 'Do they record sound?' I whisper.

'No,' Corp says, but I wish she'd said it with more conviction.

I stare at the map. 'This isn't nothing,' I say. 'We can load our cholera data into it and track the infection. At least we'll be able to warn people not to drink the bad water.'

Pat nods and starts tapping at the map, adding the information we gathered earlier in the day.

'We've got no way to treat people, not without outside help,' Corp says.

'Even if the other ships are still listening, we can't rely on them to come,' I say.

I can feel the anger building again. The frustration of having my hands tied. The need to move and act and *do something*.

'Then more people are going to die.' Corp slumps into a chair.

We sit in silence, each of us letting the enormity of what we're facing sink in. The specks on the digiplan move slowly. On the hob, the pan of water bubbles and spits as it comes to the boil.

I scratch at my ear cuff. It shows no sign of healing, and the thought of it broadcasting information back to the Coalies sends a shiver down my spine.

On the digiplan, there's a cluster of cases in Warehouse Eleven. The people we treated yesterday. We managed to get saline into some of them, and they're responding well. Cholera is a nasty disease spread by contamination, and with no latrines to speak of there's not much we can do to stop it. People can barely even wash their hands in this circle of hell.

Things are getting worse. And the Coalies seem to be taking more of an interest, as their new tracking system shows. I have no idea what's going on in the outside world. But in here the screws are tightening.

Corp shoots to her feet. She picks up her bag and swings it over her shoulder.

'Where are you going? It'll be getting dark in an hour,' I say.

'Finish getting that data into the map. Cross-reference with water sources so that we can see where the infection could be coming from. At least we'll have something concrete to show Lall if she ever gives us the time of day again.'

She slams the door behind her.

Pat's messing about with the settings on the digimap. A line of text flashes up next to each point. The font's so small I have to squint to read the names recorded for each of the cuffs. Not expecting to find them, I look for my parents' names, and experience the familiar ache. I'm not sure they even know May's dead. For them, it must have seemed like we both disappeared into thin air.

'Are we going to talk about how weird Corp's acting?' Pat says.

'We need to figure out the source of the infection,' I mutter, half to myself.

'Esther, Corp's unravelling.'

'I know,' I say.

'She's yelling all the time. She goes off in the middle of the night, trying to contact the other ships, even though we've not heard from them in months. When was the last time you saw her eat anything? And where does she go at night? Because she's not on the radio for all that time. I don't think she's sleeping either.'

I run through the past few nights in my head and realize he's right. She sits down with us, but ends up staring out of the window instead of eating.

He leans forward and looks at me earnestly. 'Where is she going now? Because she's just come from HQ, so she's not going back there, and it's six hours until she's due to do the midnight transmission.'

I add it up in my head, trying to figure out where Corp could be spending her time, and coming up with nothing. 'I'll speak to her,' I say. 'I'll make sure she gets some food in her, and I'll force her to take a nap too.'

Pat nods. 'Are you OK?'

'No. The longer we're here, the more I realize we can't wait for anyone else's help. Lall isn't going to lift a finger. If we wait for the other ships to respond, half the camp could be dead from disease. I'm sick of scurrying around at night, trying to scale the fence in the hope that one day Lall will tell us it's time to rise up.'

'I've enjoyed the scurrying at times,' he says, lacing our fingers together and resting them on his knee.

I watch the points milling about on the map.

'I'm going to get someone out,' I say.

'We talked about this –'

'I know. And you refused to help. But I refuse to sit here and wait any longer. It's my fault the camp even exists. I'm going to find a way to get one person out. And if it works, I'll get another one out. And then I'll keep going until every person in this camp is either free or dead.'

'OK,' Pat says. He sounds far from convinced. 'Say you can get someone out. Who do you start with?'

'I start with her,' I say, and I point to a name on the digiplan, a name I only learned yesterday. 'I start by freeing Margarite Stenson.'

15

MEG

This is the place they told me to come if I was ever called to a meeting. This little room (an electricity substation, they called it) is nothing more than a concrete box with a door. The big bits of machine inside send creepy shadows further into the darkness. It's right on the edge of the camp, and I'm praying it's free of booby traps. My handler wouldn't have had me come here if it was dangerous though. I pull the door closed behind me. The hinges creak like someone groaning. I shuffle into the shadows.

The air doesn't move in here, and it's dry and scratchy at the back of my throat.

I feel my way round some big metal contraptions attached to thick, rubber-coated wires that run across the floor, and, as I take a step into the darkness, I come face to face with my handler. My heart leaps about inside me. I throw my arms round his neck and squeeze him, trying to ignore the fact that he smells like he's just stepped out of the shower. What must I smell like? Doesn't matter; he won't mind.

'Meg, Meg!' he says. He gently puts some space between us. In the darkness, I can see the curve of his smile. 'You've done so well.' He's wearing his black uniform, his hair all neat and swept over to one side. Glossy. Good diet, good sleep. He hides his accent well, but I've spent enough time outside the camp to know he's still got a twang, no matter how many airs he puts on. No matter how much he practises that Federated States hoity-toity voice.

I beam back at him. 'Your Coalies almost ruined the whole thing though. Ran into them at the Pit and told them my name, but they gave me a tracker anyway.'

A flash of concern crosses his face, and he runs his fingers over the cuff on my ear. 'Does it hurt?'

'A bit,' I say.

'Ground personnel have no idea who you are. To them, you're from the ship like the rest. I'm sorry you had to go through that, but it's necessary for now. Don't want to blow your cover with special treatment.'

'I know. Rather not have their hands on me again though. So can you please sort it out?' I say. I fold my arms to show him I'm serious.

He thinks for a minute. Then he pulls off the top button of his uniform. He presses it into my hand. It looks exactly like a button, shiny and smooth, but still a button.

'What's this?'

'It's my extraction-request button. Every Federated States officer has one somewhere on them if they're going behind enemy lines.'

My ears prick at the word *enemy*. 'Never thought about

this being enemy territory before,' I say. The button doesn't feel any heavier than a normal button.

My handler runs his hands down my shoulders and pulls me close, resting his chin in my hair. 'Well, it is. The Federated States has been invaded. You and I chose the right side to fight for. You're so brave. You're a warrior.'

'Still don't understand why they let the camp stay. Can't they just give the ship people somewhere better to live?'

'The Federated States doesn't want Europeans walking about among them. But they won't tolerate killing for no reason either.'

'Those rich city people are OK with starving and freezing us to death, but draw the line at murder, do they?'

I realize for the first time that I still think of the people in the camp as us and the people outside it as them. I still think of this as home. I bite my lip. This is not home, and I owe these people nothing.

Concentrate on getting what you want, Meg.

'Now you're catching on.'

He rubs my arms and breathes into my hair, and I sink into the warmth of him. 'Once we've got Nik and Esther, things will change. We'll be able to make conditions better in the camp as soon as the danger of an uprising is gone. You're doing good work, Meg.'

'How does this button thingy work anyway?'

'Press it until it clicks. It can record a short audio message if you speak into it. An extraction team will be with you in five minutes. For God's sake, don't do it now. The last thing I need to explain is an unnecessary pickup.'

I drop the button into my pocket. Might try and find a needle and thread later to sew it on to my clothes. 'So can we go and see my brother now?'

'Soon,' he says.

My heart drops like a rock. 'But I did what they asked. I found Crossland.'

'I know, and they're grateful. We're all grateful.' He dots a kiss on to the top of my head.

'I completed my mission in less than twenty-four hours. I did what you've failed to do for months.'

He bends to look at me, skims my cheek with his thumb. 'Try not to get grouchy. I'm so proud of you. Of the way you've performed. There'll be a big pay-off for this. But I need your help for just a little bit longer, and then we can go somewhere else. We can get on with our lives.'

Butterflies beat in my stomach. He touches my chin so that I look up at him.

'Meg, we can go anywhere. We can do anything. You and me. Sebastian will be released from the prison, we'll go and collect him, and that'll be it. We'll be free. Just as soon as we finish our work here.'

'Fine. Tell me what I need to do.'

'Good girl. Your commitment will be rewarded. Now. Crossland will try to help you. She's not above taking the shady path if she thinks she's doing the right thing. I've got plans for her, but first I want to know if there's any truth to the rumours that there are ways out of the camp.'

'So what do you need me to do?'

'Stay close to her. Make her feel bad about what she did to you. If she mentions anything about how people are getting out, gather as much info as you can. Try to find out who's in charge of the escapes.'

'That's it?'

'That's it. As soon as we've gathered as much evidence as we can get, I'll bring a team down to arrest her.'

'How do you know she'll want to help me?'

'Because I know her,' he says.

His face is half shadow in this light, and I wish we could go outside and sit in the moonlight together like we used to.

'Can you stay a bit?' I say. 'I've missed you.'

'I'm expected back at the base, and I can't risk getting caught –'

There's a noise behind me, a scraping like someone opening the outer door.

'Quick!' he says.

He pulls me further into the room, behind a tumbledown wall. He pushes my back against the wall and puts his finger to his lips to shush me. The next moment, the inner door opens, and fresh light falls in.

'Meg?'

At the sound of Esther's voice, my eyes snap up to my handler's face. He looks as confused as me. He mouths *go* at me, and gives me a shove.

I stagger out from the hiding place, tugging at the bottom of my coat.

'What are you doing in here?' she asks, staring around like she might find the answer.

'Just looking for somewhere a bit warmer to sleep,' I say.

Thinking on your feet, Meg – nice.

Her eyes linger on the break in the wall behind me, right where he's hiding.

'Is someone else here?'

'Course not. How did you know where I was anyway?'

'We've got access to the Coalies' tracking data so that we can plot the cholera outbreak.'

Her eyes are still lingering on the opening behind me. She knows something's up, and I've got to get her out of here before she goes snooping any further. I'm so nervy my palms are sweaty. 'It's no good though. This place is freezing.'

'What's wrong with where you slept before?'

'You ever slept in a warehouse with thirty other people hacking their lungs up all night?'

She shakes her head like she's said something stupid. 'No, of course. Sorry.'

I cross my arms and try to look pissed off, when all I'm really feeling is the need to get her out and away from my handler before this whole thing goes up in flames. 'Don't know of anywhere half decent, do you?'

'You can stay with me tonight,' she says.

'Really?'

'It'll be better than the warehouses. And –' she pauses, and it's like she's trying to decide what to say – 'and I think I might be able to get you out.'

Well, knock me down. My handler was on the money about her. Was there a faint sigh from behind?

'You want to help me?'

'Yes,' she says. 'Call it restitution.'

'Restitution?'

'Yeah. It means I'm trying to make amends for what happened. For leaving you when I could have helped.'

'I know what the word means,' I snap.

Suddenly the old rage is back, and my voice crackles out of me like fire. She can't ever make it right. Esther Crossland will always be the girl who left me behind. The girl who destroyed my home. The girl who took my family.

No matter how kind she is.

No matter what good deeds she does.

I will bring her down.

'Lead the way,' I say.

It's midnight on Tuesday 15 March 2095. The temperature is currently -1°C.

I don't know why I make these transmissions any more. Guess the thought of you being out there is comforting, in the small hours when everything seems lost. And after yesterday I need it. I don't know how to carry on.

If anyone's listening, if anyone can help us, our fears have come true. An infection has taken hold in the camp. I can't tell you how I found out for sure without giving myself away, and the last thing I want is for someone to find me or take this equipment.

But it's true, and there's nothing any of us can do.

Days in the camp: 122

Hello. I can hear you. I'm listening.

16

ESTHER

I pretend I'm trying to sleep until milky sunlight finds its way through the cracks in the bunk-room walls. Meg and Pat have been snoring for hours, but I've been lying awake, staring at the shadows on the ceiling. I can't shake the unquiet feeling that settled on me when I found Meg in that building. There was something about that place. Like when you sit in a chair and you know someone was there until a minute before.

It gives me chills just thinking about it. Why was she in there anyway? More importantly, how has it taken me four months to realize she's in camp? Pat, Corp and I have been taking stock of the demographics. Long days spent going from tent to tent, warehouse to warehouse, figuring out who's locked in. Is it really possible I've not crossed paths with her before?

The answer is yes. Yes, it's totally possible. It's a big camp. People hide in the corners. This is just guilt putting me on edge.

I slip my feet out from under the stiff woollen blanket and push them straight into my boots, before tiptoeing to the door and easing it open. Down the landing and into the kitchen. It smells damp in here. The air never really dries properly, and everything feels soggy to the touch. I take a match from the plastic box we keep next to the camping stove and strike it, holding it to the gas ring. The ring flares to life, blue and yellow. I let the flame eat its way along the matchstick, closer, closer to my fingertips.

'You'll get burnt.' Corp's voice comes from the doorway.

The flame nips at my skin. I drop the match.

She comes further into the room. 'Did you sleep?'

I shake my head.

'Me neither.'

Corp takes two cups down from the doorless kitchen cabinet. The cups are all the same, plain white and made of chunky ceramic. While the kettle boils she adds half a teaspoon of coffee powder to each cup, followed by half a teaspoon of dried milk, then fills them with hot water. We sip the bitter brownish liquid in silence. The corners of Corp's mouth are cracked and flaky.

'What's she doing here?' she says finally.

'She needed somewhere to stay.'

'Then you should have found her a place in one of the warehouses.'

'The sub-zero warehouses with cholera in them?'

'You can't help everyone.'

'Seems to me you're happy not helping anyone at all.'

'What did you say to me?'

'Bickering again, you two?' Pat says, striding into the room and taking his own cup down.

Corp ignores him. The air feels heavy with tension. 'Why her?' she says.

'I'm a medic. It's my job to look after people.' I take a sip of coffee, trying to look like I'm in control of myself.

'There's hundreds of people in this camp. You haven't brought anyone else home.'

I hesitate. Suddenly I don't want to tell them what I did to Meg. Speaking the words will make it real somehow. Even though I'm planning to fix it, nothing will ever change what I did, not really. Nothing will ever erase the guilt.

'Tell me you've got a plan here,' Corp says.

'I'm getting her out,' I say simply.

'How?'

'Any way I can.'

'That's not a plan. Think it through. There's no way out of this camp that doesn't involve you getting into trouble. You'll get yourself killed or, worse, arrested.'

I let out a mirthless laugh. 'Thanks for your concern.'

'I'm ordering you to stop whatever it is you're doing. Send Meg back to her part of the camp. Concentrate on treating people instead of these hare-brained schemes to escape.'

'Let's just take a breath here,' Pat says.

'You've got some nerve. Your only orders for the past four months have been *wait* and *do nothing*,' I say.

'I'm your superior. Not your friend. It's not my job to mollycoddle you. Either obey my orders or leave.'

I feel my mouth drop open. Wow, that stung.

'Where is it you go, Corp? When you disappear into the camp? Why is it that you tell us to stay in after dark, and then you leave as soon as you think we're asleep? What exactly are you doing?'

Now it's Corp's turn to look injured. 'Where I go is none

of your business.' She heads for the door, pushing Pat aside in her hurry to get out of the situation.

Corp doesn't turn back, and within moments we're standing in silence in the kitchen. The kettle clicks as it cools.

'Tell me what you found out about Cuinn,' I say to Pat.

Pat looks like he doesn't want to talk. 'I asked around. People won't talk to me since I left the gang. They don't like this uniform.'

'And they don't like me full stop,' I say.

'There's that too.'

'No one's willing to talk. No one's willing to help,' I say. I lean on the counter, flexing my fingers in frustration.

'Give it a few more days,' Pat says. 'I'll take some energy bars next time. People always chat more when there's food.'

'No more days.'

I push myself up and slosh the dregs of my coffee down the sink. If no one will help, I'll do it myself. I charge from the room, into the bunk room. Meg's already awake and tying the laces of her boots.

'Ready?' I ask. My heart's pounding in my chest, and my voice comes out breathless. She's not staying here another minute than she needs to. Not another second.

'Ready for what?'

'You're leaving.'

'Did I do something wrong?'

'No, you're fine. Just come on.'

'Where're we going?'

'We're going to get you out of here.'

'Right now?'

'Right now.'

17

MEG

'We're going to get you out of here,' Esther says.

'Right now?'

This is all moving too fast. I've barely had a chance to find anything out, and now she's saying I'm leaving the camp. I need a second, a moment alone, to call my handler and tell him what's happening.

'Right now.'

Esther storms out of the room, and I hear her clunking down the stairs. Pat's standing in the doorway. He's eyeing me like I'm something to be figured out. I go to barge past him to follow Esther, but he blocks the doorway.

'What have you got on her?' he says.

I try to dodge under his arm, but he shoves me back. I push my hand into my pocket. The SOS button's there, smooth and reassuring. 'Don't know what you mean,' I say. My stomach's all knotted up. The curtains are still closed so Pat's face is lined with shadows.

'I mean, Esther's wound tighter than a spring, and she's

got it in her head to do something stupid. It all started when you appeared out of nowhere. So I want to know what your hold on her is.'

'Maybe she's just a good person,' I say. It leaves a bitter taste in my mouth, and it flashes through my head that the description feels right for Esther. She's feeling so bad about not helping me before that she's willing to put her neck on the line. Is that how an evil person would feel?

'Where did you sleep before you met up with Esther in the Pit?'

My mouth goes parched. This guy's on to me. My handler said this might happen. He warned me that one of them might be suspicious. All right, girl, time to suit up. Put all that training into practice. Body language and backstory. Don't look away. Don't lick your lips. 'Slept in a tent. Down the street from Warehouse Six,' I say.

He takes a step closer, eyes fixed on me, and it feels like he can see right into me. '*Bull. Shit.*'

I slide my thumb on to the button in my pocket and stare back at him. *Don't run your mouth, Meg.* That's what my handler said to me. *You'll want to jabber on, but less is more. Don't give them a word more than you need to.* I squeeze my lips together and look Pat right in the eyes.

'Thing is, my family lives down there. I asked around. No one knows who you are.'

'Ask the whole camp, did you? Because, if you didn't, it'll take me less than a minute to persuade Esther you're wrong, and I'm telling the truth.'

'Meg, Pat, let's go!' Esther's voice comes up the stairs.

I take the chance to push past him, but he grabs me by the

arm. 'I think you're using her. I think you're manipulating her to get what you want. And I think you're lying through your back teeth. Here's a friendly warning. Don't mess with Esther. She's been betrayed before, only this time she's got people looking out for her.'

'What, you? Cos from what I've seen that's the sum total of people who give a toss about Esther Crossland nowadays.'

He shoves me back into the door frame, so hard my head knocks on the wood. 'Yes. Me. You won't know this, but before the *Arcadia* went down I was the kind of people you wouldn't want to meet below deck. And I'm not talking about some two-bit pickpocket Neath like you, Miss Margarite Stenson. I mean if-I-gave-Silas-Cuinn-the-nod-he'd-have-you-over-the-side kind of people. If it turns out you're playing Esther, if you hurt her, I'll have you dealt with.'

I shake his hand off. 'Ooooh, scary,' I say.

I strut across the landing to the top of the stairs, trying not to let it show that my knees are wobbling. Flipping heck, I want to press that SOS button so bad my fingers are twitchy. I want to press it and have my handler come in and scare this Pat guy into next week. When I get back, I'm going to make a list of people who should be rounded up, and he's going straight in at number one.

'I'll be watching,' I hear him say as I get halfway down the stairs. So I turn, and I blow him a kiss.

He glares, fists balling at his sides. One point to me.

I trot down the stairs, and now that I'm away from him the shaking in my muscles makes me feel light and jittery. Esther's stood by the front door. I give her a smile, and when I get to the bottom I stretch my arms round her.

'Am I really getting out?' I say into her hair.

'If I have anything to do with it,' she says.

'Thank you. For everything.'

'I'm so sorry I did things wrong the first time.'

I pull away, and Esther's cheeks are flushed red, and her eyes sparkle. Is she going to cry? She opens the front door, letting in an icy wind, heavy with salt.

Pat's footsteps come down the stairs behind me. 'This is a bad idea.'

'Noted,' Esther says. 'Come with us or don't.'

Esther leads us away from the coastguard station and turns inland. Five minutes later, we're standing in front of the fence, and she's kneeling on the ground, unzipping the big bag she's brought with her. Pat stands off to one side, glaring.

'Don't like doing this in the daylight, but it's still early, and there's not another patrol due for ten minutes,' she says.

'Doing what exactly?'

'You're going over the fence.'

I feel myself blinking at her. Next thing I know, she's wrapping some sort of kneepad round my leg and fastening it with Velcro straps. I glance up at Pat as if he's going to give me some answers.

'Listen, you're going to jump for the fence, and when you hit it grab on tight. The hooks on these things should attach, and then it's just a matter of climbing.'

'I don't know about this.'

'You can do this,' Esther says.

She whacks me on the shoulder and arranges a little wooden crate a couple of metres away from the fence. She steps back, watching me like she's expecting me to do something.

Pat's found a broken bit of wall to sit on, and he's leaning one elbow on his knee. Watching the show. He's not the type to smirk, else he'd be doing it now.

I step a few paces away from the crate.

'Wait,' Pat says. He throws down the bit of grass he's been shredding and stands up. 'What's she going to do when she gets out there?'

Bleeding good question.

Esther shrugs. 'I'll go to HQ. Enid has contacts on the outside. They'll help.'

'She'll set the alarm off if she tries this. You know that, right?'

'Maybe. Worth a shot though.'

Pat walks over to Esther. He stands sideways to her and drops his voice. 'If I take you to Silas, will you give up on this?'

'Yes,' she says finally.

Girl's got him wrapped round her finger.

18

ESTHER

Wet sand weighs my boots down, sapping the energy from my legs, but I refuse to go any slower. It's not noon yet. The sun's a milky disc behind the clouds. Meg might be out of the camp before the sun sets again, and that thought's enough to keep me going.

I didn't like forcing Pat's hand, but I'm done being helpless. I won't stand by and watch this place be engulfed by disease, and I won't let Meg wallow here.

I'm taking action.

I'll focus on helping one person. When that job's done, I'll move on to the next person. Then the next and the next. And if they want me to stop, they'll have to shoot me or lock me up.

Months ago, when we were first exiled, John used a stick to scratch out a plan of the camp in the sand. The warehouses were messy rectangles at one end, and, at the other end, he left a huge empty patch. 'Don't go in there,' he said. 'Not unless you want Silas to do you in.'

Pat's walking beside me, but there's a bad feeling between us. I know he doesn't want to face Silas again. There's a hollow of sadness in my stomach, and I wonder how much damage I've done. The four months we've known each other have been the hardest of either of our lives. We were forged in fire.

Pat found us the day after the *Arcadia* crashed. His dad was injured in the collision, his tibia snapped by a fall from an upper deck. Pat and the rest of his family managed to get him off the ship and to the safety of Warehouse Eight, but then infection set in. With no antibiotics, infection is not something you want to be dealing with. Thankfully, we saved the leg, Pat got hooked on treating people, and before long Corp gave him his own uniform and a cobbled-together med bag. When the dust settled and all of Silas's people headed to his new territory in the north of the camp, Pat decided not to go with them. Most of his family stayed too, and I get the impression – although Pat won't talk about it – that the affair caused some sort of big break in Silas's ranks.

I stop in my tracks. This feels wrong. Behind me, Pat and Meg stop too. I spin on the spot so that I'm facing Pat. 'Can I talk to you a minute?'

'If you're going to listen to me.'

Meg seems to get the hint and wanders off.

Pat follows her with his eyes and then leans in to speak to me. 'That girl is bad news, and this will not end well,' he whispers.

'I'm not going to change my mind.'

'So why are we even talking about it?'

'Because ... I don't want to leave anything unsaid, OK? Because I wish I'd said goodbye to my parents, and I wish I could talk to Nik again. And because I wish I hadn't argued with my sister the day before . . .' My voice drops out, and I look down at my hands. It's still too painful to think about May.

'I don't like being manipulated. I don't deserve it either.'

'You're right. I'm sorry. But if you have any better ideas for getting her out of the camp I'm all ears.'

'I haven't forgotten last year. I was part of his gang when you broke his nose, remember? I was there when he was marching around in the dark, so angry that you'd humiliated him that he was willing to throw away a decade's work to get back at you. You should have seen them when he put that bounty on you. People were gleeful. I know how Silas works. You don't.'

'I'm not expecting you to come with me.'

'God, Esther, it's not that! I'm not scared for me. My family's still in his good books, so the worst I'll get is a clip round the ear. I'm worried he'll shoot you before you open your mouth. You're going to lose this fight.'

'I'm not scared of losing,' I say. 'I'm scared of not even fighting in the first place.'

He puts his hands on his hips and looks towards the water. Meg is picking at a piece of driftwood half buried in the sand. The muscle in his jaw tightens. 'Let me do the talking. For God's sake, try not to irritate him.'

I smile. 'Irritating? Moi?'

Pat shakes his head.

The rest of the camp shrinks behind us. In front, a line of shipping containers comes into view. Multicoloured and stacked up in towers. On the outskirts, there are old containers scattered about.

We hesitate at the boundary between the sand and the rough concrete.

Pat whistles through his teeth, craning his neck to look up at the towers of containers piled ten, twelve, fifteen high. Dense, brightly coloured walls of metal. 'It looks like a tower block.'

'More like a maze,' Meg says.

It's a rainbow of faded reds and blues, orange-streaked where rainwater runs off the sides. Patches of rust the size of cars dot the edges of the stacks. As we step between the first line, the wind dies, and the sounds of the world suddenly stop. The ground is powdery beneath my feet. 'I can't hear the ocean,' I say.

'This place gives me the creeps,' Meg says.

She's hugging herself like she's cold. There's a clanging echo behind us, and she spins to look. Eyes wide, fair skin scorched red over the bridge of her nose. Her cheeks rounded like apples. It strikes me that she looks healthier than most of us. 'Silas had a nasty reputation on the ship. What makes you think he won't just kill us?'

'If anyone can get you out of the camp, it's him,' I say.

'Much as I hate to admit it, Esther's right,' Pat says. 'Silas's smuggling operation meant he had his finger in a lot of illegal pies, and when the *Arcadia* went down he managed to keep all of his old contacts. He's got so many powerful friends the Coalies don't dare go near him. He tried to have Esther killed. More than once actually. And one time he saved her life.'

Meg stops and stares at me, open-mouthed. 'And this is the man you're going to ask for help?'

'It'll be fine. We've got Pat,' I say. There are brambles growing up from the base of the shipping containers, thorny stems bending across the path. 'But Silas won't even have chance to tell us to get lost if we don't figure out where we're going. We could be walking around here for hours.'

'We need to attract someone's attention,' Pat says.

Meg folds her arms. 'Not like there's a doorbell.'

'Get the feeling you're a glass-half-empty kind of person,' Pat says.

Meg gives him a withering look, but keeps her mouth shut.

I grab a stick and run it over the corrugated side of the nearest container. The sound reverberates through the air, and along my arm. An unpleasant scraping ring. When I get to a break in the containers, I give the wall a hard whack, and then carry on. Deliberately, marching down long rows of containers, losing myself in the warren of them.

After a few minutes, I sense movement ahead. There are voices raised, but it's impossible to pinpoint them. Eerie echoing shrieks and whoops. The hairs on my neck rise. Footsteps bang everywhere. Some higher up in the stack, as though people are running along on top of the containers.

There can be no turning back now.

Then I see one of them standing on a container, a dark shape against the pale spring sky. More and more appear, dropping to the ground.

'Dangerous place for kids like you. You lost?' one of them shouts. I squint upwards. It's a deep male voice, although I can't tell which of the figures it comes from.

Daren't look round. I sense people shimmying down from the roofs behind me.

Two men dangle their feet off the nearest platform, and suddenly things feel very, very real. They've got weapons. I see a gun. A long bat. A stick. My stomach lurches.

'Esther,' Meg whispers. 'This doesn't feel right. Let's just go.'

'What d'you want?' one of them calls. He has a roll of smouldering paper hanging from his mouth, and he eyes me like I'm trying to sell him something.

I lick my lips. 'You in charge?' I say.

'Maybe I am.'

'We need to see Silas.'

The man laughs, and the others mimic him, the noise jumping from wall to wall. 'Clear off,' he says.

'Afternoon, Jamie,' Pat says. He steps in front of us and squares his shoulders, lifting his chin.

'Didn't think we'd see you back here,' the man says, sniffing.

'Thought I'd come for a little visit. Now, run along and tell Silas that the girl who gave him a bloody nose would like a word.' A ripple passes through the circle of intimidation around us. Meg and I both stare at Pat. 'What?' he says. 'You want to see him, don't you?'

Jamie whispers to a woman standing next to him. She nods and disappears. He climbs awkwardly down the side of a container, boots squeaking as he slides. He's not agile. He comes closer until he's standing right in front of me, one thumb hooked through the belt loop on his jeans. The cigarette lolls between his lips. He stares at me, smirking, and all I want to do is drop my eyes. It feels like a lifetime until a new person jogs over and says something in his ear.

Jamie grunts. 'Right then.' He unwraps the scarf from his neck and holds it out to me.

'What's this?' I'm trying desperately to maintain control of my nerves.

Silas's people look on gleefully.

'You might be a spy,' he says.

I snatch the scarf and tie it round my eyes. It smells of something sweet and smoky. Meg and Pat get the blindfold treatment too.

'Satisfied?' I say.

'Watch your mouth.'

Jamie leads me roughly by the arm, turning at right angles so that I know we're still making our way through the street-like grid of the shipping containers, but with no chance of figuring out how to get back.

Within minutes, there's the squeak of hinges, a shift from sunlight to dankness. I'm pushed inside. And then a door closes behind us.

I pull the blindfold off.

Sitting on a chair in front of me is a broad-shouldered and thick-necked man. He's discarded the leather mask he always wore on the *Arcadia* and has grown a thick black beard since the last time I saw him. This is a man I've feared for months. A man who promised more than once to kill me. This is Silas Cuinn. Gang leader with a new gangland. The red leather chair squeaks as he leans forward to look at us.

Solar-powered lanterns are strung up in the corners, shedding dirty yellow light on to the low ceiling. It's so cold I can see my breath. Shipping containers look exactly as you'd imagine inside. Bare metal walls. No windows. People stand round the edges, leaning and lounging, and watching us like they're about to see a show.

'Nice place,' I say. 'You're thinner than I remember.' It's too cocky. But I won't be cowed by him, and this is the only way I can think of to keep myself from falling in a heap. Pat elbows me in the gut.

'You've got all of ten seconds to tell me why I shouldn't kill you.'

'What've you got me into?' Meg whispers. She's fidgeting with something in her pocket.

Pat clears his throat. He takes half a step forward. 'We've come to request your help.'

Silas's eyebrows shoot up, and even in the bad light I can see his eyes are bloodshot and red. 'Didn't fancy working for me any more, eh, Patrick?'

'I've been focusing my skills elsewhere,' Pat says.

'Apparently so. I don't like it when people don't do as they're told.'

Pat's Adam's apple bobs.

'You're right to be nervous, lad. I've been very generous with both of you. Decided on live and let live, but here you both are again, walking into my territory like you own the place.'

Pat clasps his hands behind his back. 'My grandfather sends his regards.'

'Bet he does,' Silas grunts.

'And Esther has the protection of General Lall.'

Silas lets out a hacking laugh. 'No. She does not. In any case, my patience with General Lall and the rebellion only extends so far.'

Pat closes his mouth. From the corner of my eye, I see a flicker of anxiety cross his face.

'People usually show me more respect. Take 'em round the back,' Silas says. He gives a half-hearted wave in our direction, and half a dozen of his henchmen stand up straighter.

'Oh shit,' Pat says.

The guy that led me in here kicks the back of my knees. I collapse on to the ground.

'Do something!' I say.

'Esther would like to work for you,' Pat blurts.

'What?' Silas says.

'*What?*' I say.

'Esther realizes that in the past she's acted in a manner that didn't show the right deference to someone of your rank and position.'

Silas looks interested.

'And also she's really very grateful that you were the one who fired the gun that saved her from Commander Hadley. Isn't that right?'

'That's right,' I say from the ground.

'So, she'd like to make amends. She offers her medical expertise. If there's anything she can help with, anything at all, she's your doctor. In this way, Esther understands that she's subordinating herself to you and your position.'

Silas leans back in his chair. He rests one boot on the box in front of him, fingers steepled in front of his face 'All right. Let's hear it then.'

'Stand up,' Pat says from the corner of his mouth.

I clear my throat and get to my feet, cursing myself internally for thinking bravado was the way to face Silas. He's powerful, but he's a simple creature. He believes in hierarchy based on strength and respect. He's at the top, and

I have to defer to him. But I suspect he won't react well to snivelling. I need to be strong.

'I heard you can get people out of the camp,' I say.

'Maybe I can.'

'This is Meg. I need to get her out.'

'And why would you need to do that?'

'I owe her.'

There's a long silence. I can almost hear the cogs turning in Silas's head. Meg's breathing hard next to me.

Finally, Silas says, 'All right.'

I look up at him. We lock eyes.

'You complete a job for me, everyone will know I'm your boss. And I'll get the young kit out of the camp.'

'Say yes,' Pat hisses from the corner of his mouth.

My stomach twists. 'What kind of job?'

'Don't worry. It's nothing that will hurt your upper-deck sensibilities. I just want you to get something for me.'

'That's it? I get what you want, and you smuggle Meg out?'

'Easy as that. And I'll even provide her with papers and an escort to the northern border. I'll see she gets safely to Maine,' Silas says, but he's smirking. 'I want something I lost. Something I didn't have time to get when the clearance started.'

Pat looks up at the ceiling. Mutters, 'You have to be kidding.'

'What is it?' I say.

'You want us to go back to the ship? You want us to go to the *Arcadia*?' Pat says.

A murmur passes through the people watching. The

tension in the room ratchets up. I can feel eyes on me. A lot of them.

'Not you. Just her.'

Silas stuffs a hand into his pocket and throws something down in front of me. The metal casing clinks on the floor. It's a metal ball, and I know from experience that it's a navigation orb. Programmed to guide me to whatever it is Silas wants.

'It's impossible,' I say, shaking my head. 'Most of it's below the waterline.'

'S'pose that depends on how much you want to save that girl's life, doesn't it? I'll be keeping her as collateral.'

Meg's face snaps to mine.

Someone takes me by the wrists and yanks them behind my back. They grab my hair and pull. I huff and struggle, and they drag me backwards.

'Bring the box from my desk drawer before the sun goes down, and we'll talk about smuggling the girl out. Come back empty-handed, she's dead.'

19

ESTHER

Four hours to get aboard the *Arcadia*, find the thing Silas wants, and get back to Meg before he punishes her for the things I've done.

Pat was right. This was stupid. By walking into Silas Cuinn's territory, I might have signed the death warrant for the one person I wanted to help.

Pat jogs to the edge of the water and drops a holdall on to the broken stone slabs. As soon as Silas's men threw us down outside the shipping containers, he broke into a run. He whirled through the coastguard station, collecting bits of equipment, rope, devices, while I stood there, feeling like an idiot.

A few metres away, a group of Neaths have come to watch the show. They smirk and laugh. One of them passes round a bottle.

Pat unravels a rope from his bag, feeds the end into a cigar-shaped metal cylinder, and screws the whole thing back together. 'Check it's tight,' he says, handing it to me while he goes back into the holdall.

I twist the two parts of the cylinder. My stomach's starting to wobble. I can feel tears coming up behind my eyes.

Pat takes the cylinder from me, looks up at the wreckage of the *Arcadia* and lobs the thing. It whistles through the air. There's a clunk as it hits the hull just below the rail and clings there. He attaches the other end of the rope to a huge brass mooring ring that's embedded in the quayside by his feet. When I set the *Arcadia* on its collision course, there wasn't time to choose a landing spot. It ended up crashing into this patch of dockland, slicing through the quay wall, and destroying the front of a warehouse. The *Arcadia* tipped on to its side, rubble from the waterfront building tumbling round it.

Pat repeats the process with a second cylinder, this time aiming just below the first. Now there are two ropes reaching from us to the ship. He hands me one of the old comgloves from the *Arcadia*. I slide it on to my hand, and it's like I've never been without one.

He catches my eye. 'If I could go in there for you, I would.' His voice is deep with intensity.

'I know,' I say.

I reach up and take hold of one of the ropes. The water's grey and sloshing with foam.

'Esther. Wait.' Pat inches closer to me, standing so that I can see the dark flecks in his irises. 'Say the word and I'll be at your side. They'll have to kill me to stop me.'

'Stay here in case I need you.'

He nods, but I'm sure a flicker of disappointment crosses his face.

I tighten my grip on the top rope and place my feet on the bottom one. I start to climb.

There's a cheer from the Neaths. Someone shouts, 'She's off, lads!'

'Testing, testing,' Pat says. His voice comes through the comglove.

Three sliding steps and I'm over open water. It churns beneath me. I ease myself higher, panting, trying not to look into the violent waves thrashing against the broken-down waterfront. The sea will throw me against the rocky quay wall if I drop.

Halfway there. My muscles ache, and I'm panting from the climb. I take my next step, and my foot slips, and I'm dangling from the top line, swinging my feet to try and find the bottom rope. I hear Pat yell. The Neaths shout something like, 'Way-hey!' Then I find the rope, and I hook the heels of my boots on to it, and close my eyes and breathe.

'OK?' Pat's voice comes through the comglove.

'Yep. I'm OK.'

I slide higher. So far from the water now that the height is dizzying. Gulls circle round me, cawing angrily.

'You're almost there. Another few metres.'

As I get closer, I make a grab for the rail and pull myself up. Then I'm over the other side, lying across the rail, clinging on as hard as I can and screwing my eyes shut so that I don't look down at the distance I've climbed.

'I'm aboard,' I say breathlessly into the comglove.

'Roger that. Now the fun starts,' Pat says.

I pause to catch my breath, watching the clouds spin above the ship, feeling the crush of being back aboard the *Arcadia*. I lift my hand so that I can speak to Pat again. 'Is there anything you can do for her? If I don't make it back in time?'

'You were there. It was fifty-fifty whether he let us go or shot us on the spot. Think I used up any goodwill I had.'

'Will he kill her?' I say.

There's silence at the other end of the comglove.

'Pat?'

'Concentrate on staying safe,' he says. 'We'll figure the rest out later.'

20

MEG

I'm in a tight spot, Seb, no mistake. And, yet again, it's down to Esther Crossland.

That girl's like a bad penny. She brought me down here. Disappeared. My inkling is that she's not coming back any time soon. I was starting to feel sorry for her too.

I'm sitting on the cold metal floor of a shipping container, resisting the urge to tell Silas Cuinn that my rescue party will be here any minute.

All I'm waiting for is a second to get my hand in my pocket and press the extraction button. If I can, I'll record a message into it too, but that seems less and less likely by the second. I should have done it ages ago, but I never found the right moment. And anyway, now I've got some real info that I can pass on to my handler. He'll be pleased with me after this.

Reckon it's been a few hours since Esther cleared out on her mission to the *Arcadia*. They've not done anything to me. They've not done much of anything at all really. The door opens and closes. People come and tell Silas stuff. Somewhere outside, I can hear engines moving slowly through the broad gaps between the shipping containers, which I find weird because there aren't really any cars inside the camp.

Silas sits in his big man's chair, chewing his fingernails. I knew him by name before the crash. Everybody did. He was one of the most powerful gang leaders on the whole ship, and you didn't mess with any of his people. But I'd never set eyes on him in real life. He's just as big and ox-like as people said. Wouldn't like to meet him on a dark deck, that's for sure.

Someone brings him his lunch, and the place fills with the smell of warm bread. My stomach growls at that. Haven't had a good feed since I left the training compound. The horrible stuff Esther shared with me didn't even touch the sides, and now I find I'm staring at Silas as he tears into a hunk of bread.

'Here, you planning to feed me?' I shout.

Silas blinks and looks round like he'd forgotten I was even there. 'Someone shut that gobshite up. Take her down the back where I can't see her.'

A woman pulls me up and steers me towards the back of the container. Further from the daylight. That's not a good feeling. When I get out of this, I'm going to live somewhere with big windows so that I don't have to feel trapped in the gloom ever again. My handler will make it happen. Now, if I can just get my hands free, I can call in the cavalry.

The woman leans on the wall near to where I'm sitting.

'Untie me,' I say.

'Not likely.'

'Where were you from? Before?'

She eyes me suspiciously. 'Was raised just off the main service corridor.'

I smile. 'You might know my grandparents then. Beryl and Xavier Lorca? They used to sell pinchitos out of elevator three. My mum's name was Carmen.'

'You're never baby Meg?'

I smile, broad as I can, and nod. 'That's me.'

'I remember you waddling up and down outside your granny's place. You always had a chubby little greasy face. How're your parents?' She reaches out and gives my cheek a nip with her fingers.

'My mum and dad didn't make it off the ship.'

'Oh no. Oh, I'm sorry, love. We lost a lot of people that day.'

'Yep. Couldn't you let me have my hands in front? I'm so uncomfy.'

'I can't. Silas'll have me flogged if he catches me helping you escape.'

'Not going to escape. I won't go anywhere. Promise. Just let me get my hands round the front. Maybe get me a drink of water?'

She looks round the room, checking to see whether anyone's watching. She fidgets with the end of her braid, then she crouches down and unties my hands. 'Quick!' she whispers.

I shift my hands to the front and hold them up for her to retie. Praying the whole time that Silas won't turn round and see me. She stands up, quick as a flash, and twitches her eyes round the inside of the shipping container again. Nobody saw. We did it.

The woman walks off and comes back with an empty bean can full of water. She pushes it into my hands.

I gulp the whole thing down, letting it splash over my chin, then wipe my face on my sleeve. 'Thanks,' I say.

'I'm not helping you again, so don't ask.' She gives me a look that's half irritation at being involved and half sympathy, and walks off.

Now, I need to do this sneakily. I ease my tied hands into the left pocket of my coat. It's too far. If anyone looks at me, they'll see what I'm up to. Not got much choice though, have I? Have to do it. My arms and fingers zing with the effort. Just a little further. My fingertips graze the call button. I manage to get hold of it, and press without waiting a second longer. 'Need pickup,' I whisper, my voice barely above a breath. 'I'm tied up in a shipping container at the north end of the camp. Silas Cuinn's in here with me.'

And that's all I can do. That's the only card I've got to play.

21

ESTHER

This corridor is on its side. Doors swing open above me. I'm so far inside the *Arcadia* that I can't see the sky any more. No daylight penetrates this far. I'm dripping wet and frozen through. Right now, I'd give anything to be back in the draughty coastguard station, having a cup of weak coffee next to a silent Corp.

The connection with Pat's comglove gave out about fifteen minutes ago so now all I can hear are the sounds of the ship.

I can do this. I have to do it. Meg's counting on me.

When I ran the *Arcadia* into the dock, it hit upright. But within minutes we could tell it wasn't going to sit still. It took on water, sank deeper into the ocean, tilted sideways so that it was almost lying flat. Half submerged like a grotesque iceberg. From the inside, it gives me a creeping, uncanny feeling. I've been walking on walls and climbing down through doorways.

Silas's navigation orb has led me along abandoned corridors further into his territory. Parts of the ship I never dreamed I'd set foot in. It's heady with decay, the light from the navigation orb casting eerie blue-white shadows. The constant drip of water and yawning creaks of the metal hull sound like voices in the darkness. And it strikes me now that if Silas wanted to get rid of me, this would be a pretty good plan. He could be sending me anywhere. The orb stops by the edge of a flooded corridor. Then it rolls in and starts to bob across the surface, its light spreading through the water.

'You've got to be kidding me,' I murmur.

The water's oily black and brackish. Anything could be living in there. Drips echo round me, the walls and ceiling slimy with the kind of weeds that grow in dark caves. I'm trying to keep a lid on my fear, but it's washing through me, stronger with every wave. The other end of the corridor is murky darkness, shadows stretched long and menacing by the weak light of the orb.

And now the orb is getting away from me, skimming ahead. If I don't go now, I'll lose it and its pathetic light.

I carefully let my toes dip into the water. I'm guessing it can only be a metre deep. Fresh cold floods through the eyelets of my boots, climbing over my skin.

A horrible thought looms. I'm alone. The only people who care that I'm here are Pat and Meg, and both of them have their hands tied. Meg's still enjoying Silas's hospitality, and those heavies Silas sent to watch us on to the *Arcadia* won't let Pat aboard for anything. No one's going to be launching a search party to come find me.

I take a breath and let my feet move deeper into the water.
I can do it. I can do it. I can do it.

The water reaches my calves, then my thighs, then my waist. The orb glows ahead. I wade through, using my hands to pull me along. I gulp air.

There's nothing in the water with me, I keep telling myself. Nothing. How could anything get in here? There are no tentacles and no sucking things. There's no cold flesh. There are no glassy eyes.

I pass an open door above me. The orb's light doesn't penetrate the darkness, and for a second there's so much space above that panic seizes me.

Is there anyone left inside the ship? Did everyone get out? Or are there bodies still?

I can't do this. Terror overwhelms me. I need to get out. I'll retrace my steps and find a way back.

I turn to the doorway I've just climbed through. In the weak light from the orb, I see the outline of a figure. A shadow. I falter, stepping backwards, but my foot doesn't stop and I plunge downwards. Shock forces the breath from my lungs. There must have been a doorway beneath me. There's a torrent of bubbles. My clothes weigh me down. Chest rages with fire. Panic surges through me. I can't tell which way I'm heading. I can't feel the pull of the surface.

I scream into the water.

THREE DAYS EARLIER

22

NIK

Sweat drips in a line between my shoulder blades. It's almost midnight. The darkness is busy with the chirp of insects and so hot that the air feels sticky. I slap a mozzie that's trying to take a bite out of my neck, and focus on twirling the dial on my radio. Its static fizz joins the buzz of the creepy-crawlies and flying things that make being outside unbearable even in the dark. Already my knees are aching from crouching next to the back wall of the sleeping barracks, but this is the only spot – between the building and the chain-link fence – where I can get a clear signal.

I swat another damn mosquito from my neck. This time my hand comes away smeared with sweat and grime and a crush of wings and legs. The buzzing of the radio fades as I turn the dial.

There's a sound in the deep vegetation beyond the chain-link fence. I freeze, deer-in-the-headlights style, and hide the radio behind my back. Heart's thudding around in my chest, and my hand's all clammy on the plastic casing. Don't think

I'll ever get used to places like this, where the trees are so thick you can't tell what's hiding beneath them.

Right, Nik my boy, find the right frequency, and let's get on with it. You don't need to be out here a second longer than necessary.

Truth is, I should be dozing in my bunk right now. If the Super catches me out here, he'll be asking all kinds of questions, and I don't need that sort of attention. Or, worse, someone will snatch the radio. Every night for the past few months, I've told myself it's too risky to listen. Every night, I find somewhere to hide while I twirl the dial, hoping for a single minute – five sentences – that link me to everyone back home. I can deal with the pain for that long. I can deal with the guilt.

Nothing moves in the striped shadows of the undergrowth so I push my back against the wall of the barracks and move the radio's dial again. The wall's made of those corrugated metal panels that are still warm to the touch from being in the sun all day. I turn the dial again. And there she is, the voice I recognize. Tinny and small, like it's a continent away. Corp's voice crackles from the speaker, and I get a rush of feeling that makes me feel dizzy. Guilt and happiness all wrapped up with a ribbon of pain.

. . . Midnight. Sunday 13 March 2095

The temperature is currently -2°C. I expect it to drop further before the sun rises again. Current rations provide 1,500 calories per person per day . . .

It craps out again, cutting her off mid-sentence. I slam my fist against the side of the radio until she flickers back in.

. . . Days in the camp: 120

Dammit. Missed the rest. But what I didn't miss was the desperation in her voice. Things are getting worse. When I left, my mother was planning to bring reinforcements into the camp so that the rebellion could mount a coordinated resistance and have a chance of breaking out. It hasn't happened yet, and from the sound of it Corp's not been able to make contact in a good while.

It's not my problem any more.

At the end of the building, a figure appears. It's the Super, short and thick-necked, a halo of smoke rising round his head from the vape shining between his fingers. Maybe it's the heat, or maybe it's the fact that he's in charge of a hundred guys who'd rather be anywhere else in the world than here, but that guy's constantly angry. Even now, while he's having his last smoke of the day, his free hand's clenched at his side. The Super's not a big man, but he's got enough rage to fill a room.

Easing myself up, I inch backwards. He's not seen me, so if I can make it to the far corner of this building I can sneak round the front and be in through the doors while he's still enjoying his smoke.

I get to the corner and slink round, finally out of view of the Super. Now I'm at the side, but out front I hear voices. People are standing right by the door I need to go through.

I creep to the next corner and look round. This side of the building faces the exercise yard, the bright floodlights picking up the hundreds of bugs that wheel through the air and the bats that swoop after them.

The voice I hear is Ken's. He's been my bargemate since day one out here. The other voice I don't recognize, but that's not unusual. Worker turnover is sky-high. People move on. Get better jobs. Decide they can't face another day cleaning plastic out of the ocean. New faces arrive every week.

'Told you already, never heard of him.' Ken's voice is getting defensive now, rising from the lazy grumble he usually uses.

The other voice mumbles something that could be an insult or could be a threat, then there's the padding of feet, the wheeze-slam of the screen door, and silence.

'What in God's name are you skulking around here for, Baaz?' barks the Super's voice from behind me. Baaz is my most recent alter ego, the fake name I've been using since the Coalies started looking for Nikhil Lall.

Shit. Shit. Shit.

While I was distracted by the voices and trying not to get seen, the Super finished his smoke, and now he's standing behind me in the shadows. I fix a smile on my features and turn to face him.

'Evening, Super,' I say.

'Asked you a question.'

'Just taking some air.'

'What's that?' He nods at the radio in my hand.

How can I have been so stupid? The radio should have been safely in my pocket. 'Just a piece of junk I picked up on the barge. Nothing interesting.'

'Give it.'

My hand tenses round the radio, and all I can think is if I hand it over it could be weeks until I manage to get another one. It could be months. That means it could be months until I hear Corp's voice again.

Home. Family. Esther. Sometimes, I think the loneliness is going to flood out of my mouth when I speak. But I can't go back.

My fingers creak as they tighten round the radio.

'Now, Baaz.'

Haven't got a choice. Need to keep the Super onside if I'm going to stay here. I hold it out in the air between us, faltering at the last second.

Even in the dark, I can tell the Super's face is turning purple with fury. Next second, he whacks my hand, knocking the radio out of it. It smashes on the dirt floor with a tinkle like breaking glass, the plastic casing showering red flecks, and I can tell straight off that the thing's dead.

The Super glares at me. I can see him thinking. 'Where were you before this, Baaz?'

I lick my lips and try to hide the trickle of anxiety that's running through me. This conversation has turned an unexpected and unwelcome corner. 'Did a stint in a distribution centre just outside of Federated States territory in South Carolina.'

'Interesting. They don't seem to remember you there.'

I swallow. My tongue's thick and useless in my mouth. They won't remember me there because I use a different identity every place I stop. Safer than anyone finding out who I really am.

'And before that you were . . . ?'

'Sawmill, Texas,' I say.

The foreman there didn't ask any questions, and I'd be willing to bet there isn't a single worker in the place with the right immigration docs. Decided it was time to move on when I saw the guy on the next saw take off three of his own fingers.

'Yeah, cutting down the world's oldest trees. What about before that?' The Super's smirking like he knows all the answers to this pop quiz.

Before that, I was in the camp, and before that I was on the *Arcadia*. I got out using a fake ID and took a long bus ride through the mountains. No one looked too hard at a skinny kid wearing a tattered hoody.

'I was born in Nova Scotia. It's all there in my file,' I say.

The Super steps closer to me, and I'm caught in a tunnel of his breath. It smells like warm, milky tea, and it makes me want to gag. 'I call BS,' he says. 'You're running from something.'

I stare. Not much else I can do. Knew my file was thin, but didn't think he'd go poking into my backstory. No one seems to care when it comes to these jobs. As long as you're not causing any trouble, people aren't going to look too hard. Guess I have been causing trouble though. I shrug. Give him a half-smile.

'What would happen if I radioed the Federated States and told them I had a roughneck with a lovely ship accent on one of my rigs?'

My face burns with sudden heat. Not many people can recognize a ship accent. It means the Super knows exactly where I come from. And he knows there's a good chance I did some illegal stuff to get here too. Question is, how much illegal stuff does he know about? If he thinks I'm an escapee, that's not much of a problem. The Coalies aren't all that interested in picking up straggling refugees once they get out of their territory. An escapee who is responsible for crashing a ginormous refugee ship into dry land, starting a war with Federated States forces, and who is the son of the rebel leader is another matter. They'd defo be interested to hear what the Super has to say about me.

He gets closer, and it's all I can do to stop myself from turning tail, packing my bags, and getting off this island.

'Don't want to lose a worker, but consider yourself on a warning, Baaz. Got my eyes on you. I run a tight operation here, and I don't want troublemakers. First hint of a problem and I'll report you to the Feds before you can catch your breath. Got it?'

'Got it.'

23

JANEK

Janek tugs on her collar to straighten it for the nth time, feeling the smooth pips under her thumb. Since her promotion to fleet admiral, she's worn five of the silver buttons on her uniform, and finds that she touches them in moments of high tension. She berates herself silently for the loss of poise.

'Betsy, how are you?' Janek says to the middle-aged woman sitting at the desk.

This is the office of the president's senior secretary. No one gets into the Oval Office without first passing through Betsy's, and Janek very quickly learned to keep the woman onside. In front of Janek, the door that connects the outer office to the Oval Office is solid wood and imposing.

'I can't complain, Admiral.'

'This place would fall apart without you.'

'That's very kind of you to say, Admiral. The president is getting off his call with Congressman Stokes any minute.'

Harveen, Janek's chief of staff, reaches up and pins a stray lock of hair behind Janek's ear. Harveen looks like she wants to say *good luck*, or extend some other platitude, but she keeps her mouth shut like a good subordinate. She straightens Janek's collar, picks a piece of imaginary lint from her jacket, then stands back and clasps her hands in front of her.

'He'll see you now,' Betsy says.

Harveen opens the door, and Janek marches through it into the Oval Office.

President Walsh, a man who appears much younger than his sixty years due in large part to the team of aestheticians on the government payroll, is watching the large holographic display of the Federated States. This is as famous as the Oval Office itself. Every schoolchild is fascinated by the real-life display of their country and its military forces.

Mount Mitchell, the highest point in the country, sits level with Janek's hip. Involuntarily, her eyes travel towards the part of the map that shows her hometown, nestled in the foothills of the mountain. So close to the southern border wall that she could see the wall's construction from her childhood home. If she was left to her own devices in this office, she wouldn't be able to resist zooming in on that place. She wouldn't be able to stop herself from viewing the abandoned suburbs and the bombed-out tower blocks of the city that fell during the Second War of Independence. Its destruction was the catalyst for her life of military service. There wasn't much else open to a displaced girl from the Appalachians.

Look where she is now.

The president is flanked by the red, white and blue of the Federated States flag. Heavy silk curtains hang over the windows, keeping out all but the thinnest shafts of light.

Above the fireplace, the portrait of the first president of the Federated States scowls down at them with a look of derision. The room smells of leather and beeswax and something medical. It's enough to turn Janek's stomach. The president concentrates on the map, scowling at a spot on the southern border wall, which flashes and pings with the explosions of a battle in miniature.

Janek clears her throat. 'Good morning, Mr President.'

'Nothing good about it. Not for me and certainly not for you,' he says without moving his gaze from the battle.

'I'm sorry to hear that, sir.'

'Rubbish. You want me in the ground as much as the rest of them do.'

'I can assure you, sir –'

'Do not insult my intelligence, Janek. You're waiting for me to die. I see you. You're already redecorating,' the president snaps.

His teeth shine. His lips are slightly too plump. Slightly too smooth. Rumour has it that his skin can no longer be exposed to UV light because of all the rejuvenating treatments he's had.

'As always, I serve at your pleasure, sir. As president-elect, I will take the baton whenever you're ready to pass it to me, whether that is tomorrow or three decades from now.'

Even as she says it, Janek hopes it doesn't take three decades for this creature to breathe his last. She can't face another thirty years bowing to him while trying to keep the rest of the wolves at bay. The presidency is a trophy every officer in the military wants. The chance to rule, and profit, from the Federated States. Ironically, it's also the only way to wipe your hands clean of all the dirty things you did rising through the ranks. There's no longer a court in the country with the power – or the will – to try a sitting president. President Walsh saw to it.

He snorts. There's a fresh barrage of explosions on the edge of the map. He waves a hand at them, and Janek notices for the first time the glove Walsh is wearing to control the map. 'More skirmishes on the southern border walls. The nuts wanting reunification of the Carolinas.'

Janek has been briefed on the problems of the south. The huge cost of defending the border wall from those bent on tearing it down. The Federated States armies fight an unending battle.

More explosions rock the map, and then a red X appears in the air above the location of the battle. The system beeps angrily. Lines of text scroll through the air, details of the lost battalion.

'Goddamn it!' the president shouts. He leaps out of his chair and strides to the map, fists clenched in fury. 'Every day, I send reinforcements. Every day, another loss. Another victory for our enemies.'

Reaching the edge of the map, he uses his gloved hand to select another battalion of resources from an army base in Washington, DC, and drags it to the conflict zone. He breathes through his anger, well-preened hair dishevelled by the sudden passion.

Janek waits while he removes the control glove, throws it down on the desk, and smooths a hand over his hair.

'This conflict has drained the war chest,' he says. 'Our enemies are closing in. South Carolina is emboldened with every inch they steal from us. Maine openly taunts us, spewing anti Federated States propaganda to the world. Replaying the footage of the escaped European ships arriving in their country. Our censors filter foreign news outlets, but it still gets through. I am humiliated daily, Janek. I am made fun of, and ridiculed, daily.'

Against her wishes, Janek's mind flashes to the most recent meme of President Walsh. An unflattering video of him getting a manicure. It was a deepfake, of course. Unfortunately, it barely matters. A politician's image is fragile, and once something has entered the public psyche, it can't truly be expunged.

'What can I do to help, sir?'

'Tell me you've got the ship fugitives against a wall.'

Janek feels the flash of sweat on her forehead. 'Not as yet, sir.'

'I can name another successor.'

Janek resists the hammering of her heart, demands that the adrenaline now swilling through her blood dissipates. 'If you would let me take the camp by force –'

'No!' he shouts, slamming both hands down on the desk. 'Direct action is out of the question until you've apprehended the fugitives,' he spits, flecks of spittle showering the desk. 'The three of them are too strong together. Lall gives the camp credibility on the world stage. She's clever enough to elevate the teenagers as figureheads, and she'll galvanize the people of the camp to rebel. Do not underestimate the power that teenagers fighting for a cause can have. That woman will bring disgrace on the Federated States if we don't deal with her.'

President Walsh is pointing his index finger at Janek. She resists the urge to take it and twist it.

'Congressman Stokes and the other sponsors will be introducing factory conditions within the month, and until that time you will not risk diminishing the camp's value,' he says.

Janek digs her fingernails into her palms to quell the retort she'd like to make.

'It's making me look bad. This *Arcadia* business should never have happened. Now the whole thing is playing out on our doorstep, taking up news cycle after news cycle. How did they even have the resources to start the engine? And tell me, Janek, where are they getting their firepower from? Where did Lall get a helicopter? Where did she get enough resources to persuade the world that she's a diplomat, with diplomatic immunity, instead of a housewife with a pistol? How is she in a position to make demands on us? No, don't answer. I know where the money comes from. It comes from the north.'

He's pacing now, shouting and spitting as he walks. To Janek, each step he takes makes him seem less stable. He could blow at any second. She'll need to placate him if she's to stay out of the line of fire.

'I won't give our enemies the satisfaction of seeing us scuffle with her. Take her out and make it look like one of her own people did it. I don't want anyone pointing the finger at me. She's too popular for that. Then I'll replace her with a puppet leader.'

'I have people working on it. You can be confident that the threat of an uprising will be neutralized within days –'

President Walsh takes a few steadying breaths. Janek notices for the first time a Secret Service file sitting on top of a pile of paperwork.

'My orders have been quite simple, Fleet Admiral. Subjugate the camp. Deliver the fugitives. Dispense with General Lall. You've had four months, yet there has been little progress,' he says quietly.

This man is all ego and pomposity. 'Mr President, sir, we're closing in on the key rebel leaders. Our strategy is working. Support for these leaders has never been so thin.' Janek leans forward slightly, as though she's about to reveal a secret. 'Did you know that we've been forced to replace the wanted posters in the camp?'

President Walsh raises his eyebrows. 'Why is that?'

'Because people scratch out their eyes.'

'Indeed?'

'I promise, sir, we're reaching a tipping point. Lall's support is waning, and once the teenagers responsible for the grounding of the *Arcadia* are brought to justice there'll be no prospect of an uprising coming from inside the camp.'

'Make sure of it, Janek.' The president rests a hand on top of the Secret Service file on his desk. Pointedly, Janek suspects.

She swallows, the collar of her uniform suddenly tight round her jugular. 'Of course, sir. Give me a month, and I'll have this all wrapped up.'

The president turns the Secret Service personnel file over and spins it so that Janek can see the details on the front. She recognizes the digital image of herself as a fresh-faced young woman, hair more blonde than grey, cheeks round with youth. It was taken on the day she joined the Federated States ship-enforcement division. The day she became a Coaly. That was the happiest moment of her life – back when she was ambitious because she loved her country. Before progression was a matter of survival.

The president taps the file with his fingertips. 'Secrets are part of the political game. Yours will remain secret for as long as you remain in office.'

The room spins round Janek as the thought of her self-testimony being made public washes over her. The danger to her career, and her life, suddenly brought into focus. 'I understand, sir.'

'Very good. You've got a week. If I see no successes, I'll start the deselection process and name an alternative president-elect. In the meantime, you'll go and smooth things over with the prison conglomeration. Explain to them why they haven't got a camp churning out the munitions we so desperately need. That is all.'

Janek clips a salute and spins on her heel, holding her breath until she's cleared the Oval Office and the outer office, and she's standing in the parquet-floored corridor with Harveen fussing behind her.

'What did he say?' Harveen whispers. The younger woman's eyes are wide and earnest. 'Are we safe?'

'I have him wrapped round my finger,' Janek says.

24

NIK

The barge rises on a wave the height of a truck. A rattling sea of plastic comes with it. It's not the sound of my ocean. Nothing about this place reminds me of home. Everything reeks of rotten food. Sour milk. The stuff inside nappies.

I rearrange the length of fabric I use to protect my head from the sun and run a blob of sunscreen on to my nose. The skin's crusty with sunburn, and I savour the zingy cold of the gel as I rub it over a scab. Day shift on the plastic rig is bad. The sun pounds down so hard you can barely stand up, and the stench rises in waves from the trash island. Hell of a lot safer than the night shift though. And I'd rather have this too-hot sun than the too-cold winters we get up north.

I yank at the rope tied round my waist and attached to the barge. Tight and safe. Fall in there without a safety line and I'm a goner, even if I manage to keep my head above the water. The rubbish is piled so high no one will see my hand waving in the air. My only chance would be if someone grabbed the end of my rope and pulled me out before a tiger shark got hold. Willing to bet that Ken, my bargemate, wouldn't break a sweat to save me.

We're an hour south of Tampa in the middle of the Gulf of Mexico. This patch of ocean trash is big as a city. Two hundred square miles of ancient crap. Some of this junk is a hundred years old – you can tell by the dates stamped on the outside. It coats the ocean in a suffocating layer. Colonized by seaweed, picked over by seagulls, buzzing with bluebottles. I've seen crabs wandering in among the milk bottles and toothbrushes and plastic bags, blue-orange claws raised.

'Baaz! Something trapped against the left arm!' Ken yells from inside the cab of the barge. Jowly and pale, like a witchetty grub, and wearing black-lensed goggles to keep the warm salt water out of his eyes, Ken's opened the door of the cab just enough to shout out of it.

I'm calling it a barge, but really it's a platform, five metres across, no railing, with a single-person cab at the front that looks like a toilet cubicle with windows. Extending from the sides of the platform are the arms: two long, thin strips of plastic that sweep the garbage into a concentrated pile. If I squint into the distance, I can see the next few barges. Each one's connected to the next by the plastic arm, the entire group sweeping round in an unbroken circle that traps this garbage patch in the centre.

Sloshing through puddles of warm water, I lift my hook from where it's stowed on the outside wall of the cab. There are circles of rope there too, a couple of long hooks and a tangle of net that will be useful for precisely nothing. An empty hook has the words LIFE PRESERVER printed above it and a faint circular mark where the rubber ring must have been kept. Nothing there now obviously. My employers aren't big on health and safety.

'Keep her steady, Ken!' I shout.

Ken steers this thing from inside the cab. Teams are two people. One in the cab (lucky). One on the platform (unlucky). The one in the cab sits dry and safe, adjusting the barge's position with a joystick and watching for blockages. The other one stands on deck, trying to balance, getting blasted with salt water, and hooking anything that's too big for the macerating arm to deal with. Been here two months and I've not sat in that cab once.

I inch as close to the edge of the barge as I dare. There's no point wearing wet boots all day so I'm barefoot, and the skin on my toes is wrinkled. My skin never does dry out properly. Sure I'm going to get trench foot one of these days. The surface of the barge is roughened non-slip plastic like the stuff you get at the bottom of paddling pools, and I try my hardest to grip with my toes. A twist and pull extends the handle of my hook until it bends over the surface of the water. My muscles scream from the weight of it.

All along one side of the macerating arm there are millions of tiny blades. Trash gets sucked in on one side of the arm and is chopped into tiny pieces by the blades. Once it's chopped up, it gets sprayed with a plastic-eating bacteria that breaks the microplastic down to nothing. It's when something's too big to get sucked through the arm that the problems start. A shark, for instance, would just get rolled over and over parallel to the arm without ever getting sucked through, ribbons of kelp wrapping round it like spaghetti on a fork.

Whatever's blocking us is big. Rotting shark would be my guess.

I swing my hook out over the rubbish, but the thing's too far out, and I end up splashing around in the trash. *Dammit.* Gonna have to walk the arm.

'Ken, I gotta go out,' I shout, in the hope that if I fall into that roiling sea, he'll get off his butt and haul me out. He gives a half-hearted wave that probably means get lost. 'Thanks, Ken. Thanks a lot,' I mutter.

I check my rope again, close my eyes, and breathe in time with the waves. The arm is only 30 centimetres wide, but it's more than half a mile before it connects to another barge. My foot squeaks on the slippery plastic as I take my first step. It's about twenty steps to the blockage, that's all. Twenty steps on a moving tube of plastic that's only just wide enough to walk on.

Piece of cake. Eyes forward. Arms out.

Thirty held-breath steps later, I get level with the thing blocking the macerator. Before I take a look, I plant my feet and find a good, solid position to kneel in.

I was right. It's the shape of a shark, wrapped in seaweed and fishing net. It flashes purple, yellow, green and –

My stomach lurches.

That's a face. Fishy eyes staring, the top of the head covered in short-cropped black hair that's been swept flat by the water. A jagged wound on its forehead.

Adrenaline pumps through me, and I shoot upwards and let out a yell. My feet slip from under me. I faceplant on the narrow plastic arm, chest slamming on to the surface. Pain blooms through my ribs. A knuckle of agony throbs in my chest where my scar sits. Right where a Coaly bullet was dug out five months ago.

Esther.

No. Get out of my head.

I force myself to my feet, but a wave hits and everything slows. I slide sideways, and then I'm tipped, slow motion, into the water, sploshing down into the clean side. Bubbles rush over my face. The water smells disinfectant-clean. Above me, the surface glows bright in the morning sun, and I kick towards it. Tiny particles of plastic crowd in on me. They're a sticky film in my eyes. Crawling into my ears. They'll swarm me. Drag me down. Drown me as fast as the water will.

I didn't get to say goodbye.

My legs ache from fighting against the water. Breath's burning to get out. Clothes are like lead.

I'm yanked upwards from the middle. I break the surface and take a huge gulp of air and water and tiny pieces of plastic. Then it's swim-drag-swim back to the barge. Using my nails to scrape microplastic off, panting in oxygen every chance I get.

Ken reaches for me, and I grab his hand like my life depends on it. He hauls me out. I lie on the barge, drinking in breath after breath of glorious warm air.

'Don't just lie there!' Ken shouts.

I heave myself up. My belly's full of water and plastic, and I can taste the chemicals that are somewhere between aniseed and metal. Ken's already pulling the body – the man – along with my hook. It's almost at the barge.

'Stupid idiot. Should've left you in the drink,' Ken chunters under his breath.

I reach down and grab hold of it by the shoulder. It's a new body. After a couple of days, the sharks get all puffed up, and you can hear them popping when they get too much gas inside. This body hasn't got the bloat yet. He's not been dead long.

He's face down now, and I'm glad I don't have to look at his lifeless grey eyeballs.

We heave him out. With all the water in his clothes and all the netting attached to him, he weighs a ton. He's stiff, arms and legs sticking out at broken angles. It's harder than you'd think to get him out of the soup.

Finally, we collapse down on the deck next to the body. Water pools round it, and I shudder and inch my bare feet away. Ken looks like he's about to have a coronary. He moves his goggles to the top of his head. 'Ah shit,' he says. He wipes his nose with the back of his hand.

'We gotta call it in,' I say, breathless.

'Yep.'

Ken hauls himself up and shuffles into the cab. I hear the door open, then slam shut. He'll call the Super. Standard practice when anything happens out here. The gentle whir of the macerator ceases – Ken must've hit the emergency stop button. Then there's just the gulls. The gentle shush of waves. The rattle of the plastic shifting on the surface.

The sun warms my face. This could be paradise. If I hadn't just pulled a body out of the sea. And I wasn't killing days cleaning up an island of pollution. And I wasn't hiding from my mother who wants me to go back to the camp. If I still had May.

My chest aches with loss. But if I let the thought of her creep in there'll be nothing I can do to get rid of her.

Skin's hardening with a film of nurdles – the tiny pieces of chopped-up plastic – and I can tell my ponytail's clumping with them too. They're sticky and almost impossible to get off.

A palm-sized crab crawls over the shoulder of the body. Needle-sharp feet pressing into the fabric of the dead man's clothes. It creeps me out, so I grab it by the edge of its shell and hurl it into the waves so that it can't peck at the guy. He's got a safety rope round his middle.

How did this happen? Far as I know, no one's been reported missing, and surely his bargemate should've helped him out? I pull on the safety rope until the end slithers out of the water. It's snipped clean through, not frayed. Weird. Something severed it.

Ken's voice is muffled inside the cab. I watch him talking into the radio, pink lips flapping. My eyes wander to the horizon. The other barges sit on top of the ocean, hugging the edge of the great trash island. Sucking it in, bit by bit. Day by day.

The door to the barge opens, and Ken pokes his face out. 'Super wants to know who it is,' he says.

'Come on, Ken – I don't want to touch him again.'

'Do as you're told.' He goes back to talking on the radio, letting the door of the cabin slam.

I stand over the body, looking at the back of its unrecognizable head. I'll flip him over, fast as I can, and take a peek at the name badge without looking at his face. If I don't look into the eyes, I can pretend they're not staring at me.

I grab a handful of the guy's uniform and lift until he rolls

154

on to his back. He slaps down. I keep my eyes on the sky. *Blue. Clouds. Gulls.*

As I snap my eyes to the name badge sewn above the breast pocket, the hair on the back of my neck prickles.

The name on the dead guy's badge is Baaz.

He's wearing my uniform.

25

JANEK

The vibrations from the helicopter seem to reverberate through Janek's gut. The memory of her first helicopter trip surfaces like an eel from a hole, making her heart beat uncontrollably. Forcing her to maintain a placid exterior in the face of interior turmoil.

The helicopter banks. Beneath them, a sign for the Quentin Correctional Facility stands stark in the dry ground. A chain-link fence surrounds the complex, topped with a double string of barbed wire. Guard towers keep watch over the desert. It's not a place to escape from. Felons who successfully made it past the locked doors, the barbed-wire fences and the watchtowers would find there's nowhere to go. This complex is hidden deep in the southern wastelands, where the ground is dead from chemical weapons, and the few inhabitants look like they come from some sort of dystopian nightmare. The kind of dystopian nightmare Janek herself might still be living if it wasn't for the Federated States soldier who picked her up and strapped her into an evac helicopter.

The children she grew up with were not so lucky.

The door opens before the rotor blades have slowed, and the sandy ground swirls up round them. Her Secret Service detail presses a hand on the back of her head to keep her low as they scoot under the blades to safety. Harveen follows behind. Without slowing, Janek smooths her hair, rearranges her smile and strides towards the man waiting for her at the edge of the helipad, hand outstretched.

'Congressman Stokes, such a pleasure to finally meet you.'

'Welcome to the Quentin Correctional Facility, Admiral. The jewel of our conglomeration's assets. This way, please.' His palm is damp when he shakes her hand. Janek suppresses a shudder at the sensation.

Congressman Stokes leads Janek through a fenced tunnel and into the prison building. As they step inside, the cool spring temperature drops further, and Janek finds her skin shrinking in the chill. Doors beep as they're let through. Janek counts no fewer than four locked doors with armed guards.

'You certainly run a secure operation here, Congressman,' Janek says when they come to a stop.

They're on a mezzanine looking down into a hall that's like a factory floor. Row upon row of prisoners work inside individual perspex boxes. They're all similarly hunched over tables, heads shaved, overalls sagging from thin shoulders. A shiny metal cuff is attached to each prisoner's ear.

'We keep it cold. Stops 'em fighting each other,' the congressman says.

'What are they making?' Harveen asks. She flicks her eyes over the inmates below.

'Munitions. For your president's war.'

His tone gives Janek pause, but she's careful not to let it show on her face. This congressman owns a string of correctional facilities across the Federated States. Not only does he donate significant sums of money to the president's war chest, but he deals with the more unsavoury elements of the Federated States' population – the criminals, vagrants, pacifists. The labour his facilities control produces every bullet and shell in the Federated States' arsenal. If they wanted, they could bring the presidency down within twenty-four hours.

She glances at the congressman. 'You're a busy man. I don't want to waste any of your time. Tell me how I can reassure you.'

'Give us the refugees, Janek,' Stokes says. He raises his chin in determination. 'I need inmates. Your president promised us we'd have workers, and we've been waiting four months.'

A siren sounds, and red lights flash momentarily inside each box. Without hesitation, the inmates turn away from the things they've been working on and shuffle the few centimetres to the door of their compartments. After a few seconds, the door to each one slides open. The inmates step out and form a line, heads down. They're not quite close enough to touch one another. Another siren blares, and they shuffle towards the far end of the room and begin to disappear through a dark doorway opened by a prison guard. Before the door closes behind the last inmate, more appear from the opposite side of the room. They enter the perspex boxes in silence, eyes cast down. The doors seal them in automatically.

'Why not automate your system?' Harveen says.

Congressman Stokes glares at her like she's said something about his mother. Janek takes the opportunity to ingratiate herself. 'Because, my dear Harveen, robotics are expensive. As is the power necessary to run them. In contrast, human resources require relatively little in terms of input and have the added benefit of producing more human resources given enough time . . .'

Janek places a gentle hand on Congressman Stokes's arm and pulls him round so that he can't see the flicker of disgust that crosses Harveen's face. Her deputy will need to bolster her charm if Janek's going to be president one day.

'Now is not the moment to take the camp, Congressman. The president believes – and I agree with him – that the most effective way to get you the maximum number of new inmates is to exterminate any rebellious elements before we subdue. An uprising could result in significant loss of collateral. As soon as we have neutralized General Lall, Nikhil Lall and Esther Crossland, we'll be in a position to move forward.'

'Maybe we should pull our support for this whole operation. Down tools, stop producing the munitions your president needs for the war effort. How would he like that?'

'Congressman Stokes, you have my word: the camp will be brought under control. You and the prison conglomeration have my undivided attention. I'm putting all my power behind this.'

'I want to see more, Janek. All of us do.'

Janek thinks for a moment. 'What are those things the prisoners are wearing on their ears?'

'They're tracking-and-control cuffs. Let us keep an eye on how many we've got without having to do a headcount. Stops 'em getting lost if one manages to get through the defences. It's one of the first things we do when we get new inmates.'

'What if we started the process of subjugating the camp now? Would that help to convince you of our intention to provide you with workers?'

'I'm listening,' he says.

'My Coalies could start cuffing the camp's inhabitants immediately. To front-load some of your work.'

The Congressman sticks his tongue into his cheek while he thinks, nodding. 'That would certainly speed up processing.'

'Tell you what, give me a week. I'll tag every person in the camp for you, and you'll have a fresh delivery of workers before you know it.' Janek shakes Congressman Stokes's hand. 'Why don't you tell me more about your fascinating control methods?'

26

NIK

Cook slops food from the ladle on to my tray. It covers my thumb in pinkish goo. Got no idea what this is supposed to be. Some sort of chickeny porridge? It oozes over the edge of the tray and down my hand. Cook doesn't hate me. He's this much of a jerk to everyone on the island.

Being on the run for four months has taught me that you eat when there's food because you never know when you'll get the chance again. So even though I'm rolled by nausea every time I think of that body and the way it floated, I'm going to sit, and I'm gonna eat.

I wipe my hand down the side of my trousers while I look for a seat. The mess hall's heaving with roughnecks. No one wants to miss the good slops. Plus, they might get a look at me, the guy who pulled a body out this morning. This whole thing is making me nervy – thinking I should move on from this job sooner rather than later.

I spot an empty seat at one of the long galley tables near the door. The mess hall is a single-storey building, roof of corrugated metal, army-green lampshades swinging from the ceiling. The floor's covered in a kind of plastic matting that's worn through in the busiest spots to reveal the hard-packed, dusty ground beneath. More than once, I've spotted a lizard halfway up one of the walls.

The other roughnecks keep their eyes pressed on to me, and it's all I can do not to drop my tray and run. I take a seat on the long bench that's basically a wooden plank over barrels – it's as uncomfy as it sounds – and stare into the slop.

What a day. Showered and changed my clothes and I still can't wash off the memory of the body wearing my jacket, sloshing over and over in the water. And there's the nurdles stuck in my hair like rainbow dandruff. Know from experience they'll take weeks to come free.

I dunk a piece of bread and bury the urge to hurl. Tastes worse than I imagined. An unseasoned jelly mush.

Ken appears in the big opening that leads out of the mess hall. I see him cast around until he finds me and points a chunky finger in my direction. That's when I realize he's not alone. He's got the Super with him.

Eat fast. Cold slops can't be any better than hot slops.

The Super marches over. 'Ken says the dead guy was wearing your coat. Why is that, Baaz?' he says, planting his fists on the table in front of me.

He's not messing about. No more pleasantries. Baaz is the name I put on the paperwork when I arrived, and for all the Super knows it's the name I was born with. Nobody here knows my real name's Lall. Least I hope they don't.

'This is why I love you, Ken – you've always got my back,'

I say. Ken makes a waving gesture that means get lost and goes off to get his dinner. 'Afternoon, Supervisor Reynolds. How you doing today?'

'Don't give me any lip, kid.'

He swipes my tray out from in front of me. The slops fly everywhere, splattering pink over the floor. I see it splash on to some poor guy's boot at the next table. The Super points his finger right in my face, round and stumpy like a cocktail sausage.

I stand. My fists ball up like they've got a mind of their own. I'm tired. I'm hungry. And after destroying my radio yesterday this guy is testing my patience. 'That was my meal,' I say.

We stare eye to eye. He glares. Veiny neck. Bulging eyes. Flared nostrils. I know this guy. He's the type that came out here because he can't play nice with people. All his posturing. All his swagger. All his anger leaking out all over the place. It doesn't go down well in the normal world.

'Why was the dead guy wearing your coat?'

'Lent it to him. Yesterday. His got soaked because his partner –' I pause and look round the mess hall. Everyone's silent. 'His partner couldn't control their barge, and he went for a swim. His uniform had to be decontaminated.'

'His tether was snipped. You know anything about that?'

The slops I've just eaten curdle inside me. I was right about his safety rope being tampered with.

'Nope.'

The Super slaps me. Hard enough to whip my face round. Hard enough for it to sting in a hand shape. I rub it. *Keep your cool, Lall.* This is still a good place to hide, and getting booted from the rig will mean finding somewhere new to go, with some other shitty job that might be ten times worse than this. I roll my jaw and rub my face.

'Told you before: I ask a question, you answer it. Without any cheek. Don't like it, and I can tear up your contract right now, give you a boat, and point you in the direction of Tampa.'

'OK,' I say.

'OK, what?'

'OK, Super, sir,' I say through gritted teeth.

'Good. Now, did you kill him?'

'What? Of course I didn't kill him.'

'Your name's on his jacket.'

'Because he was wearing my coat,' I say. This is starting to piss me off.

'That places you at the scene of the crime.'

'No, it doesn't. It places my jacket at the scene of the crime. Why would I give him my coat – that literally has my name stitched on the front – and then kill him?'

The Super glares. I can see him forcing his mind round the corners of the problem. 'You're the only clue I've got, so find out who killed him before the end of this rotation or you'll be in handcuffs.'

'Hang on, isn't that your job?'

'I decide what my job is.'

'Then decide to get someone else. I'm no detective, and I don't plan on spending my sleeping hours on a wild goose chase.'

I need to defuse this situation. I need to back down before the Super gets so riled up he gets on the blower to the Federated

States. I bite my tongue and turn on my heel, a fizzing ball of suppressed rage. All I want is to be left alone. Is that too much to ask?

'You find out who did this, Baaz,' he shouts after me. 'You find out or you're finished here!'

27

JANEK

Admiral Janek kneels on the cold marble floor of the cathedral. Paparazzi lights flash around her. She presses her hands together, bows her head. She remains there, in silence, for long enough to make it believable. The possibility that she's merely acting pious, rather than being pious, fades with each flash of the cameras. *Let's give it another thirty seconds, shall we?*

The silence draws her to another time she spent kneeling.

Between the shock of the blasts, dust sprinkled from the ceiling. Her friend's name is lost to memory, but Janek can feel the grip of her fingers, as though it's happening this very moment. Every shake of the building accompanied by a tightening of fear in their hands. Across from her the teacher is sheltering beneath his own desk. It feels like an eternity since the siren wailed, telling them the United States had launched a missile attack. The window glass rattles and cracks, even though they spent a whole afternoon pressing tape over the pane and painting rainbows and flowers and love hearts on to the brown paper. There's a flash. Janek squeezes her eyes tighter. She thinks of her mum and dad and baby brother as the slicing spray of powdered glass hits her.

Stay where you are, the teacher shouts. Her friend's face has streaks of dark skin where the tears are running from their eyes and streaks of red blood running from the cuts. Janek's mouth tastes of chalk.

A camera flash brings her back into the cathedral. Janek lets tears well in her eyes – these ones are real. She takes a deep and showy breath, and turns her face upwards to the elaborate golden dome that shelters the altar. She can already imagine the pictures that will be published within minutes. The purity of the gold. The solidity of the stonework. An indoor drone, sent by one of the less polite journalists, circles until it's in front of her. She wipes a tear from her cheek before getting to her feet. Pain shoots through her knees as she gets up, but she maintains the gentle smile. Nobody likes a president-elect that exhibits weakness, least of all the president himself. He understands the importance of appearing vigorous.

As she walks to the podium, her heels click on the flagstones. The tap-tap echoes round the cavernous interior of the cathedral. *Dammit, Harveen should have caught that.* Wearing heels in a cathedral is the kind of faux pas that no president-elect can afford. Only six months ago, one of her predecessors, Jocelyn Aguilar, made the mistake of dance-walking on to the stage at a rally. Her career was in tatters within an hour. Politicians rarely survive the harsh light of public humiliation in the Federated States.

For her, though, the stakes are higher. The only thing standing between Janek and an appointment with the gallows is staying in public office.

Harveen ought to have known better. No one should be focusing on Janek's footwear in this moment. It's too late now, so her aim must be to tread carefully, while not letting the fact that she's treading carefully show in her gait. The cameras will pick up any sign of change. Any stumble. Any hint of awkwardness.

The indoor drones follow Janek to the podium. They're small compared to the full-sized ones she uses for surveillance and population control, and these miniature versions are equipped with almost silent engines so as not to disrupt the audio recorders and cameras that they carry.

'Thank you all for joining me on this beautiful morning,' she says, beaming a winning smile and resting her hands on the smooth wood of the lectern.

'Admiral Janek, can you tell us what you plan to do with the cruise ship *Arcadia*?' A voice comes up from the crowd of journalists standing a few metres in front of her.

'Can you tell us how you intend to deal with the Europeans now living in the camp?' pipes up another.

Janek is careful not to let the exasperation spread to her face. When she took office, she expected to have this issue wrapped up within a few weeks. She wanted the ships gone and the people making money in the labour camps, without them being used as political capital by any of the Federated States' enemies. Instead, there are escapees spread over two states, a sprawling and disobedient camp, and a rebel leader making daily demands for supplies. That imbecile

Commander Hadley cocked up the one thing he was meant to do. Truth be told, it's a shame he's dead. Janek could use a patsy. Instead, this is what she gets. Day after day. News cycle after news cycle. A constant whine: *What about the* Arcadia?

'There are thousands of Europeans living along our coastline. Within walking distance of homes and schools. People want to know what you're doing about it.'

'You're right. And that's why this morning I will begin a programme of tagging each and every refugee in the camp.'

The crowd murmurs. The cameras flash.

'Individuals will be constantly tracked. Any escapees can be dealt with swiftly and without danger to the public.'

Harveen hurries over, carrying a cardboard box. Janek opens it and brings out a metal cuff in the shape of a crescent moon. Mutterings from the paparazzi.

'You. Come forward.' She points at a journalist. A middle-aged, well-turned-out man. Untidy salt-and-pepper hair.

He looks at his fellow leeches uncertainly.

'Come on, I won't bite,' she says. She smiles for the cameras and lifts the cuff to his face. 'Give me your age, name and occupation.'

The man licks his lips. He speaks clearly into the curved piece of metal. 'Barney King, forty-nine. I'm a journalist for FS News Twenty-four.'

The cuff opens like a clam. The spikes inside are revealed.

Gasps and a flurry of bulb flares.

'You're attaching these to people?' he says, moving his head to look at the spikes. He waves two fingers in the air, and a camera drone wheels round to get a clear shot.

'It's a completely painless procedure. It's so safe, I'll even attach it myself.'

To demonstrate, Janek pulls back her hair, lines the cuff up over her ear, and clamps it shut. There's no pain, of course, because this cuff is a fake with retractable spikes. She smoothly opens it again and leans towards King. He lets her close the cuff over his ear, touching it uncertainly.

'Now Barney King's details are stored in our central database, we can get him the food and medical help he needs, and if it becomes necessary we can locate him using GPS.'

On cue, Harveen presses buttons on a digiscreen, bringing a holographic display up in the air next to Janek's shoulder. It shows a plan of the cathedral, outlines of the pews and altar, and a single red point next to the name Barney King. Smiling, Janek spins her finger in the air. King gets the hint and walks in a circle. The point mimics his movement.

The journalist shifts uneasily. 'And if they refuse to have one fitted?' he says.

That little show will give her a nice bump in the polls and buy her favour in the eyes of the president. Now turn off the humanity and turn on the gravitas.

'The Federated States is built on the principles of freedom and opportunity. Of course these devices are not mandatory. However, registration will be required to access resources such as food, water and medical care. And why would anyone refuse? Only if they have something to hide. The beaching of the cruise ship *Arcadia* presents unique challenges of a kind never faced in the history of the Federated States. We must treat its population with compassion, but not at the expense of our own citizens. They bring the problems of the *Arcadia* on to our very doorstep, and I refuse to let the drugs, crime and, most importantly, the deadly sickness that ravaged Europe be forced upon the people of the Federated States. Many of the *Arcadia*'s inhabitants are decent, hard-working and of clean health. But it would be unwise to ignore the ones that aren't. We do not want the criminal or the contagious to be woven into the fabric of our nation. We cannot allow them to invade our shores unchecked. This is my most strongly held belief. There are those among the president's political enemies who argue that the ship people should be freed. I say that could be catastrophic.'

A cheer from the supportive journalists. A boom of the national anthem. Janek feels a surge of pleasure and determination. She joins in the clapping, raising her hands in front of her chest in celebration.

Before the music stops, Harveen taps her on the shoulder. Janek waves briefly to the gathered press before following her out of the cathedral. Harveen strides ahead, carrying the digiscreen she uses to organize the admiral's calendar in one hand. She leads Janek to a neatly kept garden of remembrance where a small courtyard is edged with leafless rose bushes. Behind them, the muddy brown stone columns of the cathedral reach into the sky like the trunks of dead trees. The sun offers little warmth, despite being high overhead. Janek finds herself inspecting one of the bushes while she waits for Harveen to deliver whatever piece of inevitably bad news she's bringing.

'What have you got for me?' she asks when Harveen isn't forthcoming.

'The assassination attempt failed.'

Janek runs her finger along the stem of a rose bush until she finds a thorn. 'It's one seventeen-year-old boy. How can it be this difficult to get rid of him?'

'He's outside Federated States territory, and you're not the president.'

Janek presses, hard, until the skin on her forefinger splits over the thorn. Blood dribbles down the woody stem. She does not allow herself to gasp at the pain. 'Yet,' she says. She inspects the deep red bead of blood on her fingertip before squeezing it against her thumb.

'Pardon me, ma'am?'

'I am not the president. Yet.'

'Of course, ma'am. Ordering his murder breaks international law. You could face extradition and be tried at the International Court. We have to maintain deniability. It has to at least look like an accident.'

'So make it look like one.'

'The covert-ops team tried, but they got the wrong person.'

Janek laughs. She turns to face Harveen. 'The ineptitude is baffling.'

Harveen nods, her long black hair bobbing over her shoulders. The woman has been Janek's chief of staff for years, and Janek has rarely seen her feathers ruffled. She's always well turned out, even on their most challenging days together. Janek's bid for the White House was born from their mutual desire to stay out of the courtroom. Because the truth is, if Janek goes down, Harveen goes down with her. They're like ivy climbing the same wall, so intertwined that one can't be removed without killing the other.

'The team is working on a new plan. It can be ready by

twenty-three hundred hours. They just need you to give it the green light, ma'am.'

'I want him dead. I don't want him back here standing trial. And I certainly do not want him before the press. He's too young and too gutsy to put in front of a camera.'

'He might be easier to control than his mother,' Harveen says.

Janek lets the thought marinate. She's been focused on terminating Nikhil Lall, but perhaps a younger rebel leader would be more willing to make concessions. If the camp can be quickly and quietly brought under control without the need for messy assassinations, it would help Janek's standing with the president.

Finally, she says, 'It's too much of a risk. There's no guarantee he'll be any easier to deal with than his mother. The last thing we need is a new icon of the rebellion. The main problem that General Lall poses is that she's a sympathetic figure. The brave widow who fought for freedom. She's popular. Her son could be even more beloved.'

'I understand.' Harveen pauses. She seems to be considering her next words carefully. 'I would be negligent in my role as your advisor if I didn't mention the fact that this goes against President Walsh's direct orders. He demanded discretion. If this reaches the press –'

'Enough,' Janek says, holding up a hand in frustration. 'I don't want to hear about President Walsh's orders. That man has tied my hands for too long. He'll be happy to ignore my methods when I finally have Nik Lall's body on a slab.'

'Very well, ma'am. The team is confident their plan will work this time. However . . .'

'Stop equivocating, Ms Atwal.'

Harveen swallows. 'There's potential for significant collateral damage.'

'Then compensate the injured parties.'

Harveen takes a step forward so that she can speak close to Janek's ear. She hugs her digiscreen to her chest. 'Every simulation of the mission has resulted in numerous casualties.'

Janek considers. 'Federated States citizens?'

Harveen shakes her head. 'No, ma'am.'

'Then I want Nikhil Lall dead.'

28

NIK

In the thirty seconds it takes me to get out of the mess hall and across the dimly lit yard outside, I've already decided: it's time for me to run. I've got no hope of figuring out which of the roughnecks has murderous intent towards me, and the longer I stay here, the more likely I am to piss the Super off. And then the big stupid ox will turn me in.

I can't get arrested. It'll take the authorities a short minute to figure out who I am. And, while I've got no idea if the United States has an extradition treaty with the Federated States, I'm pretty sure the Coalies will find some way to smuggle me across the border. Then it'll be back up north to the capital to go on trial for running the *Arcadia* ashore. The charges against me – treason, sedition, murder – are nothing to be sneezed at. If they find me guilty (which they will), I face the rest of my life doing hard labour, until they work out a way to get rid of me permanently. Some nights, I think it's exactly what I deserve.

A faint electrical buzzing sound comes from one of the

floodlights set up round the exercise yard. It sets my nerves ringing. Where I come from, that kind of hum means one thing: drones. I shake myself to relax. There are no drones here. No Coalies. No rebellion trying to make me into some sort of hero poster boy. No mother telling me how disappointed she is that I won't be following in her footsteps. No girl that reminds me of the one I lost.

The thing that's bothering me, festering like an infected wound, is the fact that the guy was wearing my uniform. So was he the target or was I? And will the murderer be giving it another go?

At the edge of the compound, there's a fence, and beyond that, wild jungle, steeped in shadows that move with the faint breeze. I speed up. Crossing the dusty basketball court in six strides, I waft away a cloud of midges that are gathered round one of the lights. It's a quiet night. Hot. Dense with pollen and sea spray. This base camp belongs to the enviro-clean-up company I work for and consists of ten flat-roofed buildings arranged round a rectangular yard. The mess hall's the biggest. The Super has his own single-storey house with an office attached. Then there's a gaggle of barracks standing round the other sides of the yard.

As I get to the door of my hut, I'm almost running. This whole thing has me spooked. I slam through the screen door that's meant to keep the mozzies out. No one's in here sleeping yet. Too hot, and they're all too busy talking about that dead body and trying to figure out if I'm a serial killer. The smell of feet and armpits never wanes. Mice scuttle in the corners. Once I woke up to find a bat circling the ceiling.

I rush between the lines of empty, unmade bunk beds, then I go out of the door at the back of the room and through the stinking latrine room where flies buzz up from the plugholes. Through the utility room where we can wash our clothes in cold brown water. Into the storeroom lined with cluttered shelves that hold buckets of that pink sludge chef calls food. I check over my shoulder to make sure no one's following me, then use an upturned bucket to climb through the ceiling hatch. At least I won't be an easy grab if the murderer does come for me.

Before I click the solar lantern on, I hold my breath in case someone's already up here waiting for me. Then pale light floods the roof space, picking out my hammock strung between two beams, my pile of clothes, and the paper bag of extra food I keep for emergencies. But no murderer, so I close the hatch carefully behind me. The roof space reminds me of my bunk back home. More importantly, it's private.

Standing with my head bent under the low ceiling, I try to figure out which of the roughnecks I share base camp with is most likely to be a killer. Problem is I keep myself to myself. Apart from Ken, I almost never talk to anyone, and I don't think he's got the energy in him to fight another man to the death so I'm pretty happy to strike him off my list of suspects. And that leaves . . . no one. I have no clue where to even start investigating.

You know what? It doesn't matter. I'm not going to be here long enough to figure it out. I grab my holdall from behind the hammock and shove my spare set of clothes into it, followed by my old boots and a packet of biscuits I've been saving for a rainy day. Then I swing into my hammock.

It creaks on its ropes. First thing, when it gets light, I'll hop on one of the transport boats to Tampa. I can get a bar job or something on a farm to keep me afloat while I figure out where I go from here.

By the time I've crunched through a couple of biscuits, my anger at the Super and the anxiety of the day are fading. The tension drains from my shoulders. The skin on my nose is tight with sunburn, and I scratch it until it's too sore to touch. There's a sound somewhere over the thick jungle. Right about now, the night shift will be heading out on to the rigs, taking their turn at cleaning up the mess made a hundred years ago.

It's warm and quiet, and my head gets fuzzy from the sway of the hammock. Her face floats to the front of my mind. Beaming after we dropped leaflets all over the Lookout cafe.

Hugging me and saying goodbye before she left the ship the first time.

Running after her sister on the Flotilla.

I jolt awake, a wave of grief crashing over me. It feels as fresh and raw as it did in the days after she was killed. Murdered. By Hadley's Coalies. I press the heels of my hands into my eyes until my vision blackens.

Somewhere in the sky, the sound of an engine gets closer. Something else joins the grief swimming in my gut. Dread and realization. That noise isn't in the distant jungle any more. It's in the air above base camp.

I drop out of the hammock and end up in a heap on the rough wooden boards. Scrambling up, I put my eye to a crack in the panelled walls, scanning the night for the source of the sound. Lights swing through the darkness, shining from the silhouette of a helicopter.

The Exiled

There's no time to run. Even if there was, there's nowhere to go. Into the forests that surround the compound – then where? It's just ocean beyond that. Too late, I realize I've trapped myself out here on this island with no way to escape.

I'm a rat in a barrel.

29

NIK

Coalies. Or my mother.

Those are the options. Not much I can do now. Whoever it is will find me the minute they start searching the place. Could go out to the rig, but it's the same deal. Just delaying the inevitable.

I grab my bag and climb down the ladder. Then I sneak out to the bunk-room doorway, where I can watch the thing coming in before whoever's flying it spots me.

It's an enormous machine, blades spinning at the front and the back. Painted all black, just how the Coalies like it. It comes in to land in the middle of the basketball court. Roughnecks are gathered in every doorway, shielding their eyes from the dust thrown up by the rotor blades. The chain-link fence that surrounds the complex jangles in the turbulence. Still skulking in the shadow of the doorway, I watch the Super steam out of his hut. Looks like he's about to tear whoever's flying that thing a new one. Ken comes out too, and all the others who were quietly enjoying their dinner in the mess hall. No way they'd miss a show. *Take a good look, boys.*

The noise slows to a low whine.

Someone steps down and takes a few running steps from the helicopter cab before straightening up. I recognize that cocky gait immediately. It's Enid. Dark hair blowing in the wind from the copter. Dark eyes ringed with black. She looks around like she owns the place, thumbs hooked in her pockets.

Even though she's found my hiding place, even though she's here to drag me back to that wretched camp, even though she's working for my mother, I want to hug her.

'Nik my boy,' she says, sauntering up to me. 'You're a sight for sore eyes. Not looking too good though, if I'm honest. Not loving the ponytail.' She lets her eyes run over my sunburnt face, taking in the nurdles still clumping like glue in my straggly, uncut hair, the slops drying on my trousers.

'How'd you find me, Enid?' I say.

'What, no small talk? It wasn't that difficult to keep track of you. You're not as stealthy as you like to think.'

I fold my arms and raise my eyebrows. Don't have the patience for her tonight.

She sighs. Rolls her eyes. 'I've found you. I've won. Can we skip the whole what're you doing here, how did you find me, yada yada yada, and just get on the copter?' She gestures over her shoulder.

'No,' I say.

'Your mother wants you home and, in any case, I've got it on good authority that I'm not the only one who knows where you are and what flimsy identity you've been using.'

The hairs on the back of my neck stand up at that. They know where I am. 'They'd be down here arresting me if they knew,' I say.

'It's not as easy as just flying down and grabbing you. They've got to be stealthy. Make it look like an accident.'

'Wait, did they try something already?'

'Just yesterday apparently.'

That explains the dead body. That poor guy wasn't the target at all. It was the Coalies coming for me. 'Who's telling you all this?'

'My source in the capital. They told me someone tried to bump you off, but they botched the whole thing, and another poor fella bit it instead.'

The Super's standing next to me now. 'I knew you had something to do with this.'

'I didn't have anything to do with it!'

'He was killed cos of you,' he says.

'Sorry to interrupt, but we really need to get in the copter,' Enid says. 'We can chat it all through on the way home.'

'No.' I shake my head. Set my feet firmer on the ground. Not going back. I'll go anywhere but back to that camp. 'Explain everything, right here, or you'll have to drag me on to that transport.'

'It can be arranged.'

'Enid!'

'OK, OK. Look, the Coalies have been looking for you. That Admiral Janek woman is convinced you're the rightful heir of the rebellion or some such nonsense, and she wants to bump you off. Someone here –' she waves around at the roughnecks who've been gathering to watch the show – 'was told to do away with you. Only they didn't get all the information, and they bumped off the wrong person. Probably want to do some checks to see which of your people are spies, by the way,' she says, looking at the Super. He shifts uneasily. 'Now, Janek is mighty pissed off that the assassination attempt was ballsed up, and she's getting agitated that you're still alive. So, she's authorized her team to take more drastic action –'

'More drastic than having me killed?'

'Apparently so.'

'How do you know all this?'

'I've got my sources. One source, actually, on Janek's staff.'

'Hey, why'd she call you Nik?' Ken pipes up from where he's standing a metre or so away.

'That's his name,' Enid says.

The Super's been slowly bubbling, and now he turns beetroot red. 'This is my yard. No one comes in here landing helicopters and taking people away. There's health-and-safety rules.'

'Ah, stop your stupid mouth,' Enid says. 'We all know there's nothing healthy nor safe about the job these blokes are doing.'

The Super's lips open and close like a fish. I can't help laughing. The people around him shuffle awkwardly. They watch with wide eyes. Drink it all in.

'This is getting silly now – come on. You've had your time to find yourself. You've had long enough hiding out. You need to come back,' Enid says, ignoring the heavy breathing sounds coming from the Super.

'Not coming back, Enid. I'm done. With the rebellion. With my mother. With all of it.'

'Don't you miss her at all?'

'My mother? No.'

'Wasn't talking about your mother.'

I don't miss her. I refuse to.

'Do what you gotta do. You're not getting me on that copter. I'm under contract anyway. Couldn't leave even if I wanted to,' I say, gesturing towards the Super, who's glaring at Enid.

'Your mother wants you home. Janek wants you dead. I'm here to make sure the former happens, not the latter, and I'm estimating that we've got –' Enid looks at her watch – 'an hour, give or take, before the Coalies start landing their own helicopters in this yard.'

A wave of heat flushes my cheeks. Coalies. Coming here. That changes things. I need to think. I need time. I could be on a boat back to the mainland in fifteen minutes if the Super will lend me one. But what then? Coalies come here and interrogate the Super? He's not going to defend me from them. Before you know it, I'll be halfway to Tampa with the Coalies on my heels. Florida's enemy territory for them, but I'm sure they'd find a way to follow me.

Enid's frozen in place. Not a speck of agitation or anxiety anywhere on her. Not for the first time it feels like I'm playing a game with Enid, except she's counted the whole deck and I've only got three cards in my hand.

There's a bang in the distance. I flinch. My heart pounds. Everybody turns towards the sound. Out over the ocean, a plume of fire shoots up into the night. Another bang. Another plume of fire.

I spin back to face Enid. She's not smirking any more; she's staring at the explosion just like the rest of us. Face lit up by the flames in the distance. Another bang rips through the night.

'Looks like my estimation was a fraction off,' she says breathlessly.

'They're already here,' I say.

'My contact wasn't kidding about it being a big attack. Well, it's a good way to make sure you can't stay here.'

I clutch my head and watch, powerless, as another barge goes up. 'There're people out there,' I say.

Ken's the first one to run. 'Get the boats in the water,' he shouts. Then we're all sprinting for the beach.

30

NIK

Six barges burn in the night, the sea around them glowing with fiery plastic. Flames are spreading from barge to barge.

Feels like the fire's in my nerves. Every neuron sparking with fear. I skid to a stop on the beach as another barge goes up. The explosion sends the platform into the air, dragging its arm into the sky. The other barges twist and thrash when the arms connecting them jerk about.

Night shift was on duty. And that means a hundred roughnecks in the water. Much as I hate being out here, I don't want to see any of those guys become shark bait.

The dinghies we use to shuttle us out to the rigs and back again are almost all gone. Out in the ocean, silhouetted figures run back and forth in front of the flames, trying to make the decision; burn or drown. Some of them jump from the rigs and swim for the shore. Between here and there is a bank where the waves roll up and crash back down. Some of those guys have just been blown up or burned, and now they've got to swim for their lives. They'll never make it.

I splash through the waves and get to the nearest dinghy, pulling the mooring rope free.

The sea is on fire. Noxious fumes thicken the air, a suffocating layer of smog above the ocean.

'Don't just stand there. Get in that boat!' a voice shouts.

Ken's wading into the shallows – suddenly he's all action hero. Who'd have thought it? He jumps into the boat with me, pushing me away from the tiller, and within sixty seconds we've got a handful of tiny boats steaming out towards the ocean-top inferno. At least half the barges have gone up. They pop like corn kernels when the fire reaches their fuel cells. Don't fancy the chances of anyone aboard one when it blows.

'Need to release the rigs or the whole thing's going to go up!' Ken shouts.

'What? You're kidding.'

Ken pushes the tiller, and we surge towards the nearest fire-free barge. We get close enough that I can feel the flames trying to bubble my skin. There are two guys from the night shift waving and shouting from the platform of the rig. We pull alongside so they can jump into the bottom of the boat. They've both got burned, their red-and-black flesh showing through holes in their uniforms.

Fumes swim round me. My stomach feels like it's about to turn inside out.

'You're up, Baaz.' Ken turns the boat so that we're facing the great arm of the rig. 'Emergency release is on the underside of the arm.'

'Get closer!' I kneel at the front of the boat and reach over the prow, trying to grab the big red lever that will uncouple the rig from the collecting arm. My eyes stream. Flakes of burning plastic fill the air like confetti. They singe wherever they stick to my skin. 'Almost got it,' I murmur. I have to lean out over the water, and in a split second my balance is gone and my stomach lurches as I tumble.

I don't hit the water. Someone's holding on to the back of my shirt. I reach the handle. Grasp it. Pull.

Ken yanks me back into the boat. 'Second time I've saved your ass today,' he says.

The collecting arm splits from the barge and floats away.

Ken speeds us back to the shore.

And then we're on the sand.

And I'm puking.

31

JANEK

Janek kicks the coverlet off her feet and paces to the window. The Statehouse, her official residence, has extensive grounds, towering trees and manicured lawns bounded by a high-security wall. In the distance are the city lights and the smudge of their reflection in the water of the bay. Above the skyscrapers of downtown, surveillance drones blink. They patrol the urban centre and the suburbs for signs of trouble.

She rarely sleeps more than three hours a night, yet navigating the situation between the president and the prison conglomeration is still affecting her rest. There's more than just her succession to president at stake here. If she loses the presidency, she loses diplomatic immunity.

Janek needs to feel the air on her skin. She pushes the sash upwards and leans on the sill to breathe in the icy spring air, ignoring the security alarm that sounds throughout the Statehouse.

There's an insistent bleating from the AI speaker on her dressing table, notifying her of a message about to be delivered. Janek sits down, catching a glimpse of herself in the mirror. Hair more grey than blonde in recent years. Face speckled with age spots.

'Room, deliver message.'

Within seconds, a tiny drone flies in through the window. It drops a metal message canister on to the table in front of Janek. She gives it a light tap. Instantly, the lid flips off, and a bot pushes two legs out. It's only the size of a playing card, one spiked leg attached to each corner.

'Do not disobey me again.' President Walsh's voice plays through a speaker on the tiny bot's back.

Before Janek has time to react, the bot lurches on to the back of her hand. In a flash, its four legs have pierced her flesh and driven themselves into the wood of the desk. She screams in agony, barely resisting the urge to yank herself free. That would only cause more pain. Instead, she holds her impaled hand still while she snatches a fountain pen from the table, and bites off the lid with her teeth. She pushes the pen between one of the bot's legs and her hand. The leg slides free, slimy with blood. Janek gasps at the pain. She moves on to the next leg. It takes only a minute to free herself. The bot is limp on the blood-spattered table. Janek wiggles her fingers. The legs have left eight round puncture wounds, each oozing blood.

Behind her, the door opens and closes.

'Do we have confirmation?' she says, without turning round. Only Harveen would dare to check whether Janek was awake without knocking first.

'Oh God . . .' Harveen starts, coming close enough to inspect Janek's hand in the low light.

'Don't make a fuss,' Janek spits. She's still breathing heavily.

'Here.' Harveen unwraps the thin silk scarf from her neck and wraps it round Janek's mangled hand. 'Was this the president?'

'It appears he's unhappy with my decision to take a more drastic line on Nikhil Lall. Now would be the perfect moment to report that he's been obliterated.'

There's a short exhale of breath. Not quite a sigh. 'There was a lot of wreckage –'

'I didn't ask about the wreckage. I asked whether you were here to confirm Nikhil Lall's death.'

Janek is losing her cool. Not something she's used to. Not something she intends to allow.

'The teams are doing what they can.'

'I want them both dead. Why is this so difficult . . . ? How can it be so hard to find . . .'

Janek looks out of the window and breathes. The icy air works to soothe her nerves. 'Did I ever tell you the story of how my hometown fell, Harveen?'

'No, ma'am.'

Even now, Janek can taste the dust that showered from the ceiling. 'I grew up in the shadow of the Blue Ridge Mountains. Did you know that?'

'I did, ma'am.'

'My town was on the front line between the Federated States and the United States, and the spring before the ceasefire we were really getting hammered. I'm talking air-raid sirens in the middle of the night, drills in our classrooms, people walking away from town with nothing but the clothes on their back, just hoping to go far enough that the shells wouldn't get them.'

Harveen shakes her head, and in the darkness Janek can see the expression of sympathy on the younger woman's face. 'I've heard the horror stories of what happened. It must have been difficult for someone so young.'

'After four weeks, the United States had us over a barrel. Surrounded by their forces, civilians starving and dying from disease in their hundreds. The town was being held by a small militia made up of locals. They were spread out and hiding in the suburbs. The United States got a message to the rebels that if they gave themselves up, the civilians would be spared.'

'Interesting. They relied on the emotional response of the rebels.'

'Exactly.'

'Did it work?'

'Yes and no. Conditions were so bad that the rebel leaders were *persuaded* by the civilian population. It took less than forty-eight hours for them to walk up to a United States checkpoint and lay down arms.'

'That must have been terribly difficult for you.'

Janek holds her injured hand to her stomach. 'Indeed. But it also taught me that sometimes all that's needed is the correct motivation. I wonder if the people of the *Arcadia* might be similarly persuaded to give the teenagers up.'

'A direct threat against the civilians in the hope that Nikhil Lall and Esther Crossland will give themselves up or be betrayed. I doubt the president will sanction it. The public reacts badly to morally ambiguous policy.'

'We have to be subtle about it. If we push the right buttons, the camp inhabitants will come to the right conclusion on their own. Let's see if we can find a way to flush them out, shall we?'

Harveen nods curtly. A question seems to hover between the women.

'Something further?' Janek asks.

'What happened to the civilians?'

'Some, including me, were rescued by a Federated States soldier and evacuated.'

'And the others?'

'There were few survivors once the United States forces moved in. You won't find many Janeks in the Federated States.'

Harveen clutches her screen to her chest.

'Let's see if we can flush the rebels out without having to flatten the place,' Janek says.

32

NIK

Barely got enough energy to drag myself up through the hatch to my bunk, but, when I see Esther, and she smiles, I throw my arms round her. I bury my face in her neck. Tears build behind my eyes until it aches to hold them back. How did she even get here?

'So you do miss her,' she says. In the wrong voice.

I shove her away. 'Enid, what the hell?'

She reaches behind her ear and unpeels a flesh-coloured circle. A wire trails into her hair. Esther's face ripples and disappears, revealing Enid's smiling features underneath.

'Neat, huh? It's an augmented-reality mask. Just a party trick really. Won't stand up to much scrutiny, but it's enough to fool the Coalies if the need arises.'

'That was cheap,' I say.

'Ah, don't be like that, Nik my boy.' Enid looks round my room. 'Nice place you've got here.'

'I'm not coming back. Doesn't matter how many stunts you pull, or how many people you pretend to be.'

I rub the layer of grime on my face. My stomach's still churning from the smell of the plastic burning. It's a miracle that we managed to drag everyone out of the water, but some of those guys were burnt so bad they'll be in the ICU for months. The Super's already been on the phone to his superiors to request full evacuation. There's a convoy an hour out. Whether he'll let me get on the transport, I don't know.

I start taking my filthy clothes off. Between the ash and the nurdles, it's probably time to brave the brown water that dribbles from the showers downstairs.

'Sure you're not coming back. I hear you. Only . . .'

'Only what?'

'Your mother wants you home.'

'Nope.'

'And she's tasked me with bringing you.'

'I said no.' I pull a clean T-shirt on without bothering with the shower. Not convinced it would help at this point anyway.

'But you know how snippy she gets when she doesn't get her own way.' Enid hops up on to my hammock. Swings her legs. My towel's hanging from a hook by her head, and she grabs it and throws it at me.

I catch it and rub my hair. It's matted into thick, crunchy strands. 'Is she OK?' I say without looking up at Enid.

'Who?'

'Not my mother obviously.' Wish I could pretend I didn't care what's happening to Esther Crossland, but that ship sailed when I thought I was giving her a big old bear hug.

There's silence for a few too many seconds. 'Your mother's

got her hiding out in a shack on the edge of the camp. Girl's going stir-crazy. You going to offer me any refreshments?'

'Energy bar in the bag,' I say.

'And of course the Coalies are up to their usual tricks. Most recent thing is tagging everyone. Giving them these cuffs pinned right through their ears so they can see where everyone is at every second of the day and night.'

I stare down at the towel. Just like I expected, hearing about home hurts. 'Does she know about the boyfriend?'

'No. She's been asking John to keep an eye out for him, but I've told him to keep schtum. She doesn't want anything to do with that scumbag if you ask me.'

Well, that's something.

'Rumour has it she's met someone new. Not that you're interested in that.'

And there's another ripple of pain followed immediately by the guilt.

I stick the corner of the towel in my ear to clean out the nurdles. 'None of my business.'

Enid smirks and chomps an energy bar. 'OK. So, what's it going to take to get you back to the camp?' She drops the crumpled wrapper on to the floorboards.

'Apart from hell freezing?' I say.

'Come on, your rig's gone. The Coalies are certainly going to have another crack at killing you. What have you got to stick around here for?'

'They're transferring us back to Tampa. We'll wait for a new assignment there.'

'Ah no. That's not going to work.'

'It's not your decision.'

'OK.' She shrugs.

I let out a sigh because I know for a fact it's not OK. She's not letting this go.

Ken's head pushes up through the hatch in the floor.

'Ah, there he is. My latest minion,' Enid says. She jumps down from the hammock.

'What's that supposed to mean?' I say.

'Say hello to the newest member of my team. I've just purchased Ken's contract from your Super. For what was it, Ken?'

'Two years and four months,' Ken says.

'Leave him out of this,' I say.

'Ken here is heading off on an assignment. Sadly, it's going to be a lot less pleasant than this one.'

'Huh?' Ken says, his mouth flapping open.

'Got your stuff, Ken?' Enid says.

'It's by the copter,' Ken says. 'This is your doing, Baaz. I was meant to be going home in two weeks. Had a cushy factory job lined up near my mom's house.'

'Now, now. It's not like Nik here can do anything about your situation. You'll be fine. Those Australian lithium mines are way safer than they used to be.'

'Let him go,' I say.

'It's a contract. Signed and paid for. He goes where I tell him.'

'We both know you aren't going to make him honour his contract.'

Enid stares me dead in the face, not a flicker of humour in her eyes. 'Try me.'

I screw the towel up and throw it against the wall. She always wins.

Enid smiles. Holds out her hand for me to shake.

'Your mother's expecting you tonight.'

33

JANEK

The man from the camp stands on the marble floor of 30th Street Station with his shoulders up round his ears. Janek watches him on the large conferencing display on her desk. He looks like he's recently woken from a deep sleep. Three hours ago, he was inside the camp. Now, he's standing in the busiest train station in the Federated States, surrounded by rush-hour commuters. Janek planned every detail: from the quiet tranquillizer dart in the night, to the secret transport, then the bleary-eyed release into a very public place as the man was coming to.

Early sunlight slices through the towering windows flanked by columns of polished stone. Behind the humpbacked figure of the European, the names of Federated States cities flash on the destinations board.

He's as disgusting as she'd hoped. Baggy trousers held up with a piece of sandy rope. Dirty shirt open to reveal a pigeon chest. He's sweating for good measure, so much that his hair is slick and stuck to his forehead. He'd fit right into one of the anti-ship caricatures the Sunday epapers run.

'Everything's ready, ma'am,' Harveen says from behind the conferencing screen. Over the top of it, Janek is aware of Harveen's neat figure in a silk blouse and two-piece.

'Did I detect a hint of reprimand in your voice?'

'Not at all, ma'am.'

Janek stands and steps round the desk so that she can see Harveen clearly. 'Your hope of a pardon lies in me becoming president, Ms Atwal. You'd do well to remember it.'

Harveen swallows. 'Yes, ma'am.'

'This will help our people experience the fear of having Europeans walk among them. It keeps them supportive of the regime. It improves the president's ratings, which reflects well on me, which reflects well on you, and so on.'

'I didn't suggest –'

'Your tone suggested it,' Janek snaps.

Harveen clamps her mouth shut, but the expression on her face remains antagonistic.

'I do not feel any remorse for taking action to protect this country,' Janek says quietly.

'Due respect, ma'am, it's not protecting the Federated States that I take issue with. It's lying that I find dangerous. If people find out we orchestrated such a cruel –'

'If people find out, we'll spin it. You graduated top of your law class, and you've been dealing with the press expertly ever since. I still remember that first press conference. The lies you told on my behalf came so easily. I have every confidence that you'll be able to weather any storm that comes our way.

Now, let's see if we can send Nikhil Lall and Esther Crossland a message.'

'We won't be able to spin it forever. At some point, a lie will be revealed that we can't cover up,' says Harveen.

The two of them stare at each other, Janek letting the hint of a smirk lift her. She steps closer to her chief of staff. 'Don't ever forget who got you here.'

Harveen breathes through her nose. She lifts her chin defiantly. 'Believe me, Admiral, I know exactly who's to blame for getting me here.'

Janek slams her hand down on the desk, the impact so sharp that her palm stings. She grits her teeth as she composes herself. 'You're trying my patience –'

'*Awaiting your order,*' comes a voice from the screen.

Janek clears her throat, pats down her hair and retakes her seat. 'Very good. Just give me a minute,' she says to the monitor.

Harveen drops her eyes and clutches her digiscreen to her stomach. Janek's chief of staff has these outbursts sometimes. These little displays of compassion. It's the stress of their situation.

Janek smooths the non-existent wrinkles from her skirt, composes her face and settles back into her chair. 'You have permission to begin the mission. And connect me directly to Lieutenant Grimson. I'd like to oversee the operation personally.'

'*Roger that,*' comes the disembodied voice.

Harveen moves so that she can see the screen. She slides her digiscreen on to Janek's desk, pushing a book askew and nudging the floating glass orb that is Janek's award for valour out of its stand. The orb drops from the air, chinking on to the desk without breaking.

Janek's fingers twitch with the impulse to straighten things up, and it crosses her mind that perhaps Harveen did that deliberately. She forces her attention to the screen and away from the disorderly arrangement of objects on her desk.

The refugee isn't infected with *the bane of Europe*, as some of the press call the Virus. But he could be. The Virus hasn't been found on any of the European ships in forty years. But one of her scientists claims that viruses could remain dormant in populations over generations, so Janek will use these snippets of information to her advantage. Whether Harveen thinks it's a good idea or not.

Harveen watches over Janek's shoulder.

The commuters are beginning to notice the man. The circle of empty space around him broadens as though it carries contagion in the very air. Normal people stare; some of them sip from travel mugs. Some of them clutch their briefcases to their chests and speed up, pretending to run for a train when in reality they're running from trouble.

The man's shoulder blades stick out through his thin shirt. He fidgets with the rope that holds up his trousers, bony fingers worrying the frayed ends. It makes him look even more threatening. It gives him an unhinged air.

There's a commotion off screen. Commuters who had been watching from a safe distance suddenly decide the situation has become too dangerous and scurry away. No point getting caught in any crossfire when they can rewatch whatever comes next in the comfort and safety of their locked homes.

The man seems to realize something is happening, although he clearly doesn't know what it is, or why he's at the centre of it. He sways and works his mouth. A bitter taste after the sedative, Janek assumes.

Black-uniformed retrieval officers appear at the edge of the feed.

'On the ground!' one of them shouts as they near the man. He stares blankly.

'Get on the ground! Now!'

The man takes another look around, and Janek swears, although it's almost impossible, that he looks at the camera – looks right through it to her face – and, for a split second, makes eye contact. And in her chest there's a flare of disgust. So sharp and deep it's like a splinter. She is not one of them.

She jerks her head, and presses her fingernails into her palms until she feels the pop of skin breaking.

It's them or me, she reminds herself. Once she claims the White House, she'll quietly and officially pardon herself for all crimes. Including this one. She may even pardon Harveen at the same time, if the woman can hold her nerve long enough.

Janek presses unmute. 'You're authorized to complete the objective,' she says.

On screen, one of the Coalies raises their rifle in a smooth motion, aims and pulls the trigger. There are screams from the commuters. As one, they drop to the ground, shielding their heads with briefcases and paperbacks.

'Target neutralized, ma'am.'

'Thank you for your service, Lieutenant Grimson.'

By her shoulder, Harveen lets out a shuddering breath.

'Harveen,' Janek says.

'Yes, ma'am?'

'You're fired.'

Harveen reaches forward and turns off the digiscreen. It folds neatly in on itself and vanishes inside the desk top. When she gets to the door of the office, she turns back.

'You can't fire me, Janek.'

34

NIK

'Eat this,' Enid says. She tosses me a sandwich wrapped in plastic. After how long I've spent fishing plastic out of the sea, these things are enough to make me gip. But nothing can be as bad as slops and I'm starved so I tear into the packet and pretend I haven't seen a thousand of these decaying on top of the water.

'Thanks. Where are we?' I say through a mouthful of egg salad.

'About a hundred and sixty miles south of the border wall.'

Halfway back then. My chest tightens and the bite of sanger in my mouth turns to dry cement. All the way here I've been telling myself I'll only ever go back for as long as it takes to tell my mother to stick her job offer. Maybe she'll get the message. If she doesn't, I'll sneak away again. So, for now, I'll go along with whatever Enid tells me to do.

'We just going to fly over the wall?'

'That's the plan.' Enid looks out through the slats in the

blind, letting a line of midday sun through. She takes a seat on an upturned bucket.

We landed here forty-five minutes ago, and she ushered me across an empty car park and into this building. Half the room is taken up with piles of moving boxes, the other half stacked with mops and industrial-strength toilet rolls. When she went back out, I didn't hear the door lock, but there was a shadow on the other side that made me think someone was standing guard there.

'Was it necessary to keep me holed up in here like I'm a flight risk?'

'Are you a flight risk?'

I study the black-and-white linoleum tiles on the floor. There are worn patches where people have come and gone. When I look up, Enid's watching my face. I swallow and take another bite of sandwich just to deal with how awkward this is. I hadn't thought about running. But if the opportunity came about I can't say what I'd do.

Enid reads it in my face. There's a millisecond of . . . what? Pain? Betrayal? She stares at the door like she can't stand to look at me. 'We'll refuel here, cross no-man's-land, then sneak over the wall before the Federated States can look at us twice.'

Someone hammers on the window from the outside.

'Time to go.'

Enid opens the door to the building and strides across the tarmac, so fast I have to jog to keep up. We pile back into the chopper. Next second, we're lifting into the air.

She doesn't speak to me. Not a single word. For 160 miles. Eventually, the tree farms and fields give way to what can generously be described as a wasteland. Either side of the border wall got nuked to hell during the Second War of Independence. All that's left are patches of dry yellow earth with the odd scrappy weed bursting through. Trees that look like driftwood, all bleached and cracked. Not a living thing for miles. A ribbon of dead land running from the Atlantic to the mountains. Gives me the creeps.

The outline of a city grows in the distance. A cluster of skyscrapers like the ribs of a dead animal sticking up into the sky. 'What's that place?'

'Used to be a city before the war,' Enid says. 'Not much of it left now though. We'll be flying low so as not to attract attention. Might get a bit choppy.'

I pull the seat belt over my shoulder.

'Here comes the wall,' she says.

That's not a wall. That's a cliff face.

When I say it's big, I'm not kidding. You could stack three *Arcadia*s on top of each other and still not reach the top. It's made of black metal and smooth as glass.

'Holy crap,' I say. 'Look at that thing.'

Enid raises an eyebrow at me.

At the top, there's a spiral of evil-looking barbed wire, but God knows why. There's no way anyone's getting close to climbing up. As we get nearer, we start to rise, taking a long arc upwards so that by the time we reach the wall we could skim the top.

The co-pilot swivels round and taps on the window separating us from the cabin. Two taps. Enid taps back. 'Ready?' she says to me.

'For what?'

Enid pulls a mask down from the ceiling above her seat and straps it over her face. She's grinning through the glass. Then something thuds into us, hard, and the helicopter lurches sideways. Orange smoke flashes outside. An acrid smell like burning soap fills the air. Enid points up.

I grab the mask down, fumbling in my panic so that by the time I've pressed it on to my face my eyes are stinging. Another blast hits us. I grab the edge of my seat. The dark shadow of the wall passes beneath, and at the same moment the booming intensifies. Orange clouds gather round us.

'Federated States anti-aircraft cannons,' Enid says. Her voice is muffled, but just as calm as ever. 'Fully automated. We usually manage to dodge through a sparse patch, and they rarely get a direct hit.'

'Usually?' I shout back.

At that moment, there's an almighty bang right under where I'm sitting. My heart jumps into my mouth. *I'm going to die. They're going to bring this helicopter down, and even if I survive the crash I'll have fifty miles of wasteland to get across before I find so much as a plant alive.*

Then, just like that, the cannons stop. The clouds clear. Enid smiles through her gas mask. 'Welcome home,' she says.

And I'm back in the Federated States.

35

JANEK

The press corps is arranged in row after well-shod row. Standing with her hands relaxed on the edge of the podium, Janek flicks through her mental list of soundbites. The press room is small. Only one camera hovers in the air directly in front of her face. A screen below it shows an image of her, hair neatly arranged in a bun and suit unwrinkled. Just enough effort to be respectable without suggesting vanity.

Harveen points at a journalist with his hand raised.

'Good evening, Admiral Janek. What can you tell us about the sick refugee that was found wandering around Thirtieth Street Station this morning?' he says.

'I'd just like to reiterate that although the Virus is highly contagious, it can be effectively contained through social distancing and quarantine measures.'

The news ticker underneath the camera scrolls her soundbite perfectly. *Admiral Janek: the Virus is highly contagious.* She can hear the journalists tapping on their phones and digiscreens, filing the story milliseconds after she speaks. Within a minute, every news station in the Federated States will be delivering that soundbite to the public, playing it over and over.

'If that's the case, then why was the man killed?'

Janek glances at Harveen standing by the wall of the press room. There's no flicker of emotion from the woman. No indication that Janek might be performing well or tanking. A chill runs down Janek's spine. She and Harveen are like ropes knotted together. Their shared fate has kept them close, but sometimes Janek wonders: if they weren't fighting the consequences of their shared crimes, would Harveen be at her side at all?

The truth is the man wasn't killed because he was sick. He was killed so that Janek could finally put an end to Nikhil Lall and Esther Crossland. How long will the teenagers last once inmates of the camp start being picked off and publicly executed?

What Janek needs to get across is the soundbite that she and Harveen prepped before the press conference: *The sickness could mutate and become airborne*. While the ultimate aim of this side venture is to lure the teenagers out of hiding, Janek can use it to make sure the public understands the importance of keeping the refugees permanently isolated.

'Our very strict rules on containment are a sad necessity. Earlier today, I met with top doctors at the Federated States Disease Control Laboratory. Unfortunately, they raised the concern that illnesses such as this have a high potential for mutation. My first priority will always be to protect the people of this country. I would rather be strict than face the possibility that the disease could mutate and become airborne.'

The camera flashes. Its ticker switches to: *The disease could mutate and spread through the air.*

This is too easy.

'Admiral, could you tell us what conditions are like within the camp? Could this outbreak have been averted if more resources had been given to the people there?' That's Barney King. Janek makes a mental note to keep an eye on him. He errs towards empathy.

'We must be clear about this point. The sickness is caused by poor hygiene.'

The camera flashes again: *Poor hygiene among refugees caused Virus outbreak.*

Good. Now, round it up. Make it about piety.

'The people of the *Arcadia* are in our thoughts and prayers during these challenging times. Please, join me in praying for the sick within the camp.'

Janek drops her face and presses her palms together. She feels the lights of the camera blink.

When she opens her eyes, Lall is standing in the doorway of the press room. Her hair falls over the collar of her jacket in a wave of black and silver. A grim smile tugs at the corners of her mouth, but her face is drawn with tiredness. Those elegant cheekbones are sharper than the last time they met.

Janek steps down from the podium, crossing paths with Harveen, who hurries to take her place. Lall trails Janek down the corridor.

'That was very clever. The way you spoon-fed the media

while remaining pious and compassionate. The way you made it clear that ship folk are dirty, disease-ridden heathens.'

Janek enters her office and takes a seat behind her desk. She doesn't offer the other woman a chair. 'And I didn't need to tell a single lie.'

'We have different definitions of the word *lie*.'

Janek smiles at General Lall. 'What can I do for you, Mrs Lall?'

'I've come to arrange the release of prisoners, as agreed. One hundred to begin with.'

'As you will have gathered from the press conference, the disease outbreak your people have identified in the camp makes any release impossible.'

'We had a deal. I had my people stand down while you carried out the tagging operation. You faced no resistance. There was no trouble to be reported in the press. No embarrassment for your president.'

'And for that I'm grateful. It is better for everyone involved if my Coalies can carry out their work without violence. But circumstances have changed.'

In reality, Janek was never open to the idea of releasing prisoners in exchange for cooperation. The outbreak of disease in the camp is a serendipitous coincidence, something she can use to explain her about-turn.

Harveen enters and closes the door quietly behind her.

'The government in Maine have agreed to take the people of the *Arcadia*,' says Lall. 'Let us go, and we'll be out of your hair in a few days. No more food, no more supplies, no more disease.'

Janek smiles. 'My dear, how will you get all the way to United States territory?'

'You don't need to be concerned with that.'

Janek's eyes slip to Lall's. 'You seem supremely confident that you can facilitate the movement of hundreds of people through six hundred kilometres of Federated States territory.'

General Lall doesn't falter. She stares at Janek with steely, unblinking eyes.

'Well, Mrs Lall? Are you planning to walk all the way?'

Lall closes the space between them and leans her fingertips on the desk. 'That is not your concern.'

'Without some indication of how you intend to move hundreds of sick and undernourished people, I'm afraid it's unconscionable that I would drop my security system and let you walk out into my country. My citizens would never allow it.'

'They're undernourished and sick because you've held them hostage for four months.'

'The president has asked me to bring those responsible for the grounding of the *Arcadia* to justice.'

'Then put me on trial. Have me answer for the crimes committed during the operation I was overseeing.'

Janek can't help rolling her eyes. 'Mrs Lall, even if you weren't immune to prosecution as a diplomat, the news is already out. It was your dashing son and his promising young friend who destroyed the ship.'

'The girl is dead.'

'As you've informed me. And your son is still missing.'

'Correct.'

Janek indulges in a broad smile. 'I'm sorry to inform you that you could soon be getting some rather bad news on that front.'

Lall straightens like she's been electrocuted.

'Here's the thing. I'd be much more inclined to negotiate improved conditions for the camp if you could help me tie up these loose ends. Hand the teenagers over to me, and I give you my word that they will be removed from the equation with as little fuss as possible. It's in nobody's interest to have a protracted and public trial. Afterwards, I can announce that I have dealt with the culprits from the ship. I'll release details of their demise, and we can move on to more pressing matters.' *Such as introducing full prison conditions immediately and selling off your people as inmate workers.*

General Lall snorts mirthlessly and crosses her arms. She's remarkably calm while discussing the capture and execution of her only child. 'I agreed to the tagging of the whole population in exchange for the release of a hundred prisoners. You went back on our deal. I won't be fooled twice, Admiral.'

Janek taps a fingernail against her desk. 'What you do or do not believe has little bearing on my actions.'

General Lall slams her hands down on the desk, making the stationery rattle. 'Let us go, Janek,' she snarls.

Janek lets out a peal of laughter. 'Have the Secret Service show Mrs Lall out.'

Harveen opens the door.

Lall grits her teeth. 'Another one of your assassins failed yesterday. If you're so determined to kill me, why don't you just do it now?'

'That wouldn't create the right optics at all. I'd be painted as a bad host. A bad person. You were betrayed.

You were double-crossed. Most unsportsmanlike. But, if you're assassinated in your own house, by one of your own people? Well, that's just bad housekeeping on your part, isn't it? The internal squabbles of the ship people. Most savage. Primitive almost.'

'Another leader will take my place.'

'Maybe. But I doubt you have anyone suitable. The camp will wither and die without its head and those two rebellious children, and we'll subjugate it for the next thirty years without any of your demands. Just enough food to keep it going. Just enough resources to keep it productive. Oh, and Lall, just so that we understand one another: I can come and take those kids any time I want,' Janek says.

Lall gives Janek a final acid glare and turns tail. She stomps from the room, leaving the door ajar. Janek sees the Secret Service detail trail after her.

'It's oddly satisfying to see that woman struggling when we know she's never going to get free,' Janek says.

Harveen raises her eyebrows in reproach.

'Oh, Harveen, you really must deal with that empathy of yours.'

36

NIK

'Nice of my mother to be here when I got back,' I say to Enid.

She looks at me from the blackened liner at the edge of her eyes. Her hair's flowing back in the cold breeze that seems to come straight off the ocean and up on to this rooftop. 'You've been AWOL these past four months. You expecting a ticker-tape parade?' She raises a pair of binoculars to her face.

I shove my hands in my pockets and bob on my toes, trying to keep warm. From the roof of HQ, I can see the city, all lit up in the waning sunlight. If I leaned over the low brick wall at the edge of the rooftop, I'd be able to see down into the streets and alleys of the main camp. In the distance, the *Arcadia*'s almost on her side in the water at the border of the dockland. And I can just make out the front line between us and the Coalies. Nothing more than a shimmery fence and the odd patrol of our friends in black who won't actually set foot inside the camp unless there's trouble. My mother's hastily agreed ceasefire saw to that.

'Where's she been anyway?'

'If I told you, I'd have to kill you.'

'Brilliant. She's expecting me to get involved in the rebellion again without knowing what the score is.'

'She is. And I'm with her on this point. You want out of the rebellion, that's your call. But you can't expect us to be giving you any kind of information about our operation if you're determined to be an outsider.'

'I'm her son. And I've been your friend for longer than I can remember.'

'A lot's changed, Nik my boy. It's not like it was on the ship. If you hadn't noticed, we've got God knows how many people being held prisoner here. So, you'll forgive us if we ask for a few words from you to tell us we're still fighting for the same team.'

Enid goes back to watching through the lenses. She's angry. I can almost feel the ice radiating from her. And it gives me a nasty feeling of dread in my gut because, if Enid's rattled, things are way worse than I thought.

'Will you at least tell me when the reinforcements are coming?'

Silence.

'Enid, are the other ships coming or not?'

Silence.

Now I'm starting to panic because, when we got off the *Arcadia* and pulled ourselves together, it was pretty clear we wouldn't be able to fight our way out again. Not without outside help. So we hatched a plan. When I left, it was all set in stone. Now, Enid's body language is giving some bad-news feelings. Guess I should have known from Corp's radio announcements that things weren't going to plan.

Somewhere in the distance the buzz of a helicopter starts up, and the next second a black dot comes into view. The chopper gets closer until I can feel its rumble in my gut, and when it sets down on the roof its blades flick my hair about. The door opens, and my mother steps down. She's thinner than when I left; her face has lost some of its roundness; the furrow between her eyes has deepened. She's wearing a formal coat over a white shirt, collar turned up against the cold. She could pass as one of the Federated States politicians she hates so much.

For a second, I think she's going to march right past me, then she stops and looks me over. 'You need a shave and a shower.'

'Nice to see you too, Mum,' I say.

That's all the interaction I'm gonna get. She carries on walking. A group of our people in suits that look suspiciously like a DIY security detail crowd round her.

'What just happened?' I ask Enid.

The helicopter blades whine back up to full speed, and we're forced to close our eyes against the rush of air as it takes off.

'Looks like you need to freshen up, boyo.'

'She wants to talk, she can talk without me putting on a suit,' I say.

Enid gives me a look and starts after my mother.

'Charming as usual,' I say under my breath.

Should I follow them? I know what my mother's going to say: join the rebellion, blah blah blah, it's your duty, yada yada yada. I look round the empty rooftop for a sec, then run after them, catching the door just before it slams closed behind the last of the people in suits. 'Hey, Mum, wait!' I shout.

Down the other end of the corridor, I see my mother disappear with her security detail, followed by Enid. By the time I get there and push my way through the unmarked door, my mother's already removed her coat and is standing beside a long table.

A glance of disdain, and she goes right back to looking at whatever it is she's looking at on the table. This room is set for war. There are piles of paperwork and maps strewn over the table and the floor. The end wall is taken up by a huge map of the camp showing every building inside the boundary, every centimetre of fence we know about, every booby trap we've located.

'Whoa,' I say, staring up at the map. 'Someone's been busy.'

'The fruit of Enid's labour,' my mother says. 'Her team has worked hard to understand the Coaly security system.'

There's way more detail on the digimap than when I left. Even so, some big gaps exist. Places where we don't know exactly where the fence runs. Quadrants with no booby traps marked, not because there are none in there, but because locating them is the kind of work that can get you killed a thousand times a day. One in a long line of ways the Federated States keeps us exactly where it wants us. And then there's the gang territory at the north end of the camp that's completely blank.

Enid's unfurling an enormous digiplan on the table, anchoring the corners with cups and books and whatever else she can find. Hundreds of lights flicker over its surface.

One for each person captured, cuffed and released by the Coalies during the first day of their tagging operation.

'How could you let them do this?' I ask.

My mother doesn't look up. She runs her finger over the digiplan, inspecting each pinprick of light like she can see the person it represents.

'We can talk when you look like an adult.'

My fingers twitch in anger at my sides. My mother knows how to put you in your place. 'I don't need a shower to talk to you,' I say. 'My answer's the same as the last time you tried to force me into being your second in command.'

'Don't be silly. Enid is my second in command.'

Enid snorts and goes back to the digiplan.

'They could do with more hands up there,' my mother says, pointing to a patch on the map.

'I'll ask around, but we're going to be scraping the barrel. We've tapped up most people who have any kind of mechanical knowledge. It's going to be a matter of training people up, and the truth is we mightn't have the time any more.'

'What're you talking about?' I say.

'None of your beeswax,' Enid says over her shoulder. 'Oughtn't you to be doing as your mother's asked and having a shower?'

From somewhere lower in the building, there's a blast of something like corn popping. My mother looks at Enid, who shifts uneasily, then moves to the other side of her like she's positioning herself between her and the door. And that's the second time I've seen Enid nervous today. Anxiety squirms in my stomach again.

'It's going to be harder to hide the fact that people are working in that part of the camp now that the Coalies can see where each person is at every second of the day. Last thing we want is them getting curious and stumbling into Silas's place. We need to put some manpower into figuring out how the cuffs work,' Enid says, still studiously ignoring me.

'Agreed. Let's pull someone from the vehicle crew to look at it.'

'Hello. Son who's been away for months over here,' I say, pointing at myself. 'Why don't you tell me what you want so that I can get on with refusing to do it?'

My mother switches her focus to me for the first time, getting closer so that she can pull a stray nurdle from my hair. She inspects it on her fingernail and flicks the tiny piece of plastic away. 'I need you to be a symbol.'

'Excuse me?'

'I want you to be leader of the rebellion. I want you to take my place as the representative of the people in this camp.'

'I'm not doing that.'

She nods, lips slightly pursed. 'Nikhil, why did you come back here?'

'Because you sent Enid after me, and the Coalies destroyed the barges I was working on.'

Mother looks at Enid. 'That was a bold move from Admiral Janek. It also explains why she thought I might get news of Nikhil's death today.'

'Sure was bold. Reckon she wants to make sure the rebellion's leaderless. And, according to my source, she's getting her knickers in a twist every time one of her plans doesn't go right. We should expect retaliation when she finds out Nik's safe at home,' Enid says.

My mother crosses her arms and taps her fingers on her sleeve. 'What will it take for me to persuade you? I need someone to be the face. I need someone who fits the Federated States' image of a young person with great potential. Someone who will deal with negotiations and press conferences while I get on with other things.'

'Other things like what?'

'I can't give you the key to the kingdom before you agree to take charge of it.'

I shake my head. 'Enid can do it. There, problem solved. Goodnight. God bless. See you around.'

I give them a two-finger salute and start for the door. A good night's sleep, some food, then I start looking for a job somewhere far away from here.

There's another round of popping. Close enough this time to set my nerves on edge.

'Enid can't do it. She would excel in the role, I have no doubt, but she's not the kind of person the Federated States approves of. Enid, could you perhaps find out what the disturbance is?' My mother speaks softly, but her voice is hard as diamond.

Enid disappears through the door.

'I need someone to act as the voice and face of the camp. You will be doing good work, Nikhil. You would be helping.'

'You seem to be doing just fine by yourself.'

'I will not be around forever. You should begin shadowing me now. Sometimes, it's necessary to play in somebody else's sandbox, and for that you need to understand the rules.

Admiral Janek won't go easy on you because of your age.' My mother takes a step closer. 'We are in danger, Nikhil. It's time to come out of exile.'

Urgent voices rise from the other side of the door. My mother's eyes stay fixed on me. The door swings open and a man runs through, blood pouring from a gash on his forehead, dripping on to the shoulder of his shirt. He's followed by Enid and a gang of people in suits. He stops. Takes in the room, my mother, me. Then he charges, letting out a roar like a bull and aiming his head right at my mother's middle.

Next thing I know, he's lying on the ground and twitching, wires trailing from his back to the taser Enid's pointing at him. My mother hasn't flinched. Not even a flicker. Still as bedrock, and pale too.

'Get him up,' one of the suited guards says. They lift the man by his shoulders, ignoring the wet patch that spreads from the seat of his trousers to the floor, the sharp smell of pee.

'See he's not hurt,' Enid shouts after them.

My heart's pounding around in my chest. 'What in hell was that?' I say.

'It's nothing to concern you. You've made your position quite clear,' my mother says.

'Was that guy trying to get at you? Was he trying to kill you?'

'I have work to do. You are welcome to eat in the mess hall, and you will find your room as you left it.'

My mother returns to the table, lifting paperwork to read it more closely. 'Enid, I'd like the daily report of Coaly numbers policing the border to be separated into sections from now on.'

'Of course,' Enid says.

'Could you show Nikhil out, please?'

Enid ushers me towards the door. 'Time to go.'

'Tell me what's going on,' I say as she pushes me out of the door.

'You have to leave. She won't have you here until you decide which side you're on.'

'It's not about being on a side. I'm not against the rebellion. I just don't want it to be my life any more.'

'Ah, Nik, we both know that's not how it works. It's never how it's worked. Either you're in it or you're not.'

She starts to close the door, and I jam my foot under it to hold it open. 'At least tell me who that guy is.'

'I've no idea who he is.'

'Has this happened before?'

She hesitates. 'He's the third one they've sent.'

37

JANEK

There are men in Harveen's office. Men in the cheap suits of lower-level public servants. Men who don't make eye contact with Janek when she glares at them – not avoiding her gaze through fear, but through indifference. She was reading new legislation in her study when they hammered on the door of the Statehouse. Three loud booms that said, *Open up! We won't take no for an answer.* The digiscreen is still in her hand, and now she presses her thumb against the glass, willing it to fracture, calling for the slicing pain in her fingertips that would help to channel her anger.

One of the men opens a filing-cabinet drawer and pulls out a brown folder that's bulging with paperwork. He licks his thumb and flicks through the pages. The sight of his tongue threatens to send Janek into a rage spiral.

'Gentlemen,' she says, maintaining a level voice, 'perhaps one of you could enlighten me. On whose orders are you conducting this search?'

None of the men look up. The air is full of the sound of paper shuffling. The wheeze of metal drawers being opened.

'We'll be needing access to the admiral's office next,' a suited man says.

Janek opens her mouth to reply, but Harveen takes her firmly by the arm and steers her out of the office and into the wood-panelled corridor.

Harveen keeps her hand on Janek's arm until they reach the privacy of Janek's office down the hall, and the door is closed firmly behind them.

'There's nothing for them to find. So you're going to let them conduct their search, and you're not going to do anything stupid like incriminating either of us. Do you understand me?'

Janek reels like she's been slapped. Her chief of staff is ordinarily careful to maintain their respective positions, even behind closed doors. But recently she's shown frequent and worrying signs of disrespect.

Harveen looks at her digiscreen. 'They're from the Supreme Court of the Federated States and they're investigating what happened eight years ago.'

'The *Ithaka*?' Janek says.

'Yes. The president signed the search warrant.'

Janek's shock gives way to rage, and in the privacy of her office she feels her surface beginning to crack. 'The *audacity* of that man! To raid my offices as though I'm some sort of employee to be watched and reprimanded.' She's losing composure, so she turns her graduation ring into her palm and squeezes her hand into a painful fist.

'He already knows everything there is to know about what happened that night,' Harveen says.

A bitter film coats Janek's tongue. She has no desire to think about the night she ordered the clearance of the first ship. No desire to be reminded of her failures. Or the things she and Harveen have done to keep the events secret.

Janek paces to the window and looks out at the rose garden that's still in the grip of winter. Before she turns back to Harveen, she resets her face. Panicking won't help the situation. She's going to need a level head to work with all the moving parts. 'Why don't you enlighten me as to what those men are really doing here?'

With unfocused eyes, Harveen stares at the wall behind Janek, thinking. 'He knows the details of what happened that night, and what you did –'

'What we did.'

'What *we* did in the aftermath.' There's a flicker in Harveen's face as she speaks. It's impossible to tell whether it's a flash of anger or defiance. Janek doesn't like either option. 'But there's no physical evidence of what happened, apart from the self-testimony you recorded when you became president-elect.'

Janek gets an intense flash of memory: the day the president announced that she would become the Federated States' most recent president-elect. At the time, giving up her most damaging secret had seemed like a small price to pay for a chance at the presidency. After all, every president-elect in living memory had done the same. The president called it his way of ensuring a 'collegiate working relationship'. Janek knows his secrets; the president knows hers. It's how the political system works, and she's been happy to play the game. Until the rules changed, and suddenly her secrets are being held over her neck like the blade of a guillotine.

'The president already controls my self-testimony. He keeps it locked in his safe in the Oval Office. He's got everything he needs to destroy both of us if that's what he wants to do.'

Harveen's face seems to spark with understanding. 'I think this is a message. From him to us.'

'And what, pray tell, is this message trying to communicate?'

'It says *you're running out of time*.'

38

NIK

The basement of rebellion HQ is a museum to Coaly technology. There's everything in here. Helmets, uniforms, the tiny snake-shaped bots they use to unclog the drains. My mother and the other members of the rebellion picked up everything they could get their hands on after Landfall.

Enid clicks on a lamp over a cluttered metal workbench. There's a bank of shelves stacked with gadgets. The wall at the end has tools on little hooks, outlined in black so you never put anything in the wrong place. Most of the spaces are empty.

'Cool place,' I say.

'Need to get you kitted out if you're sticking around. And I thought you could make yourself useful down here anyway.'

'You're giving me a job?'

'It's a volunteer role. No salary. No benefits.'

'Tempting.'

'Now we're on land, we can get our hands on more of the tech the Coalies kept from us when we were stuck on the *Arcadia*. We haven't got a hope in hell of manufacturing any of this stuff, but with that big brain of yours we might get some of it working. Your girl Esther was particularly thrilled when we got our hands on some of those nanobot things they use to figure out what's ailing someone.'

I pick up a gadget, wires trailing from a flat metal disc. 'So why are you sending mechanics up to Silas Cuinn?'

She looks at me for a second. 'Intrigued, are we?'

'More surprised than anything. Thought he'd have been off by now. With his contacts, he could have set himself up anywhere.'

'There's this concept you might have heard of. They call it loyalty. Even gang leaders like me and Silas understand it.'

'Ouch,' I say. Enid gazes at me until I can't stand the pressure any more, so I throw the bit of machinery down on to the workbench. 'This is junk.'

'For the most part.' She shrugs. 'There's a vest for you hanging on the shelf. Stab-proof – won't stop a bullet, but it'll slow it down.'

'And, given the fact that there are assassins running round HQ, I'll take as much help as I can get.'

I lift the vest down and head behind a set of shelves to change. It's made of a thin mesh that shimmers in the basement's bulb light. I pull my shirt back on over it and find Enid sitting on the workbench, tapping something on to a screen.

'Now. Where can I find Esther and Corp?' I say.

'How should I know?'

'Because, unless you've had a personality transplant, you'll have spent the past four months making sure you know everything that goes on in this camp.'

She looks at me square for a minute, then seems to make a decision. 'Couple of days after you left, your mother suggested it might be better for them to find alternative accommodation. Once the Coalies started plastering those posters of you lot up everywhere, she knew they were on to you. She thought it best if they were to lie low so as not to get arrested.'

'And then what happened?'

'Nothing. That's where we're at. Your mother hasn't let them back in since.'

'So you just cut them off? Left them to fend for themselves?'

'Hey, I get stuff to them, all right? If it was up to your mother, the two of them would be eating limpets and seaweed. I have John take them food on the daily. I've been getting them medical supplies as and when they come in. And, being frank, I don't think you should be calling anyone out about the cutting-off-contact thing.'

We stand in silence. Not sure what to do now. On the workbench, there's a metal cuff like the one most of the people in the camp are wearing. I pick it up and start trying to prise the thing open.

'If you're interested in going to see them, they're staying in the old coastguard station about halfway down the camp.'

My gut twists. I'm not ready to see Esther.

Enid turns halfway round on the bench to look at me. 'Are you? Interested, I mean.'

I try squeezing the cuff. Nothing happens.

'Course, your mother wouldn't like you running down there on a visit.'

'My mother doesn't like much of anything I do.'

'You're right on that count.'

More silence. Was it always this hard to talk to people? It's like there's a mile between me and everyone else.

'How have you been these past few months?' I say.

'Right as rain. Anyhow, your mother wants to brief you on the cholera situation this afternoon. If you can find your way to the war room about teatime, that would be grand. And figure out how to open these things too,' she says, pointing at the cuff.

'Wait, we've got cholera? When did this happen?'

'Corp got word to us yesterday. She's sending updates every hour, but it's like watching the tide come in. We've got hundreds down with it in less than twenty-four hours and almost no means of treating them. The way it's going, there won't be anyone fit to fight if the Coalies launch their attack.'

Enid starts for the door. 'Hey, Enid, are we OK?'

She stops. Turns on the spot. 'Why'd you ask?'

'Because you can't stand to be in the same room as me for more than five minutes at a time. Because everyone around here seems to resent me as much as the Coalies. I can feel it when they look at me.'

'You've been gone for months. Most people here haven't had that luxury.'

'OK –' I start.

Jeez, this is not like Enid. In any situation, she's the one you can count on to hold her nerve, but now she's getting agitated in a way I've never seen before.

'And while we're on the subject: you've been off licking your wounds, focusing on your own pain, and that's fine and all, but in those four months you acted like the rest of us didn't exist. You and Esther were responsible for something pretty monumental. Esther lost her sister. Your mother lost her oldest friend. But all you could see was yourself.'

'OK, I get that I should have been in touch –' I grab a screwdriver and push it into the thin gap in the cuff, and give it a twist. It makes a faint buzzing sound like a digiscreen powering up.

'No, you should have done more than that. Did you consider, even for a second, that Esther and your mother might have needed you to help get them through it all?'

'Enid –' I stare at the cuff. The sound's gathering momentum, rising to a whine.

'No, you didn't think. You just went off and did your own thing, footloose and fancy-free –'

'Enid –'

'– while the rest of us stayed here and put up with the Coalies, and the lack of food, and –'

'Enid!' The cuff's volume increases until it's an ear-splitting squeal.

Enid grabs one of the stab-proof vests from the shelf and throws it over the cuff. There's a thud, and the vest bursts outwards. I shield my eyes. In a split second, a shockwave ploughs through the room. My ears ring. When I open my eyes again, the air's hazy with smoke.

Enid pulls my face round so she can look at me. She inspects my head for wounds. 'You OK?'

'Ears ringing, but apart from that.'

Enid lifts a corner of the shredded vest and peers underneath. 'If we didn't already know – the Coalies are a nasty bunch.'

What's left of the cuff is mangled and bent into strands. I pick it up to inspect the charred metal.

'I'd better get the word out that no one's to try and open these things unless they want their head removed,' Enid says as she makes for the door. 'If you could figure out how we do it without decapitation, that'd be grand.'

'No problem,' I say, and I throw the broken cuff on to the desk. 'Hey, you didn't answer my question.'

She narrows her eyes at me and sighs. 'No, Nik my boy, we're not OK.'

39

NIK

It's taken me hours, but I finally managed to open one of the cuffs without causing an explosion big enough to take my own head off. A magnet of the right strength was all it needed. Coalies must've figured we wouldn't be able to find the right equipment in here, and they didn't much care how many of us died trying to work it out. *Take that, Coalies.*

I throw the open cuff on to the desk. It clatters into the remains of the fifteen others I accidentally set off. The skin on my face is itchy and singed from the time I didn't get behind the shelves fast enough.

That thing Enid said about me ignoring everyone else's pain is gnawing at me. Partly, I'm pissed off because I don't want people thinking the worst of me. Partly, I'm pissed off because it's true, and no one likes having the cold light of truth shone on them. I got swallowed by grief after I lost May. I couldn't handle seeing the people I love suffer. So I pretended none of them existed.

And then there was the other thing that I've done my best to pretend never happened –

No. I'm not going to think about it now.

I'm back. Even though I'm not planning on sticking around long term, I also don't want to live with this hanging over me for the rest of my days. Don't want people hurt and angry and thinking I abandoned them. Much as I don't want to admit it, there's someone in this camp that was hurting just as bad as me. Someone who I didn't even say goodbye to when I left. I'm ashamed of that.

I grab the digimap from the wall above the workbench. Time to put things right.

Even though we're heading for spring, the air's crisp as frost as I walk from HQ down towards the waterfront. Enid told me Esther's been going by the name Kara, one of her classmates who died when Hadley attacked the market last year.

I unfold the digimap as I'm walking. It shows everything in the camp from the air, but it's short on detail. The *Arcadia*'s labelled, obviously, and the warehouses are numbered. But the coastguard station Esther and Corp have been living in is nothing more than a rectangle, and the area occupied by Silas and his people is all but blank. A week after the *Arcadia* crashed, my mother negotiated a *no-surveillance* clause into the ceasefire agreement. Enid spent weeks shooting down every drone that strayed inside the camp. Eventually, the Coalies took the hint, but not before we'd brought down about fifty of the things.

My mother's endgame is still a mystery, and she's not

willing to bring me in from the cold until I pledge my allegiance to the rebellion again.

We are in danger, Nikhil. It's time to come out of exile. That makes me shudder every time I replay it in my head. The way she looked at me when she said it. It was like she was vulnerable – and I can count on one hand the number of times that woman has let anyone see that part of her.

The quayside's up ahead. A seagull flaps out of my way as the water comes into view. I turn left at the bottom and there it is. The *Arcadia* up close. Suddenly I can't face looking at it so I lift the digimap and watch the dots moving.

May lived there and died there, and in my nightmares that's where she still is. Skin the colour of bruises, swollen and rotting –

The name Kara lights up over a dot on the map.

I freeze, squinting at the tiny mark on the plan. Can't be right. I flick the refresh button and watch the camp disappear and reappear. Esther's bright white spot isn't in the camp. It isn't on land at all. She's on the *Arcadia*. Nobody should be aboard that ship now. My mother got off everyone she could, then sealed it up. Too dangerous. Too unstable.

Esther wouldn't be that reckless, would she? Last time I checked, she wasn't an idiot.

Then I remember how she acted when May died. How wild she got when she didn't have anything left to lose. I remember her being fearless and stupid, and altogether too unconcerned with her own safety. Hyper-focused on completing our mission.

She'd be exactly that stupid.

I break into a run, stuffing the map into my coat pocket as I go.

There's a group of Neaths sitting on the broken rubble by the ship's prow. Laughing and joking like hyenas. And, further away, a kid I don't recognize in a medic's uniform, arms folded, chewing the corner of his mouth and listening to one of the old-style comgloves.

'What's so funny?' I say when I get close to the Neaths. I was right: Silas's people.

'Hey, it's Nik Lall. Nobody's seen you in months.'

'I've been busy. What's going on?'

'Silas has sent a girl in there.'

What the hell has she got herself into now?

'Tell me why, fast, or things are gonna get difficult for you around here.'

Silas's people get to their feet and walk towards me menacingly. 'Oh yeah? Who's going to make things difficult for us?' one Neath says. 'Cos I heard you're a nobody. I heard your own mother won't even give you the time of day.'

'Hey, you know who I am?' the guy in the medical uniform says.

'You can get lost as well. Silas's given us permission to cap you if you step out of line.'

'You're obviously a new recruit, so I'm going to let that slide. My last name's Huang. Recognize it?'

The smile drops from the Neath's face.

'Thought so. My family isn't afraid of anyone, not even Silas. Unless you want to meet one of my cousins on a dark night, I suggest you answer his question, and we can all go back to minding our own business.'

The Neath gives me a momentary blank look before deciding he'd better talk. 'He sent her to look for something in one of the cabins. Was told to give her a couple of hours and then call her done.'

I turn to the medic. 'Is she on audio?'

He scowls at me. 'You're Nik Lall?' he says, like he knows exactly who I am. Not only does he know who I am, he already hates me. Is this the someone new Enid was so eager to tell me about?

'That's right,' I say.

'How about you shut your mouth so I can hear?' He holds the comglove to his ear. The only sounds are incoherent fragments of Esther's voice, then static, then splashing.

In the five seconds I've known him, I've already had enough of this guy. I snatch his hand and mash the audio button on the palm of his comglove. 'Esther? You there? Dammit, Esther,' I say.

The guy pulls his hand back, squares his shoulders like he's ready to fight me. Couldn't care less. Esther's gone aboard a ghost ship, and he's standing here, watching.

I shrug off my jacket and take hold of one of the ropes that stretches from the quayside up to the *Arcadia*.

'This is none of your business, Nik,' the medic says.

'Esther is always my business,' I say. I start to cross the rope. It scrapes the skin on my hands, and I feel the burn in my arms before I even get halfway.

Without warning, the ropes bob lower. Esther's boyfriend is climbing up after me.

40

ESTHER

My head breaks the surface. Someone's holding me. I erupt in coughs as I try to get the water out of my lungs.

'All right. I got you.'

Hands drag me through the water and heave me out on to the wall.

I rub my eyes, trying to make them adjust to the gloom. Nik's here with me aboard the *Arcadia*, and I don't think my heart can take it.

Happiness, anger, relief battle to come to the surface. Anger wins. My heart burns with it.

Hot enough to throw a wave of black ship water straight into Nik Lall's stupid face.

He shields himself as the wave hits, so I switch to slapping him with the flat of my hands. But I'm exhausted, and every smack is as weak and pointless as the water.

'Stop, doc! Stop!' he shouts.

'You're such a jerk!' I scream back, and now there are red-hot tears running down my face, and I can add humiliation to the list of emotions coursing through my blood.

'What? What did I do? I pulled you out of the water!'

'You left me!' I shout. 'May died, and we crashed the ship. And then you left, and everyone else acted like I don't exist!' There's water dripping from his hair. I slap his chest again. 'Say something!'

'I . . . I . . . didn't know what was going on in the camp.'

'Don't play stupid, Nik. You ran away. You left us without looking back.'

He rubs the water from his face. At least he has the decency to look ashamed.

'Did you even think about me?'

'Honestly, I tried not to.'

I slump to the ground, and that's when I feel an arm round me, someone crouching next to me. I look up and find Pat. As soon as I see him, everything bubbles to the surface, and I bury my face in his neck and just cry. I cry for my family. I cry for everything that's happened over the past four months. The hunger and the cold and the Coalies piercing my ear. I cry about the cholera. About Meg held hostage by Silas. I cry so much my chest aches, and my head throbs. By the time my tears run out, I can only breathe in shuddering gulps.

Pat holds me in silence. The warmth of him like a balm on the parts of me that are most damaged.

'I'm sorry,' Nik says. 'I did all of it. Everything you said.'

'But why?'

His eyes dart to Pat and back to me. 'You know why.'

I search his face. 'Enlighten me.'

He looks at Pat again. 'Because of what happened on the roof.'

Pat's arm drops from around my shoulder, and in that moment I realize what Nik's talking about.

'What are you, twelve?' I say.

'Let's get into this some other time.'

'No, seriously. You abandoned everyone who loves you, everyone who needs you, because of one stupid misunderstanding?'

'It wasn't just a misunderstanding. You know it wasn't.'

I'm standing up now, pacing in the tiny space. Pat's moved away from me and is watching, an expression on his face that looks like pain. I can't make myself stop talking. I'm too angry and frustrated and relieved that Nik's come back. 'All of this drama over five seconds.'

'I wasn't ready.'

'Ready for what? It wasn't like I was asking to be your girlfriend.'

'I wasn't strong enough to live with my heart in someone else's body again.'

I stop pacing and stare at him. His eyes are glistening with tears. 'I'm so sorry,' he says.

I sniff and rub my nose.

Pat clears his throat. 'Silas gave us four hours to get back. We should move,' he says and starts off into the darkness without waiting for me.

I take another long look at Nik's face, then follow Pat into the shadows.

Everything's changed.

41

ESTHER

The three of us wade through black water in silence. After my last fall, I put each foot down tentatively in case there's bottomless water underneath. The thought of being pulled down again is like an icy hand round my heart. The water gets shallower and deeper. More than once, we have to climb over floating debris.

'Silas's place was up ahead,' Pat says. His voice is hollow, sucked into the darkness that surrounds us so that it sounds weak. There is a constant *drip-drip-drip* that echoes through the deserted corridors in an eerie soundtrack.

I wade into the next stretch of dark water. It comes up to my waist so that I'm walking with my hands in the air. Pat follows after. Nik comes up behind.

'You seem to know a lot about Silas Cuinn. In his pocket, are you?' Nik says.

'Not any more,' Pat replies. 'You planning on doing a runner again?'

Nik laughs mirthlessly. 'Apparently, your friend has a problem with me, Esther.'

'Too right I do.'

I realize they've stopped, and Pat has turned to face Nik. Quietly, I take Pat's hand and lead him onwards.

'What's that stuff all over you?' I say to Nik.

Pat goes ahead. I can't be the only one that dreads the awkward conversation that's ahead of us. I should have stopped speaking the second I realized what Nik was talking about, but it felt impossible. My anger was so strong, my relief at seeing his face again so powerful, it wouldn't have mattered who was watching. In that moment, it was just me and Nik.

Nik scratches the back of his neck as he walks.

He's unshaved and stubbly, and I have the urge to run my finger over his jaw.

No. I do not have feelings for Nik Lall. I never had feelings for him. We just went through something monumental together. We shared the pain of losing May. We got caught up in a moment. I'm with Pat, and he's steady and reliable, and he didn't run to the other side of the continent the first time we kissed.

'It'll wash off,' Nik says.

It takes an age to find Silas's cabin. It's a total wreck. In the centre of the room, slowly spinning in the water, is a big wooden desk. A stream showers from the ceiling, and the water around the desk is mulchy and thick with all the stuff that's bobbing in it. Pat splashes over to the desk and floats it round. He pulls it closer to me so that I don't have to get into the chest-high water. My heart breaks a little.

There's a small drawer in the desk, and that's where Silas told me I'd find what he needs. A box containing I don't know what. My breath flurries with apprehension. When I pull on the drawer handle, I find it's stuck fast.

Nik takes his multitool from his pocket and slides a flat blade in between the drawer and the wooden frame of the desk. There's a creak and a snap as the lock gives, and he shuffles the drawer open. Inside is the box Silas sent me to get. The wood's swollen and damp, but it's not flooded with water. I lift the lid, and my heart sinks. It's empty.

'What?' I say.

My guts crunch with fear. What does this mean? Do I need to look somewhere else? But what was I even looking for? I search through the drawer, but there's nothing else in there.

'There was never anything to find,' Nik says quietly.

'Why did he send me down here?'

'To humiliate you would be my guess. To show everyone how strong he is.'

'I . . . I don't know what to do next,' I say.

There's nowhere else I can go for help. Meg is going to die in this camp because I broke my promise to get her out.

'Come on,' Nik says. 'There's somewhere else we need to go.'

I stare down at the door, so familiar it's like I saw it yesterday, the memory of it so ingrained it's like a part of me. When the *Arcadia* toppled into the ocean, our cabin stayed high and dry. It took a lot of climbing to get here, using the ropes and buckles that Pat brought with him to find our way through the wreckage. Every step closer made my chest clench tighter.

Our front window is smashed, and through the shattered glass I can see the curtains hanging down into the cabin. Above my head, the rail is as solid as it ever was, the sky beyond it darkening in the late afternoon.

'You plan on opening it?' Pat says with a fraction less compassion than usual.

'Just give me a minute,' I say.

'I can go in first if you want,' Nik says.

'What if they're in there?'

Nik shakes his head. 'I don't know. Can't stand here forever though. You're on a deadline.'

I crouch. Now that the ship's on its side, I have to stand on the door frame. The weirdness of it all makes my head spin. I try the handle, and my stomach flips over when the door drops open.

We all look down into the gloom. The far wall, the one that has the doorway through to my bedroom, seems impossibly far away.

Nik attaches a rope to the rail above our heads and lets the end drop through the open door. He holds it out to me.

'I'll stay here,' Pat says, and he takes a few steps away from the door to my cabin.

Nik catches my eye with a look that says, *Well, this is awkward*.

I shimmy down the rope, each movement snagging the skin on my hands. Finally, my feet touch the wall, my boots crunching on broken glass. I find my footing, and then move out of the way so that Nik can follow me down. The place is destroyed. I'd been holding on to a mental image of the home I grew up in, the place that was mine for almost seventeen years. It still felt real in my memory. I hadn't seen the destruction, so somehow I could still believe that it existed.

Tears build behind my eyes; my throat aches with the pressure of trying to hold them back. The Federated States flag is still in place on the wall, sagging now and spotted where the rain got in through the broken window. Our sofa – my parents' bed – is on its side and resting against the wall, the covers crumpled and covered in a fuzz of green mould. But there's no smell. There's no buzz of carrion flies.

Nik slaps me on the back. 'OK?' he says.

I nod.

'I'll take a look in the back.'

He moves on, using the rope to climb further down into the cabin, where he'll find the room I shared with May. I don't have the strength for that. I expected to start throwing things into a bag and hauling everything back to the camp with me. But it's so dead in here. It doesn't feel like this stuff has any trace of May or my parents in it. The thought of touching the smashed plates or the rotting bedsheets makes me shudder uncontrollably. I don't want to be in the same room as these things.

The sound of Nik moving around in the next room is strangely comforting.

There's a creak, and a whine, and the place shifts beneath my feet. It's just the ship settling, but it makes my stomach lurch and my head spin. The disorientation's too much. I try to steady myself by taking deep breaths, and I tilt my head to look straight up through the front door. Past the rail, white and like the bars of a cell, to the blue-grey of the sky.

I shouldn't have come here. There's nothing of my family left. Just ghosts.

Something white flaps in the breeze above my head. A piece of paper, folded in half, taped to the wall above the sink. I snatch it. On the front, in my mum's handwriting, the word: *Esther.*

I unfold it to read the lines of frantically scrawled text on the inside. *We're with Mrs Lall's people. They're taking us somewhere safe. We love you.*

The rope wobbles, and Nik climbs back into the room.

'We need to go,' I say. 'My parents are alive.'

42

NIK

When we jump on to the quayside, Silas's goons are gone. Pat got down first, and now he turns back to help Esther. She's silent, face as still as a statue. Part of me wishes I hadn't walked into this mess. Part of me wonders whether Esther likes me at all.

Esther's not said anything since we left her cabin. She couldn't look more like she was going to murder someone if she had a knife in her hand.

Pat glances at the sky, and I follow his gaze upwards. More than one drone is zipping around tonight. 'It's getting hot out here,' he says, and even as he's speaking a drone circles round the back of the ship and sprints towards us.

Esther touches her fingers behind her ear, and an AR filter creeps over her face. It's of a pale-skinned, freckled girl. This must be Kara. Her face is familiar, and I realize I saw her once before, after the market on the *Arcadia* was bombed. She was one of Esther's classmates.

My clothes are heavy with water. What I wouldn't give for a warm meal and a change of outfit.

'Let's go,' Esther says to Pat. They both march off along the waterfront.

'Where're you going?'

'I'm going to get Meg back,' Esther shouts over her shoulder.

'Isn't she being held by Silas?'

'Yup.'

'You're going back there?'

'That's right.'

'Silas sent you to get something. You're going back with an empty box, even though you know he set you up. Sounds pretty stupid to me.'

Esther stops and spins round to face me. 'I'm empty-handed because there was never anything for me to find, remember? He gave me until sundown to get back there. I'm not leaving May for a second longer than I have to.'

'May?'

Esther looks flummoxed. 'What?'

'You said, *I'm not leaving* May *for a second longer than I have to.*'

'Meg. Obviously. I meant Meg.'

We stare at each other until it gets awkward. I know what she said, and suddenly this whole thing clicks into place. The reason why Esther went on a suicide mission to the *Arcadia*. She's trying to save Meg because she couldn't save her sister. She's trying to save everyone. The realization feels like an icicle through my heart, and all I want to do is fold this girl in my arms. Tell her what happened wasn't her fault.

'What if he kills you?' I say.

'So what if he does?'

'God, Esther, you're infuriating.'

'Yeah, well, you've been MIA for four months.'

I scratch the back of my neck. Pat's watching us like a hawk. 'How long until you get over this?' I say quietly.

'Let's start with four months and see where we're at.'

'What about your parents?'

'Meg first. Then my parents,' she says.

'At least call for backup. Let me contact Enid, and we can go get Meg with more firepower.'

'I've been trying to call for backup for months. I've been telling them I can fight, that I can be involved. Enid, your mother, the rest of the rebellion left me to rot. Like they're suddenly going to jump into action for one ship girl.'

'He's too strong.'

'Maybe Lall's right,' Pat says. He said my name like it tastes bad.

'You two go to HQ. I'll see you later.' Esther strides away. Pat gives me a look, then marches after her.

'You'll lose,' I shout.

Esther waves over her shoulder.

She's going to get herself killed. This is not my problem. I turn towards HQ. I've done my bit. I worked on those cuffs, and I ran aboard the *Arcadia* when it was the last thing I thought I'd do in my entire life. She's made it abundantly clear that she doesn't need my help. I've saved her ass twenty times. If she wants to be stupid and go up against Silas Cuinn by herself, there's nothing I can do to stop her. Just because

I abandoned her doesn't mean I have to put my own neck on the line.

Just because I spent my teenage years in love with her sister doesn't mean I owe Esther anything.

Just because I think I love Esther too doesn't mean I have to fight Silas.

Just because I'd walk through fire for that girl, just like I would have done for her sister, doesn't mean I have to go down in a shower of bullets.

I bunch my fists and watch Esther and Pat getting smaller in the distance. The sun's sinking behind the tall warehouses of the camp, and it's freezing in these wet clothes.

'Dammit, Esther,' I mutter.

I jog after them towards Cuinn's territory.

43

MEG

Silas Cuinn crouches down in front of me. His eyes are bloodshot, and he smells of smoke and tobacco and booze.

'Time's up,' he says.

My rescue team will be here any second, and then Silas Cuinn will be my prisoner instead of the other way round. That gives me a bit of a thrill, truth be told.

I look at his boots. Funny, the leather's still smooth and uncracked. Makes you wonder where he got them from – in this prison where the only people getting perks are the ones working with the Coalies. Maybe he really has got another way to get out of the camp. Maybe we even share a boss.

He takes me by the scruff of the neck and pulls me to my feet. I'm still holding the SOS button, and I press it over and over again.

My handler will come for me. I'm sure of it. We've made plans together. He's done everything he can to look out for my brother while I've been getting ready for the mission.

He even tried to get him out of the prison, but in the end his hands were tied. His superiors said the mission was too important, that I needed to focus on getting the job done, and then we'd all be free. Me and my brother and my handler.

My shoes scrape across the floor as Silas drags me. My stomach's swimming with a horrible dread feeling because this is all going a bit further than I'm happy about. And I thought, by now, I'd be able to hear backup coming.

Silas throws me down and takes his seat on the big chair again. People look at me with hunger on their faces, like they're waiting for the entertainment to start. They're all twitchy and tense. Even the woman who was our neighbour on the *Arcadia* is watching.

'Why's Esther Crossland trying to help you?' he says.

'Feels bad, I guess.'

I listen for the helicopter. For the sound of boots running. For the hammering on the door of the shipping container, and the crash of it breaking open, and a flashbang rattling as it's thrown in. None of that happens. My mouth's dry.

'Does she owe you something?'

'She let me get taken by the Coalies when she could have stopped it.'

Too late, I snap my mouth shut. Silas Cuinn doesn't just want to kill Esther. He doesn't just want to humiliate her. He wants to destroy her. And, if he thinks I'm important to her, he'll want to destroy me too.

He leans forward. 'Getting you out of here was her way of offloading her guilt.'

Where are they? My heart is pounding in my throat now.

'Kill her,' Silas says.

Immediately, the woman from the service corridor steps forward and pulls a gun from the holster at her waist.

'Wait! Please, you knew my grandma!'

The woman looks down at me with something like pity. 'Nothing personal, love,' she says.

'Not in here, imbecile. It'll make a mess,' Silas says.

The woman who was once my neighbour drags me towards the door, the sunlight, and I feel like I'm not touching the ground, like there's nothing keeping me weighed down in the world. And I'm grateful really that I'm not panicking. I'm not afraid of what comes next. I only wish I'd managed to see my little brother again.

We go out into the sun and turn down the side of the container. They stretch as far as I can see in all directions, stacked high to the sky. The woman pushes me against one of them, a sunny yellow wall of metal. And I see that there are already bullet holes scattered all over the yellow paint. Little black holes circled by orange rust.

I turn round, and I'm looking into the sun.

Others have followed us outside, and one of them is smoking. The tobacco smell scratches at my throat, and I wish that wasn't the last thing I'd ever smell.

There's a helicopter in the distance, I think, but I can't see it.

He didn't get to me in time.

The woman raises the gun and points it square at my forehead. And now I close my eyes because that's too real, the urge to hide is too strong, and I'd rather not look in her eyes while she kills me.

'I really am sorry, love,' she says.

There's a thud. An *oof* of air leaving someone's lungs. A shot.

I open my eyes.

44

NIK

By the time I realize what's happening, Esther's on the ground, fighting tooth and nail with some woman. Esther gets on top of her. She thuds her hand into the hard, cracked concrete once, twice, until there's the bang of a gun, and everything seems to pause.

Esther's face whips round to look at a fair-haired girl standing by the side of a container riddled with bullet holes.

'OK?' Esther says. The girl nods.

Esther gets hold of the gun and pushes herself up. This whole time Pat and I are standing, gawping.

'I'm going to see Silas whether you like it or not,' Esther says to the woman on the ground. 'Put the code in at gunpoint, and we'll pretend you put up a fight.'

'Or what?'

'Or I'll deal with you,' Patrick says quietly.

The woman gets to her feet, eyeing him. 'Ain't much of a choice,' she grumbles.

'Esther, it's time to go. We've got what we came for. No need to antagonize the man even more,' Pat says.

Esther ignores him and follows the woman to the door of another shipping container. The woman beeps the numbers into the code panel and pushes the door open.

Esther grabs the woman by the back of her coat and pushes her ahead, holding the gun against the woman's chest so that it's visible to everyone.

The girl, who I'm guessing is this Meg person, trails with her head lowered and one hand clutching the other elbow. A picture of anxiety. She did just have a brush with death, so I guess it's understandable.

Esther's gone inside, marching like she's possessed. Pat and I trot in her wake. She walks right up to Silas, who looks more shocked than I've ever seen him. Esther doesn't stop when she gets to him. He leans back, trying to get as far away from her as he can, but she brings the gun up to his face. She's right up in his grill.

Now I notice the people around him. They go from lounging to weapons drawn in a second. I raise my hands. Pat and Meg do the same. Silas waves his people back and seems to regain his composure.

'Enjoy your excursion?' he says.

'Hilarious,' Esther says through clenched teeth. She brings out the empty wooden box and throws it on to Silas's lap. 'There. I did it. You had your fun. You and your people can have a good laugh. But I want this over with, Cuinn. I'm taking Meg, and I'm leaving. I'm not coming back. But I want this to be the end, got it? You're not sending anyone after me. I'm not looking over my shoulder. What's it going to take?' She backs away, letting the gun drop. 'What do I need to do to put an end to this vendetta?'

He looks at her for a few seconds. 'That's not how this works,' he rumbles.

'I bloodied your nose. Do you want to punch me in the face? Let's go.'

'Esther,' I say. 'Now you're being ridiculous.'

'Mind your own business, Nik.'

Ouch.

'Might not be his business, but it is mine,' Pat says. 'And I agree with him. You've got Meg. Walk out of here now. All this eye-for-an-eye crap. You're as bad as he is.'

Well, that's a turn-up. Didn't expect Patrick Huang to be agreeing with me any time soon.

Silas is out of his chair. His people come closer. Esther's face tightens with determination. She grips the gun at her side. Her shoulders heave, but she doesn't break eye contact with Cuinn.

Silas marches towards Esther, fist pulled back. Then Pat steps between them. Shoulders squared.

Silas hesitates, hand still ready to strike. 'I let it go when you and your clan broke ties, and this is how you repay me? A public challenge?'

Patrick glares into Silas's face. Not a single muscle twitching.

Feels like every person here is holding their breath.

'No one touches her,' Patrick says through gritted teeth.

'You'll start a war – your lot against mine – for that girl?'

'I'll start a war to protect her.'

Looks like there's a battle going on inside Silas. Finally, he sniffs and turns away. 'No honour in punching a slip of a girl. Anyway, she's been adequately humiliated today. If you come back, I'll have you shot on sight.'

Behind us, someone opens the door, flooding us with sunlight.

I don't waste a second. I unpeel Esther's fingers from the gun and pull her by the hand. She's trembling.

'You've got a death wish,' I say.

It's midnight on Wednesday 16 March 2095. I don't know what the temperature is.

Over the past two days, things have got worse, far worse.

A cholera outbreak that began in Warehouse Eleven is tearing through the camp. The death rate is alarmingly high – almost fifty per cent don't recover.

I have lost all hope of outside help arriving.

We are utterly alone.

I gave up. I couldn't see any way forward.

Then someone threw us a lifeline. A way to really help people.

But I don't think I can make the choice they want me to make.

I don't know what to do.

Days in the camp: 123

45

MEG

By the time we got out from among the labyrinth of shipping containers and away along the beach, I could hardly walk I was shaking that much. Esther put her arms round me as we walked, whispering, 'It's OK – you're OK.'

I let her think I was shaken by the whole situation, which I was a bit, obviously. Not even I can come that close to a bullet in the brain without it having an impact. But what's really keeping me quiet, though, is trying to figure out what went wrong with my handler and why I wasn't picked up when I called for help. The button could be broken. But what if something's happened to him? He's military after all. What if he's been shipped off somewhere to fight? What if his base has been attacked, and he's lying in a pool of blood? Because, if he knew I needed him, nothing in the universe could have kept him away.

In the darkness before dawn, I can see the shapes of Esther and Nik and Pat, all sleeping in the bunk beds around me. There was a weird atmosphere between them last night.

Esther barely spoke to Nik. And every time she tried to speak to Pat he gave her single-word responses. Haven't got time for whatever it is. I need to get out of here and head to the meeting place. My handler will be there. I'm sure of it.

There's a thump from somewhere downstairs. They call her Corp, and I've only had a glimpse of her so far. She gave me the creeps, looked like she hadn't slept in a week – her eyes were all bloodshot and staring. Bet it's her who's making the racket downstairs.

I slide out of bed and pull my arms into my coat, then pick my boots up, sneaky-like.

It's too early for the sun to be rising, but now I see a flash of light pass behind the thin curtains. Holding my boots in my hands, I go to the window and pull the curtain enough to look through the crack. There are lights on the beach.

He's here.

Earlier was a mistake. Something made him late, that's all. My head goes all thin with happiness. This is over.

I've done it, Seb. I'm coming to get you.

I turn to run for the door.

'What's wrong?' Esther's standing behind me.

'Jeez, you almost gave me a heart attack,' I say, clutching the bottom of my throat.

'You're dressed. Are you going somewhere?'

'Someone's out there,' I say. Trying to sound scared rather than elated. Don't want to give the game away too early just in case. Not now, when I'm seconds away from running to him. Inside, I'm screaming.

More lights move back and forth outside, coming in round the edges of the thin curtains.

'It's the Coalies,' Esther says.

There's another sound beneath us, a shuffling and banging.

'They're inside,' Esther says breathlessly. She looks round at her friends still sleeping peacefully.

From my pocket, there's a whisper of a voice. Esther's face snaps to mine and the realization that floods her almost makes me laugh. Looks like I don't need to pretend any more.

'What have you done?' she whispers.

Can almost see her heart beating, feel the adrenaline stampeding through her. I take the earpiece from its place in my pocket and hold it out between us.

'Go ahead,' I say.

I can't help the little smile that's pulling at my mouth. I realize it probably makes me look unhinged, but I can't find it in myself to care. It's done.

'Could you ask Ms Crossland to come in here, please?' My handler's voice comes through the call button.

My heart's fit to burst. *Be patient, Meg. All in good time.*

Esther takes a gulp of air. She drops my hands. And walks out without saying a word.

46

ESTHER

I'd know the voice that came through Meg's earpiece anywhere.

He's in the lounge. Sitting in an armchair. A steaming cup in one hand. Alex Hudson. The boy I loved.

He's looking better than he ever did at home. Better than the last time I saw him anyway – when his face was a mess of bruises from the beating the Coalies gave him. Peeking from beneath a dark woollen overcoat, I can see the high navy blue collar of a Federated States military uniform. A single brass pip on each collar. The blue sets off his fair hair, which has been cut and styled. He's indistinguishable from a land person.

I'm suddenly conscious of the fact that I haven't washed my hair in weeks. I resist the urge to fidget with my lousy clothes.

'I made tea,' he says.

A shiver runs down my spine. To hide it, I open my arms. 'Welcome to my home.' My voice drips sarcasm. 'You look like you've done well for yourself since the *Arcadia* crashed.'

'I know which side my bread is buttered.' He looks round the hovel we call home, but there's no trace of distaste on his face. I know from experience what a good actor Alex Hudson is. How skilled he is at manipulation. He picks up the second cup of tea and holds it out to me.

'I'll make my own. Not sure I'd be able to stop myself from throwing it in your face,' I say.

He grins. 'Don't be like that. We were friends once. More than friends.'

'And don't I regret the fact.'

He takes a sip. 'Don't you want to know why I'm here?'

'Not overly,' I say. But I do. The question's burning through my mind.

It's infuriating how calm he is. How is he this OK? My old hatred of him had been dampened by the cold and the hunger, but now it catches again. There's something else too. The faintest pang of loss for the Alex I loved for so many years. I'd give anything to feel safe with him – at home again on the *Arcadia*. But that Alex is long dead, replaced by this monster dressed up in a costume and preened and primped like a show dog.

'You look ridiculous in that uniform. You look like a pig on its hind legs.'

'And you –' he looks me up and down – 'you look like a Neath. It pains me to see what you've become,' he says easily.

'The feeling's entirely mutual.'

I go to the stove and fill a kettle from the bottle we keep by the front door. My hands shake. Water sloshes over the sides.

Don't let him see that you're rattled. Don't let him see that you feel weak.

The next second, Alex is standing next to me, so close I can smell whatever it is he sprayed on after his shower this morning. He takes the handle of the pan, letting warm hands brush over mine. Making my skin crawl.

'Here, let me,' he says. He takes a lighter from his pocket and turns on the gas of the single-ring camping stove we use to cook. 'Your hands are freezing.' He pushes me gently into a chair, taking a hand-warming pack from another pocket in his coat and snapping it once, twice, to activate the heating chemicals inside. He presses it into my hands and a flush of warmth sets my palms tingling. He takes two more, cracking them to activate, and pushes one between my jumper and my coat at the back, and another between my collarbones, taking care not to let his skin touch mine.

'Don't,' I say. But the packs are so warm I could cry.

He sits down opposite me. The emergency heating packs spread their warmth through my clothes. Steam from the tea swirls round my face.

'I've missed you,' he says.

I let out a laugh.

'You don't believe me?'

'What do you want, Alex?'

'What makes you think I want something? Maybe I just wanted to see you.'

'If you were here to arrest me, I'd be in a cell by now.'

'Thought I'd see Corp here. How is she?'

'Don't talk about her.'

'I've heard she's not handling this cholera outbreak too

well. Heard she spent most of last night walking along the seafront with tears streaming down her face. What a sad, helpless little figure.'

That information rattles me. I know Corp has trouble sleeping, and she goes out at night. But the thought of her walking and crying, all alone in the dark, breaks my heart.

'Get on with it, Alex,' I say so that he won't see how much Corp's downward spiral affects me.

'I've come to talk to you.'

'About?'

'About what's going on in the camp. About what General Lall's doing. Or not doing, I should say.'

That piques my interest, and I can't help sitting up straighter in the chair. Four months we've been trapped here, and some days it feels like all Nik's mother is doing is shaking hands with politicians and promising that none of us will try to escape.

Alex leans forward so that we're too close, hands together and elbows resting on his knees. He raises his eyebrows so that his forehead scrunches up and gives me an open-faced look that I imagine he thinks makes him looks sincere. It does make him look sincere. But I stopped falling for Alex's manipulations a long time ago.

'Lall has betrayed you. All of you.'

A twist of pain in my gut because I believe him. 'She's in negotiations,' I say.

'She's filling her belly and staying comfortable by schmoozing the people in power.'

'She needs to schmooze,' I say. 'She's trying to get us released.'

He leans back and shakes his head. 'Nope. She agreed to these barbaric tags you've all been fitted with. Within a few days, she will announce a complete end to the hostilities, and the rebellion will be disbanded.'

I lick my lips and find they're dry and rough. 'What about us?'

'You have already been sold to a prison conglomeration. Just like everyone else here. The cuffs are the first step in introducing prison conditions.'

My head spins like the steam. I suddenly feel too hot. I drop the heat pack and throw off the blanket, not caring if Alex sees me flustered now. 'You're lying.'

'OK.' He takes another sip of his tea.

It makes perfect sense though. Her clothes, her hair, the helicopters in and out. The refusal to give details of the negotiations. She won't give us the details because she's not working for us. She's working for herself. Then there's the total silence from the other ships. She's abandoned the plan to get us out of here. We've been waiting for the end of the camp without even realizing it.

'I don't believe you,' I say. But I clutch at my chest because I do believe him. It makes me feel like my heart's been ripped out.

'I understand,' he says. 'But that doesn't change the fact that it's the truth. I'm going to lay everything out for you. Lall is lining her own pockets. Her power relies on the presence of the camp and the people of the ship. If this place is liberated and the people allowed to disperse, she loses any kind of control she has. She needs the ship people right here. And she needs them to be suffering, otherwise –'

'Otherwise, she's just a refugee.'

Alex doesn't speak.

I need to move. I stand up and pace the couple of steps across the room with him watching me.

'I hate to see you struggling like this. You've tried everything to get Meg out, and you've failed. You've had every door slammed in your face. We both know Lall has kept things from you, important things, like the fact that your parents are alive. Tell me I'm wrong.'

I hate that he's right.

'I've come with a deal. We need to get rid of Lall and replace her with a leader who will genuinely want to see a change in conditions in the camp. Someone who's willing to negotiate properly.'

'I can't help you.'

'You've not even heard what I have to offer.'

'No, I mean I can't help you. She's kept me out for the past two months. I'm not allowed anywhere near.'

'You'll find a way.'

I stare at the ground. I'm not even considering it. I won't help them. I won't collaborate, not even if our own leader has become a self-interested despot.

'In return for your assistance, the Federated States will introduce a new visa system. A small number of refugees will be released each year and allowed to enter society.'

'No. All of them.'

I turn round to find him shaking his head. 'This isn't a negotiation, Esther.'

'The rest of us just stay here? Have you seen this place? Have you smelt it?'

'We'll free five skilled and disease-free refugees at a time.'

'*We*,' I say, and I can't help the air that puffs from my nostrils. 'What?'

'You said *we* will release five at a time. You're really one of them now.'

Alex frowns almost imperceptibly. 'At the same time, we're willing to improve conditions in the camp significantly. Proper shelters. Proper food and sanitation. A clinic. Maybe even a school.'

I can't help staring at him, trying to find out whether he's telling the truth. He looks trustworthy, but then I always thought he was. More fool me for believing him again.

'Just think of all the good you could do with proper medical facilities. All the people you could help. All the suffering you could ease. Things could be good for people here. They wouldn't be free, but they'd be safe. And isn't that better than this?'

His breath smells clean. Like toothpaste. A smell I haven't encountered in four brutal months on land.

I turn away. 'You expect me to trust one of your deals again? After May?'

If he cares about hearing her name, it doesn't register on his face.

'Deep down, you know I'm right,' he says.

He moves so that he's standing behind me. I feel his breath on my neck, and I get a thrill of disgust as he runs a hand down my arm. Then he's moving towards the door.

'Go to headquarters. Do it tonight before she leaves for dinner with Admiral Janek. And keep your eyes peeled for an act of good faith from my superiors.'

'What kind of act?'

'Just a little treat for the people here. Something that will help to arrest the infection of cholera.'

I hear him put something down on the coffee table and then walk to the door. When I turn round, he's standing in the doorway. On the table is a gun.

'Ask yourself: if she kept the fact that your parents are alive from you, what else is she hiding?'

47

MEG

The slam of the front door wakes Nik, and he shoots up, banging his head on the low ceiling above the top bunk. He swears, rolls off, lands in a groaning heap.

Until a second ago, I was listening at the door, trying to snatch any little bit of the convo between Esther and my handler in the room down the hall. Now I run to the window, and see him striding away from the coastguard station without me.

I bang on the cracked windowpane with my hands, each slam making the old glass rattle in its frame. 'Alex!' I shout. Panic's welling inside me now. I have to get to him. He hasn't realized I'm here.

Nik's beside me now, and behind us I hear Pat say, 'What's going on?'

I'm halfway down the corridor before I can think. Esther's in the living area, staring at something in her hands. I sprint past, down the stairs, through the equipment room, and out of the front door. I take the ladder, splinters catching my hands like tiny daggers. I'm on the sand. He's still here.

The muscles in my legs tremble, and I'm not sure how I keep moving, but I do. Further down the beach is a helicopter. Its blades turn lazily. The sun's still coming up over the ocean, making everything seem thin and unreal.

Alex is halfway to the helicopter. His long woollen coat blows back as he marches away, and it feels like I'll never catch up. I'm so desperate to reach him, but the sand is wet and heavy, and it feels like every second he gets further ahead of me.

'Wait!' I shout. My voice carries on the thin air.

He stops. I'm so relieved I let out a little laugh, and I wave both hands in the air.

He doesn't react until I'm getting right up close to him. My feet are leaving deep prints in the ground.

That's when I notice the look on his face. It's a horrible sneer of disgust like I've never seen before.

'What's wrong?' I say.

When he doesn't answer, I run to him and grab his hand. And he pushes me so hard that I fall back and thump into the wet sand.

'You disgusting creature,' he says. His face all twisted and ugly. A monster.

There's a bloom of pain in my chest, and my mind flicks between the things I know and the things I can't figure out. I can't piece them together. He loves me. He trained me. He made plans with me.

There's sand under my fingernails. 'I don't understand.'

'That is not a surprise. You aren't the sharpest pencil in the box.' He stands over me and the look on his face is one of pure hatred. Like I'm worse than nothing. Sea scum. 'Did you really think I was planning to make a life with you?' He comes closer, looming over me so that I'm looking up into his face.

'No. You said we'd leave together,' I say, shaking my head.

'You're never leaving. None of you are.'

Everything's broken. Everything's rotten and rancid, and nothing, nothing, nothing is ever really good.

'What about Seb? What about my brother?'

'I don't know where your runt brother is.'

'But you've seen him. You've talked to him.'

'Of course not. My guess is he's still floating inside the *Arcadia*.' He waves a hand to where the wreck of the ship is. 'But you were so very easy to control once I made you think he was alive.'

'No,' I sob.

Oh, Seb. I want to die.

He climbs on to the helicopter. The door slams, and he doesn't even give me a final glance. The helicopter takes off. It circles over the main camp and shrinks to a dot before it blinks out of view.

Sadness rushes out of me, and I crumple on to the sand and cry and cry. Eventually, I start to hear the waves crashing again.

'Want to tell us what's going on?' Esther says.

They're all looking at me. Fire and stone on their faces. My cover's blown, and the only person who could help me escape has just flown off in a helicopter.

I run.

The beach is like wet cement dragging me down. Don't know where I'm going, just know I don't want to be anywhere near these people and the kind of questions they're going to ask.

Stupid, Meg. Stupid. Nobody, in this entire world, is looking out for you. Seb's gone. You're not a citizen of the Federated States. You're not a ticket holder like Esther. You're not part of the rebellion like Nik. You're not even a criminal like Pat. You're nobody.

I make it to the ocean and leap into the shallows. The sea's better than what's left on land.

But Nik's fast. Can hear his feet thundering behind me. My feet splash through the foam, and then he slams into the back of my knees. I'm in the freezing water, brine soaking through my clothes.

'Get off me!' I scream. Salt water splashes into my mouth.

I hear Esther shout, 'Nik!' Then she's pulling him off me.

All of them are standing over me now, looking down while I try and get my breath. Esther glares under her eyebrows. 'What else did you tell him?' She says it quietly, like she's disappointed in me instead of angry.

'Told him everything I could,' I say. It gives me a little thrill of satisfaction.

'The name I was using? Where to find me?'

'All of it. That you'd gone to Silas. They knew where you were the whole time.'

Esther crouches in the sand. 'But why, Meg? I was trying to help you.'

'Why? Because my life turned to crap the day I saw you in the Lookout. You could have helped me. You could've stopped me getting arrested. You could've stopped Hadley popping my fingers out one by one.' She flinches at that. 'And then you and him crashed the ship. You two are the reason my family's dead. Of course I wanted to help the Feds get you.'

Esther's face seems to crumple.

'What's she talking about? How'd you even know each other?' Nik says.

'I don't know her. We were just in the same place at the same time. And I could have helped her. But I didn't. I'm sorry,' Esther says finally to me. 'For that day. I'm sorry I crashed the ship. I'm sorry your parents died. I'm sorry for dragging you to Silas's. I'm sorry he tried to kill you. I'm sorry Alex betrayed you.'

She takes a few steps away, hands on her hips, looking down like she can't keep control of herself.

'How did you communicate with him?' she says when she turns back to face me.

'Call button,' I say.

'Give it to me.'

I get it out my pocket and slap it into her outstretched hand.

She takes it. Presses it.

'Won't work,' I say. 'He won't answer.'

Esther presses it anyway. It makes a faint crunching noise. 'Alex. Listen up. She's done. She'll never get close to me, or Nik, or General Lall. She'll never get any information about what we're doing. She's excommunicated. Cut off. So you leave her alone from now on. Got it?'

And then she lobs the call button into the waves.

'No!' I shout. My last chance of contacting someone outside the camp is gone.

Nik grabs my arm and pulls me up. 'Move,' he says and he starts dragging me along the beach towards the main camp.

'Where we going?' I say. 'Don't let him hurt me, Esther!'

'You're going to a prison cell.'

'No,' Esther says from behind us.

'You got a better idea, doc?'

'Leave her here.'

'Not sure I get it,' he says. He's still holding on to me like a vice.

'Alex tapped her for everything he needed. She's no threat to us now. She doesn't know anything that could interest them. Taking her to HQ will give her another chance to gather information. Leave her here. Alone.'

Nik looks at me, then releases his grip, and I almost fall again. 'If I ever see you sneaking around, you ever go after her again,' he says, pointing at Esther, 'I'll let the rebellion deal with you. They don't take kindly to traitors. Understand?'

Then they all turn their backs and walk away.

48

NIK

When I saw Alex jogging down the steps from the coastguard station, it was all I could do to stop myself charging him. Hoped I'd never set eyes on that guy again.

Meg's snivelling on the sand.

It's a damn mess. Seems like everything that could go wrong while I was away did.

'Who was that?' Pat says. He's crossing his arms, watching the helicopter shrink into the distance.

'That was the reason everything went wrong with the *Arcadia*,' I say.

'Thought things went wrong with the *Arcadia* because the Coalies launched the clearance early.'

Jeez, this guy keeps poking me. 'Why don't you shut up about things you know nothing about?'

'I know plenty about what happened out there. Because I've been here, with Esther, for two months. Want to hear what I think?'

He's stepping up to me, lips tight as he talks.

'Enlighten me.'

He pokes me in the chest, and this guy is getting on my last nerve. 'Things would have been a whole lot better if you'd dealt with that snake Alex Hudson when you had a gun pointed at him.'

'Enough!' Esther says. She forces herself between us, one hand on my chest the other on his. 'You two need to stop whatever this is. We've got more important fish to fry right now.' She pushes me further away, and I can feel the imprint of her hand on my ribcage.

I laugh and rub my nose. 'You are not wrong, my friend. If I had the moment again . . .'

Meg's stumbling away along the beach. Not sure whether we should be turning her loose when she's clearly a double-crossing traitor. But Esther's right. If there's one thing I learned last year on the *Arcadia*, it's that you don't give people access to the rebellion unless you're one hundred per cent sure they're not going to gather info and hand it to the enemy. We stop when we're far enough away that Meg won't be able to hear us.

'What did he want?' Pat asks.

Esther hesitates, chewing the inside of her lip.

'Come on, doc. Need to know what went on in there.'

She drags in a deep breath.

'Look, I know I messed up,' I say. 'But, for the time being, we're in this together, and if something's going on with Alex that might affect the rebellion I really need to know about it. Come on. You know you can trust me.'

She looks at me, and her eyes are just as hard as they have always been. 'For the time being?'

Oh. Shit.

'You're leaving again,' she says. 'Wow, what a shocker.'

'I didn't mean to . . . I shouldn't have told you like that . . .'

She snorts. 'Beats last time.'

'What happened last time?' Pat says.

'Last time, Nik kissed me and I didn't see him again for four months.'

Pat raises his eyebrows. 'He kissed you?'

Esther seems to realize who she's talking to. 'Pat, I'm sorry. I shouldn't have said that.'

'You two obviously have stuff you need to work through,' he says. 'I'll see you later, Esther.'

'Hey, I don't want to get in the middle of anything,' I say.

'Nik should go,' Esther says.

Now it's my turn to feel crushed.

'He's so determined to get away from me, it'll be a relief to him. So go, Nik. You get a free pass. Thanks for the help with Silas. Have a nice life.'

'Don't be like this.'

'What am I being like?'

'You're being childish.'

'I'm being childish? You're the one who ignored me – over a kiss – for four months!'

'I've said I'm sorry!'

'Oh right. OK. Well, Nikhil Lall's sorry. Everyone bow down because he's back now, and he's sorry.'

I don't know what to do. Guess I thought things would be the same as before I left. Didn't know everything would be so broken. 'What did Alex want?' I say.

Esther laughs. She folds her arms.

'If the rebellion's in danger, you need to tell me. No matter what you say, no matter what they've done, I know you still love those people. So, if Alex is planning something that might affect them, I have to warn them.'

Esther looks at me from the corner of her eyes. 'He offered me a deal. I spy for the Federated States; he tells me where my parents are.'

'Wait, your parents?' Pat asks.

'I found a note . . . in our cabin . . .' She takes the piece of paper from her pocket, unfolds it, hands it to Pat. He scans the words.

'So they were alive. And they were with some of Lall's people?'

'Yep,' Esther says. 'I don't know where they went, or if Enid got them to safety. One of the many things General Lall decided I couldn't know.' Her cheeks are all red, and her eyes are filling with tears, and it's enough to break my heart.

No. I refuse to have feelings for May's sister. She's with Pat. End of story.

'Alex seemed to take it pretty well,' I say, trying not to look at her face.

'What?'

'You saying no to him. From what I remember, he never much liked you thinking for yourself.'

Esther looks at her feet, kicks the sand.

In the sky, shining black against the grey dawn light, a drone arrives. Instinct tells me to get as far away from it as I can. As it hovers closer to us, I pull my hood up. But something catches my attention. Underneath, it carries a box.

'What the hell's that?' Pat says.

'I'm guessing it's Alex's gift,' Esther replies.

'His what?' I say.

'He said he'd send something. A show of good faith.'

The line carrying it snaps, and the box drops on to the sand with a dense thud. It settles at an angle. Relieved of its cargo, the flying thing whizzes off towards the edge of the camp and disappears.

Esther runs over to it and drops to her knees. It's no bigger than a shoebox.

'Whoa,' Pat says. 'Tell me you're not about to open a box sent to you by the Coalies. Did you learn literally nothing from the other night?'

'What happened the other night?' I say.

'Got shocked trying out a new way of getting through the fence,' Esther says.

'You were trying to escape? You know what they'd do to you if you were caught?'

'Save your concern for someone else.'

'Fine. But, for what it's worth, I'm with this guy. Alex has proved he's pretty much a sociopath, and even more sociopathic when it comes to his ex-girlfriend. I say we leave that box exactly where it is.'

Esther shrugs. 'It could be a trap. But, if he wanted me dead, why all the theatrics? He could have killed me. He could have had Meg kill me. If Alex wanted to hurt me, he could have done it a hundred times over.'

'At least let me have a look at it first,' Pat says.

'No way. If anyone's opening that thing, it's me.'

'Let the guy do something useful,' I say.

He throws me an acid glare.

283

'Look, don't touch,' she warns Pat.

'Fine,' he says and drops down next to her, his knees making circles in the sand. He gets close to look round the edges of the crate, scanning every surface before standing up and shrugging. 'Can't see anything suspicious. No obvious booby traps. That's not to say it won't explode if we try to get inside.'

'Satisfied?' Esther asks.

'Nope. But you're going to do it anyway.'

She carefully lifts the lid off the crate. My heart pounds.

Nothing happens. No explosion. No spider bots. Esther drops the lid on to the sand. Inside, cradled in cut-outs of black foam, are five long plastic packages.

'The hell are they?' I say.

We grab one each. I turn mine over to read the instructions, written in twenty different languages.

'SafeStraws,' I say.

I rip open the wrapper to reveal a plastic rod with a hole in one end and a drinking straw at the other. I walk a few steps out into the wavelets, put the straw end in my mouth and bend down to drink. It's crisp, cold and sweet. I straighten up, and wipe my mouth with the back of my sleeve. 'Clean, salt-free water wherever you go.'

'Not enough to help the camp though,' Esther says, looking down at the straw in her hand.

'As grand gestures go, it's not really got the wow factor, has it?' Pat says.

'Maybe Alex hasn't got the clout to deliver what he's promised,' I say.

Esther's still looking at the SafeStraw in her hand. 'This

could save lives. A lot of them,' she says. 'Only there's not enough. We'd have to share them out. Just one per family.'

'One per warehouse,' Pat replies, looking into the box.

'It'd have to be organized. And it could cause more trouble with infectious disease if people share,' Esther says.

'We can deal with that if it happens. But we can stop them getting sick from the dirty water and that's the main thing.'

'You're taking his help?' I say.

Esther's face is pale in the grey light. She looks like she's about to hurl. She takes the straw from my hand and slides it back into its wrapper.

'I'm going to take whatever help will save the most people. And, if that means taking these straws to the warehouses and making people line up to drink, that's what I'm going to do.'

A buzz starts in the distance, not drones this time, but helicopters, half a dozen of them. They swoop low over the beach, carrying enormous crates, so close we all duck. We watch them in silence as they reach the main camp, and then the crates drop, one by one.

'Pat, I need you to find Corp. Tell her where I've gone.'

'And where's that?' Pat says.

'I'm going to HQ. Nik's going to get me in to see his mother.'

'Can't do it, Esther,' I say.

'You'll think of something,' she says.

49

ESTHER

The gun is heavy under my coat. I don't know what I'm doing. All I know is that I trusted the rebellion, and I trusted Meg, and in the space of a few hours it's all crumbled around me. In a bizarre twist of reality that I never saw coming, Alex seems to be the person levelling with me. He told me we would never be allowed to leave, and I believe him. He told me General Lall is doing nothing to help the camp, and all evidence supports that. He told me if I helped the Federated States he could make our lives better. He helped the Federated States. They made his life better.

Nik leads us to the door of HQ. A tall, nondescript metal thing set into the ground-floor wall of a warehouse in the west of the camp. It echoes dully when he hammers on it with his fist.

I don't know what I'm here for. I'm not here to kill General Lall. It's a monstrous idea. But I took Alex's gun and hid it in the back of my trousers, and when Nik asked what Alex wanted me to do I lied, and I don't know why. If I had no intention of carrying out Alex's orders, why did I lie to Nik about it? And why am I now so determined to get into HQ and speak to General Lall?

Because I need answers, that's all. General Lall will answer my questions. She'll explain what's been happening. That will be the end of it.

Obviously, I'm not going to kill Nik's mum.

Obviously.

There's a squeak, a roughly cut hatch opens in the middle of the door, and a pair of eyes looks out. 'What you want?'

'It's Nik Lall. Let me in.'

The eyes swivel to me. 'Not her.'

'You know who I am? I'm your boss. Now open the door and let us in.'

'Not yet you're not. And I'm more afraid of Enid and your mother than I am of you.' The hatch snaps shut.

He hammers on the door again.

The hatch opens. 'What?'

'Let me speak to Enid.'

The man behind the door sticks his hand through the hatch, grubby and wrapped in a frayed comglove. It's making a *boop-boop-boop* sound, then there's a beep, and the click of a call connecting.

'Yep?' Enid's voice comes through.

'Enid, it's Nik. I'm at the front door, and this guy –' he throws the eyes in the hatch a pointed stare – 'won't let me through.'

'Of course he won't let you in. You're not one of us. And he'll be especially reluctant if you're with Esther Crossland. Nice job, by the way, Derrick.'

'Ta, Enid,' the face through the hatch says.

Nik bites his teeth together in frustration. I can see the little muscle in his jaw working. 'I gave five years of my life to the rebellion. I don't bend a knee to my mother, and suddenly I'm *not one of you*?'

'Fact is, everyone in here is offering their lives for the cause right now. Can you really blame us for not trusting you?'

He throws his hands up and paces away. 'Not trusting me? You've known me my whole life. I took a bullet for the rebellion –'

'Two bullets,' I say.

'Two bullets! What else do you want from me?'

'So she is there with you. Nice to see you, Esther, though I'd prefer it if you were hiding like we asked you to two months ago. You've been a right pain in my neck, you know?'

'We need to speak to my mother. Esther's just had a visit from Alex Hudson.'

'The ex?'

'That's right.'

'How's he looking?'

'Enid!' Nik shouts.

'What? Just want to know if the girl still fancies him. I'll let you in soon as you agree to your mother's terms. We want you to choose the rebellion.'

Enid ends the call. Derrick pulls his arm inside the hatch, smirks and closes it, twisting the latch to keep it shut.

Nik stares at the door, hands on hips.

'You can change your mind later,' I say.

'Can't. Won't happen. They're like a web I've been struggling to get free of, and all of a sudden I'm stuck right back at the centre of it.'

'If they start doing stuff you're against, back out. Better yet, make them change. But right now I need to get in there and speak to your mother. Please. I think she knows where my parents are.'

He sighs and rests his head on the metal of the door. Then he raps it with his knuckles, and when the hatch squeaks and Derrick opens his hand, Enid's already on the line.

'Good choice, Nik my boy,' Enid says. 'Let them through.'

Inside, HQ is the same as the last time I was here. It's clean compared with the rest of the camp, and brightly lit. The walls are a kind of faded white that must once have been crisp. Noticeboards still line some of the walls, safety notices and ads for yoga classes secured by drawing pins. I'll probably never know why this part of the city was abandoned by the Federated States. Maybe they just didn't need it any more – they've got so much of everything that they could afford to let it fall down.

Nik doesn't wait for the man at the door to show him the way. Instead, he marches ahead, then leaps up a flight of stairs two at a time. We end up in a long loft space, skylights flooding the place with mid-morning sun.

Enid stands up from the table when we enter. A guard at the door flinches forward, but Enid dismisses him with a shake of her head.

'Nice to see you, doc,' she says, although the way she keeps her face blank makes me think she's not all that sincere.

'Where's General Lall?' I say.

'No small talk? OK. For what precisely?'

'I need to ask her something.'

''Fraid you're going to have to be a little more specific. She's a busy woman.'

'Busy planning her political career now she's in Janek's pocket?' I say.

Nik shoots me a look. 'You told me you wanted to ask about your parents.'

'I'll get to that. But Alex told me a number of interesting snippets this morning.'

'Now, just hang on –' Enid starts.

'Get her. Now,' Nik says. And, for the first time, I see Enid waver. Nik usually shows more deference to Enid, and his tone has clearly set her off balance. Good. It's about time someone shook this place up.

Enid nods at the guard. When he's gone, she drums on the table with her fingernails.

After what seems like an age, Enid keeping time with her fingernails, Nik breathing quietly at my side, General Lall appears. Her appearance shocks me and does precisely nothing to persuade me Alex was lying. She's as neat and polished as any land person. To look at her, you'd never guess she's spent the past half a year living in a squalid camp. Guess some people have an easier time here than others.

I'm not going to kill her. She'll explain everything. I probably won't even need to get the gun out. When it gets dark, I can take it down to the quayside and throw it in the sea without anyone knowing.

'Ah, Nikhil. You've seen reason and decided to throw

your hat into the ring. Good. Ms Crossland, you can leave,' General Lall says with barely a glance in my direction.

I steel myself for an argument. I've never been strong enough to push back before. This time will be different because it has to be. 'I have some questions,' I say.

'As I understand it, you ask John questions regularly. He communicates all of the information that we are willing to share. Please make your way to the front entrance, where someone will give you some extra food to take with you.'

'You're kidding,' I say.

Keep going. At the very least, she's going to hear my questions. I'm not going to kill her. That would be murder, and I'm not a killer. But now I'm in front of her, and she's so cold, so aloof, so *uncaring*, maybe I could just show her how serious I am . . . show her that I won't be ignored. I'm here. I'm alive. I'm important.

'I made my position perfectly clear when I ordered you into hiding a few months ago. You and Corp are wanted fugitives. While there's any danger that you could be arrested and interrogated, it is imperative that you have no access to confidential information. That includes access to headquarters, and specifically to this war room.' She gestures round the room at the maps and plans, the digimap of the camp shining ocean blue, bone white. 'Nikhil should have shown better judgement than to bring you here.'

'Does everything I sacrificed count for nothing? The people I lost. The life I gave up. The danger I put myself in. Does it mean *nothing* to you people?'

She looks at me straight on. 'It means very little.'

'Mum,' Nik says.

'It's a fact. Perhaps one that makes Esther feel underappreciated, but a fact all the same. In the scheme of things, her sacrifices meant a great deal four months ago. Now they mean very little. Esther was instrumental in getting the people of the *Arcadia* off the ship. She is of little consequence now. We have other more pressing concerns than the legacy of a girl who took action only when she was left with no choice. Your actions, your losses are in the past. Now we must look to the future. It's a sad fact that you are entitled to nothing from me. The rebellion is not obliged to involve you in any way.'

Anger threatens to burn me up. 'I've been here,' I say, and my voice is screaming to get out of my throat. 'You say it's in the past, but I've been here, waiting to help. Asking what I can do. Asking how I can serve.'

Enid takes a step forward. 'I think what General Lall's trying to say – and frankly butchering the delivery – is that we're grateful, really, for what you did, and for what May did, but it's over now. You're retired. End of the road for you and the rebellion. It's for everyone's good.'

The door to the next room opens, and John's head pokes through. 'Enid, I've got Corp and some kid downstairs wantin' to be let through.'

'Why not? The more the merrier at this point. And maybe she can calm Esther down a bit,' Enid calls over her shoulder.

'You owe her,' Nik says.

'We owe her nothing,' says General Lall.

'You're collaborating with the Coalies,' I say.

General Lall looks at me in surprise. 'I have frequent

contact with them as I negotiate the terms of the ceasefire and our release from the camp.'

'And you've abandoned the plan to bring the other ships here,' I say.

She turns her eyes on me. 'This is not a conversation I intend to have with you.'

'You know all about Janek's plans to sell the camp to the prison conglomeration, and you've taken no action to prevent it.'

General Lall considers me. There's a flicker of something on her face that could be guilt or the setting of her features in advance of a lie. 'I won't be held hostage by an irate teenager.'

'You were happy enough to work with teenagers when it suited you,' Nik says.

'And perhaps that was a mistake. This meeting is over.' She starts to leave.

All at once, I'm sure: General Lall keeps her silence because she's guilty of every crime Alex outlined.

'Where are my parents?' I say, my voice shaky. I pull the gun from its place at the back of my trousers. I point it at General Lall. And I feel fear and a cold certainty. I will shoot this woman if she doesn't give me the answers I want.

As soon as she sees the threat, Enid grabs a taser from the table, flicking the switch to charge it, so that a faint whistle lets me know it's the real thing. 'I'd take no pleasure in shocking you, girl. But I will if you don't stop this silly business right now.'

'Everybody take a breath,' Nik says. 'Nobody needs to get shot. Nobody needs to get tased.'

'You're taking what you can for yourself while the rest of us drop like flies. You're working for the Coalies.'

'Esther, she's not working for them. And you can't go threatening people with guns. Where did you even get it?' Nik says.

General Lall raises her hands in surrender, one eyebrow cocked. She doesn't believe I'll do it. 'He's right. I'm not working for them. But I don't owe you any further explanation. And I certainly won't be revealing the ins and outs of our organization's activities to a teenager who's holding me at gunpoint.'

'Due respect, General, but I think the time for being cryptic is over, don't you?' Enid says. 'It was a ruse, girl. All the dinners, all the clothes, all the endless talking and meetings and press conferences.'

'You're tricking them?' I say, but I don't let my hand drop. Not until I'm sure she's telling the truth.

'She is. We all are,' Enid says. 'Esther, I'll level with you. We scrapped the idea of bringing the other ships here months ago. It was never going to work.'

My stomach plummets. 'I knew it,' I say, shaking my head. I tighten my grip on the gun. 'I knew she wasn't working to bring the others here. That's why the transmissions stopped.'

'That's right. They stopped because we cut them loose. They've gone off to Maine.'

There's a flurry of hope in my chest, small but enough to make me want to cry.

Enid carries on, 'There wasn't enough time, and what Janek's got planned for the camp is coming much sooner than we'd thought. Bringing in reinforcements would've meant a lot of bloodshed and almost no chance of survival.'

'At least we would have gone down fighting,' I say. There's a lump in my throat and tears are aching behind my eyes.

'Hey, don't you start with that crying nonsense. We've done a lot of compromising, and we've done a lot of placating, but we've done it all in the service of the people in this camp. If you can take a minute and listen, I'll fill you in on what else we've been doing. But I'm going to need you to point that weapon at the ground –'

The door opens. Corp and Pat storm in, cheeks ruddy from running. Pat comes to stand by my side. Corp takes in my shaking, outstretched arm. I have to steady my elbow just to keep the gun from sagging.

'Finally, someone to talk some sense into the girl,' Enid says. She doesn't take her eyes off me. 'Tell your subordinate to drop her weapon.'

'Put the weapon down, Esther. That's an order,' Corp says. Her eyes are wild, and her hair's pulled free from its ponytail.

I drop the gun, so relieved I could laugh out loud. I sense Pat relax next to me. Enid lowers the taser and hooks it into her belt.

I don't see where the weapon comes from, but suddenly there's one in Corp's hand. And it's pointed at General Lall.

Someone shouts, '*No!*'

The shot is like the universe cracking in two.

PART TWO

ESCAPE

50

NIK

For a second, I can't figure out what's happening. Sounds so loud it's like it's inside my head. Then my mother's dropping like a bag of wet sand. And there's blood. Lots of blood.

Enid rushes Corp. Grabs the gun.

Corp lets it go easy. She's staring at me, eyes like saucers, saying, 'I'm sorry, I'm sorry.' Over and over.

People dart through the door, plough into Corp, lift her and carry her away, even though she's offering absolutely no resistance.

I'm not really touching anything. Not really solid.

Esther's already in action mode. Her hands press against my mother's stomach. She turns to face me, and her mouth's moving up and down like she's saying something, but all I can hear is the shot ringing and ringing in my ears.

Sound floods back in. 'Nik, get a medical kit. Now!' she says.

On the ground, my mother pants like a fish out of water. Eyes roaming the ceiling in confusion. All I can think is, if this is her last moment, I don't want her to be alone. Please, don't let this be the end. When I take her hand, the fingers are cold.

Pat disappears out of the door, and it could be a minute or it could be an hour before he's back at my mother's side. A pile of medical gear cascades on to the floor round her. Esther yanks open the suit jacket my mother wears whenever she's going to meet Federated States officials. Underneath, the crisp white shirt is turning brilliant red. Esther uses a pair of scissors to cut the shirt open, and I get a glimpse of loose stomach skin bathed in blood. Frantic movement up and down. Hands limp like every bit of life has rushed to her core so that she can fight on for a second longer.

My mother is dying.

51

ESTHER

My hands are slippery and warm. 'Get that scanner on the wound,' I say.

Pat crouches on the other side of General Lall. He arranges a field scanner over the wound. I stare as the image flares, knowing that every second my hands aren't pressing the wound it's another second closer to General Lall bleeding out.

'OK. We're leaving that bullet where it is,' I say.

No point messing about with something that's already done as much damage as it can. If she lives – and it's a big if – I'll keep an eye on it and go back in if I need to. Pat whisks the scanner away, and I press my hands back over the bullet hole, kneeling up to get in a better position.

The last time I treated a gunshot wound, it was her son lying on the floor, and his mother hoping for a miracle.

'As soon as this is over, we're going to have a conversation,' Pat says. He's unwrapping a white dressing, waiting for me to move my hands so that he can press an absorbent pad over the wound. He opens another with his teeth.

'Now's not the time,' I say.

Pat throws stuff out of the med bag. 'There's no blood replacement.'

My heart sinks. General Lall's blood is seeping away. At thirty per cent loss, her blood pressure will plummet. At the same time, her heart rate will skyrocket. But if I can get fluids into her it might buy me enough time to plug the hole.

'We're doing this the old-fashioned way,' I say. 'Nik, hey – I need to know your blood type and your mother's. Hey! Hey!'

Nik doesn't react. I click my fingers in front of his face. He's staring at his mother, catatonic.

'Check his blood type,' I say to Pat, cocking my head at Nik.

Pat grabs a testing needle, and presses the punch into Nik's fingertip without asking permission. Nik doesn't blink. That's a problem I'll deal with later.

'Enid, hands on this wound and press, hard. Don't be shy.'

Enid puts her hands over mine, and I ease myself free. I snatch another testing needle. No need to punch the general's finger – there's enough blood around here. I drop the end of the needle into a pool of blood on the general's belly button and then insert it into the hole of the field scanner.

'She's blood group B,' I say as the result flashes on to the scanner screen.

'Yep, group B blood over here too.' Pat drops Nik's hand. 'Is there a transfusion kit?' he says to himself, going back into the med bag. He finds a long plastic tube, a catheter, a tourniquet. It'll have to do.

I take the long plastic strip from him and tamp down a surge of horror. The person who taught me to do this is the same person that inflicted the damage. How did things go so wrong with Corp? How did they go so wrong with me? Because, if I'm totally honest, I was almost willing to do the same thing. Now, facing the injury that's torn through General Lall, the thought makes my head spin.

'People were trying to get her ... Didn't think Corp ...' Nik says.

'I need you to focus for ten seconds.' I steer him over to General Lall and push him on to his knees. Get his coat off, still soggy from our swim on the *Arcadia*. As I strap the tourniquet round his bicep, pulling it tight, I turn this whole thing over in my head. I didn't pull the trigger. Corp did. *Did someone get to her too?*

I press the needle against the bulging blue vein in Nik's arm, hard enough to break the skin, gently enough to enter the vein but not pierce the other side. The catheter slides into position, and I hold my breath while I wait for the swirl of blood that will tell me I'm in the right place. It creeps into the tube like a lava flow. I flick the knot off the tourniquet and let go of Nik's arm, and then the blood's flowing from Nik's body into General Lall's.

Pat's already activating a suture bot over the wound on General Lall's gut. Within three seconds, the bot is exploring the damage with its legs, testing to see where the repairs need to be made. I tape the catheter on to Nik's arm so that it can't slip out.

There's nothing else to be done. The suture bot is doing its repair work. Nik's blood is replacing what General Lall has lost. Already, her breathing seems less chaotic, the puffing less frantic.

The front of Enid's clothes are covered with streaks of blood. Just like mine. Just like Pat's. 'Come on,' Enid says to me. 'We're going to talk to Corp.'

52

JANEK

There are already crocuses under the yew tree, signalling the start of spring. Janek sips her tea – Earl Grey, lemon – and tries to keep her cool. Things are moving at once too slowly and too quickly. The president's patience is thinning faster than the firestorm engulfed the *Ithaka* eight years ago. Meanwhile, the prison conglomeration want their workers working. Her plans to bring the rebellion to heel are foundering. Every day that passes without her delivering the heads of the key players is another chance for the president to name an alternative successor. If he does that, there's more than just her political career on the line. Heads will roll, literally and figuratively. And if Janek is facing the gallows, then Harveen will be swinging right there next to her.

If she can't kill off Crossland and the Lalls soon, she may need to take more drastic action, even if it's against the express wishes of the president. But the destruction of the camp and its resources will mean a loss of profit for the prison conglomeration. After populating their prison factories with the Federated States' criminals for years, the conglomeration has their sight set on a jackpot. Hundreds of new workers all at once. Stokes and his cronies already have the president in a chokehold. Handing him donations with one hand, selling him munitions for the war effort with the other. That's where the real power in this country lies.

To top it off, there are those among the ruling elite who believe the ship people should be well treated and who hold General Lall up as a symbol of good. That element must be appeased and coddled, assured that the government are the *righteous* characters in this story. The need to hold on to their approval is one reason why Janek can't just shoot Lall in the street.

Not for the first time, Janek curses the fact that the *Arcadia* landed so close to the city. A few miles to the north and it would have been safely out of sight, out of mind. She could have had this all wrapped up in a matter of days.

Behind her, the French doors to the Statehouse open and close, and footsteps bring someone to the table. Janek looks up to find Harveen and a fresh-faced kid who can't be more than seventeen.

'My mood depends on whether you're bringing good or bad news,' Janek says, placing her teacup carefully on to the saucer.

'This is Alex Hudson, ma'am. He's one of the agents we recruited after the grounding of the *Arcadia*.'

The boy steps forward and gives a tidy bow.

'You don't look like a ship kid.'

'I'll take that as a compliment, thank you, ma'am,' he says, smiling.

'Aren't you charming? Tell me some good news, Mr Hudson.'

The boy glances at Harveen, who nods her assent.

'After Esther Crossland and Nik Lall crashed the *Arcadia*, I was given the opportunity to serve the Federated States, and for that I will be eternally grateful –'

'I don't need your life story, Mr Hudson.'

'Yes, ma'am. I was close to Esther Crossland and Harriet Weston aboard the *Arcadia*.'

'Close how?'

'Mr Hudson was on the medical-track training programme. Esther Crossland was his classmate. Corporal Harriet Weston was his trainer,' Harveen says.

'I've been using my knowledge of them to guide the search.'

'He's been running a number of agents within the camp with the aim of locating the fugitives without the need to launch a large-scale military operation.'

'Why is this the first I'm hearing of it?' Janek says.

'There are a number of operations being carried out, Admiral, and frequent dead ends. We don't need to brief you unless one of them bears fruit.'

This is true. Janek can't and shouldn't be briefed on the details of every operation being undertaken. It would be unnecessary and taxing. However, the thought of Harveen overseeing operations that she has no knowledge of gives Janek a faint prickle of uncertainty. Has she given this woman too much freedom? What other missions are being undertaken in Janek's name she has no knowledge of?

'I assume that your presence here means there's been a development.'

'As of this morning, we have located both Esther Crossland and Harriet Weston,' Alex says with another winning smile. The kind of smile any Federated States mother would be proud to see on her son.

Janek's surprise must be evident from her expression because both Harveen and the boy grin. 'Well, Mr Hudson, that is good news! And some impressive work, I must say.' Janek stands and shakes Hudson's hand.

'Thank you, ma'am.'

'Harveen, make arrangements for me to go to the White House right away. No point sitting on good news. The president will be delighted that we have not one, but two of the Federated States' most wanted in custody.'

This is exceptional. Her past failures will be forgotten. She'll be back on the presidential track. More importantly, her life will be safe, and all she'll need to do is wait for the current occupant of the White House to keel over – whether his death is a natural one is something she will need to consider.

'Actually, that's why I've brought Mr Hudson here. His operation is ongoing.'

Janek sags under a sudden heaviness. Of course it is. She was so close. 'How so?' she says, retaking her seat at the table.

'May I speak freely, Admiral?'

'I think you'd better, young man.'

'I've been informed that your task is to retrieve the fugitives, and in addition neutralize General Lall, who has become the figurehead of the rebellion. But that you are restricted from taking direct action against the general.'

'That's correct.'

'And – pardon my bluntness – your attempts at neutralizing her have failed.'

'We have sent a number of assassins from within the camp to take her out. By all accounts, some have come close.'

'From the start of my mission, I've wanted to take control of the rebellion from the inside. To turn them against one another and use their own strength to destroy them. My plan puts someone inside rebel HQ. Right into the heart of their operation.'

'You had the location of the fugitives, yet you didn't arrest them?'

'I gave them the means to kill General Lall. And I gave them incentive enough to pull the trigger.'

'This is quite the gamble, Mr Hudson. They could slip through our fingers.'

'It is a gamble, ma'am, but one that I'm confident has paid off. Just fifteen minutes ago, I had surveillance-bot confirmation that both Esther Crossland and Harriet Weston have entered rebellion HQ.'

Alex places a digiscreen on the table in front of Janek and taps the screen so that a video plays. It shows bot footage of Harriet Weston entering a plain metal door. Hudson flicks the screen and another video rolls, this time showing Esther Crossland.

'Wait, who's that with her?'

'That is Nikhil Lall,' Hudson says.

His voice drips with pride. He's enjoying the slow reveal. He's enjoying his own success, but also that he's bringing welcome news to Janek. This teenager might be an extremely useful asset.

Janek grips the arms of her chair. 'He survived the attack. We failed. Again.' She glances at Harveen, who drops her eyes. 'Mr Hudson, are you telling me that in one afternoon you've located the top three most-wanted fugitives in the Federated States, and you've put in place a plan to remove General Lall from her position of influence?'

'Yes, ma'am.'

'This kid might give you a run for your money, Harveen.' Harveen's cheeks redden, either in humiliation at having failed again, or anger that this teenager is showing her up. 'Do you have any other revelations for me, Mr Hudson?'

'I'm pleased to report that our surveillance picked up at least one shot being fired inside HQ.'

Janek gets out of her chair. 'Let's not count our chickens, Harveen, but I think Mr Hudson might have solved a number of our problems.'

'Yes, ma'am,' Harveen says.

'You certainly are impressive, Mr Hudson. Especially for someone who grew up in less-than-ideal circumstances. And you can take that as a compliment.'

'Thank you, ma'am.'

Janek turns to Harveen. 'Set up a call with General Lall. Let's see if she's still standing. Mr Hudson here is going to take tea with me.'

As Harveen leaves, Janek pours a second cup of tea and adds sugar without asking Hudson how he takes it.

'May I ask what your plans for Nik Lall are, Admiral?'

'That's very forward, Mr Hudson, but I think you've earned it. My hope is that Nikhil Lall will become a valuable asset. General Lall has always been prickly, but I sense Nikhil isn't bound by the same sense of duty as his mother. If I can bring him under control, he'll lead the camp in whichever direction I demand.'

'A puppet leader.'

'Exactly. Now, tell me, Mr Hudson, what do you want?'

'Ma'am?'

'Out of life.'

'I just want to serve the country that has given me so many opportunities.'

'No. That's how you're going to get what you want. But what's the *thing*? What keeps you trying?'

He looks at the flowers nestling among the exposed roots of the yew tree. 'I want power. A lot of power. I want to be so strong people will be terrified to disobey me.'

Janek considers the boy, the neat, wholesome, healthy features of a patriot.

'That can be arranged.'

53

ESTHER

We march down a flight of brightly lit stairs and through a set of doors. 'Where is she?' I ask Enid.

Enid's paler than I've ever seen her, chewing on the corner of her lip in a way that makes her seem uncharacteristically shaken. 'Locker room in the basement. Jeez, what happened to the pair of you?'

'What happened is you made us feel so powerless that when the Coalies came knocking with a deal Corp took it.'

'Now hang on a minute. You can't blame this on us. If Corp picked up a gun, she did it of her own volition.' Her voice is weighed down with anger. 'Why in hell didn't you stop her if you knew what she was thinking?'

'I didn't know what she was planning. But they offered me a deal too.'

Enid stops in the centre of the corridor. As she turns to face me, the full reality of all this washes over me again. I didn't pull the trigger, but I came here not knowing what my choice would be. There will be consequences.

'The Coalies offered you a deal, and you turn up here with a gun. You were planning to do it.'

'No.'

'That's a lie.'

'I don't know, Enid. I honestly don't know,' I say. My mouth's as dry as dune grass.

'It's a damn mess,' she says, shaking her head. 'I told the general it was a mistake. I told her she shouldn't excommunicate you. I should have you arrested. You know that, right?'

I take a deep breath, raise my chin, stare straight back at Enid. I'm ready to take anything that's coming. Right or wrong, I made a choice. I have to face it.

'I don't know if I would've pulled that trigger if she'd given me different answers. But I took the steps. I took the weapon Alex offered me. I hid it from everyone, from Nik, until I got into the room. Then I pointed it at General Lall. All of that is true. I'm willing to face whatever punishment you dole out. But right now General Lall's out of action. So is Corp. And you have to know that what I did, whatever I would have done, was in the service of the people of this camp.'

Enid stares at me. 'You're being stripped of your rank.'

'I don't have a rank –'

'Don't interrupt me, girl. You're now a private. That means you obey my orders. You do what I say, when I say it. You will not be privy to any information I deem it necessary to keep from you. And, next time your ex comes beckoning with promises of free stuff and comfort, you come directly to me and report it. If you don't, I'll have you up on charges faster than you can say *I sank the* Arcadia, and you'll spend the next fifteen to life on latrine-digging duty. Do you understand?'

I clear my throat. 'I understand.'

'I beg your pardon?'

'I understand, ma'am.'

'That's better.'

She carries on marching down the corridor, muttering to herself, 'Should've taken charge of this from the start.' Her hands are clenched into fists at her side. We reach a door guarded by a couple of Neaths, arms crossed. One of them swings the door open for Enid. 'She's been searched for transmitters and the like?' Enid says to one of the guards.

'She's clear,' he replies.

The room inside is lined with lockers, and wooden benches run down the middle. At the far end, there's a tiled area with showerheads pointing down from the walls. It smells faintly of disinfectant. And on the floor, bleeding from a split in her lip, is Corp. Someone's bound her hands and ankles with duct tape. The room spins round me, and I think I'm going to be sick. Pressing my hands into my knees, I breathe until the swaying stops. This is Corp. Teacher. Friend. Traitor.

She looks up when she hears us come in. 'Is she dead?' she says.

Even though I've known this woman for years, I can't tell what answer she wants to hear.

I stop at the edge of the shower room, not wanting my toes to step on to the tiles. 'She's not dead yet,' I say.

'You controlled the bleeding?'

'Transfusion from Nik.'

'It would have been better if she'd died.'

Enid snorts. 'Think General Lall would disagree with you on that point.'

'What did they offer you?' I ask.

'Nothing. I did this on my own.'

'They tried it with me too,' I say, and I pull my jacket back to reveal the gun Alex gave me, hastily holstered and clipped in. 'For me, they sent Alex. And they promised to help us fight the cholera.'

She looks up at me, bleary-eyed. Under her eyes, her face is all puffy and swollen from crying.

I take a step forward, my shoe echoing on the white tiled floor. There's a drain nearby, and the faintly sulphury smell of sewers. I bend down next to Corp, close enough that I could take her hands if I wanted to. 'How did they make reach you?'

'Through the radio I'd been using to contact the other ships. I'd given up hope of anyone answering, but it made me feel better to say it all out loud.'

Corp lifts her tied hands to her face and rubs her nose. Her fingers are bruised purplish around the duct tape.

My heart feels like a shard of glass in my chest. I try not to breathe too deep in case it cracks and slices into me. I can't stand the sight of those hands tied together so I reach for them and start unpeeling the tape.

'Esther, leave it on,' Enid says quietly.

'She can hardly fight her way out of here, can she?' I say.

Corp stretches her fingers. She scratches her hands through

her hair. I look over my shoulder at Enid. Apart from the slightest line between her eyebrows, there's no hint of emotion from her.

'So what happened?'

Tears stream down Corp's cheeks, running into the creases of her nose and over her lips. 'I've been doing it for months, and I've never had any clue that someone was listening. Until two nights ago, out of nowhere, there was a voice.'

My scalp tingles at the thought of a strange voice coming through a radio at night. Persuading Corp to do something terrible.

'It was an old friend I knew from med school. She said she'd been listening for a while and that she'd persuaded her superior to help us.'

'All you had to do was help them replace General Lall,' I say. My voice is barely a whisper.

'The general had already refused to do anything about the cholera. She said there was no way to get the things we needed to keep the outbreak under control. So, when the Coalies said they could help, and then I saw the SafeStraw drop, I knew I had to do something.'

Corp's head sinks to her knees. Her shoulders rock with sobs.

I lean forward and stretch my arms round her, kneeling as close as I can. She smells of salt water and cold.

The door slams back against the wall, the sound clattering round the bare tiles of the shower room. Nik comes in, all pale and sweaty, his sleeve still rolled up to the elbow and hands stained red.

'We've got this!' Enid shouts. She tries to get in between

Nik and Corp. Nik pushes her away. His face is twisted with rage.

'This really is not the place for you right now, Nik my boy,' Enid says. Somehow, she's managing to keep her voice calm.

'I'm sorry. I'm so sorry. But she wasn't *doing* anything. Everyone's dying, and she just went off to dinners at the Statehouse. And I had to do something. I couldn't wait any more.'

'Tell her Enid,' Nik says.

Enid takes a breath. 'Her schmoozing the Coalies, it was all a ruse. The other ships aren't coming. We were trying to buy enough time to get an evacuation started.'

Corp seems to crumple. She lets out a cry and clutches her hair, shoulders shaking.

Nik takes a few strides away. He's bristling with tension, shoulders hunched and eyebrows heavy with anger. He points at Corp. 'As soon as my mother dies, I want her taken out and executed.'

'Nik, take a breath –' Enid starts.

'That's an order.'

54

NIK

Enid pulls a fresh shirt over my arms, and I button it up while she straightens the collar.

My stomach's roiling with the memory of my mother getting shot. The memory of Corp crying on the tiles of that basement shower room. And, not for the first time, all I want to do is talk to Esther. But she's somehow wrapped up in this plot to kill my mother. Even if she wasn't, I think I've destroyed what we had.

We got a missed call from Admiral Janek's office five minutes ago. Enid reckons they'll be on the line again any second.

Sure, the plastic barge was gruelling, but at least there were moments of blissful boredom. Moments when I could turn my head off and forget about everything. But somehow my mother is lying in a pool of her own blood and a woman I counted as a friend until an hour ago is tied up in the basement. Even Enid seems rattled by it all. Somehow, the Coalies have infiltrated the camp in a way none of the rebellion ever suspected. They've turned our closest allies.

'Your mother's stable. They've moved her to her bedroom so they can start thinking about bringing her round.'

A flicker of relief, and my eyes go to the stain on the floor of the war room, hastily wiped and now drying to a muddy red-brown.

Enid's got a face on her like she sucked a lemon. She blames me for all of this, I can tell. And the dark and painful voice in my head says, *Maybe she's right*.

If I'd come back when they asked me to, maybe this would have happened anyway. Or maybe I would have told my mother to stop pissing about and bring Esther and Corp back to HQ where they belong. They wouldn't have been out there so desperate for help that they thought about murder. More than thought about it. Corp pulled the trigger. It's a freaking mess, and all I can do is keep my head above water while I try to fix it.

Enid holds a dark grey jacket up for me to slide my arms into. She loops a tie round my neck.

'You've met this woman?' I say.

'They say psychopaths walk among us, and that woman is a case in point. But don't let her faze you. Paste a smile on your face. Keep it short and simple. She'll know something's up when your mother doesn't answer, so the aim now is to put her off as long as you can. If she thinks she can get in here and take over without making any ripples, she'll jump at the chance. For the next five minutes, just concentrate on keeping the wolf from the door. Got it?'

'OK. Short. Simple. Get off the call as soon as possible. Got it.'

She slaps me on the top of the arm, hard. 'You can do this. You're made of strong stuff.'

I take a breath and shove my hands behind my back to hide the blood under my fingernails just as the digiscreen in front of me lights up. There's a sound like a gull shrieking, and a green phone icon throbs at the centre.

'Show time,' Enid says. 'Everyone out of shot.'

She runs around, gathering the last bits of paper, pushing my mother's desk out of view. She stands to the side behind the screen, breathless. 'Ready?' she says.

'Nope.'

The screen goes from blank to a view of a desk in front of a picture window. There's a woman sitting behind the desk, flawless grey-blonde hair pulled back in a neat bun, tiny hooked nose in the centre of a high-cheekboned face. She smiles like a saint as she watches me.

'Why, this is a surprise,' she says. Almost purring.

Feel like a mouse in a trap. 'What can I do for you?' I say.

'I assume I'm speaking to the infamous Nikhil Lall.'

'Assume makes an ass out of you and me,' I say, and I curse myself the second it's out of my stupid mouth. Behind the digiscreen, Enid throws her hands in the air. Not the tone we were going for.

Janek allows herself a laugh, a high, bright sound like wind chimes. 'You're not wrong. Well, in that case, why don't we introduce ourselves? I am Admiral Janek of the Federated States navy, and I have been given the task of overseeing the various refugee camps that have sprung up along this stretch of our territory.'

'I'm Nikhil Lall. I'm standing in for my mother, General Lall.'

'A pleasure to meet you, Mr Lall. I hope your mother isn't ill?'

I look at Enid. We've had no chance to devise a story. Now I've got to make something up on the fly.

'She's not ill. She's –'

Enid gesticulates, miming spooning something into her mouth. 'She's eating.'

Enid drops her head into her hands.

'Eating?' Janek says. 'Perhaps you could run along and get your mother, Mr Lall. The grown-ups have important business to discuss.'

I pause, trying to think about the words before they come out of my mouth. 'What I mean is, General Lall is busy dealing with a food-distribution issue. She asked me to take your call while she's occupied elsewhere, and I thought it would be a good opportunity to introduce myself now that I'm back.'

'Ah yes, your hiatus. Where have you been hiding?'

Janek sits up straighter. She's an unnervingly composed woman. There's no fidgeting or scratching. No noticeable tics. It's like she's in control of everything, right down to the molecules.

A band of sweat pops up on my hairline. 'That's not important. What's important is that I'll be shadowing my mother from this point forward.'

'Learning the family business. You have something on your collar, Mr Lall.'

Sweat trickles down the side of my face, tickling all the

way. Enid's eyes go to the collar of the shirt I'm wearing, and I just know there's a smudge of blood there.

Janek leans forward, hands clasped on the desk, and it's everything I can do not to take a step back from the screen. 'I'll be honest, I'm rather concerned for your mother's safety. Should I send a team to check on her?'

My heart hammers. Don't let it show. You know the answer to this. 'As we both know, any entrance of your forces into the camp will constitute a violation of our ceasefire agreement and will result in a forceful response.'

'Very well,' she says, smiling. 'Your mother was due to visit the Statehouse this evening. Perhaps if she's still indisposed you would like to attend in her place.'

'I won't be visiting the Statehouse tonight.'

A shadow, momentary but cold as ice, passes over Janek's face. 'I wasn't asking for your RSVP, Mr Lall. You'll be quite safe. As I explained to your mother just a few days ago, I'm not in the habit of inviting diplomatic leaders into my home in order to arrest them. The usual rules of international relations apply here.'

Can't think of anything else, so I say, 'It would be an honour, Admiral.'

'Excellent. I'll have my staff arrange for transportation.' The display blinks off.

Enid and I stand in the silence left behind.

'You think she bought it?' I ask.

'Not a chance,' Enid replies. 'Looks like you're going in, Nik my boy.'

55

MEG

The only thing I can think to do is go back to the Pit. My stomach's growling and my fingers are numb, even though I'm exhausted from walking around all morning. Haven't got anyone I can go to now. No family. No Alex. What an idiot I was to trust him. Everything he said, all his promises: lies on top of lies.

Going to the Coalies is off the cards. Alex made it clear that our deal is over. That it was never on in the first place. And I wonder now, with a pain in my chest like a knife twisting, whether my brother is even alive. Or was Alex just using him to manipulate me? And all the stuff about how our life would be. How we'd find somewhere quiet and safe to live. Together. Now I realize he wouldn't put out his hand if I was drowning.

I've got no one, Seb. All this time I've been talking to you in my head, I might have been talking to a ghost.

The memorial wall looms in the shadows at the back end of the Pit, the pieces of paper and dead leaves and photos lifting in the breeze. My family aren't there – I've looked for my mum and dad, even though I know for certain they're gone. Haven't got any photos of them.

There's a pencil stub lying by a tiny teddy bear and a pile of bruise-coloured mussel shells at the bottom of the wall, so I grab the pencil, and I write their names straight on to a brick. Scratching the words so hard the wood splinters with the pressure, and specks of brick flick on to my hand. Mum, Dad, brother. It's barely anything. Less than a slug trail. Even if they're looking really closely, no one's going to see it. But these few scratchings are better than no trace of them existing at all.

Then I write the names of my gran and grandad. And my cousins, all gone. Then Sim from the Lookout and our neighbour who taught me my letters when I was a kid. Soon I've written the names of everyone I can remember from the *Arcadia* – every Tom, Dick and Harry I ever knew or spoke to or just passed on the deck sometimes, and by the time I'm finished tears are streaming down my chin, and I have to keep wiping my nose on the back of my hand. Finally, I write May. Esther's sister that she lost.

Last off, I write Alex and my chest gets tighter with pain, and the numbness in my hands seems to spread up my arms. I trace my fingers over the letters. Then I use what's left of the stubby pencil to scratch a line through it. Over and over, until it's just a groove in the wall, and my fingers are scraped clean of the top layer of skin, and the nails are ragged and broken, and my knuckles are bleeding. And I throw the pencil at the place where his name was.

I've got no one and nothing.

I crouch down with my back to the wall.

56

NIK

As I step down off the chopper and on to the garden helipad, two guys in dark suits wearing earpieces run up to me. Can hardly tell them apart. Cropped hair and bulky build hidden under bad suits.

Just manage to say, 'Whoa!' before they've grabbed me and started running, one of them holding my head down so I don't get decapitated. There's a flash of tall white columns, of Federated States flags flapping in the wind from the chopper. Then they pull me through a glass door and into a marble-floored corridor. Pictures hang heavy on the walls, gilt frames over richly decorated wallpaper. I've never been somewhere so fancy. Even the ballrooms on the *Arcadia* had nothing on this.

Up a flight of carpeted stairs and into a room with an enormous four-poster bed and a chaise longue and curtains so big they could be made into tents. Suddenly the men are gone. I listen for the turn of a key in the lock, but it doesn't happen. When I twist the handle to see if I'm a prisoner, the door opens. I slam it shut. Not under arrest, but I have a feeling I wouldn't be allowed to walk out of here. The not-knowing in this situation has got me in fight-or-flight mode. Have I really got diplomatic immunity? Or am I Janek's prisoner? She's played by whatever rules govern international relations until now, but that's not going to help me if she suddenly decides it's my time to go.

I do a quick scan of the ceiling corners to see if I'm being watched. No cameras in sight.

The bedcover is the same flocked pattern as the curtains. On a glossy round table by the sofa there's a cake stand, three tiers, piled up with enough pastries to feed a family for a week. Piped icing in swirls of pink, yellow, white. My mouth waters. After months eating whatever the canteen dished up at the plastic rig, I could devour it all.

Tucking in wouldn't be sensible. Could be poisoned. Then again, if Janek wants me dead, there's not much stopping her from offing me. I take a bright blue macaron and pop it into my mouth. Crunch-smush and then the sweet blueberry flavour floods my taste buds. *OMG*. I take another one.

There's a gentle knock at the door. A pause. Another knock.

'Come in?' I shout, almost choking on the meringue.

The door springs open, and a woman in a suit and heels hurries into the room, carrying clothes on a hanger.

'I'm Harveen Atwal. I'll be your liaison today – anything you need, anything at all, please don't hesitate to ask,' she says, speaking so fast it feels like standing on the edge of a tornado. She blinks at me.

'Nik,' I say.

'Always nice to meet a fellow Punjabi. That's right, isn't it?'

'Can we get on with whatever it is I've been summoned for?'

'Of course. Here are your clothes for the function. We didn't have your exact measurements on file, so this is as good as I could manage. Someone will be in to fix your hair in a moment, and yes, I think we'd better give you a shave too.'

I run a hand over my chin.

Harveen unzips the clothes bag and lays a high-necked tunic and trousers on the bed. She looks at me like I'm supposed to answer.

'Thanks,' I say.

'I just thought you might like something traditional. I'm a child of the diaspora too. Maybe I can introduce you to some people. We can get a bite to eat. They make great halwa at this restaurant round the corner. Your mother has enjoyed it on a number of occasions while she's been here.'

'Wow.'

'What?' she says, and she smiles pleasantly at me.

'I just can't believe your generosity.'

She grins. 'You're very welcome.'

'No, really. These clothes. The little pastries.' I wander over to the table and grab another macaron, stuffing it into my mouth. 'And you're even willing to introduce me to the community.'

Harveen's smile falters. Finally, she gets my tone. 'You're under no obligation, of course.'

'Do you people really think you can buy me off with a bit of sugar and some fancy clothes?'

'No one's trying to buy –'

'And then dangling the promise of community in front of me like I'm some culturally starved orphan exiled from their heritage.'

'I apologize. We didn't mean any offence –'

'Where is she?'

Harveen clasps her hands in front of her. There's a hint of a frown line between her eyebrows. 'If you mean the admiral, she'll be at the function tonight.'

'I won't be attending a function. I won't be wearing your suit. I won't –' My eyes rest on the cake stand. 'I'm going to eat the cake, but only because it's wrong to waste food.'

'Of course. I understand.'

'Don't appreciate being summoned like a naughty schoolkid. Get her in here so I can hear what she's got to say, and I'll be on my way.'

'The admiral is keen to continue the negotiations between the Federated States and the insurgency.'

I snort. 'Insurgency? Is that what you're calling us? A thousand starving people trying not to get clapped in irons against the might of the Federated States. You people have some nerve,' I say. Getting into my stride now. 'Explain it to me. And remember I'm a ship kid – don't have the benefit of an expensive education, so make it simple. My mother has asked Janek to let us go. What's stopping her?'

Harveen pauses. 'You have to wear the suit. You have to cut your hair.'

The whirlwind persona is the surface of something intractable.

'Or what?' I say.

'Or you won't be meeting with Admiral Janek tonight.'

'Or ever. Am I right?'

'I think, perhaps, if you refuse, the admiral would extend her hospitality to tomorrow. And then the next day.'

'And the day after that? I'll stay here until I play by your rules, that it?'

'Admiral Janek will be at the reception. There'll be a number of community leaders, and there'll also be press. While I sympathize with you not wanting to capitulate to our suggestion –'

'Demand,' I say.

'– *suggestion*, there is a dress code. It wouldn't do to have you in front of the cameras looking like this.' She waves a hand over me.

I get a rush of heat in my face when I realize my hair's still covered with nurdles from when I fell in the ocean a few days ago. Don't even remember the last time it was cut.

Harveen goes to the dessert stand and uses a silver cake knife to ferry a slice of sponge on to a plate. 'Nik, a lot of important people will be attending tonight. Not everyone in the Federated States agrees with the admiral's tactics.'

Hang on.

Harveen holds the yellow cake out to me. 'You could be very comfortable here, you know. And you could really make a lot of difference to a lot of people if you take advantage of the support and resources available in the Federated States. Your mother seems to understand that.'

My mother does understand it. She also understands that she's entering a den of vipers every time she comes here, and that any second they might turn on her. She's been going along with their pretence, playing for time. And it sticks in my throat ... but maybe I should be doing the same thing.

'I won't betray the people of the ship.'

'No one expects you to. We're just asking for compromise.' I take the cake from Harveen and slice a piece off with the stupid tiny fork. I know that if I put it in my mouth it's going to taste like sawdust. Everything in this place is toxic.

Harveen heads to the door, gives a shrug. 'You know, you can always find new people,' she says.

She closes the door behind her. This time, there's a click as a key turns.

57

NIK

'Good evening,' the guy holding the door open for us says.

Harveen ushers me into a huge, high-ceilinged room that's dripping with gold. I'm not kidding: it's everywhere. The curtains. The wallpaper. The swirly fancy bits of plaster on the ceiling. Through the crowd, I even catch a glimpse of a plate piled up with little gold-topped cakes.

There are so many people it feels like the service corridor on the *Arcadia*, except here I'm overwhelmed by sickly sweet perfume, and everyone's got ridiculous haircuts.

Harveen puts her hand close to the small of my back, not quite touching. I pull at my collar. My ponytail's gone, not that I'm too sad about losing it, but it's been replaced by the same haircut Alex Hudson sports. I wear it better, obviously.

'The outfit suits you,' Harveen says.

'It feels like a straightjacket.'

A tray of drinks floats past at eye level, carried by a man in a black tux. Harveen grabs two glasses without even making eye contact with him, hands one to me.

'Thanks,' I say to the server. He gives me a weird look before moving on to the next guest.

'In a moment, I'll take you to speak with the admiral.' Harveen pauses, watching me. 'Down the hatch.'

She tips the gold-coloured liquid into her mouth, touching the corners delicately with a napkin. I follow suit. It's thinner than I expected, less gloopy, and, even though the liquid is cold, it gives a pleasant, warm sensation in my chest. I smack my lips.

Harveen's looking at me. Eyes shining in the candlelight. 'You like?'

I clear my throat. 'Yeah. We, um, we only really got moonshine on the *Arcadia*, and you only drink that if you're happy to go blind.'

Harveen shakes her head, 'God, what a life you've had.'

'I guess –'

'There are perks, you know, to living in the Federated States.'

My head's fuzzy. The edges of me blur. 'Yeah?'

'There's usually enough food. We have power cuts sometimes, but no more than the rest of the planet. And, for most of us, the opportunity to do what we want with our lives.'

'Sounds pretty sweet. Apart from the fact that I know you're always either at war with the south or at war with the north. Must put you on edge thinking you're one bad battle away from enemy tanks rolling along Main Street.'

Harveen raises an eyebrow at me.

'What? You think I've not picked up any news in the past few months?'

'It's true that we're surrounded by enemies. But we haven't lost any ground in the south in a number of years.'

I laugh. The wine's making me light-headed and invincible. 'You're holding on to Charlotte and the other southern border cities by the skin of your teeth. Not that there's much left to hold on to now. It's all crumbling around you.'

Harveen stares me dead in the eye. 'Aligning yourselves with our enemies was your fatal mistake. Taking help from Maine destroyed any goodwill the Federated States had for the ship people.'

'Bullshit. Our fatal mistake was not fighting our way off the *Arcadia* right at the start. We spent forty years waiting on your promises and lies, trying to play your game by your rules because you told us that was the way it needed to be. We're not going to spend the next forty years waiting for you to let us out of the camp. As far as I'm concerned, the enemy of my enemy is my friend.'

Harveen sips her wine. The thin layer of shimmer she's applied across her cheekbones glows in the candlelight. 'The president is a vain man. He won't allow you to humiliate him by taking refuge in Maine. Can you imagine the propaganda material they'd produce if the people we've held for decades found freedom in the arms of our enemy?'

I lean closer. 'Maybe you should have thought about that before you caged us like animals.'

She drains her glass and grabs a couple of tiny pancakes topped with bright pink salmon – hands one to me. 'We're going to carry on this conversation. First, eat. It wouldn't do to slur in front of the admiral.'

She pops a pancake into her mouth in one go. I copy her

and – holy wow. 'That's the best thing I've ever eaten,' I say, mouth still full.

Harveen laughs. She shoves a napkin into my hand and discreetly points to the corner of her own mouth.

'How can you stomach it though? Knowing that there are people suffering on your doorstep? Not just that they're suffering, but that you're part of the system that keeps them under lock and key?'

She turns serious again. 'You just have to hope that the best way to make things better is to work within the system.'

Well, that took the wind out of my sails. Harveen has something like a conscience. It's crooked and messed up, but still a conscience. She takes two more glasses from a passing tray and gives one to me.

'Guess it helps, being surrounded by all of this,' I say. 'Easier to pretend the bad stuff isn't real if you've got everything you need to keep you comfy.'

For a split second, she falters. She looks into her wine glass and presses her lips together like she's tasted something bitter.

'I'll take you to see the admiral now.'

The atmosphere has dropped a full ten degrees as Harveen leads me through the crowd. Her sleek ponytail sways. I've offended her, that's for sure, but I can't find it in me to care.

We get to the far end of the room and stop in front of a couple of creamy gold settee things with sweeping wood frames set opposite a massive fireplace.

The woman I recognize as Admiral Janek is sitting on one of them. Wearing an evening gown, with hair done and make-up applied so she looks like a movie star, she's surrounded by land people who're all equally fancy. She must be in the middle of a story: everyone's looking at her, but when she sees me she smiles and gets up.

'Ah, Mr Lall. What a pleasure to finally meet you in person.' She holds out her hand for me to shake.

'I'll shake your hand when you promise you won't sell the camp – and everybody in it – to the prison conglomeration,' I say, loud enough for everyone to hear.

The sound seems to get sucked from the room. Someone coughs. Janek's face loses its good humour, the mouth locked in a mirthless grin.

'Let's take this conversation somewhere private, shall we?' she says.

As we move, the crowd parts ahead of the admiral. She leads me to an adjoining room.

'Thank you for coming, Mr Lall,' she says when Harveen closes the door quietly behind us, the chinking glass and hum of the party cut off.

This room's smaller than the last, but equally opulent. Even the wallpaper is patterned in gold leaf. On the wall above the fireplace, there's a painting of some old guy in a white wig and tight trousers, talking to a load of other guys in wigs. Beyond the French doors, there's a garden that's flooded with light from the party.

'Wasn't really given a choice.' I'm trying to force as much power into my voice as I can. My mother would call it gravitas.

'Indeed. Well, I trust your visit is a pleasant one. Is Harveen treating you well?'

'As well as any jailer could.'

'Let's cut to the chase. You're a clever man. I believe that something has happened to your mother, and that you are now the leader of the insurrection.'

'It's not an insurrection, and we both know it, Janek. We're not attacking you. All we want is freedom. We're only asking to be released from your custody.'

'It's Admiral Janek. And I'm afraid release is out of the question for myriad reasons.'

'Seems pretty straightforward to me. You open the gates. We walk out.'

'And go where?'

'Maine.'

'Ah yes. Your ally in the north. How will you get there precisely?'

That I don't know, and I have a horrible feeling it's showing on my face.

'Without a guarantee that everybody from the ship will travel north immediately, I cannot possibly allow people from the *Arcadia* out of the camp. What if some of them decide to hide themselves in the Federated States? It happened just a few days ago with an escapee who had to be neutralized in our main station.'

A shudder runs down my spine. Don't know what she's talking about, but I can imagine some poor fella from the ship met their end from a Coaly gun barrel. 'I assure you, we have the necessary resources to give our people safe passage to Maine.'

'And then there's the question of the Virus.'

'There hasn't been a case in the entire history of the *Arcadia*. It's almost like someone was making the whole thing up as a reason not to let us leave.'

'Our research indicates that the Virus could have entered a period of dormancy. We are not willing to take the risk of it spreading to our people.'

I sip my drink. The alcohol's starting to go to my head, lifting me, making me feel like I'm wearing armour.

'We can discuss all of this later. Now, I want to hear about you. The enigmatic Nik Lall. The boy who destroyed a ship and then disappeared.'

'Almost permanently.'

'I'm afraid I don't know what you're talking about.'

'So it wasn't you trying to kill me a few days ago? I think it was. And I think the only reason you're not killing me now is that it would look bad if you offed me while I'm visiting.' I sit down as heavily as I can on the sofa. Its thin wooden legs creak under my weight.

I sense a shift in Janek. A measure of discomfort. There's a plate of those small cakes on the coffee table in front of her, so I take one, smearing jam on to my thumb. Then instead of taking a napkin, I wipe my fingers on the cream fabric of the sofa.

Janek's face is a picture. She's trying really hard not to react. She and my mother have plenty of buttons in common. Both sticklers for order. Both neat freaks. Both easy to wind up. I lounge back on the sofa.

'I was so sorry to hear about the sad demise of your mother, Nikhil.'

She already thinks my mother's dead. Interesting. I'm not going to enlighten her. 'It was quite a shock, as you might expect.'

'Indeed. A tragic loss. In time, I hope that we can forge a similar relationship.'

I lean forward so that I'm looking straight at her. 'You mean you want me to smooth the way for you in the camp.'

'I can make things easy for you, and for the people of the camp, or I can make things difficult. I'd prefer the former. And I believe with the right negotiations we can come to an arrangement that balances the needs of the Federated States with the needs of the camp.'

'Aha. I scratch your back, you'll scratch mine kind of thing?'

'You have a way with words, Mr Lall.'

'What makes you think I'd watch while you imprison the people I grew up with, the people I love? What makes you think I'd be OK with the prison conglomeration taking over? What makes you think I'd betray them?'

The alcohol's making my head spin. Got to be careful I don't give her any unnecessary info.

Janek smooths her dress and perches on the chaise longue opposite me. 'Your mother has briefed you on our plans for the camp, I see. But come now, there's no need for hyperbole. Looking out for your own interests hardly constitutes a betrayal. Anyone in that camp would do the same thing. It's about helping yourself so that you're in a position to help others. Your mother understood that.'

'So you're expecting me to live in luxury while everyone else is scraping around for crumbs.'

'I'm expecting you to be sensible and to use the resources and wealth I'm offering you to make a difference in the world. Or are you planning to feed all those people with platitudes and determination?' She leans forward so that I can see all the lines on her forehead, all the shine and gloss of her make-up. 'I know you're willing to ignore what's happening in the camp because you've done it before. Now, tell me about your friend Esther Crossland.'

My heart drops. I don't want Esther anywhere near Janek. I don't want Janek talking about her. I don't even want her thinking about her. 'Esther died just after the *Arcadia* was scuppered,' I say.

'Interesting. One of my agents claims to have spoken to her in person just this morning.'

I get to my feet. 'That's a breach of our ceasefire agreement.'

She smirks. 'Then attack us, Mr Lall. Rise up. Bring your little army of fighters and show us what you're made of. Believe me, an excuse to come and subdue the camp would be immeasurably helpful at this moment.'

My mouth feels like a desert, but I've got to keep my cool.

'Can I tell you what I think is happening in that camp right now?' she says. 'I think my assassin has done their job. I think your mother is either dead or very close to it. And I think you are out of your depth. You're not a leader. You don't want all of this. So let me make things easy on you. Enjoy the benefits of close friendship with the Federated States. Let me make you all more comfortable. Be my guy in the camp, and you can have a pleasant life. All of you can have a pleasant life. There will be adequate food. We can build clinics. Sanitation. Proper housing.'

'And beatings and disappearances and punishments for anyone who doesn't toe the Federated States' line,' I say. I'm having to grit my teeth because I'm shaking so bad.

Don't let her see it. Don't let her know you feel weak.

'It will be an acceptable existence.'

'It'll be a hopeless one.'

'Take some time to mull things over. Sleep on it. Send me a message by sunrise.'

'What kind of message?'

Janek stands, takes my arm, and herds me out through the French doors and on to a lawned area. There's already a circle of photographers arranged on the grass. She urges me forward until we're standing in front of them, the warmth of the Statehouse replaced by a biting-cold night.

'Friends, I'd like to present to you Nikhil Lall.'

The cameras flash, and through the searing bulb light I catch a glimpse of someone standing at the edge of the crowd. Of neat blonde hair, a smart uniform. Glaring at me. Alex Hudson.

Janek puts her arm round my shoulder and smiles at the photographers. 'Give me Esther Crossland, and I'll give you the world,' she says so that only I can hear. She waves at the cameras.

'And if I refuse?'

She closes her hand on my shoulder. One of her rings presses through my sleeve until it's jabbing my skin painfully, so the skin almost breaks. 'If you refuse, there will be no way for us to work together. I'll be forced to come and get the girl myself, and that will be the end of life in the camp. And it will be the end of you.'

58

ESTHER

Paper stands in wobbling piles on the table. My eyes droop, and I force them open again, rubbing with my thumb. The flat panes of glass that make up the ceiling of this room give a view of the sky. Cloud-covered and dark in the middle of the night, the moon an eerie circle that appears momentarily and vanishes just as quickly. I'm piecing together the activities of the rebellion in the two months since General Lall and the rest exiled me. Nik's gone off to liaise with Admiral Janek on some errand he won't tell me about. Enid's still dealing with the fallout from Corp's attempt to assassinate General Lall. Corp is still down in that cold basement shower room.

I don't care if I get caught in here. I need to know exactly what's been going on in this camp. What did General Lall agree to? What did she trade? Where did the collaboration end and the double-crossing start? Most importantly, if they've abandoned hope of reinforcements coming to help, what are they really working on?

I run my finger down a long list of names: a census of

people living in Warehouse Nine. On the next sheet, there's a pencil sketch of an alley near to the fence at the southern end of the camp, the booby traps marked by little grey circles and annotated in shaky handwriting with the words *electrical*, or *personnel trap*, or *incendiary*.

It's crossed my mind that I might find evidence of my parents in this lot too. There's a small voice telling me that these people know more about everything than they've been willing to say.

I bite my lip and suppress a twist of anxiety. Nik's order still rings through my mind. *I want her taken out and executed.* Do I think Nik will go through with it? Yes. I remember him going after Alex last year, and only the fact that May wouldn't have wanted Nik to kill Alex saved him. I won't let it happen to Corp. I'll stand between her and the bullet if I have to. We've had too many losses already. We've been fractured and broken apart. We're weaker because of it. I need Corp. I love her. I won't let them hurt her. She deserves another chance.

Maybe Meg deserves a second chance too. Was Meg's betrayal any worse than what I was planning to do?

The maps here make the efforts produced by me and Pat look like they were drawn in crayon. There are detailed headcounts. Records of deaths. A handful of births. All information collected quietly by Enid and her people without making it obvious what she was doing. It brings a bitter taste to my mouth. All that time we wasted. All those people we could have helped if we'd had this information.

As well as the tents and Silas's shipping containers and the warehouses that take up most of the camp, the big digimap on the wall shows the people tagged by the Coalies. Small bright spots moving round the camp, in and out of buildings. There's something irritating me about it that I can't quite put my finger on. Like I'm trying to remember a word that's just out of reach. I look at the list again. There are names I recognize. The Huangs are listed, Pat included. Little Dylan is recorded as living in a tent across from theirs.

It feels like there should be more.

I take another sheet – the title tells me it's a list of people living in Warehouse Five. The list ends after two full sheets, but the last names – fifty or so at a guess – are crossed out.

The door to the war room opens, and Pat comes in. 'Soup,' he says, pushing a cup into my hand.

'I'm not hungry.'

'Cos it's gonna help if you keel over.' He crosses his arms.

'Your hair needs cutting,' I throw back.

Pat runs his hand through the mop on his head. I take the soup.

'It's past midnight. How're the general's stats?' I ask.

'She's stable. Suture bot's done a tidy job.'

'I'll go down and keep an eye on her, but it'd be easier if we had monitoring equipment to report her condition. You should sleep,' I say.

Without thinking, I take his hand. He's warm, the skin slightly rough and in need of moisturizing. Maybe one day we can think about all of those things again. Hand cream, and shampoo, and washing in something that isn't seawater.

He doesn't move, pretends not to notice that I'm holding on to his fingers, and then he shakes his hand free. My heart cracks a little.

'What's all this?' he says.

'Lists of people. Maps of the camp.'

I swallow the lump in my throat and try to move past the moment of rejection. We're both exhausted. We've both spent hours trying to save a life. He's looking at the digiscreen, but it feels more like he's focusing on anything that isn't me.

I clear my throat. 'I'm glad you came up though.'

'Yeah?'

'Do you remember the other day when we were in Warehouse Five, there were families in there named Singh and Ahmed?'

'Yep. All the kids had chickenpox.'

I search through the papers on the table until I find the one I'm looking for. 'They're on this list, but they're all crossed off. At first, I thought maybe it was deaths, but they were all alive three days ago. And we'd notice, wouldn't we? If we suddenly lost a whole floor of people?'

'Weird.' He looks up at the digiplan for another second, then he's off towards the door like I've offended him.

'Well, thanks for your help,' I mutter.

Pat whips round. 'What do you want me to say? I don't know any more than you. And from the look of these plans we've spent two months trying to map the fences and booby traps, and it's already been done. We've wasted two months of our lives.'

'Something on your mind?' I say, although I'm not sure I want the answer.

He rubs his chin. 'You and Nik.'

'No,' I say as fast as I can. 'Pat, it was nothing.'

'You can't pretend it's nothing.'

'I'm not pretending. Nothing happened.'

He frowns over my shoulder, doing everything he can not to look me in the face. The light flashes off his skin, and I watch him trying to find the right words. I wish I knew how to persuade him I don't have feelings for Nik Lall.

I wish I knew how to persuade myself.

'It's hard enough in here to think about having a normal life,' he says.

I lick my lips. My breath feels hot against them, and I'm trying desperately not to move because, if I do, it might make him talk again, and if he talks again he's going to say –

'I don't want to chase someone who's into someone else.'

'There's nothing –'

'Stop it!' he almost shouts, and he pushes a pile of papers off the table. They stream to the floor, rustling in the silence. 'Do you think I don't see it? You've been waiting for him.'

'Nik and I haven't stopped arguing since he got back.'

'And I'm the idiot stupid enough to think this time we've spent together actually meant something.'

'It has . . . Pat, I would never . . .'

'Don't. We're going to skip the part where I watch the two of you making eyes at each other.'

'Making eyes? What does that even mean?'

'You know what it means. You kissed. He'll look at you, and you'll look back at him, and I'll be standing off at the side like a spare part, watching you looking at each other. And everyone will see it, and I'll be the dumb-ass pretending not to. And Enid will make some snarky joke like, "Your girl's really playing the field, Nik my boy."'

It hurts too much. I open my mouth, and nothing comes

out. I push my fist against my stomach to try and staunch the pain.

Pat looks up at the digiscreen again. Above him, the night's clearing, stars revealing themselves, crisp and silver. It'll be cold by the morning.

I can't tell whether Pat's sad or angry, or both. Whatever rope connected us has been sliced through, and I don't know exactly what did the cutting, but it's total and irreparable, and he's completely out of reach.

'Is that it?' I say. 'We don't even try?'

'Guess not,' he says.

59

NIK

Harveen's decidedly cold as she walks me back through the shadowy garden to the helipad. I don't have time to care.

First priority is to go back and get Esther the hell away from the camp. She needs to be on the first vehicle I can get my hands on and running in any direction as long as it's away from Janek. By the time the Federated States rocks up at the camp, Esther needs to be half a continent away. Enid will know what to do.

The chopper's not here yet, and we're surrounded by weird manicured bushes that are straight out of a haunted-house story. Never thought I'd be so keen to go back to the camp.

Just thinking about Janek gives me the creeps, and there's zero chance of me handing Esther over to her. Can still feel the sharp point of that ring on Janek's finger. All the charm on the surface, the viciousness oozing underneath. Bet you any money you'd find a handful of mysterious pet deaths in that woman's history. She's the kind of person who'd hold a kitten underwater just to see it struggle.

I bob on my toes. Click my fingers. 'Where's the chopper?' I say.

'It'll be here any minute.'

After Esther's safely away, I need to figure out what to do to defend the camp. Those reinforcements would have been nice right about now. Haven't got the resources to get everyone out of the camp, so my only option is to warn them about the storm that's coming. Maybe I can get them into the basement of HQ. Least then if Janek's bent on fighting we can defend the place. Second thoughts, maybe they're safer away from HQ. Maybe I should send them up to Silas's shipping containers and have them wait it out.

I can count on one hand the number of times I've wanted my mother's advice, but tonight I wish she could tell me exactly what to do.

Harveen's looking around, arms crossed like she's trying to keep herself warm. She's barely said two words to me since I called her out for enjoying a life of luxury as a member of the Federated States' upper crust.

'Look, I'm sorry,' I say, and instantly regret it. Shouldn't be treading on eggshells around these people. 'You've got to understand that I came from a place where half the people didn't get a meal today, to a glitzy party where you lot ate enough to feed the camp for a week.'

'I get it: you didn't enjoy the party. No further discussion is necessary.' She looks over my shoulder, into the long shadows surrounding the helipad. A shiver runs down my spine, and I find myself glancing that way too.

'It's not that I didn't enjoy it – don't even know why I'm

348

trying to explain this to you. You can't get it. You'll never know what it's like to be hungry.'

She looks up at me like she's about to say something. Like she's just seeing me for the first time. In the cold, her breath trails like fog between her lips. 'I'm sorry about the headache.'

'What?'

Something sharp scratches my neck. Someone's at my back. The world spins. The ground swoops towards me. Everything goes black.

'Did you get the dosage wrong?'

'Of course not. Give him a minute.'

Feels like I'm on a carousel. My stomach lurches, and I have to bite my teeth together so I don't lose all those cakes and wine I had earlier. When I open my eyes a crack, I see a ceiling fan, an overhead light. It's too much effort so I let them fall shut again.

'Not sure it was necessary to drug the kid. Couldn't you have explained where you were taking him?'

'It's not your neck on the line, B. If this goes wrong, I'll get the death penalty. Forgive me if I take extra precautions to make sure he's not going to scream for help or try to escape.' That's Harveen's voice. Fuzzy and far away, but defo her.

Last thing I remember I was talking to Harveen, then something stung me.

'OK. OK. Relax. He's coming round.'

The blurred outline of a man swims into view when I open my eyes again. He's got glasses and a five o'clock shadow and a shirt so crumpled he can't be a politician. He hands me a glass of water, and I take a swig, letting it run out of the corners of my mouth. Whatever I'm lying on is soft. Cushions. A sofa.

'My name's Barney King. You aren't in danger.'

'Under arrest?' I croak.

'No.'

'We're friends,' says Harveen.

'Needle in the neck is a funny way of being friends. Where are we?'

'A hotel room. In the city. Away from the camp and the Statehouse and anywhere else Janek might have bugged,' Harveen says. Is it me or is her tone towards Janek particularly salty?

I sit up and swing my legs off the sofa. 'If you're friends, and I'm not in danger, take me home.'

'First, we need to talk. There's not much time. In fact, there's almost no time at all.'

'So friends willing to take me hostage and demand I listen to them then.'

I stand up and sway, grabbing the arm of the sofa. The curtains are drawn over a floor-to-ceiling window. The light's low and hazy. I wobble over and make it just in time to hold myself up on the curtains.

'Room, windows open,' Harveen says behind me.

The curtains and the glass glide sideways. There's a rush of wind. I take a few steps forward and catch myself on the waist-high glass rail that acts as a safety barrier. My hair whips round my head, and the wind's so strong it snatches my breath away.

This apartment must be 200 storeys up, so high it makes my head spin. Air rushes upwards like we're trapped in a wind tunnel. The sound of helicopters and traffic from the streets below makes the air vibrate. There are lights everywhere. Millions of them in the air and on the ground. I didn't realize everything was so big.

Without warning, a drone zips upwards, so close to my face the blades almost slice into me. My heart hammers, and I dodge backwards, letting go of the rail. My foot catches on something, and I fall away from the open window.

'It's just a delivery drone,' Harveen says.

She offers me a hand and helps me to my feet. My knees shake beneath me.

I need to think. Need to formulate a plan. Need to get back to Esther and warn the camp. But first I need to get my body obeying orders again.

Harveen closes the window. The glass cuts off the sound of engines and the bluster of the updraught.

'We're here to tell you that you're too late,' Harveen says.

'For what exactly?' I say. My breath clouds the surface of the glass. My tongue feels like stale bread crusts.

'The clock's run out on your plan to get people out of the camp,' the guy says.

I turn my back on the city and let my head rock back on the glass. 'Cuinn's smuggling operation? Hardly think a handful of people getting out and running for the border constitutes a plan,' I say.

Harveen and Barney share a look.

'Your mother hasn't told you anything?' That frown line's back between her eyebrows.

'My mother is indisposed.'

'It's true then? Your mother's gone?' Barney says. He's

been lounging on the low coffee table, but now he sits up straighter, a spark of excitement in his eyes.

'Don't get too excited, B,' I say.

Under the blank digiscreen on the wall there's a mini fridge. I go and search through it until I find something cold and sweet-looking with a picture of an orange on the side. When I crack open the can, it fizzes.

'I apologize. That was insensitive,' Barney says.

'You people really struggle with being human beings, you know?' At least the guy has the decency to look shame-faced.

I pace as I drink. My head's banging from whatever crap they injected me with, and all I can think about is the fact that a) I don't know where I am or how I'm going to get out of here, and b) this might be an elaborate trick. I know from experience that Federated States officials aren't above smoke and mirrors. Just look what Hadley did to the market on the *Arcadia*. Bombed it to smithereens and made everyone think it was us with blood on our hands. This could be them trying to get answers out of me. Some weird interrogation technique where they get you to trust them and then pump you for information.

I drain the can, crush it, throw it.

'Nikhil, please, can you just try and put your dislike aside for a few minutes and listen?' Harveen says, and I can tell from the ripple of strain in her voice she's getting frustrated. Apparently, this isn't going as well as she wanted it to.

Good. If they're going to pull shit like a kidnap, I'm going to make their lives as difficult as possible.

'If you don't hand the girl over, Janek will enter the camp by force tomorrow.'

'I know all of this. And from where I'm sitting it's you and this guy stopping me from getting home and warning them.'

'We're here to offer our help,' Barney says.

Interesting. 'Say I believe you can help. What's in it for you two?'

'He wants a story,' Harveen says.

'Actually, I want a Pulitzer Prize for Journalism. She wants Janek dealt with.'

I look at Harveen.

'Let's just say I'm tied to the admiral in a way I'd rather not be,' she says. 'And I need to start taking responsibility for the morally grey things I've done to reach the position I'm in.'

'So all that stuff about community and going for halwa together was . . . ?'

'Necessary, to be sure you weren't going to take Janek's offer. I threw everything at you to see if anything would sway you.'

'You were playing games.'

'We're not playing games now. And we don't have much time. She gave you until sunrise. If we're going to make preparations, we need to do it now.'

'Why should I trust you? Suddenly grown a conscience?'

'Actually, I've been helping you for quite some time.'

Something in the back of my fuzzy mind clicks into place. 'Enid's contact at the Statehouse. The one who gives her a heads-up when something big's gonna happen. The one who told her they were gonna try and off me last week.'

'Yes.'

Out of the window, I watch a bus turn a corner between two skyscrapers, all lit up from the inside – the people are like dolls they're that far away. In the reflection, I see Harveen and Barney throw another glance at each other. I need a second to get all this straight in my head. I need to let them wait.

Harveen's got her arms folded like she's trying to hide herself, fingers tapping against the sleeve of her jacket. 'Janek's over the coals. The president will deselect her if she doesn't get control of the camp by the end of the week.'

'And she's that attached to her career that she'll use violence if she doesn't get what she wants?'

'Without hesitation. This isn't just a job, and she's clinging on to power by a thread. If she loses, she'll be destroyed.'

'Destroyed how?' I say.

'So far, all deselected presidential candidates have been arrested, tried and executed within twenty-four hours.'

'Now you've got my attention,' I say. 'Keep talking.'

'Your mother's out of action, and you're pretty much untouchable unless she wants to explain to the world why she's murdering people with diplomatic immunity. If Janek gets Esther, she wins. I've known the woman for longer than I care to. I know she's getting desperate, and when she gets desperate she'll go to any lengths to get what she needs. With your mother out of the way, she's convinced she has you over a barrel. She will take the camp by force,' Harveen says.

'Giving it the hard sell, Harveen,' I say. 'Say Janek goes in guns blazing, gets Esther. What does the president do?'

'Hard to tell,' Barney says. 'Maybe he deselects her for disobeying him.'

'Or maybe he's so pleased that all is forgiven and he and Janek are best friends again. Either way, Esther's dead, and the camp's on its knees,' Harveen says. 'I'd rather make sure Janek fails and liberate the camp at the same time, wouldn't you?' She checks her watch. 'Nine hours.'

'Let's get back to Cuinn. And explain it to me like I've been out of the loop for two months.' They're throwing each other looks again, and it's really starting to piss me off.

'Silas Cuinn has been arranging transportation out of the camp,' Barney says.

'Tell me something I don't know. Cuinn's been smuggling people on and off the *Arcadia* since before I was born. It's not news that he carried on once we got ashore. But why are you interested in the two dozen people he's managed to free?'

'According to our intel inside his gang – and yes, we're running spies in the camp – he's been working on vehicles to transport people *en masse*. As of yesterday, we believe he's managed to get three large vehicles out.'

I stop pacing. 'Wait. He's got three large vehicles out of the camp? How many people?'

'One hundred and forty-two,' Barney chimes in.

'A hundred and forty-two of my people have escaped? Where are they now?'

'North,' Harveen says. 'Safe.'

This is what my mother and Enid have been working on. This is why my mother's been wining and dining and playing the Federated States' game. She's been keeping them busy while people sneak out of the back door.

'As far as we can tell, he has two or three more vehicles that could be ready to evacuate people by the morning.'

There's a grain of excitement in my stomach. One minute I'm wondering how I protect Esther and keep people alive for the next twenty-four hours. The next I'm talking about evacuation.

'Don't leave me hanging, B. Have you hatched a plan?' I say.

'We can get more buses. Greyhounds to be exact,' Barney says. He's smiling like a crocodile, a row of neat, well-cared-for teeth.

And that's what I wanted to hear. A way out. A glimmer of hope. An option that isn't just telling my people to duck when the fighting starts. 'How many more?'

'Enough to transport everyone in the camp,' he says.

My head swirls again, and this time it's not because I've been drugged. 'Harveen, you've been messaging Enid. You've got a line to her. I need to tell them to get ready. We're leaving.'

60

ESTHER

'I've been looking for you.' Enid saunters into the war room.

She clocks my red, puffy features and hesitates, letting her eyes linger long enough to confirm that she's noticed.

I've got the kind of face ache that only comes from spending hours crying. I rub my nose with the back of my hand. 'What do you want?' I say.

'You can pull yourself together for one. And, for two, you can play this video. For the record, I didn't agree with General Lall's funny business with regard to you and Corp, and I told her as much. She shouldn't have left you out in the cold, and that's going to change, starting now. In the spirit of full disclosure, here's something she's been keeping from you.'

She presses a data disk into the side of the digiscreen above the table. The plan of the camp disappears. Instead, there's my mum and dad jumping off a bus. They're dishevelled, but they don't look hurt. My mum turns to whoever's filming and says, 'Where's my daughter?'

'Give her details in at the registration tent, and someone will be assigned to find her,' the camera operator says.

My mother nods and strides off towards a large military tent while the camera swings back to the bus to watch other passengers climbing down. They blink in the sun.

'When was this? Where are they?' I say, my voice cracking as I try not to break down.

'They're safe. This was filmed at a camp just the other side of the Maine border. In all likelihood, they'll have been rehoused by now, but I've sent some people up there to try and find out more.'

Nik marches through the door to the war room. He's wearing some sort of formal suit with a high neck, and he's had a clean shave. Something warm and sweet-smelling radiates from him.

'Set countdown timer for sunrise,' he says to the screen as he walks. My mum and dad are replaced by green numbers: 08:00.

'Wow, you can wear a suit, can't you?' Enid says.

'What was that?' Nik says, glancing at the screen as though he's not really interested in the answer.

'Footage of my parents when they arrived in Maine,' I say.

'After tonight, nothing surprises me any more. When were you going to tell us about Silas's smuggling operation?' he says to Enid.

'Was planning to tell you just as soon as you decided you wanted to know. As it happens, there hasn't been that much time between you saying *let's go* on being leader, and your mother getting a bullet in her belly, and then you going off to your soirée tonight.'

'What smuggling operation?' I say.

'How did you go off to the Statehouse and come back with information like that?' Enid says, ignoring me completely.

'I met your contact tonight. In fact, she jabbed me with a tranquillizer and took me on a trip to a hotel in the city.' Nik yanks his collar down to show a red dot circled by a bruise.

'What the hell?' I say. I take a step closer, planning to check him over, but he inches out of reach.

'I honestly did not see that coming,' Enid says. 'Glad it was just a kidnapping, not an assassination.'

'Thanks for the concern,' Nik replies.

'So, you've got the identity of the person sending me info. I'd be interested to know.'

'A woman by the name of Harveen. She's Janek's chief of staff.'

Enid raises her eyebrows. 'Why would Janek's second in command help us?'

'Because she's not as evil as her boss, and she's not interested in being second in command much longer. She'll help us if it means Janek gets what's coming to her.'

I feel like I'm being pulled in every direction at once. 'Hang on. Will one of you please fill me in? Enid's got a contact in the Federated States? And what's this about Cuinn's smuggling operation?'

They don't bother looking at me this time. It's like I'm not even here. 'I want you to organize a transport out of here. A helicopter. A car. Anything. I don't care how she gets out, I just want her out. Understand?'

'Me?'

'Nik really found his bossy self out there,' Enid says to me, a smirk lifting her eyebrows. 'No problem, boss. And where's she going?'

'To her parents. I'm assuming from that footage they're over the border?'

'You'd assume right. But listen: the reason your mother didn't want her knowing her parents were alive is because she knew the girl would be off looking for them. She wanted her safe in the camp where she could keep an eye on her. Once she's out there, alone, the Coalies could snatch her at any minute. Even with Silas's help, it would have been too dangerous.'

'Wait, a transport for me?' I say. My heart's doing tiny thumps, and I can feel my anxiety rising as I scramble to understand what's going on.

Nik turns his back and takes a rolled-up digiplan from the table, flicking the elastic band off in a single motion. He spreads it out on the table and weighs the corners down, leaning over to get a better look.

'How many people have we got in the camp?' he asks Enid.

'According to the Coalies, a little over a thousand.'

'No. I need numbers. Exact numbers. No, wait. Forget it. We'll just go room to room and tell them what's happening.'

'What *is* happening?' I say.

'Your guess is as good as mine,' Enid says. 'Might need to give us a little more info, Nik my boy.'

'You've been getting people out, Enid, correct? And so far you've freed a hundred and forty-two people by walking them up to Cuinn's territory where there's less security, then putting them on to buses, and driving them all the way north. Right under Janek's nose.'

'All correct.'

'When they get to the border, the driver flashes fake papers at the guard – who's in our pocket – saying the coach is full of agricultural workers going to the potato farms, and gets waved through. The Federated States and Maine are enemies, but they're not actively fighting right now, so there's trade and movement.'

I can feel my mouth hanging open. 'That's why there aren't enough people in the camp. That's why their names are crossed off the lists.'

'It's also why my mother and Enid were happy to let everyone get tagged. Because it made the job of figuring out how many people we had, and where they were, infinitely easier,' Nik says.

'Once you used that clever brain of yours to figure out how to open the cuffs, we were raring to go. Our next step was to remove people's tags and keep them here in the camp. We were even planning to have people walk them around so it looked realistic.'

'It would've seemed like there were hundreds of us in here still. But it's too slow, and now Janek's on the warpath,' Nik says. His eyes are shining. He's more excited than I've seen him since the night we launched the Landfall mission. He's alive again. 'Wish it hadn't taken me getting kidnapped in the dead of night and a couple of strangers to fill me in on it.'

'That's history, Nik my boy. Let's focus on the positives. You've finally had your interest piqued. I'll be thanking that Harveen woman if I ever meet her.'

'It was a good plan. But it failed.'

'Explain,' Enid says.

'Janek offered me everything. Wealth, food, comfort. If I do what she wants.'

'And what's that?' Enid says.

Nik flicks his eyes to me and back to Enid. 'I need to speak to you. In private.'

They walk to the other side of the room.

Pat comes in carrying a digiscreen that I'm guessing has General Lall's medical notes on it. He hands it to me in silence. We avoid looking at one another, but I catch a glimpse of his eyes, and I'm sure he's been crying too.

'You'll tell her, Nik Lall, or, God help me, I will.' Enid's voice rises up from the edge of the room.

'Haven't got much choice now,' Nik says. He's got his hands on his hips, and he's glaring at Enid like she's asked for his firstborn.

'Tell me what?' I say.

'Janek's coming for you,' Enid says.

My stomach drops. 'And if she doesn't get me?'

'Her forces come in, guns blazing.'

'Let me guess: that timer shows the deadline.'

'Yep. Sunrise. Eight hours from now.'

'Seven hours, fifty-four minutes,' I murmur. Adrenaline spikes in me. The bitter taste. The thumping in my temples.

'I'm guessing from your tone that she'll not be handed over?' Enid says, glaring right back at Nik.

'You guessed right. Which is why I want her as far away from here as is humanly possible before Janek's even had her morning coffee. Then we need to get everyone de-cuffed and start moving them up to the north of the camp. Get your people to go tent to tent, starting with this area.' He points at the plan with a pen, circling the part of the camp he wants evacuated first. 'Take the cuffs off, and leave them in their beds. To anyone that's looking at the cuff feed on a digiplan, it'll look like everyone's sleeping in. By the time the Coalies realize what's happening, it'll be too late.'

'Got it. Stealthy-like. But I know for a fact that Silas only has three coaches ready to move. That's only another hundred and fifty passengers, give or take. Your new friends got a plan for the rest of them?'

Nik nods. 'Yes, more are coming. As soon as I give Harveen and this Barney guy the signal that we're ready, the coaches will start arriving. One at a time.'

Enid whistles. 'This is a hell of a gamble. Janek could notice at any moment.'

'I'm not leaving,' I say. 'Hey. You two. *I'm. Not. Leaving*. No way. You're telling me to go free when everyone else is facing life in a prison camp.' They turn round.

'It's not up for discussion,' Nik says, and he turns back to the digiplan like he's too busy to even talk to me.

'You're doing it again,' I say. 'You're doing exactly what your mother did.'

Now Nik throws his pen down on the table and turns round again, folding his arms. 'Come on then. Explain to me what I'm doing.'

Enid steps away. She grabs an apple from the bowl at the other end of the table, sits down and puts her feet up.

'You're pushing me out. You've decided you know what's best for me, and you're going to try and force me to do it. No matter what I think, or what I want. You're treating me like I don't count. Like I'm someone who can be told to get lost.'

Anger's firing me up. *How dare he? How dare any of them?*

'She's coming for you. And, if she gets you, your execution will be live-streamed to the whole of the Federated States,' he says. 'I won't have that on my conscience.'

'You feel guilty about May.'

'Shut up.'

'She's dead because of you, Nik. There's no way round it.'

He slams his hands down on the desk. 'I said *shut your mouth*, Esther.'

'But you wouldn't have stopped her, would you? You wouldn't have turned her into someone obedient?'

He rests his knuckles on the table. I can just see his shoulders rising and falling.

'If she gets me, Janek will call off the attack. Everyone will be safe.'

'Wrong. If Janek calls off the attack, we're stuck here. Indefinitely. The president will sell the camp off to whatever rich prison corporation bids the highest. It'll be another forty years.'

'You'll have more time. Breathing space to get people out. You can carry on doing what you're doing.'

'Still wrong. This is a one-time offer. If Janek gets to you, she wins. The people helping us won't be willing any more.'

The tears are creeping up on me. 'I can help,' I say.

Enid's crunching through her apple.

'We don't need your help. You're a problem if you stay. You're the reason all of these people are in danger,' he says over his shoulder. 'Either go up to the roof and wait for your transport, or I'll have you removed.'

Enid's not crunching any more. I look around, desperate

for something to change Nik's mind. 'If you make me go, I'll hand myself in.'

'You're stupid, but you're not that stupid. I'm in charge now. You're all going to start doing as you're told.'

'Try me.'

'You're bluffing,' Nik says.

'I'm with Nik on this,' Enid says, taking another bite of apple before tossing the core down on the table.

I take a step towards him, ball my fists. 'I swear, on May's memory, that if you force me out of this camp I will fight tooth and nail to get back into the Federated States.'

Nik folds his arms and rests his butt on the table. As he looks at me properly for the first time since he got back, his face seems to soften.

'That makes literally no sense.' He grins.

It feels like the sun has come out for the first time in weeks, and I have to stop myself from running to him.

'It sounded better in my head,' I say.

Enid's smiling now, eyes crinkled like paper.

Nik marches over and, before I know it, he's hugging me, lifting me off the ground. I can't help thinking about the night we kissed up on the roof of HQ. The way his lips were warm and soft. The way his breath smelt like cinnamon. I can't help thinking about doing it again. He breathes on my neck, and everything falls out of my mind.

'Don't suppose you'll leave even if I ask nicely?' he says against my ear.

'Not a hope in hell.'

'You win. You can stay. But no heroics. You're not giving yourself up, deal?'

'Deal.'

'I miss May,' Nik says.

I know without looking at him that his face is tight with sadness. The way he has to hold himself together whenever he thinks about her.

I poke him in the ribs. 'All right, Lall, no need to cry about it,' I say in my best impression of May's voice.

Nik laughs and sniffs. He picks me up, spins me round, and drops me back on my feet, keeping his arms round my waist.

I put both hands on his chest and look up at him. 'I won't let you kill Corp,' I say, almost whispering.

'She tried to murder my mum.'

'I know. But you can't kill her. Not unless you punish me too.'

He nods, pressing his mouth into a thin line. 'I'll deal with her once this is over. But no executions.'

When I turn round, Pat's staring at me. His face is angry red. He throws me a glance so loaded with acid it makes me wither. The elation of making amends with Nik morphs into guilt because I hurt Pat.

Nik claps his hands and goes back to the digiplan. 'Right. Esther wins this round, although I still think she's an idiot for putting herself in danger. First point of action: we're not going to let Janek take Esther without a fight. Second point of action: we're going to get as many people out of this camp as we can. We've got eight hours –'

'Seven hours, forty-five minutes,' Enid says.

61

MEG

Couldn't fall asleep on the ground. It's so cold it leaks into my flesh everywhere I touch. My feet, my thighs. I shiver worse than I did when that Coaly dropped me in the ocean the other day. And I think maybe I deserve everything I get. I thought Esther Crossland was my enemy, and I was happy to throw her to the lions if it meant I got to see my brother again. More than happy. I was over the moon. Would have probably helped them get her even without the promises Alex dangled in front of me.

I wanted revenge. I wanted to see her suffer.

Something rustles by my leg, but I keep my eyes closed and my head down on my knees. Don't dare look up because more than once I've seen rats running along the bottom of the opposite wall.

Just now, I'm starting to realize Esther isn't the monster they've painted her. She wasn't even the bad guy when she let me get arrested half a year ago. She was just a girl trying to make the best of a shitty life. Same as me.

There's nothing here but cold loneliness. My stomach's

shrivelled and empty, and even though I'm parched I can't bring myself to move. Can't even cry any more because I've got nothing left for tears. The thought of whether my brother's alive keeps stabbing at my heart.

Someone's standing over me. An energy bar drops on to the ground by my boots.

'Get up,' Esther says. She plops a bottle of water down next to the energy bar.

'What d'you want?'

'I've got a job for you.'

She grasps my hand and pulls me up so that we're standing right next to each other.

'I don't understand.'

'Something big's about to happen, and I need to get a message to as many people as we can in the next –' she checks the time on her watch – 'six and a half hours. It's all hands on deck.'

'Why would you trust me after I gave you up to Alex?'

'I don't trust you. But I figure you've not got any way to communicate with them even if you wanted to give us up. Have you?'

I shake my head.

'Good. Let's go.'

'But why?'

'Because there have been too many people left behind already. Because the more of us there are, the stronger we'll be. Because I ... well, I think you're a good person even if you did a bad thing. And I hope that maybe one day you'll be able to say the same about me.'

I grab her, and now the tears are flowing down my cheeks.

We hold on to each other in the dark.

62

NIK

'Put your hoods up, will you?' Enid says.

'Hoods won't help if they're watching,' I say.

'It'll help me feel less like we're about to be nabbed, so be a good lad and put your hood up.'

I flick my hood over my head. Esther does the same, and her boyfriend hunkers down into his scarf so that I can only see the top half of his face.

We're heading down to the far end of the camp, keeping to the shadows and the sides of buildings, and hoping we don't get spotted on the open sand of the beach. Behind us, there's a straggling line of ship people who we unceremoniously roused from their beds, gave them two minutes to grab stuff, and removed the cuffs from their ears. Also behind is my mother, carried on a stretcher by two people. She woke up just after I got back from Janek and gave me a dressing-down for all the things I'd done wrong in the past few hours. I let her have a go. Figured she should enjoy herself.

Enid leads us between the first of the shipping containers,

following directions she knows by heart. Five minutes later, we round a corner, and we're confronted by something different. Bigger. A low building with a corrugated-iron roof, no windows, and a door that rolls up into the roof.

'Get everyone inside,' I say.

Enid goes straight for the door and pulls it up above her head without checking over her shoulder. We're running out of time. She's feeling the pressure. I know because I'm feeling it too.

It's been a slow, anxiety-inducing night. Harveen came good on her promise of more buses. A whole fleet of them. Enid's people have herded three busloads so far. Problem is we can't have a fleet of buses leaving all at once, so we're having to load people on and wait for the bus to get far enough away before the next one rocks up. The whole thing organized and paid for by secretive sponsors in Maine. We could get everyone out of here if only we had a bit more time.

People climb aboard a big Greyhound bus in the middle of the garage. Its engine purrs, and the air's thick with exhaust and soot. The smell of freedom.

I check my watch. By my estimation, we've got three hours until Janek comes for Esther. I want as many people out of gunshot range by then as I can.

'Have you arranged those extra trucks?'

As I say it, a white bus trundles through the big door at the opposite end of the garage. The driver cuts the engine, and a couple of Silas's people jump out the back. They call to half a dozen of the ship people who're resting their legs on the ground, helping the frailer ones to get up. Passing out bottles of water for the road.

'Even with the extra Greyhounds, it's going to be tight. Silas has called in every favour he has, but it's not easy getting people to help. Especially since we don't know what the Feds are going to do once they get to the border.'

The people we've brought with us climb on to the bus. A woman stops before she gets on. She's been walking with Pat. Now they whisper to each other, just urgent enough to make it obvious they're arguing. Esther watches them from the corner of her eye.

'You're going to stay here and risk your life for a girl who's dumped you for someone else?' the woman shouts. Pat scratches his head.

Enid's eyes dart to mine, and she's got that little smirk on her face that makes me want to throw a bucket of water over her. She winks.

I know the feeling of getting called out by your mother in public all too well, so when Pat marches over I keep my eyes off him and pretend I wasn't listening. I hate that for him. But if they're not together any more then maybe . . .

No. Now's not the time. You've got shit to do tonight. People to look after.

'Everything OK?' Esther asks him.

'She wants me to go with them.'

'No one would think the worse of you if you did,' Enid says.

Pat's mum climbs aboard. The door closes behind her, and the engine cranks into life. At the other end of the garage, the door is rolled up, opening on to the night. A knot of tension releases from my shoulders when the bus hisses and starts to move. These fifty people, at least, are getting out of here.

We've done what we can for them. Now it's someone else's job to get them over the border.

'They'll keep the lights off till they get out of the camp,' Enid says.

'How are they going to get through the defences?' Pat asks. 'We've been looking for weak spots, but there's nothing.'

'Guessing you haven't mapped Silas's territory, have you?'

'We assumed the fence went all the way round.'

'There's the remains of a railway station – nothing more than a pile of bricks. But it's got a tunnel that leads out. When the Coalies sent their fencing bots to lock us in, they either didn't notice or didn't care that the fence went right over the top without blocking off the tunnel. We kept an eye on it for a few weeks to be sure it wasn't a trap. Then Silas took a wander through.'

'Why didn't he leave when he had the chance?' Esther asks.

Enid shrugs. 'Contrary to what you might believe about Neaths, doc, we aren't just out for ourselves.'

'Maybe you're not. Not so sure about Silas,' Esther says.

Enid shrugs again. 'He stayed. Honoured the fact that we were all in it together. And got in on the plan to start getting the civilians out.'

My mother's brought to the loading area on her stretcher. It'll be a relief when she's on the road and safe.

Esther turns her eyes on me, face all stern in the torchlight. 'Nik?'

Everyone looks at me. 'What?' I say.

'Something's on your mind. Tell us.'

I sigh, put my hands in my pockets, and wish Esther

couldn't read me quite so easily. May could do it too. It's infuriating. 'It's taking too long.'

'It takes as long as it takes,' Enid fires back.

'We need to speed things up.'

'There's no way I can think of,' Enid says. 'Far as I can see, soon as the Coalies spot what we're up to, we're done for. So we could charge out of here, but they're going to nab hundreds of us on the way out. Or we could take it slow and hope they don't notice.'

'Or we could buy more time,' Esther says.

The door at the opposite end of the garage whines open. The white bus leaves. Another group of people on their way out.

'Tell me what's got you worried,' I say to Enid.

'Nothing and everything, Nik my boy. Janek wants us locked up indefinitely. There's a whole lot of Federated States territory to cross before we get anywhere near the border. Small-scale people smuggling is one thing; it's another getting a whole camp to disappear without them noticing. Can't help thinking this is the end of the line for us. If we'd had a few more weeks, we might've got closer.'

Janek wants us locked up. She also wants us quiet. The seed of an idea sprouts in my head.

'What if we're going about this all wrong?' I say.

'You're of the opinion that we should be attracting more attention?'

'Maybe.' I chew my lip.

Esther comes back from checking my mother. 'I gave her morphine to help her sleep. She'll be pretty out of it for a few more hours. What're we talking about?'

'Nik here's about to have some sort of revelation,' Enid says.

Esther looks at me. 'Well?'

'My mother's whole thing has been sleight of hand. Acting one way while Janek's watching, doing something completely different behind the scenes.'

'Creating a distraction,' Esther says.

'Exactly. So let's make some noise. Get Janek to look exactly where we want her to look.'

'Not much to lose at this point. What have you got in mind?' Esther says.

I shake my head. Didn't get that far along the train of thought.

'I know how we can do it,' Pat says.

63

NIK

The night's still dense and dark when we get to our first target. 'Do we know what type it is?' I ask Pat.

'Nope. Could be electrical charges. Could be smoke. No way to tell until they go off.' He crouches down like Spider-Man, fingers touching the ground. Wasn't thrilled when I got teamed up with him, and it's been super awkward. But Pat point-blank refused to go with Esther, so now it's him and me. Neither of us wanting to talk about the fact that I kissed his girlfriend. Most annoying thing is I can see why Esther likes him.

'You sure it's not going to kill me?' I say.

'Pretty sure.'

'Not filling me with confidence here, Patrick.'

'Go fast and you'll be fine. Or you won't. Which I'd be totally OK with actually.'

I stretch out a crick in my neck and wonder whether this guy's angry enough to let me get 'accidentally' killed. No, doesn't seem the type. He was one of Silas's guys back on the

Arcadia, and I don't reckon he'd hide it if he wanted me gone. There'd just be a knife in a dark alley.

Across from the Pit, halfway up the wall of a warehouse, there's a dome of red glass. Like half a basketball stuck on to the wall. And that, my friends, is a Federated States anti-personnel booby trap. There's a bunch of them along this whole stretch of buildings, sending a clear message: *You can go this far. No further.*

'What does this one do?'

'Impossible to tell. Could be tar. Could be a snare. Could be fire.'

'Fire? Just when I think those scumbags can't get any worse.'

'At least we agree on that.'

'You've tried throwing stuff at it?' I ask.

'Of course.'

'You've poked it with a stick?'

'I'll set the thing off if you're chickenshit.'

Ouch. Maybe he's not such a good guy after all.

'Something on your mind, Patrick?'

'I'm not in the habit of being besties with someone who kissed my girlfriend, then ghosted her for months, then came back and acted like they could pick up where they left off.'

'Heard she wasn't your girlfriend any more,' I say.

'Why don't you just leave her alone? You've hurt her and her family enough.'

'Sure, no problem,' I say, smiling. 'The minute Esther tells me to get lost, I'm gone.'

He grits his teeth, glaring at me. Enemies it is then.

'Not gonna lie, we were a bit shaky for a second at the

start. But she came round. And now I reckon we're closer than ever. Seemed pretty happy when I got back from the Statehouse. You were there.' Maybe I've gone too far. He's looking out for Esther, and here I am throwing what we've got in his face. I shrug. 'How about we let her decide who she's friends with?'

The guy's about to go off. He's all pent-up energy and twitching. 'It crushed her when you left.'

'Yeah, well, I am sorry about that.'

'And I'm glad you're back,' he says.

I turn to look at him.

'She built you up into this huge deal while you were gone. She held on to you like you'd fix everything. But you're back now, and nothing's better. It's only a matter of time until she sees how poisonous you are. No one gets close to you without getting burned, do they, Nik?' he says.

Not going to let him see how much that stings, so I fix my eyes on the booby trap. 'Let's get this over with,' I say.

'Try not to get blown up,' he says.

I jog a few times on my toes, staring at the trap. Then I run, aiming for the space right under it. Need to get going fast enough so that when it activates, I'm already on my way out of its range. Obviously, the Coalies designed their traps to be activated by humans only. Wouldn't expect anything less from them.

When it happens, I don't even realize I'm in range. There's a pop. A surge like a wave, and something hits me. It carries me up into the air, my view of the alley from above terrifying and fast, and I crash down on to the hard brick. I lie there. My head's ringing from hitting the ground. All the air's gone from my lungs. And there's a smell like burning oil. Faint wisps of black rise from my clothes.

'Get it off!' Pat screams. His footsteps hammer towards me. 'Nik, move!'

Then I feel the heat. All over my back, my head, my neck.

'Get your jacket off!' Pat yells again, and now he's wrestling me out of my coat. He drops me back on to the alley floor, swings my smouldering jacket round his head once, and launches it away. He grabs me, pulls me and we run. By the time we turn back, my jacket's an inferno. A patch of burning ashes, flames higher than my head, thick black smoke climbing into the sky.

'Hey, thanks,' I say.

'That was a freebie. Won't be saving you again. Let's do the next one.'

64

ESTHER

Somewhere behind us there's a thud like a broken bell. Shouting, then a stack of smoke. The smell's prickly and singed. My pockets are weighed down with clicking ear cuffs. We have teams going warehouse to warehouse, tent to tent, getting people up and moving. All without arousing suspicion. Me and Corp, Nik and Pat, Enid and John have loaded our pockets with the cuffs, and we're attacking the Coaly defences. I can imagine them in black uniforms, watching the display, spitting out their cups of tea or choking on bagels as soon as they realize they're under attack.

From a digiplan, all they'll be able to see are the bright spots – ten here, another ten there – of gangs running around. Activating booby traps, cutting their carefully placed fences. It sends a thrill through me thinking they'll be watching. Even if we lose, even if they take the camp – arrest us, kill us – we'll have that single moment where the Federated States went, 'Oh shit.'

We're close to the fence where I managed to climb a few

days ago. Feels like a lifetime has passed. We were trying to stay hidden then. Now we're trying to draw as much attention as possible.

Corp swings the wire-cutters off her shoulder. 'One cut ought to do it, right?'

'It did last time,' I say.

She hesitates with the wire-cutters resting against the fence. 'I need to explain why –'

'No, you don't,' I say. It's the first time we've been alone together since Corp attacked General Lall. 'You don't need to explain it me. Your reason for going through with it was the same as mine.'

'If I could take it back, I would.'

'You can't. But it's in the past. As long as you're not going to do anything like it again, it's over.'

She lets the cutters sag away from the fence. 'Not sure Nik sees it that way.'

I rub my forehead. 'You tried to kill his mother. He's not going to shrug and say no harm done.'

Corp chews her lip, frowning.

'They're still going to put you on trial. This isn't going away. But maybe if you can rebuild some trust with Nik and Enid we can keep you out of the ground,' I say.

Corp stares at her feet.

'Out of interest, what was on the table?' I say.

'They promised everything. They said they'd help with the cholera outbreak. Said they'd bring food. They even said they'd take me to see my family.'

I feel my eyebrows shoot up. 'Your family from the *Oceania*?'

Corp grew up on the next cruise ship along from the *Arcadia*. When it got cleared, the rebellion smuggled them off, and they went into hiding.

'They had video. Footage so real I was certain it was them. And they knew things about me too. The agent told me they'd been arrested and were in custody, awaiting trial.'

'Was it true?'

She shakes her head like she can dislodge the thought of them in prison. 'Don't know. I was convinced, but now I don't know. It was more than that . . . They offered . . .' She shrugs and looks at the ground.

'They offered hope,' I say.

Corp looks at me. 'I hadn't felt it in such a long time.' Her voice cracks. Her eyes brim with tears.

I reach out and take her free hand.

There's another explosion in the main camp, somewhere near the Pit. This time followed by a high yell of triumph.

'Let's move,' I say.

Corp places the wire-cutters over the lowest portion of the fence. She snips. There's a flicker, but no alarm. 'Did it work?' she says.

'Guess we'll find out.'

'There's a line of traps in that alley.' Corp points to an area across from the fence. 'We can set them off on our way back to HQ.'

We walk to the end of the alley, the street lights painting everything in eerie shadows. The glass dome is halfway up the wall, and another a few metres further down.

'They'll activate as we run. If we're fast, they'll cascade behind us,' Corp says.

'And if we're not fast?'

'Then we're going to find out exactly what each of these weapons can do. Ready?'

'Ready.'

We run. So fast it feels like I'm going to faceplant. My heart hammers with adrenaline. After all this time, we're finally doing something. I don't know how today will end or what the Coalies will do to us, or even if I'll be alive in a few hours. But I'm alive now. Every time I hear another group of five or ten or a hundred of us have left the camp, it chips away at the guilt I've been carrying for four months. I won't save everyone, but the act of trying will help me to rebuild myself.

We pass the first trap, and there's a *phut* as something shoots out of it. No fire or smoke, no buzz of electricity. The next one activates as we sprint past, and this time I feel something fly past me. They're getting closer.

The end of the alley comes into view. A few more traps to get past and we'll be safe.

I'm hit. There's no pain. One second I'm running, the next I'm slammed to the ground. Through the blur of the impact, I see Corp sprinting ahead. The fall knocked the wind out of me, and I've nothing left to shout with.

Body check. Everything's where it's supposed to be, but my veins flow with ice when I realize I can't move my foot. Can't roll over, can't get up. Looking back, I find the bottom of my leg's covered with black-brown tar, thick as molasses. In panic, I pull my leg away, but the substance seems to expand, sliming its way over my boot. Now I realize that heavy patch on my arm is more of the sticky stuff, and it's moving too. Creeping over the sleeve of my jacket. I swipe with my other hand, and then it's on my glove too.

'Don't touch it!' Corp shouts.

She skids down next to me, and the relief of having her here is like drinking cold water. It washes away the last of my uncertainty at giving her another chance.

'It's getting bigger,' I say. My voice wobbles, my panic intensifying as the stuff grows.

'Listen to me, Esther. Look at me. Stop struggling. We think fast, we act fast, but we never panic.'

I do as she says, breathing through my nose, forcing myself to put all my fear aside.

Corp peers at the tar. I will myself to keep still, even though the thought of the stuff sticking me to the ground makes me want to scream, even though I can imagine it growing up my leg and over my body and over my face –

'Wiggle your foot.'

I do as I'm told.

'It's a snare trap. The more you struggle the tighter it holds on.'

She produces an army knife from her pocket and selects the blade attachment. Then she slices through the laces of my boot.

I close my eyes. Each pull of the knife makes the substance constrict round my foot until it's so tight I gasp with pain, the bones of my foot crushed tighter and tighter.

After a lifetime, Corp says, 'OK. Ease your foot out. Slowly.'

It takes every drop of willpower I have not to yank myself free. I wiggle and pull until my socked foot emerges from the top of the boot. The second I'm free, I jump away from the stuff.

'Jacket!' Corp shouts.

I throw my jacket and gloves off. These final movements activate the slime. In three seconds, it's completely swallowed my boot. All that's visible of my jacket is a centimetre of frayed hemline.

'What happens to people if they don't stop struggling?' I say.

'Something not very pleasant.'

I look along the alley. Already, there's daylight rising bright and clean over the ocean. 'One more to go.'

Corp looks at the final glass dome, sets her face, nods.

We run.

65

JANEK

Admiral Janek puts on her field uniform, using the mirror on her dressing table to straighten the line of medals on her chest. No office attire this morning. She's going into battle. The Lall boy has shown no sign of handing the fugitive over, and so Janek will go and retrieve her. He's probably been spurred to rebellion by the death of his mother.

Outside, it's only just getting light, and the bulbs round the edge of the mirror are kind. Janek looks good. Not tired. Not ill. Strong. Still, she dots make-up round her hairline with a brush. This is the biggest gamble of her life. Disobeying the direct orders of the president is a dangerous game. The fact that General Lall is out of the way will help her case, and she's gambling that the president's anger will be assuaged by the victory she's about to secure.

She grins into the glass and makes a final check of her teeth, then trills her lips and starts her vocal warm-up routine. The press will want to speak with her today.

'One rebel leader down, two to go,' she says to herself.

'Unique New York, unique New York, unique New –'. She hums the national anthem tunelessly.

There's an insistent knock at the door that can only mean bad news. Harveen enters without waiting for an invitation.

'Tell me this is a good day, Harveen. Tell me I'm going to take the girl, take Nikhil Lall, and take control of the camp all at once. The president will be pleased, the prison conglomeration will get what they want, and I can put the whole saga of the *Arcadia* to bed,' Janek says.

'Admiral, there are gangs attacking the fence. The defensive system in the southern part of the camp has been activated.'

'Gangs? Of how many people?'

'I-I don't know. A lot. Look.' Harveen tilts the screen in her hand so that Janek can see a plan of the camp, bright spots glistening.

'This doesn't make sense. There must be fifty of them. A hundred. What are they doing?'

'It's a coordinated attack, ma'am. They've breached parts of the fence, and they've been attacking the booby traps.'

'A handful of booby traps is hardly a concern.'

'No, it's systematic. They're going street by street.'

'Do we have eyes on what's happening down there?'

'No, ma'am. It's part of our ceasefire with the rebels that we won't use surveillance in the camp, and we have a limited number of patrols on the ground.'

Janek turns back to her dressing table and smooths her hair. She eyes Harveen in the mirror, that alarm bell of suspicion sounding again. 'We've been sending surveillance in as necessary, irrespective of the agreement. If they're trying to escape, we need to see what's going on. Arrange for a drone flyover,' she says quietly.

'Yes, ma'am.'

'How many traps have they sprung?'

'Almost the entire system.'

'At my last briefing, the Coaly leader informed me there were more than thirty streets protected by the booby-trap system.'

Harveen's face remains impassive in the mirror.

Forget about the deadline. If there's an uprising, Janek wants to be on the ground when it's quashed. She'll look like Queen Elizabeth going out to face the Spanish invaders.

'Unique New York,' she says to her reflection. She pinches her cheeks to bring a pinkness to them. 'Get me Air Force Command.'

Harveen doesn't move. In fact, she stares at Janek in the mirror. 'No.'

Janek lifts the lid of her jewellery box, searching for her graduation ring. She slides it into place on her finger and admires the way the light plays on the metal.

'There is an active uprising in the camp. The rebels have activated all zones containing our booby traps. You're choosing this moment to oppose me?'

Janek spins to face Harveen. Now the woman keeps her eyes lowered beneath her thick lashes, obviously uncomfortable under Janek's stare.

'I won't let you destroy us both. The president's orders are clear. You do not have the authority to attack the camp.'

Janek slaps Harveen with all the force she can bring to bear. She feels the impact of her ring on Harveen's cheekbone, a blow so hard that Janek's skin thrums with the violence of it.

Harveen staggers, clutching the side of her face. A long gash has opened up and blood is dribbling in streaks down her face.

'You vile, treacherous –' Janek composes herself, breathing through her nose. 'You would have been next in line for the presidency.'

Harveen's face is ruddy with fury, her eyes wide and watery. 'This is completely unsanctioned. If you attack and fail, you'll have nothing. Not the Lalls, not the girl, and there'll be nothing left for the prison conglomeration to use. I won't watch you go rogue. I won't go down with you, Ania.'

A bitter film coats Janek's tongue. She and Harveen have walked a long road, tethered together by their shared sins. Janek ordered the destruction of the *Ithaka*, despite the fact that an entire Coaly unit was still aboard. But it was Harveen who helped her cover it up afterwards. Harveen who carefully researched every witness present and made a list of each person who could feasibly know something about their error. Anyone who could point the finger of blame at them.

There were eight Federated States officers watching the operation from the shore that night, all of them a threat to Janek. But it was Harveen who insisted that each life had to be ended differently. That they must avoid any hint of a pattern. One officer disappeared while hiking. A second passed of natural causes. Another drowned in a tragic boating accident on Lake Erie. Commander Hadley was the easiest. He got involved with that insurrection business and was discredited. All Janek had to do was whisper in the right ears, and he was shipped off to the *Arcadia* indefinitely. At the time, Janek had wanted to dispense with the man, but Harveen had got cold feet. She thought it would appear suspicious if every witness to their most bloody mission turned up dead. It was a peculiarity of fate that his entanglement with the rebels saved his life once.

Janek sits back down in front of the mirror at her dressing table. She presses powder into the crease of her nose with a sponge. 'You're quite right about one thing: I have gone rogue. This is all or nothing. Either today ends with the fugitives dead and me in control of the camp. Or it ends with us both in manacles.'

'You're utterly deranged.'

'Quite the conundrum. How to dispose of a pernicious subordinate before she can spill her guts about your past. Room,' she says, speaking to the AI assistant embedded discreetly in one corner of the mirror, 'please ask Mr McGarry to see me in my dressing room as a matter of urgency.'

Behind her, Harveen's face is a picture of emotion. She's vibrating with anger, eyes filled with tears, fists clenched. Janek plucks a tissue from the box on the dressing table and holds it out to her.

The door opens, and Mr McGarry, Janek's chief of security, looks in. He clocks Harveen's bloody face. 'Everything OK, Admiral?'

'Everything's fine, Mr McGarry. Ms Atwal has decided to leave my employment. She needs to be debriefed. Please see to it that she is held under house arrest until I can complete the formalities of terminating her position.'

'Certainly, madam.' McGarry opens the door wider and holds an open hand out for Harveen to leave.

'This isn't over, Janek. The whole world is going to see what kind of monster you are.'

66

ESTHER

From the roof of HQ, I can see Janek's forces massing. The cheap plastic binoculars show a large tent, camo brown and green, and a checkpoint set across a road. Coalies mill about, not worried about us at all. I watched them rolling back a section of shimmering fence, gloved hands clumsy but efficient. Whatever goes down in this camp, it's just another workday for them.

The fire-escape door squeaks open, and I sense someone crossing the rooftop towards me. I close my eyes and find I'm hoping for Nik.

'That's everyone up and out of bed,' Nik says.

My stomach flips.

He rests his hands on the wall that runs waist-high round the edge of the rooftop. 'We've put a load of the cuffs in the Pit, and a load in the basement so it looks like people are taking shelter. Just sent Meg and that kid Dylan downstairs with the final load from Warehouse Two.'

'It'll look like most of the camp's moved in,' I say. 'Meg

and Dylan both need to get out of here before trouble starts.'

'Told them already, but neither of them do well with taking orders. Starting to be a thing with you people.'

'Hey, I'm fine at taking orders. I follow every order I agree with.'

From the corner of my eye, I see a smile break through Nik's grim expression for just a second. 'They'll drop the last of the cuffs in the basement and then hotfoot it to the transports.'

'I'd feel better if Dylan had gone hours ago.'

'Like I said, stubborn. Told me he wanted to help.'

It's a relief to hear they'll be gone soon. Two fewer people to worry about this morning. 'How long until everyone's clear of the camp?'

'Couple of hours. Maybe more.'

'Plenty of time for Janek to get her ducks in a row.'

'And that's if we can keep them looking our way long enough. Someone clocks them moving around down there and it's game over.'

I go back to watching the Coalies. The camo tent billows in the wind. All we can do is wait for Janek's next move. At least we've got her attention. At least now she's looking at us in HQ, and hopefully not at what Silas is doing at the other end of the camp. This is how the moments before a battle must feel. A strange sense of pent-up energy. Fear of what's to come. Anxiety. But also the calming certainty that something terrible is about to happen, and there's no way to escape it.

'Is it too much to hope she's not going to attack?' I say.

Nik hesitates, looking in the same direction. He puts his hand on the wall next to mine so that there's only a few millimetres separating our little fingers. He wants to say something.

'So, what's the deal with you and Pat?' he asks finally. He takes the binoculars and stares through them.

A lump rises in my throat. I don't trust myself to speak.

Even without the binoculars, I can see the big black car pulling up close to the tents. It shines like the person inside is important. A security agent opens the back door, and there's a flash of white-blonde hair before whoever was inside is ushered to the safety of the tents.

'That's Janek,' Nik says. 'Coming to watch from the front line.' When I don't answer, he carries on talking. 'Look, I never meant to get in the middle of anything with your boyfriend . . . Is he?'

'Is he what?'

'Your boyfriend?'

That's the question I've been asking myself. 'No. Not any more,' I say.

I can't stop the tears gathering in my eyes now, so I focus on what's happening below. The guilt's overwhelming. Pat's such a good guy – such a good friend – and as soon as Nik came back I treated him like he didn't matter at all.

'Is it my fault?' His finger twitches so that it's touching mine. It feels like electricity, and I have to stop myself moving away.

'This probably isn't the moment to be talking about it.'

'We might not have that many moments left.' Then he takes my hand and pulls me round so that we're facing each other. He must have dropped the binoculars because they fall from the side of the wall and clatter off the roof.

'Nik –'

'Did you break up because of me?'

He doesn't wait for me to answer. His hand's in my hair, the other sliding round to the small of my back, pulling me closer. He kisses me. Softly first, and when I don't pull away he kisses me again.

My breath hitches. This feels . . . right. I let my hand fall on to Nik's chest.

At that moment, there's a whoosh somewhere in the distance. On the horizon to the south, over the city we're so desperately cut off from, three specks appear.

'The hell is that?' Nik says.

He squints at the source of the sound. Then his expression changes, and he seems to realize what he's looking at. In the distance, the dots form into triangles that turn my blood to ice.

'They're bombers. Go. Now. *Go!*'

67

NIK

I scream so loud my voice scratches through my throat. '*Move!*'

Esther races ahead of me, through the fire-escape door I propped open when I came up to the roof, into the dark stairwell. We run. We fly, spinning round the turns. My fear is like an animal, strong and terrible and chasing me. I can't get everyone out. My mind flashes to the people I know are in this building. *Enid. John. Esther. Pat. Dylan. Meg.*

We might be safe out of the building. These stairs zigzag down, eventually opening on to an alleyway through a heavy metal fire door.

Neon emergency exit lights point the way to safety. Their light is so weak it makes everything ghostly. My throat's burning from running. There's a whoosh from above. Was that the bombers or the blood roaring through my head? In my mind, I see the planes taking their first run over HQ, dark silhouettes against the dawn sky.

Esther stops dead in the dark stairwell. I run into her, barely holding us both upright.

'Don't stop!' I yell.

I only realize what she's stopped for when an alarm cuts through the air. The ringing so loud I can feel my brain vibrating.

I grab Esther's sleeve and pull, and now we're falling down the stairs again, as fast as we can move. We stumble, holding on to each other, then we're up again and running, hands knotted together. Her face a pale mask of fear.

Halfway down.

People come from one of the corridors, dawdling to start with, but when they see us running the fear infects them, and they chase after us.

If those planes took a turn, we might make it. If they swung out over the ocean to get their approach right, we'll have a chance.

My breath rakes my chest. Heart's beating so hard it's going to break through my ribs.

We're at the ground floor. There's the fire-escape door. Please, please let it open.

Esther slams into the door, pushing the bar down. Sunlight streams in. We keep running. The others follow. Soon as we step outside, the blare of the fire alarm is joined by the sound of plane engines. Right here. Right above us. A glimpse of the underside of a bomber, wings outstretched. A black shape against the washed-out sky.

All I can think is *run*. And then the air shatters, and the world shakes, and somewhere above there's an explosion. I take Esther's hand again. Force myself to move.

I'm hit from behind, from above. I slam into the ground. I taste dust and blood.

I see Esther lying in the rubble.

68

MEG

Ringing. Like my head's on vibrate. Can't lift it. Everything twists around.

Ran when I heard that alarm. Me – and Dylan too. Not stupid. Neath kids don't stick around when there's a hint of trouble. You hear an alarm, you leg it.

Almost made it too.

I wiggle my fingers and feel them grating through dust. My eyelashes are sticky.

Try to remember. You'd stashed the last of the cuffs and were going to find some food. The racket started. You ran like Hadley himself was following you. That kid, Dylan, was right behind. Then *smash*, like everything got sucked in and blown out all in the same second. Too much for anyone's ears to handle.

The ringing's getting stronger. My hearing's coming back, but now everything's too loud.

Where is that kid?

'Dylan?' I shout. Try to push myself up, but there's something on top of me. Heavy.

Can't hear my own voice. Too much pain in my head. So much dust it's like I'm in a blizzard. I manage to heave myself up, and whatever was pinning me slips off. Glassy sound of rubble sliding and dropping. Metal creaking. Feels like it's going to come down on me, but I sit up anyway because I can't stay here. Everything's dust. When I move, it puffs up from my clothes. I rub my eyes, all caked in dirt.

Half the building's gone. The sky's blotted out by a thick white cloud. And, as I look upwards, I see a hand poking out from underneath a pile of broken building. And I can't help but let out a cry.

Esther's next to me. There's blood trailing down her chin. She wipes the wet thing that's dripping down my face.

'Dylan,' I say. My voice is a tiny croak.

Esther's face drops. 'Where is he?'

I point to where the hand is, further up the rubble pile.

'Esther, don't,' Nik says. 'The rest of it could come down. I'll go.'

But she's already climbing up the side of what was once a building. It's cut open like a pumpkin, insides spilling out. Esther looks tiny scaling the side of it.

Pat helps me get up. My legs shake out of control. He steers me to the edge of the HQ yard. There's people running about now, back and forth, carrying stuff. He makes me sit down and pours water from a bottle over my face. It feels good. And with every swipe and rub, and every 'you're gonna be OK' that comes from Pat's mouth, I want to cry more.

69

ESTHER

My heart's about to explode from my chest. I let myself be overtaken by the calmness needed to deal with this. There's a kid trapped in the rubble of a destroyed building . . . and I'm going to get him out.

Meg pointed up at the building, and when I followed her hand, I saw the end of a sleeve and fingers covered in white powder.

Now, I shake off my jacket and put my foot on the first solid-looking piece of building I can see. It doesn't move. So far so good.

Stepping as fast as I can, concrete to girder to smashed fragment of door, gambling which piece will hold me. All around, the debris shifts with a shushing as loud as the ocean. Risking a glance upwards, I see a mess of steel beams and bricks, floating floors and walls suspended in mid-air. It's about to come down.

I leap to a huge shard of cement, a wall broken and dropped on its side, wires trailing from it. As soon as my foot touches it, I know I'm in trouble. It shifts like sand under my feet, and suddenly I'm cascading downwards with the wreckage flowing round me. I drop into a crouch. Dust rises in clouds, and there's a horrible creaking and groaning. Then it's over. I daren't breathe, daren't move in case it starts up again.

A few more metres and I'll be with him.

I fix my eyes on the hand. The fingers twitch. Alive? Or was that just the movement of the building?

Trying to gain my balance, I push myself to my feet. If I can make it to that girder, and it's solid, I'll be able to shimmy along it.

I jump and grab. There's the sound of metal grinding on stone, but the girder doesn't move. I wrap my legs round it and reach upwards, then pull myself along until I'm level with the tiny white fingers. There's enough flat space next to Dylan for me to stand.

I lift the first piece of rubble. Then the next. Then I can see brown hair covered in dirt, matted with blood.

Say he's alive, say I pull him out – how am I getting him down from here? He's only eleven, but I can't climb *and* carry him.

Next second, Pat's with me, and I'm relieved and angry all at the same time. Why the hell would he follow me up here?

We scrabble through the debris. The ends of my fingers are being scraped away, but I ignore the sting and focus on digging.

The building rumbles, and we freeze, staring at each other with wide eyes, waiting to see if it's going to fall. Pat breathes through his lips. 'Keep going,' he whispers.

I grab the next big stone off Dylan's body. He groans, and I could cry with relief.

Pat rolls Dylan's head over so that we can see his face. I wipe dirt from the kid's mouth and nose, and he lets out a rattling cough.

Together, we ease Dylan free. The medic in me screams that we shouldn't move him, that he could have any number of spinal injuries and broken bones. But what's important right now is getting him away from here before this dying building crashes down on us.

'Help me lift him,' Pat croaks.

He's covered in building dust himself, his black hair white and gritty. He folds Dylan over his shoulder and grabs one arm and one leg.

'Get down first – don't wait,' Pat says. He's already panting from the weight of Dylan, the sweat on his forehead soaking through the cake of dirt.

I lower myself on to a patch that was stable on the way up. Each time Pat moves behind me, shadowing where I step, there's a landslide of bricks. Tiny pieces of debris like an avalanche.

Inch by agonizing inch, we make our way towards solid ground.

After a lifetime, I jump down and turn. Pat tips Dylan into my arms, and I stumble away from the wreckage of HQ.

70

JANEK

As the HQ building falls, Janek breathes a satisfied sigh. One way or the other, this all ends today.

In hindsight, she should have done this four months ago. She could have subjugated the camp within hours of the grounding of the *Arcadia*, and offered the prison conglomeration whatever workforce she was able to pick out of the wreckage.

She no longer cares about the opinions of those in charge of the prisons, and the president can whistle if he thinks she's obeying any more of his demands for discretion. Today, she'll focus on getting the job done her way. None of the rebellion will be alive at sunset.

The business with Harveen is unseemly, and Janek isn't yet certain how best to do away with the woman. Harveen's high profile makes killing her hazardous – another skeleton to be found in another closet – but equally, keeping her alive is altogether too dangerous. She could go public with Janek's sins at any moment, and that can't be allowed to happen. Not after everything Janek has sacrificed to get here. Not after she's dragged herself from the ruins of her hometown to be within reach of the presidency of the Federated States.

Another plume of dust rises into the sky along with the clinking rush of a building collapsing in the distance.

'Is she still moving, Mr Hudson?' she says, turning to the kid. He's bent over a digiplan on a hastily unfolded table.

The boy frowns. 'Hard to tell. The cuff's moving round the edge of the HQ building complex, but it's not clear whether that means Esther's still attached to it.'

Janek watches a white haze spreading over the sky just a few blocks from here. The air is tainted with destruction, and she's dragged back to the hours spent as a child, huddled beneath her school desk, while the sirens blared their airstrike warnings.

It is an invigorating moment. She will hand the girl to the president. He'll be pleased. Janek will end the day victorious.

'You've pitched yourself as the expert on all things Crossland and Lall. If they're both alive in there, what's their next move?'

He thinks for a minute, squinting up at the dusky sky. 'They'll fight if they're cornered.'

'You don't think, in the panic following the complete destruction of his headquarters, that Nikhil Lall will see sense?'

'I don't think Nik Lall has the IQ to make a reasoned decision under normal circumstances, and now he'll be picking up pieces of rebels from the rubble. If he's not dead, he'll fight like a wild cat.'

Janek smiles. 'I wonder if your dislike of Mr Lall might be clouding your judgement on this point.'

She signals to the personnel standing around, waiting for orders. 'Send in a loudspeaker and prepare to move into the vicinity of HQ.' Someone hands Janek a helmet and a flak vest. 'Let's find out if you're right, Mr Hudson.'

71

ESTHER

He's alive.

By some miracle. He's got a couple of broken ribs and concussion, and we won't know about internal damage until I can get him to a hospital.

He opens his eyes as I clean up the wound on the side of his head. 'Thanks for coming to get me,' he says.

'Always in trouble.'

He smiles.

Nik comes up behind me. 'Just got word from Enid. Screw trying to be quiet. They're running.'

My knees creak as I stand. My whole body feels like it's tensed up: every part of me's just waiting because I might need to move any second. 'She's leaving a driver behind to get us out if we can make it that far.'

Everyone we managed to drag out of the building is huddled against the wall of an alley opposite HQ. None of them are unscathed. There are bloody temples and broken bones. And there are people missing too. There's a single rifle between the lot of us, propped up against the brickwork. We're not fighting our way out of this.

I grab Nik's sleeve and pull him to the other side of the alley. Pat's eyes follow us as we walk, and I crush the desperate urge to go to him and tell him I'm sorry. That this wasn't how I wanted us to end.

'He needs a hospital. A better one than me and Pat trying to stick plasters over broken bones.'

'If the Coalies get him, they're not going to rush him to the ER. More likely he'll die on the floor of a jail cell. Let's get everyone moving,' Nik says.

'They'd stand a better chance of making it if someone stayed here.'

Nik nods. 'Delay the Coalies.'

'Order them to go. Pat too,' I whisper.

Nik raises his eyebrows. 'You want me to order Pat to leave you behind?'

Dylan hacks up dust.

Pat's watching us. He gets to his feet.

I feel the prickle of urgency in my chest. Janek's coming for us. Now we've got our breath back, we need to move.

Somewhere nearby there's a sound. A loud, low voice.

'*Esther Crossland and Nikhil Lall are enemies of the Federated States. Anyone harbouring them will be arrested.*'

Then there's the rumble of vehicles.

'When they get here, they're going to take us all,' I say. I'm staring up at Nik. 'I can slow them down.'

Pat's already getting everyone ready to move. The metallic

voice comes again, this time closer, bouncing between the buildings.

'Go with Dylan. Go with Pat. Find somewhere safe,' Nik says. 'I've been a shit leader to these people for four months. The least I can do is give them a fighting chance.'

I shake my head. 'No, Nik. I can't. They want me too.'

The ones that can walk hustle away from the voice.

'Take the alley in front of Warehouse Three. Then go straight through the tents and behind the coastguard station. Pat knows the way,' Nik calls after them.

'Come on, Esther,' Pat says. He starts to leave, making towards the nearest alley.

'Just give me a minute,' I say.

There's a blast of that voice again, saying, '*Esther Crossland is an enemy . . .*'

Pat's eyes widen. 'We haven't got a minute. Come now.'

'Esther, you have to run. Please. I can't watch it happen again,' Nik says. He grips my shoulders and looks into my eyes like he's saying goodbye.

My soul splits because he only just came back, and it's already over.

He gives me a gentle shove towards Pat. 'Don't make this any harder than it needs to be, doc.'

I walk to Pat and take both of his hands. I kiss him, even though I'm crying. 'Goodbye, Patrick. Thank you for everything,' I say.

Pat's face drops. He gives me a final look, and even through the tears I can see this is destroying him. He turns his back and runs after the rest of the survivors.

I wipe my face.

The sound of vehicles gets louder. Across the broken remains of HQ, I spot a dark black Hummer enter the courtyard.

I'm going to give Janek what she wants.

72

MEG

'OK. Let's give Janek what she wants,' I hear Esther say.

'No, you don't,' Nik says. He gets hold of her arm and pulls her back.

Right then, Seb, I know what I've got to do.

I push myself up from the wall. Esther and Nik are arguing, still holding on to each other. Arguing, both of them desperate not to let go. Wish I had someone who'd hold on to me like that. That one person who'd rather die than be separated from me. Too late now.

Cars, big black ones, all shiny and expensive-looking, rock into the courtyard. They skid to a stop, blocking the entrances to the yard in front of HQ. If I wanted to escape, I should have done it by now. The others have already gone. All on their way to safety. Well, that's the decision made for me at least.

Nik and Esther aren't taking any notice of me. I grab a gun that's resting against the wall of the alley. I've got to do this before they can stop me.

'Hey, Esther,' I say. 'Hands in the air.' I brandish the gun. My arm's shaking a bit already.

'Don't be stupid. Go after the others,' she replies.

'I said put your hands up otherwise I'm going to shoot you. Both of you.'

'You have to be kidding with this,' Nik says. 'Running straight back to the Coalies first chance you get is on-brand for you. We're about to give ourselves up. You don't need the weapon.'

That stings. Stings so much it brings a tear to my eye. Won't matter in a minute though. 'Just get your hands where I can see them, or I'll fill you full of holes.'

Nik smirks. Can't say I really liked him so I'm not bothered what he thinks now.

'So, what – you're gonna hand us over and hope Alex puts a ring on it?'

Esther snorts, but she's not laughing. She looks like she's been betrayed all over again. Her hands are in the air, and I take a step closer, close as I can without risking them taking the gun away.

'Give me that mask,' I say.

73

JANEK

Esther Crossland walks out into the front of the courtyard that runs round the HQ warehouse, toting a rifle. She's rather smaller than Janek expected. Time to tie up the loose ends efficiently and without fuss. No more bowing and scraping to the press and the president and the prison conglomeration, twisting herself in knots trying to keep them all happy. She'll get the results they want, and if they don't like her methods they can whistle. She'd like to see any of them do a better job.

'Seems you were wrong, Mr Hudson. They've decided not to fight after all,' Janek says.

He's in the next seat of the Hummer, frowning out of the window as the small figure of Esther Crossland waves a weapon around. Good thing these vehicles are bulletproof. Explosion-proof for that matter.

'Tell me, Mr Hudson, where do you see yourself in twenty years' time?'

The boy turns in his seat to face Janek. His eyes sparkle, and his cheeks have a healthy pink tinge. 'In your seat,' he says without missing a beat.

Janek lets out a laugh. 'Very good. But Federated States politics asks a lot of its diplomats. You'll be ordered to do things that perhaps you're not comfortable with. Manipulating old friends, for one.'

'On the contrary, ma'am. I've enjoyed messing with Lall, Crossland and the others.'

'I continue to be impressed. As the next step in the realization of your ambitions, I'd like you to carry out the execution of Esther Crossland.'

The kid meets her eye. 'Yes, ma'am,' he says, unwavering.

The choice of him as the executioner is deliberate. If the public view the killing favourably, she can raise him up as her protégé. If they condemn it, Janek will distance herself and blame the vile tendencies of the ship folk. It's what they call a win–win situation.

Hudson opens the door and steps out into the morning air. For a second, the familiar smell of crushed stone and fire seeps into the car. He slams the door behind him. The girl sees him, her face lifting in recognition.

It's an exhilarating thought that this will be over in a matter of moments. Janek will march into the White House, declare the endeavour a success, and be welcomed by the president. She's dealt with the rebel leaders, she's removed Harveen as a source of negativity, and brought the camp to its knees. Nothing can stand in her way.

Hudson walks directly over to the girl. According to his

file, they were in a relationship before the sinking of the *Arcadia*. Janek wonders whether he'll be able to –

He lifts his hand and pulls the trigger. Then, without hesitation, steps forward and shoots the girl twice more.

74

NIK

Alex gets out of the gigantic black Hummer.

Esther takes a step forward. I sense the uncertainty in her.

Alex raises his hand. I grab Esther, pull her back to me. Hiss a frantic, '*Shhhhhh!*' against her ear.

Before us, exposed in front of the wreckage of rebellion HQ, is Meg. She's wearing the AR mask she stole from Esther. Reprogrammed in seconds to display a version of Esther's face.

Alex pulls the trigger without flinching. Bang. Meg drops. Alex takes a few steps closer and shoots once, twice more.

'No!' Esther screams.

I drag her backwards into the shelter of the alley, pressing my hand over her mouth. 'Esther, don't!' I whisper into her hair.

We stagger backwards. Gotta get away before they realize that girl on the ground isn't Esther.

Alex hesitates over Meg's body, looking down, frowning.

There's movement behind him. Black uniforms spreading out and taking up position round the remains of HQ.

Esther's sobbing, breaths tearing out of her throat.

I take her hand and run, squeezing too tight, pulling too hard, because if they get Esther they're going to kill her. They'll kill her right there, just like Meg. Blood draining out over the dusty ground.

We run along the alley away from them, and every step I pray we're not going to find Coalies blocking our way.

Think, Nik, think. Which way's safest?

We dodge in front of Warehouse Three, down another alley, and we're almost among the tents. It's harder to run here. The sand sucks you down. Takes all the energy from your legs. Makes it feel like you're running against the current.

Don't slow down.

Abandoned tents flap in the wind. There's no sound of kids playing out on the sand.

We pass the coastguard station. It hurts to breathe. Hurts to move. My legs shake out of control. In the distance, I get a glimpse of a bright red shipping container on the outskirts of Silas's territory.

75

JANEK

Hudson crouches next to the body of the girl, the gun lolling in one hand. He reaches down to touch something, then springs to his feet. Before Janek realizes what's happening, he's running back towards the car, shouting. He yanks the door open.

'It's not her!'

Janek's out of the vehicle before he can shout again. 'What in hell's name do you mean?' she snaps.

'It's not her. They've been using AR masks to hide themselves from surveillance. That is not Esther Crossland.' He's out of breath. Whirling round to look at the various entrances to the courtyard.

Janek strides to the body and roughly brushes the hair from its face so that she can see. Sure enough, as Janek's hand passes through the AR filter, it glitches and reveals a different face beneath. 'Then who's this?'

'It's one of my agents.'

'What was she doing?'

'I don't know. She didn't say anything.'

Janek shoves Hudson. 'She was buying them time. One of *your* agents distracted us to let them escape. You idiot!'

Janek walks in a circle, kicking rubble out of her path. The place is silent, save for the gulls circling above the camp. No survivors are groaning among the wreckage or trying to break free of the debris trapping them. Janek has lived this scene before. She's been at ground zero when shells brought down tower blocks. It was part of daily life for her until she joined the military. She understands the aftermath. With eerie certainty, she realizes this isn't what a building looks like if there were civilians nearby. People shout after an attack. The survivors help the trapped, or litter the ground, or call for help. This camp is quiet as a grave.

'Where is everybody?' she snaps.

Janek looks around. She hasn't seen a single person since she pulled up here. Not a single one other than the girl lying dead on the ground.

'*How can that be?*' she whispers to herself. 'How can that be?'

She spins round, staring into the shadows. Searching for evidence of life. The Coalies turn round too, mimicking Janek's movements.

'They've gone. Find them!' she shouts.

76

ESTHER

I stumble into the wall of the tiny derelict substation, letting myself fall to the ground. Nik drops down next to me, his back against the breeze blocks, his chest heaving. This is where I found Meg a few days ago, and now my mind replays what's just happened. Flashes of Alex's blank face as he pulled the trigger. The way Meg dropped like she'd been unplugged. Dylan's hand twitching among the rubble. My vision swims from the mixture of exertion and horror at what we just witnessed. *Poor Meg. Poor, poor Meg.*

How can I carry on when everything's so messed up? In my most terrifying nightmares, I never conjured Alex as a monster. But that's exactly what he is. Merciless and cruel. Willing to murder.

We're clear of the tents and warehouses, and among the small tumbledown buildings on the western edge of the camp. Ahead, the shipping containers of Silas's territory are almost within reach. But it feels like an impossible distance to cover, and I don't know whether my body will get me there. There's no way to disguise ourselves now. No places to hide as we run. All we can do is keep going and hope.

Will help still be waiting for us when we get there?

'We have to keep going,' Nik says. He can barely catch his breath, and he squeezes his eyes closed and rests his head against the wall.

Back where we came from, a hazy dust cloud among the warehouses marks the remains of HQ. This feels worse than drowning. I turn my eyes away. There's nothing back there for us but death. Focus on what's ahead. The people waiting for us. Pat . . . and my parents.

Nik pushes himself up, and we drag ourselves onwards at barely walking speed.

The multicoloured shipping containers rise ahead of us. I never thought I'd be so relieved to see Silas Cuinn's territory again. Dusty and dirty, with the promise of salvation. If we can get to the tunnel. If we can get to a bus. If we can get –

'Don't slow down,' Nik says.

There's a flash of movement ahead. A human shape forms out of the shadows at the edge of one of the shipping containers. There's a whistle that cuts the air, and I know it's our people. They waited for us. They know we're coming. The sight of them gives me a final burst of energy.

We run on to the first patch of concrete between two lines of shipping containers. The people gather round us. People I recognize as Neaths from Silas's gang. A woman with braids knotted close to her scalp removes the cuff from my ear as we walk. There's a beep, and a rush of relief as the cuff drops from my ear, clattering on to the concrete.

'There's one vehicle left,' she says, and she gives me the kind of slap on the back that means *keep moving*, but also *you've got this*.

We're joined by more people as we get further into the maze of Silas's territory. They run behind us, yelling, gathering the last of them into the group as we flee. Then we're walking down the long, straight stretch that feels like an avenue, and at the end the big double doors of the garage. That's the jumping-off point for freedom. Inside, a glint of metal, a blinking red light. A bus. One final tiny little bus. Waiting.

From the corner of my eye, I see a streak of black. Halfway up the wall of stacked shipping containers, something catches up with us.

The woman with the braids yells. Then there's another one on the opposite side of the avenue. They're high up, but running and coming lower. By the second.

'Leg it!' someone shouts.

From the sound of feet clattering on metal, there are more behind.

One has got ahead of us, and now it springs from the wall at head height.

I lose Nik's hand. By the time I skid to a halt and turn, he's already on the ground.

'Esther! Go!' he shouts.

Some of the Neaths dash back to help Nik. The woman jostles me onwards. Now there are more of those bots jumping down from the walls, and the Neaths are losing the fight.

Nik's got a bot between his shoulder blades, its long legs

pinning one hand to his side as he tries to free his other arm from a second bot. The bots' spiked feet press divots into Nik's jacket.

Another bot jumps down from the side of the shipping-container wall and pounces on a man who went back to help. The man lets out a yelp of panic as the thing drags him to the ground.

I don't care if they get me. I'm going to help. A memory flashes into my mind of the stabbing, slicing arms of the spider bots that almost killed us once before.

By the time I get to Nik, the bots have him face down on the ground. Their feet leave scuttling trails on the sandy concrete. The other people are in various stages of restraint, but not a single one of them looks like they can win the fight against the bots.

I cast around for anything that might help and find half a brick. I slam it down on the bot attached to Nik's back. Again and again. One of the legs loosens its grip, and I pull it up and outwards the way Pat showed me.

Nik manages to get up on one knee. 'Take her!' he shouts to the woman. 'Esther, I'm coming! Just go!'

The woman tries to pull me away.

Far down the end of this row of containers, black figures swirl. Knees bent as they run. Crossing from left to right. Waving their weapons around.

I shake off the woman's hands and run to Nik. Even though it's damaged, the bot's climbing up his neck, each foot pressing horribly into his flesh. Touching the delicate jugular vein that's straining through his skin. I try again to pull it off, but it's too strong.

The other Neaths have stopped struggling, and I realize with horror that the bots have covered their faces.

I push my fingers under the bot's legs and try to prise it back. But, even as I'm trying to loosen its grip, a flap opens in the casing of its body. More legs emerge. They crawl over Nik's shoulder until they find his face.

'No,' I manage to say. My voice cracks and I can't stop the tears running down my face.

One of the new legs flattens out and presses itself over Nik's mouth.

His eyes widen in terror, and he huffs through his nostrils as the metal plate attaches itself to his mouth.

'It's OK. I'm going to get you out. OK? I'm going to get you out.' A plate extends over his eyes, pressing painfully into the skin on the bridge of his nose. I watch until he can't see any more.

People are scattered over the ground, arms and legs held tight by the bots, heads covered by horrible masks.

The woman's next to me now. 'You can't help him – come on,' she says.

'I'm not leaving him!' I cry.

She ducks as a bullet whips past and thunks into a metal wall somewhere behind us.

'They're coming!'

Something thuds into my arm. My head knocks against the ground. Then pressure squeezing round my bicep like a rope being pulled tighter and tighter. Pain blooms, stretching up to my shoulder, down to my fingertips.

My ears ring. I feel the woman pushing herself under my arm, and someone dragging me over the concrete.

The Exiled

The sunlight disappears. There are flashes of a metal roof. Red lights blinking. The thick smell of exhaust. A door slams. An engine growls. Urgent voices shouting.

We're moving.

The camp has fallen.

77

ESTHER

The motion of the bus makes me sick.

It's moving downhill, bumping and swaying over things lying in the way.

The ground flattens out. Outside the windows is black. All I can see are the reflections of the last few people to get out of the camp. We're driving through the tunnel that will lead us away. Enid stands at the front, peering over the driver's shoulder. Pain pulses through me with each rumble and jolt of the old bus.

I force myself up. My stomach roils with nausea. Pat kneels in the space between the seats and checks my eyes, gently pushing one eyelid up with his thumb and then the other. I can hardly see him in the low light of the bus, but his face is tense, and the line between his eyebrows makes him look like he's about to cry.

He's knotted something round my arm, a piece of fabric, in a makeshift tourniquet. My sleeve is wet all the way to my hand, and even in the dark I know it's blood. My blood.

We hit something big, and the bus rocks from side to side, the headlights swinging through the dark. Roots or vines slap into the windscreen and flick back. The driver dodges round a massive pile of rubble beneath a hole where the sunlight leaks in.

I clear my throat, trying to speak. Enid looks back over her shoulder. Without a word, she takes a bottle of water from a bag and holds it out to me. I glug. It's icy – its only effect is to sharpen me to the pain radiating through my arm.

'I left him,' I whisper to Pat.

Pat presses his lips into a line. 'It wasn't your fault,' he says.

Enid tramps to the back of the bus and leans over the back seats, glaring into the darkness behind us. 'No sign of them following yet.'

'Another mile and we'll be clear of the tunnel,' the driver says over his shoulder.

'That's when the fun starts,' Enid calls back to him. She takes a seat on the opposite side of the narrow aisle and eyes me. 'Your boy Patrick insisted we wait for you.'

Pat presses a syringe into the crease of my uninjured arm. Two beats of my heart and the relief floods through me.

Up ahead, a faint smear of sunlight picks out a ramp climbing upwards.

'Dylan?' I ask.

'Wasn't looking good. He went into cardiac arrest, but Corp managed to get him going again. You should sleep,' Pat says.

I rest my head on his shoulder and wish I hadn't made it this far.

78

NIK

Gotta save my energy.

This thing's so strong it's pointless even trying to get free.

Can hear nothing through the metal mask that's covering my face. Can't move my lips, although when hands grip me by each arm and leg and lift me like a trussed hog I can't help the groan that sounds in my throat. Apparently, my vocal cords still work in this thing, even if I can't form words.

Can just about breathe, but there's nothing in the way of smell.

I think I'm upright.

Did she get away?

I'll be OK. It'll be worth it if she got away. That'll be one last jab at Janek.

Whoever's got me left me sitting on the cold ground long enough that my body aches. Motion is one thing they can't block out, and I can tell we're moving. My guess would be a truck from the swing of it. Someone else is here. I can feel the warmth of them next to me. Their thigh pressing into mine as though we're sitting side by side. Guessing it's one of the people who was trying to get me free. That turns my stomach. Didn't want anyone else getting caught up just to save my sorry ass. But we're definitely moving. And, if she's making the effort to transport us, that means Janek's not going to kill us.

At least not yet.

79

JANEK

Janek bites her teeth together so hard she can hear the enamel creaking. 'What do you mean the camp is empty?' The field tent is open on one side, though the air is stuffy and oppressive.

The Coaly shrinks from her as though he can feel the heat of her rage.

'We're searching the area. Apart from a few stragglers and the prisoners we picked up earlier, there's no one in there.'

'Before the airstrike, there were hundreds of them in the basement of Lall's HQ. I saw them with my own eyes. They were –'

'They were just cuffs, ma'am.'

Janek's vision blurs. She sees the man through a heat haze, and before she can stop herself she flies at him with her nails, scratching at his face until he drops to the ground, shielding himself with his hands.

Other officers run into the tent and stop short, clearly at a loss.

The man on the ground waves them away. He gets to his

feet and straightens his uniform. 'What are your orders regarding the fugitives, ma'am?'

Janek rolls pieces of the man's skin between her fingertips, trying to find a place of calm. Panic won't help matters now. Damage control is key. She needs to keep this escape secret for as long as possible. The president will step in as soon as he's aware. She has to get the Lall boy in front of the judges as soon as possible. All eyes on a public trial, a public execution, while she gets enough prisoners back to prevent utter humiliation.

'There has been a large-scale breach at the camp. Pursue the escapees. Do it without drawing attention to your efforts. Get them back, do you understand me?'

'Yes, ma'am. Which direction should we focus on?'

The rage wells up again. This time she swipes her arms across the top of the table, sending a computer and a pile of paperwork crashing to the ground as she screams. 'Which direction? *Which direction?* Any direction! They could be heading anywhere. And they have hours of head start.'

'And what vehicles are they travelling in?'

Janek looks at the man with undisguised disgust. He recoils. The scratches on his face are lines of tiny bloody beads.

'Take Lall directly to the courtroom,' she orders.

80

ESTHER

The bus pulls into the car park of a diner that's all closed up, swings round the back and stops. Pat helps me down. My fingers are caked in blood, and my arm's numb from the wound downwards. That's not a good sign. Would rather keep my arm, so I need to get the tourniquet off sooner rather than later.

The other passengers file out behind us. The driver stopped the bus under a carport – a flimsy plastic roof held up by wooden uprights. Enid keeps watchful eyes on the trees that circle the diner on three sides, and the road that runs in front of it. Once everyone's off, the driver pulls a tarp down over the front of the bus.

'Get inside,' Enid snaps.

The back door of the diner creaks open, and a woman in a pink waitress uniform holds it open for us. Her hair's grey beneath her cap, and the badge on the front of her blouse says *Hi, I'm Chelsea!*

Inside, the blinds are down over the windows, and the

lights are off, giving the place a closed-up, sleepy feel. Camp people huddle in the booths, nursing cups and plates of food. My people. And now I realize for the first time: free people. My breath catches in my throat. Right at this moment, we're free. Even if we get caught before the sun goes down again.

'Where is my son?' a voice booms from behind me.

I spin round, and I'm face to face with General Lall. She's pale, face drawn in pain, and she's holding herself up on a chair, but she's just as imposing as ever. I throw myself at her. Her arms wrap round my waist. She pulls back and lifts my face in her hands. 'Esther, where's Nik?'

'They took him.'

For the first time ever, something like devastation shows on General Lall's face. 'He's alive?'

'Last time he was seen,' Enid replies.

General Lall pushes me away. She's like a storm. 'Where?' she demands.

'That's the million-dollar question,' says Enid. 'They don't mess around with long trials. My guess would be he'll be going straight to a prison cell at the central courthouse.'

General Lall crosses to the window and stares out, one hand on her hip.

The woman in the waitress uniform is staring out of the diner's front door. Keeping watch along the coastal road.

It feels like noon. Even though it's cloudy, the sun's high overhead. 'How far have we come?' I say.

'Twenty miles, give or take,' Enid replies. Her eyes hover towards General Lall and back to me again. 'We're switching vehicles here before we carry on north, and I'd like it done pretty sharpish. Pat, get the girl's arm sorted and then grab yourselves some food for the road.'

'What about the people who have gone before? Did they make it?' I say.

'First of the buses will be getting to the border any time now. Banking on Janek taking a minute to realize what's happening. Others'll be hitting different spots on the border, presenting different papers.'

General Lall paces up and down the chequerboard floor between the tables. The smell of old cooking oil and fresh coffee turns my stomach.

'You'll go north. That is an order,' she says to Enid.

'While you're doing what?'

'I'm going to get my son.'

The diner goes quiet.

Enid's mouth sags open. It might be the first time she's ever been lost for words. 'What?' she manages to say.

'I am going to retrieve my son.'

'It's a suicide mission,' Enid replies. 'And I'm not one to shy away from a good suicide mission, God knows, but this is just stupid. We'll all go north. Get out of here, then we turn round and negotiate the boy's release.'

'There will be no negotiation. There'll be a show trial, and then there'll be an execution. I intend to stop it.'

'What about all the people you've set running and then left to fend for themselves?' Enid says, pointing out of the window as though there might be refugees fleeing along the road.

'I've done my part. I have given my life to the rebellion, and, more than that, I have given my son's life. Nik's childhood was sacrificed to this cause. I won't let it take his future too.'

'She's gone berserk. Stark raving. Talk some sense into her, Esther.'

'You're going back for him?' I say.

General Lall stands taller. 'I am.'

'Want an extra pair of hands?'

General Lall breaks into a grim smile.

'So you're going too? This is . . .' Enid throws her hands in the air.

'Enid is going to take the rest of these people north and continue with the planned escape over the border to Maine. I have every confidence that she will succeed in getting this group to safety.'

Enid shakes her head, walking around, too agitated to stand still. 'Let me come with you, General. I've served as your second in command all these months. My place is at your side.'

'Your place is guiding these people. You were never that good at being a deputy.'

'You're kidding!'

'I don't kid. You're far better as a leader. You led the Flotilla for decades. Now someone needs to lead the last of our people.'

'And what are we going to do?' I ask.

The waitress has left her place by the window. She's gathering up the cups and plates, making it clear it's time for us to be making tracks.

'Shortly before the attack on HQ, Enid got a message from her contact inside the Federated States. Harveen, Janek's second in command, has been placed under house arrest. I believe she'll help us if we can get to her.'

'Help us how?' I say.

General Lall gives a tiny shrug.

'She hasn't even formulated that part of the plan yet,' Enid says with an edge of derision.

'We will deal with the details when we need to,' General Lall says. 'Perhaps Patrick could treat that wound before we leave.'

He pushes me towards a bar stool at the counter, the red plastic cover creaking as I sit. His eyes stay fixed on the wound while he unties the tourniquet.

I shrug out of my coat. When he pulls the last layer of clothes off my arm, it hurts so much it makes me suck air through my teeth.

'Sorry,' he says. 'It's still bleeding. Put pressure on it.'

He bends down to where his med bag is on the floor and rummages through until he finds a field scanner. It's cold when he presses it against my skin. I focus on the physical pain and keep away from the memory of Nik struggling against that bot.

'You took a bullet for Nik Lall,' Pat says.

The field scanner beeps. From this angle, I can't see the rectangular screen, or what diagnosis it's giving.

'I'd take a bullet for you too.'

Pat's eyes flash up to mine. The field scanner beeps again, and he looks down to see what it shows. 'Despite the fact that you're thinner than the coffee they serve here, that bullet went into and out of the flab of your arm without hitting anything important.'

'Feels like it pulverized the bone,' I say.

'It will feel like that for a few days. But it'll be healed in no time. The dressing will knit it back together. Doesn't even need a suture bot.'

'You sure? Because it feels like a pretty serious injury. And you know you're not a real doctor.'

He smiles thinly and sits back on a bar stool. 'Oh, now you're bringing up credentials, are you? Because I'm not the only person who didn't graduate. So who's technically not a real doctor?'

He opens the packet of a wound dressing with his teeth and spits out the fragment of plastic, then presses the dressing over the bullet hole, flattening the edges to seal them. Instantly, the anaesthetic in the dressing kicks in and the pain dulls.

I press the edges down. 'I'm serious.'

'You'd take a bullet for me?'

'In a heartbeat.' My voice hitches in my throat.

'And you'd die for him too?'

'Yes.'

He looks down at his hands, and I can tell his heart is just as broken as mine. 'Pretty confusing situation for you to be in then.' He throws the crumpled bandage wrapper on the floor, gets up from the bar stool and brushes past me.

'Pat, I'm sorry. I didn't want to hurt you ... If Nik had never come back –'

'Dammit. You're making it worse. I don't want to hear that you'd have settled for me,' he says over his shoulder.

'No, I didn't mean that –'

'We should leave now,' General Lall calls to me.

I watch Pat walk to the other end of the long diner. He pushes through a door marked KITCHEN without looking back. The door swings shut behind him.

I feel like I'll never see him again.

'What if she won't help us?' I say to General Lall.

'Then we will have failed, and Nik will die.'

81

NIK

My eyes ache in the artificial light, but jeez, it's good to see again. Thirty seconds ago, I was manhandled on to a chair, the pressure of the bot on my shoulders eased, and the bit of mask covering my eyes slid away.

I blink. Bright halogen light. The sound of people moving around. The mask moves down further, and my mouth's free, so I can stretch my face.

Tiled floor. Hair in my eyes. Heeled shoes. I follow the legs up and find Janek.

'Good to see you, Admiral,' I say, testing my voice.

My throat feels like I drank bleach. The fact that she's here, not some lackey, brings me out in a hot sweat. Things aren't going to go well for me if she's holding a grudge. I've heard about Janek's methods before, and I have no desire to end up as one of her public displays of justice.

I don't see a door. Not that it would do me any good to know where the exit is when my hands are still caught behind me.

'Mr Lall. What a shame you decided to fight when this could all have been wrapped up diplomatically. Your bloodlust will have consequences.'

'Funny. I thought it was you that sent an airstrike to destroy a building with all my people inside.'

Janek watches me. I can't focus on the detail of her face, just the vague outline and the pale skin. She's got her hands behind her back.

'I understand that you were trying to flee in the company of Esther Crossland when you were apprehended. I must say that I expected more of you, Mr Lall, than saving your own skin while your people were dying in the streets.'

'She gave you the slip then?' I say.

'On the contrary, Esther Crossland was shot and killed even before you were detained.'

Janek's words hit like a punch in the stomach, and I can't keep the pain from my face. Even so, I manage to say, 'Nice try, Janek.'

A guard in the black uniform of a Coaly steps forward from the edge of the room and passes a screen to Janek. She taps the glass, then holds it up a few centimetres from my face. 'If you didn't know, many of our personnel have cameras. It often helps to revisit video footage of our operations. It lets us learn from our mistakes. In this case, it let us confirm the tragic passing of Esther Crossland. This video was taken from the chest camera of the officer who fatally injured your friend. There you are, fighting valiantly against the anti-personnel bot . . .'

It's grainy and taken at distance, but I recognize myself kneeling on the ground. Looking stupid while I try and wrestle the thing off my back. The Neaths return to help me, and get taken over one by one. Then I'm on my knees, and a small figure runs towards me. I remember the sensation of the mask clawing its way over my face. And, as I drop to the ground, there's a bang, a thud, and Esther falls to the ground.

Bile floods my throat. I clench my teeth. Janek won't see me break down. I refuse to give her that.

Janek presses the screen again. 'Take another look, Mr Lall.' She moves the video back, and zooms in so that the image is even more pixelated. 'There. She runs to help. And then, sadly, is terminated.'

I fix my eyes on the floor. I force myself to stay quiet. My hair trembles over my face.

'Your mother. Your friend Enid. The scandalously untrustworthy Corporal Weston. All met the same fate earlier today. The people you helped to escape are being rounded up as we speak. It's time for me to acknowledge that I have failed to bring the camp and its people under control, and the Federated States' plan to give them meaningful lives of labour has been thwarted by your efforts. Every fugitive will be executed. There will be no more ship people in the Federated States. You should be very proud of your actions, Mr Lall. It's all because of you.'

82

ESTHER

Just looking up at the townhouse makes my mouth dry from anxiety. The black spike-topped railings are like prison bars. The columns holding up the portico stand guard.

General Lall stops the truck on the opposite side of the road, a few huge houses away from Harveen's home. That's where her brief message told Enid she was being kept. There were no other messages. Guessing they took her screen off her or she can't risk trying to communicate again.

The indicator *tink-tink-tinks* in time with my heart. I can't drive a car so General Lall had to suffer through the pain of getting us here, even though she's injured. By the time she pulls the handbrake on, there's a sheen of sweat on her face and an unpleasant pallor to her skin.

By far, this is the craziest, most doomed-to-fail scheme we've ever thought up. But it's our last-ditch attempt to save Nik from the execution we all know is coming. Weirdly, the fact that we have almost zero per cent chance of succeeding is what's keeping me calm.

This truck was lent to us by Chelsea, the pink-uniformed diner waitress. She explained that twenty years ago she met and fell in love with a man who had just escaped from a ship called the *Ithaka*. They quietly ran the diner and kept their heads down until the news came that Janek had cleared the ship. The next day, they went looking for the rebellion, and their diner has been a safe stopping place for escapees ever since.

On the drive from the diner, I held my breath at every police car we passed. Every time we stopped at a red light, I pushed myself deeper into my clothes, hoping no CCTV cameras would be interested enough to look at our faces.

We've driven round this block three times already, me and General Lall, both scanning the house perimeter for places we might be able to get in unnoticed.

'How will we know what room she's in?' I ask.

'We don't until we get inside. My instinct is that security won't be a high priority when it comes to protecting a disgraced former employee,' General Lall says.

'We could try to take the security cameras out first,' I say.

'Not without equipment. In any case, it might attract more attention if their CCTV suddenly fails. We'll have more success if we sneak over the back fence and use the trees as cover. Unless someone's watching, they're unlikely to notice.'

'I'd feel better about this if we could get her a message to say we were coming,' I say.

'Enid's contact with her has always been one-way,' General Lall replies. She takes a weapon from the glovebox of the truck and hides it in her coat.

Things just got real. I open the door, letting in a blast of cold air. The wind tangles the branches of the trees. General Lall slams the door behind her, and we cross the empty road that runs behind the fancy gardens. Acting like we're going for a walk.

General Lall takes a final look up and down the street. Without hesitating, she kneels by the fence. I put my boot on her knee and pull myself up. Halfway over, I find a position between two spikes where I'm not going to impale myself, and lodge my boots between the bars of the railing. I reach down to help her climb up, and that's when I realize there's no way she can make that climb. It's tricky, even without a major injury.

'Keep the car running,' I say.

She looks as though she's about to protest, then she nods quickly and turns back to the road.

I drop down and creep to the edge of the garden. *Imagine being able to afford flowers that are just for decoration.* The back windows of the house stare down, watching me.

A dark-haired woman moves around on the other side of the window.

As she turns to pace away, she spots me crouching in the dirt. I lift my finger to my lips and hope she understands I'm here to help. Not help her. I couldn't care less about getting her out of whatever game she's losing with Janek. But, if helping her helps Nik, then I'm up for it. I catch the tiniest shake of her head, and the next second a man in a suit comes into view. I duck back behind a bush. Seconds later, the swoosh of the window being pushed open.

'He's gone!' the woman calls out.

I peer round the leaves, and, when I see it's safe, I creep up to the window. By the time I've pulled myself inside, the woman is standing across the room, wielding a book like it's a baseball bat. 'Stay right there,' she says.

'Why did you let me in if you're just going to threaten me?' I ask.

'Tell me who you are. And don't even think about coming closer. I sent my Secret Service guard to the other room, but if I scream he'll be here within ten seconds. Now start talking, or so help me you'll be in cuffs before the end of the day.'

'I'm Esther Crossland,' I say, folding my arms. 'And I need you to help free a friend of mine.'

'Nikhil Lall,' she says. She lowers the book a fraction.

'Where is he?'

'He's being held at the courthouse before his trial this afternoon.'

'This afternoon? Don't you people have to build a defence or something first?'

She lets out a laugh. 'Tell me you're from a ship, without telling me you're from a ship.'

'What?'

'Our legal system allows for trial by self-testimony.'

'I don't understand. What does that mean?'

'It means, in cases where there's little doubt that the accused is guilty, we access their memory of events directly. The stream, invariably, removes any remaining doubt.'

A chill runs down my spine. 'What's the stream?'

'The accused is hooked up directly to a computer system so that their thoughts can be streamed publicly. It's not a pleasant experience for the defendant, but it doesn't really

443

matter. Execution takes place immediately after the trial, so the suffering is finite.'

My head spins. 'I thought we'd have more time,' I whisper.

'Even with all the time in the world, there's nothing I can do for him. I'll be lucky to get out of this alive.'

'I don't believe that for a second,' I say.

'What makes you say that?'

'You're still here.'

She raises her eyebrows.

'Come on. You don't think this is the end for you. The window's open. I got in, so you sure as hell could have got out.'

'I have no desire to be pursued by the Secret Service.'

'No. You still think that playing by the rules is an option for you. You still think there's a chance your life can be salvaged. You're not desperate. You're waiting.'

'That's irrelevant. I don't intend to make my situation any worse by throwing my hat in with escaped refugees. I've done my part to help you people. I'm not obligated to put myself in any further danger. If you leave now, I won't call the guards.'

'So it doesn't matter that he's going to die?' I say. The heat of anger's rising over my collarbones.

'I like Nik, truly, but I've done enough damage to my life trying to help you.'

I bring the gun out now and point it at Harveen. She shrinks under the threat, but her face is still hard as stone. 'That won't achieve anything. If you shoot me, the Secret Service will burst through that door, and you'll be dead before you can take another breath.'

'Worth it,' I say, and I tighten my grip round the handle, my fingers twitching to the trigger.

Harveen raises her hands.

'You were willing to help us before – what changed?' I say.

'My plan worked.' She shrugs. 'All I have to do is wait. The president will be livid that Janek disobeyed him, and he'll name another successor. With any luck, it'll be me.'

A shiver runs down my spine. 'What if she isn't humiliated? What if the president decides to keep her around?'

'He won't.'

'I've heard different,' I lie.

'From who?'

'Doesn't matter. What matters is whether you're willing to leave what comes next up to chance.'

For the first time, Harveen seems to falter.

'I'm safer here.'

'Maybe. But only for another few hours. By which point, Janek will have solidified her position with the president, and will be busy deciding how to deal with you. It'll be too late to do anything. And you've seen how she punishes people.' I lower the gun so that it points to the ground. 'All I'm asking is that you get us inside that courtroom so we can help our friend. We get Nik. You finish Janek. Win–win,' I say.

83

NIK

'Not a chance,' I say, smiling at the guard. It's good to be up and on my feet. My back feels like it's made of a single piece of metal, and every time I move, the bones crack. For an entire day, I was in that mask with the restraints holding me in place. It was a day too long.

'Prisoners are required to shower before court,' he says.

He's a tired-looking man with nicotine-stained teeth, and I can tell he'd rather be doing pretty much anything than working here. Poor guy just wants to go home for the day. Shame he decided to be the henchman for a murderous regime.

They're planning to kill me. Not gonna make life easy for them.

'Do what you gotta do. But I'm not taking orders until I get legal representation.'

One of the other guards laughs. 'That's not how this works, kid.'

'Last time I checked, the Federated States still had the whole trial-by-a-jury-of-their-peers thing in place.'

'Not for people like you.'

'Ship people?'

'Terrorists.'

The younger of the guards pushes me towards the shower block. Still fully clothed, trainers squeaking on the tiled floor.

'I'm not a terrorist,' I say.

'I don't give a shit,' the guard replies.

The blast from the hose is like being hit with a stream of concrete. The force takes my feet from under me, and I crash on to the tiles. Water hits my face. I crawl to the back of the shower area, trying to find space to suck some air in. Freezing cold. My clothes do nothing to stop the bruising lash of the water. I curl against the wall, making myself as small as possible. The sound of the water is white noise. When it's finally turned off, I wobble to my feet and wipe the stream from my face.

'Question,' I say, trying to breathe.

'What?' the guard barks.

'Can I have some soap?'

He turns the hose back on.

84

JANEK

She takes her seat early so that she can watch the judges enter the courtroom. It's a strange mix of modern and traditional, the building designer clearly having tried to incorporate vintage elements to give the new courtroom gravitas. The reclaimed wooden bench where the five judges will sit is bathed in light from a glass skylight. The antique wooden stand has been upgraded with the installation of retractable glass walls. Alex Hudson occupies the seat next to her. He's neat as a pin in his dress uniform, long white fingers folded on his lap.

'Do you feel ready, Mr Hudson?'

'I do. Thank you for allowing me this opportunity, Admiral. I won't disappoint you.'

'See that you don't.'

The Hudson boy is uniquely equipped to lead the interrogation of Nikhil Lall. Another prosecutor would have done adequately. However, Hudson's personal history with Lall means he should be able to provide some uniquely insightful queries.

Lall is already restrained on the stand, the ornate wooden box coming up to his waist. His hands are held down by metal gloves, one on either side of the stand, so that he can only face the judges.

It's little wonder that he looks so tired. They scrubbed him top to bottom before his court appearance, and dressed him in new clothes. The public doesn't like to think of prisoners being mistreated, even ones who will be executed within the hour.

Janek's teams have apprehended a portion of the escaped refugees. A few more hours and she'll have enough in prison camps that she can pretend this whole fiasco was planned. The president might never even hear about the breach. She'll silence Harveen with a syringe of opiates, and her body will be found surrounded by the paraphernalia of an addict. Evidence will be brought to light that Harveen was the one responsible for the *Ithaka* disaster, and for the deaths that followed. Janek will finally be freed from the shackles of her past.

She breathes in and lets the air flow calmly out through her nose. The courtroom is filling with people. Nik Lall strains to look over his shoulder.

The judges enter, long black robes trailing over the ground. Three men, two women, all serious.

Janek stands out of respect, and the oldest judge, a retired colonel, halts in front of her to salute. She salutes in return and feels the swell of pride and success lifting her.

None of the judges look at the defendant.

85

ESTHER

My eye itches, and I rub it vigorously. The press credentials are contained on a lens that was awkwardly put in place by General Lall as we stood in the street outside the courthouse.

'Don't fiddle with it,' she says.

Two steps ahead of us, a man we met three minutes ago leads us into the heavily guarded courtroom. I feel like I'm walking into Janek's office. I wanted the freedom of the Federated States. I never imagined I would be here like this.

The man leads us up granite steps and through the colonnade. He holds the heavy glass door open for me, and I struggle to find the strength to keep it open.

'Remember, I get you in, and that's it. Whatever you've got planned in there is nothing to do with me. If they take you, you keep my name off your lips.'

'Until you want an exclusive interview,' General Lall says.

'Mrs Lall, I can tell you, without a hint of doubt in my mind, that you will not be giving interviews after today. I'm doing this because Harveen asked me to, and we've got history, not because I think you're going to succeed.'

We march onwards. I'm shaky with adrenaline.

Less than an hour ago, Harveen grabbed clothes, climbed out of the window of her house, and got into the car where General Lall was still waiting for us.

I concentrate on the way the too-big shoes clip on the flagstones. Before, on the *Arcadia*, I dreamed of places like this. The majesty of the architecture. Never thought I'd be an enemy of the state, on the run, and planning a stupid, futile jailbreak.

Just inside the glass entrance of the courthouse, there's a security station. Guards in uniforms watch as each visitor steps up to the scanner and lets it read their credentials. Barney King, Harveen's reporter friend, goes first. He stares into the scanner lens. A green light pans over his eye. His image flashes up on a screen, and the guard nods him through.

King doesn't wait for us. He disappears up the broad staircase, washing his hands of us and any responsibility for what we're about to do. No matter. He's done what we needed him to: got us into the courthouse.

'I'll go through the security gate first. Any sign of trouble, you turn round and leave. Do you understand me?' General Lall says.

'Yes, ma'am.'

She walks as though she belongs here. Her hair's neatly pinned into a bun on the back of her head, and Harveen's clothes make her look every bit the Federated States citizen. She brings her eye to the scanner. It scans, beeps, and she's through.

I follow and, by the time my face has been flashed over the security screen with a fake name and journalist credentials beneath it, courtesy of Barney King's employer, I can barely take the pressure in my chest any more.

'Hold your nerve,' General Lall says. She squeezes my arm before we climb the stairs to the courtroom.

The sight of Nik freezes me to the spot in the doorway so that the person behind me stumbles into my back. They tut and push past.

He's in the middle of the room, elevated on a small wooden stand just big enough for one. His arms are stretched to either side of the stand so that he's forced to stay in one position. I want to shout to him. I want him to know he's not alone. In front of him, the judges' podiums are flanked by Federated States flags. Behind him, rows of plastic seats are filled by the audience. Men and women in military uniforms and what look to be court officials sit along both sides of the courtroom.

On the other side of Nik, smirking to himself, is Alex. It flashes through my mind that if I'm going to be arrested, charged and executed today, I could take him with me. I could jump over the barriers and wrap my fingers round his neck. Janek's too. It could be over before anyone tries to stop me.

General Lall nudges me forward until I drop my head and walk to the press gallery at the back of the room. Rows of uncomfortable plastic chairs separated from the rest of the court by a low barrier.

We sit two rows back from the front. Barney King carefully avoids making eye contact. I've barely had time to process anything when everyone around me stands, and a line of judges files in from a door at the front of the room. Nik's shoulders tense. I wish I could tell him we're here. That we're going to try, even if we fail.

The general taps her fingers against her thigh. Waiting, just like me.

Come on, Harveen. Nik's counting on you.

86

HARVEEN

The girl was right. My choice was to hope that Janek would fall off a cliff, or give her a little shove. I couldn't risk her not falling.

My credentials are still active, so I walk through the security barriers and into the West Wing of the White House without being challenged. I'm the president-elect's chief of staff. I could be here for any number of reasons. No one's going to stop me.

Getting into the Oval Office is another matter.

My legs have never trembled on this walk along the corridors of power before. But then I've never had sinister intentions before. I smile and say *good afternoon* to the staffers who see me.

Everyone here is in office wear. It smells of coffee and floor polish. The president's secretary, Betsy, occupies the outer Oval Office, and this afternoon she's at her desk. *Dammit.* My first obstacle. Manicured nails click on her keyboard.

There's no Secret Service guarding this door. Why would

there be? They're surrounding the building. Every entrance and exit is covered. If I'm caught, there'll be no getting out of here. I don't have a getaway driver sitting with the engine running.

'Good afternoon, Betsy,' I say.

'Harveen. You do not have an appointment,' she says without looking up from her screen. 'We do not presume to walk into the Oval Office without scheduling a meeting through me. All staffers know this. My house, my rules.'

'Rest assured, I would never dream of going over your head,' I say with the itch of a smile.

'Then you can have a cookie.' She lifts the glass lid of the jar on her desk and waits.

I plunge my hand in and retrieve one. 'I'm not here for the president,' I say. There's a tremor at the end of my words, the slightest hint of anxiety. It's because I'm being duplicitous, but now I realize it will play to my advantage.

Betsy looks at me, eyebrows arched. I lean forward on the desk and tilt my head down as though I'm sharing a secret. 'I was coming through the assistants' pool just now, and one of them was crying.'

'I'm not interested in the dramatic exploits of the assistants,' she says.

She goes back to her work, using a finger to slide dates round a calendar on the screen. All I need is five minutes, with her away from her desk.

'Only I did hear one of them saying they'd go to the press –'

Her face snaps up. That did it.

'They're in the toilets by the lobby.'

Mrs Turner slides back on her chair and steams out of the office.

I ease the outer door closed behind her and take the few steps to the closed door of the Oval Office. Time to make the decision. *Am I really going in there?*

I've come this far. I'm this close to destroying Janek – and saving myself in the process. All I need to do is give her that little shove.

The ancient wooden door opens with a turn of the handle, and two steps bring me into the personal office of the president of the Federated States.

There's no time to take a breath. The room is dominated by his enormous wooden desk. Flags on long poles stand in front of the windows.

This is why I do the things I do. Janek seemed like a good bet at the start – thought I'd ride her coat-tails into power. Instead, I've spent years cleaning up her mess. Doing things that no decent human being would even consider.

Concentrate, Harveen.

I ignore the draw of the leather chair and cross to the portrait hanging by the fireplace. It's a well-known secret that this portrait hides a safe. Every schoolkid who's been escorted round the Oval Office on a class outing knows about it. Still, my heart thrills as I pull the corner of the frame, and the portrait swings back on hidden hinges.

I take the code breaker from the pocket of my suit and attach it by the keypad of the safe. A press of the button and numbers flash over the screen as it finds them: 0–8–0–7 . . .

'Come on,' I mutter to myself. Sweat's gathering between my shoulder blades and slithering down under my blouse.

'Zero eight zero seven eight zero. The date I was inaugurated,' a voice comes from behind me.

I spin, heart like a block of ice in my chest. My breath catches in my throat. I'm finished.

'Or didn't they teach you that in your political-science classes?' The president is smiling at me, white teeth shining.

He reaches over my shoulder, standing so close I can smell his musky aftershave, and adds the last digits to the keypad. I hear it beep and then the puff of the safe door popping open.

'I suspect this is what you're here for.' He reaches past me into the safe and then waves a data disk in front of me. 'Although I am mildly curious as to why Janek sent you to launch the *coup d'état*. Clandestine murder is more her style. Here I was expecting arsenic in my dinner followed by a swift burial. Care to elaborate before I have you hauled off?' He leans back on the desk, tapping the disk against his sleeve.

'I'm not here on Janek's behalf,' I say. My throat's like sandpaper.

He raises his eyebrows. 'Expand.'

'She's failed to bring the camp under control. The entire workforce is scattered. There's nothing left to offer the prison conglomeration. Her last effort to keep hold of her position is the trial of Nik Lall, hoping you'll be so pleased with the results that you'll forgive the disaster she's overseen.'

'You're a clever girl. You must know it's over for Janek. I'll wait for her to finish with the camp before I fire her. The only question is whether she takes the ship people – and you – down with her.'

His eyes bore into my face, and it feels like I'm under

threat. The very next thing he does will mean my death. The president stands up and walks towards the door of the Oval Office.

'I want to humiliate her,' I blurt, almost tripping over the words. The president stops short of the door. 'I wasn't here to destroy it. I was planning to release it.'

The president laughs. 'Well, well. Janek's most trusted comrade is also her most lethal enemy.'

I glance at the disk and then back up at the president's face. He's no longer laughing. Now he's staring at me with such intensity that I want to shrink into my clothes.

'Catch,' he says, and he tosses the disk to me. I catch it and hold tight. It's warm from his hand.

'Janek is finished. I've not been enjoying her work for quite some weeks, and I felt it was time for a change. The only reason I haven't named another successor is that there hasn't been a clear replacement in the line-up. A series of tiresome military personnel – empty, bloviating uniforms. Unwilling or too narrow-minded to take any action likely to rock the boat. I want someone fierce. I want someone who will leave the safety of the road to tread their own path if necessary.'

I blink at him.

'And naturally I want someone who isn't going to poison my dinner at the first opportunity.'

'You want me to take Janek's place?' I say, and my voice is hardly more than a whisper.

'You're the next in line. What's your plan for releasing that testimony? I hope it's not destined for some dull exposé in the Sunday papers.'

'No, sir. It's going to be released somewhere more impactful.'

He circles the desk and sits down in the shiny leather chair. 'Let's start by tying up the loose end that is Admiral Janek. Then we can talk about your role in government.'

My fingers shake. I try not to let him see the tremble as I take the mini-screen from my pocket, slide the disk into the port, and click the green send button that appears in the middle of the screen.

The president smiles at me. This is turning out even better than I planned.

87

NIK

The sky's a kind of washed-out blue through the skylight. They haven't given me any details of what's going to happen now. And really it doesn't even matter. They're going to kill me.

Esther's gone.

My mother's gone.

Enid's gone.

Corp's gone.

I don't have anything left to cling to. I'm like one of those astronauts in a sci-fi flick watching their home planet disintegrate into crumbs. Never understood what the point in carrying on is if everyone you've ever loved is gone.

There's a spiral of seagulls above the building opposite.

Kind of wish I could turn round and see what kind of sociopaths come to a trial, but my hands are stuck fast inside these weird metal gloves and attached to the walls of the stand. Janek's smirking over at the side of the courtroom, whispering in Alex's ear. It's more than a little irritating that

Esther's ex is going to be the only one of us to survive. The smug creep. Haven't seen Harveen; maybe she wasn't an ally after all. Maybe she's realized our escape plan was doomed from the start, and she got out while the going was good.

Behind me, there's the sound of people standing up, and from the corner of my eye I see Janek get to her feet. If I could give her one last jab, I would. A final kick as I'm going down.

Five judges file into the room, long robes swooshing over the marble floor. They take their places behind the bench at the front of the courtroom. They sit. I wiggle my fingers.

'Nikhil Lall. You are charged with acts of terrorism against the Federated States. How do you plead?' That's the one that seems to be in charge. The oldest and crustiest one. He looks about a hundred.

'I've got no idea what charges you're bringing. I don't recognize this court. Everything I've done was in self-defence. Oh, and screw you.'

The judge stares straight at me and, under the folds of his eyelids, the corneas are a pale blue.

'That language will not be tolerated here. I'm adding contempt of court to the charge list.'

'That's accurate. I do hold you in contempt.' I wiggle my fingers again. Wish I could just get one hand out to scratch my nose.

A murmur runs through the crowd gathered behind me. The old judge watches me beadily for a sec before deciding I'm not worth bothering with. Janek's got her eyes on me too. I can feel them.

The old guy waves a hand. 'Who is acting for the prosecution?'

Alex stands up. 'I am, sir.'

Oh great, this is all I need. Not only am I going to be executed, but I've got to spend my last few minutes with that guy.

'Begin the testimony,' the judge says.

Alex skips down to the centre of the courtroom and grabs a goofy-looking thing with wires trailing from it. As he gets closer, he leans in to me. 'You should know I played a role in killing every single person you love. How does it feel to realize I won?'

'I feel great,' I say, breaking into the widest grin I can manage. 'I feel peachy. Although if you could scratch my nose I'd appreciate it. I'm a bit tied up.'

Hudson grimaces. 'The more you fight, the more it will hurt. So struggle away.' He lifts up the weird-looking visor thing.

'What's this?' I ask. Don't like the look of that thing one bit.

'It's how we get the lenses on to your eyes.'

'I'm going to pass on that,' I say.

He looks at me and drops his hand slowly to the taser at his side. He flicks his thumb over the clip that's meant to stop the weapon getting stolen, still looking straight at me.

'OK, I get the picture,' I say.

He places the visor over my face. The inside has circles of foam that fit round the bones of my eyes, and as soon as they're in place I sense them move. First, there's pressure as the visor attaches itself to my face, then it seems to suck outwards, pulling at my eyelids until my eyes are stretched open. There's nothing to see but black inside the mask. I try to blink, but the mask holds my eyelids in place. And now I've got the scrabble of panic running round inside me. The only thing keeping me calm is Alex.

Things move over the surface of my eyes. Things attach to my forehead. Worst of all, things slide beneath my eyelids. Feel like crushed glass. *Don't you dare give them the satisfaction of screaming.*

Then I'm blinking in the light, and Alex is packing the visor back into its case, clicking the clasps closed and walking away.

My eyes are hazy. Whatever this thing is they've installed, it feels like I'm seeing everything through a camera lens.

'Please begin with the afternoon of Sunday the twenty-fourth of October 2094,' the judge says. He's speaking to Alex, not me.

The world sways. The courtroom, the judges, Janek are all still here, but there's another world superimposed on them. I'm standing inside it. Janek's a pale ghost. The judges' robes make them look like wraiths.

Then I smell the ocean. The sun's dropping over the city. I lean over the ship's rail and beneath me is the Lookout. There's Sim, the owner, going from table to table, filling people's cups with coffee. I can almost taste how bitter it is. In my hand, there's a pile of leaflets. And I don't want to look at the person I know is standing next to me.

My heart cracks, and I force myself to look at her. Her face is covered with a scarf, so all I can see are her eyes. Press pause, I think. Just press pause for a second, and let me look at her. But the memory barrels on, and I can't find a way to slow it down. May's eyes crease at the edges. Her scarf moves as she lets out a breath. Now, just like then, she's a ball of fizzing exhilaration.

'Ready?' she says.

'Ready.'

She throws the leaflets into the air.

88

ESTHER

General Lall grabs my thigh and digs her fingernails into my flesh. 'Keep your seat,' she whispers.

I can't breathe.

At the front of the courtroom, surrounding the stand where Nik is being held, is the *Arcadia*. And, next to Nik, something that drags my heart like barbed wire – May. Like she was a few days before she went to a Federated States training facility.

General Lall increases the pressure on my leg. The pain grounds me and stops me from running to her. 'This will be over in minutes. As soon as Harveen sends the recording, we will move. Hold your nerve.'

She's not real. She's hazy and glitchy and not solid, but she's the closest I've come to seeing my sister since she was murdered by the Coalies as we tried to leave the ship.

'Get your breathing under control. It's a technological trick, and if you can't keep it together you're going to lose Nik.'

I bite the inside of my mouth. Concentrate on the sensation

of my teeth slicing into my cheek. Drop my eyes and stare at the too-big shoes that Harveen gave me, until I'm strong enough to look up without a single tremor or shake.

The judge's voice is a distant drone. I catch words like *propaganda* and *lies*. Nik's face is turned to where the figure of May is smiling at him, and I realize they're replaying what happened in the Lookout when they dropped the leaflets on us. I was in the cafe below. I've never seen it happen from up here.

Nik's fixated on May. She leans on the rail and tosses a handful of leaflets. The image disappears, and I'm sure Nik's shoulders sag under the grief. For a second, the air is blank, then it's replaced with an image of Nik working on a piece of machinery. An engine, higher than his head, with tubes and wires connecting its different parts like the veins and arteries of a heart. This must be the *Arcadia*'s engine room.

The metal door opens and the captain enters. General Lall lets out a tiny gasp. 'They're making him relive the crimes,' she says.

Before the captain speaks, the image changes again. Now May's sitting cross-legged on the floor, a textbook open on her knee. She disappears, and reappears standing on the rail, wind blowing through her hair. 'You think you're really funny, don't you, Lall?' she says. Her voice is disjointed. It fades and glitches like there's a bad connection.

The judges shift in their seats. Janek frowns. Something's happening.

'Take control of this, please,' the main judge says. 'I would like to see the interaction between Mr Lall and the captain of the *Arcadia*.'

Another version of May flashes up. She's on one side of Nik's cabin, with him on the other. They're throwing a ball between them. May tosses it straight at Nik's face. He dodges. The ball slams into a clock on the wall behind him, glass showering down from its smashed face. May's hands fly to her mouth.

The image resets, the scene starting over. May throws the ball; the clock smashes; she covers her mouth with her hands.

'Mr Lall!' the judge cries. 'Hijacking the testimony like this will achieve precisely nothing. The only outcome is that you will remain on the stand until you are too exhausted to resist, and we will see the testimony we require anyway.'

Nik doesn't speak. The scene resets.

'He's fighting them,' the general says. She's got a tiny, grim smile on her face.

89

NIK

Not gonna lie, the sight of May almost floored me. Half of me can't stand to see her because she's gone. And the other half never wants this to end. I could stay in here and just wait to die. I can feel the court official trying to direct my memories. It's like waves pressing on my mind. Strong and insistent. But I can let it wash right over me.

So I'm choosing which memories they see first. Because, if they're going to execute me right here in this courtroom, I will sure as hell spend my last minutes of life looking at happy memories.

From his place on the other side of the room, the court official prods me to remember the moment Esther and I charged through the door of the bridge on the *Arcadia*. That's an easy nope. It was hazy to begin with, and it's no problem to brush away. Instead, I focus on Esther. We're standing on the roof of HQ. The sky's pink and purple, and she's telling me about how some guy called Patrick has taught all the kids to deal with surveillance bots. There's a plate of fruit on the wall in front of us, and she's laughing while she's describing the kids. How they scream with delight when they manage to destroy them. And she puts her hand on my arm while she's talking, and the smile is so real and just so normal I could cry. And that's the moment I decide to kiss her. If she's the last face I see, it won't be so bad.

I'm sure I catch an exasperated grunt from Alex as I rewind and start the memory over. It's not as clear as real life, and, if I look through the image of Esther, I can see the wall of the courtroom beyond.

Tiredness leaks into my body, and my eyes are starting to burn like I've looked at the sun.

'Enough.' That was the judge's voice. The images disappear, and I'm back in the courtroom properly. Janek's face like lava in among the other politicians and officials. 'In light of Mr Lall's failure to cooperate in the trial process, I move to pronounce a guilty verdict. Do my fellow judges have any objection?'

None of them speak.

From behind me, there's a rumble of voices, and I'm sure I hear a muttered, 'No!'

'Carry out the execution order, please.'

My hands are released from the cuffs, and in the same moment the panels on the sides of the stand seem to get taller, until I'm encased in a glass box. A roof shimmers above me. I spin round, looking for an exit, seeing for the first time the crowd gathered to watch my death. There are two faces I recognize. Esther and my mother. I'm so happy to see them I could cry. I press my hands on the glass.

'They told me you were dead!' I shout. My voice bounces

back, and now I realize there's no noise entering the box. I'm sealed in.

So what's this gonna be? Slow asphyxiation? Some poison?

Even as I'm thinking it, I hear a hissing sound inside the box. So that's the way. I run my finger over a line of tiny holes in the top of the wooden stand, just inside where the glass meets the wooden frame. Air pushes past my fingers. Except it's not air.

There's no point trying to cover my nose with my clothes. No point trying to block the holes the gas is coming through. It's over.

I fix my eyes on Esther and my mum. Trying to drink in the last view I'll have of them.

I rest my forehead on the glass.

I take a long, deep breath.

And then they both look up.

90

ESTHER

Around Nik, the memory stream has flashed to life again. But this time the memory is of an office. Tiled floor, broad wooden desk. Harveen sits in a chair on the other side of it. 'If we send in the airstrike now, we risk the personnel already aboard.'

'If we don't, the rebels will take the ship. I'll be a laughing stock.' Janek presses a button on her screen. 'Begin the airstrike.'

Harveen purses her lips. 'Those are our people. At least warn them to evacuate.'

'It will take them half an hour. I'm not willing to lose the first battle on the first ship that I'm responsible for clearing.'

'What happens when people find out?'

'We'll do a little clean-up afterwards. There should be very few witnesses.'

'If you won't warn them, I will.' Harveen gets up from her chair and takes a small screen from her pocket. She taps with her thumb.

'If you warn them, you're done. It doesn't matter how many degrees you have from prestigious institutions, I'll make sure you're back in the Upper West Side before the end of the week. You'll spend the rest of your life discussing which shoes go with which handbag. Or you could let this go.'

Harveen lets the screen drop to her side.

The image falters and is replaced by Janek and Harveen talking about the death toll on the *Ithaka*.

I suppress the urge to punch the sky. *Harveen did it.* She got Janek's testimony. She streamed it into the courtroom's system.

The judges watch with their mouths open like stupid fish, apparently unable to comprehend what's happening. Janek too. She's as shocked as the rest of them.

'Turn it off!' she screeches. Then she's pushing through the people in front, trying to get to Alex.

There's no movement from the gathered press. Everyone's rapt by the streaming memories.

Everyone apart from Nik. He's banging silently on the glass of his glass prison. His face is a violent red, and he's clutching his throat with one hand.

'General!' I say, but she's already running to him. Over the low barrier that separates us from the rest of the court.

She slams her hands on the glass. Then she turns and shoves a reporter out of the way, grabbing a chair from the press gallery. She swings it and smashes it into the glass. Nothing happens. Not a dent or chip. Nik's bent double, looking a sickly purple, saliva and snot streaming down his face. General Lall swings again, and this time there's a crack in the glass, but the legs of the chair shatter from the force of the blow. Nik disappears from view.

'The smoke!' she shouts.

I feel in my pocket for the hastily thrown-together smoke bomb. Pat said it's low on power and won't do much. But all we need is confusion. I take the cylinder he gave me from my pocket, twist the two halves of the plastic bottle in opposite directions, and shake to let the two liquids inside mix. Then I throw it on to the floor in the middle of the courtroom. It froths and spews out grey smoke. The smell of sulphur hits me immediately. It's totally harmless. But totally foul.

People run for the exit.

General Lall grabs another chair. The crack flashes longer with each strike.

It's too slow. It's taking too long.

The judges are on their feet and shouting.

I need to open that box. Now.

I leap over the barrier, pushing people out of the way as I go. Barney King runs past, covering his face with his tie. I push him aside too and carry on, wading through the smoke that's rising from the canister and forming a dense grey cloud. Behind the bench, Alex is still sitting by his control console.

'Let him out!' I scream.

Alex stares at me like I've got two heads.

I give him a shove to wake him up, but when he doesn't move I grab the taser that's strapped to his belt. The idiot didn't fasten the clasp to secure it when he was done threatening Nik. He puts up no resistance as I pull the taser out of its place and hold it up to his face. 'Open it. Now.'

He does as I say, and over my shoulder I turn to see the glass retracting into the wooden stand.

'You did this!'

Janek is standing two steps away from me. Her hair's a tangled mess, the bun sagging down over one shoulder. She launches herself at me. She slams me into the ground, and then she's on top of me. Her fingernails score lines in my cheeks. She yanks my hair, and I feel a handful tugged out. All I can do is hold on to her wrist as she pulls me from side to side. Then she's got her skinny fingers round my neck, impossibly strong. I can't breathe. Pressure like my head's going to explode. My vision blackens.

I swing a fist and get a lucky hit, just hard enough to send her off balance. I push her off and scramble away. Panting. Trying to get enough air into my lungs. There's pain where she scratched my face. Pain where she tried to strangle me. She stands over me, heaving with rage, eyes ablaze.

She jerks. Straightens. Eyes wide. Arms like planks at her side. Then she falls.

General Lall is standing over her, the long rod of the court official's taser in one hand.

'Thanks,' I say.

General Lall looks at Janek lying on the marble floor of the courtroom, one leg bent underneath her, hair falling over her face.

'It's you . . . how?' Janek groans up at General Lall.

The general tasers her again.

NIK

Sirens.

My lungs burn like I've swallowed lava.

The lights in the courtroom are flashing. Janek's voice saying, 'No one can know what we did, Harveen.'

Don't know whether it's real or in the memory being streamed. Above me, there's the skylight of the courtroom, but – thank God – no glass box any more. Was just about done for. Then there was a moment when everything seemed to get sucked down into the bottom of the stand. When I opened my eyes, the walls and ceiling holding the gas in here with me were gone, and I was lying on the floor.

Esther stares at me. Her eyebrows are knitted together. Then she's under my arm and my mother's under the other, and there's smoke swirling all round them.

'Took your time,' I croak, and my voice is like metal.

They pull me into the throng of people who're all running for the exits. We take marble steps down, people slipping and leaving behind their stupid shoes. Everyone's careening downstairs. Seems like the whole building's running for it, not just the people in my courtroom. There's a judge in a long gown among them. A guard in a Coaly uniform. Loads and loads of people in suits.

No security at the front of the building any more. Apparently, there's only so much danger the guards are willing to put up with, and a terrible-smelling smoke bomb couldn't keep them at their posts.

By the time we get out on to the street, I'm feeling almost like I can walk under my own power. Esther and my mother seem to know where they're going. We get to the edge of the crowd of people who fled the courtroom – gasping for breath and looking back at the building and vomming on to the pavement. We keep going. Down a side street. My mother lets her hair down. Esther takes off the suit jacket that looks suspiciously like something Harveen would wear, and shoves it into a bush as we pass. My mother presses a baseball cap on to my head, partially covering the lenses that I've still got pressed horribly to my eyes.

There's a truck on the opposite side of the street, and, as we start to cross, a man gets out and circles the front to open the passenger door for us. My mother climbs in. Me behind. Esther last.

The driver's back in the front, and then the engine's purring, and we're driving along the road as though we're any other Federated States citizens.

Esther peels the sticky strips from my head. I try to pull the lenses from my eyes.

'Hold on,' Esther says. She stares like she's trying to figure out what they did, then finally she pokes her finger right into my eye. I try not to retch. She pulls the first lens from my eyeball, long wires trailing goo and blood. 'Animals,' she mutters, dropping the lenses and their wires out of the truck window.

I rub my eyes and blink.

'They told me you were all dead.'

Esther doesn't say anything. Her face is set, and she's got the same expression as my mother. Hard. Like the only way she can deal with all of this is if she makes herself as unyielding as the thing she's fighting against.

By the time it's dark, we're driving through the comfortable houses of the suburbs. We stop for petrol at a service station where the city meets the trees. My mother fills the tank while Esther inspects my throat. She gives me service-station painkillers washed down with Coke. None of us say much. I wake up a few times and find the driver has switched places with my mother, or the radio's playing, or they're whispering. The Federated States flashes by outside the window. The big roads lit from above by towering street lights. The small ones only visible because of the truck's headlights.

It feels like we've been forgotten. Maybe whatever happened back there means they've got bigger fish to fry. Maybe they aren't interested any more.

It's after midnight when the floodlights of the northern border checkpoint come into view. There's a wall, two storeys high and made of solid concrete. The road passes through, to a small windowed building. Cars stop one at a time to wait for the barrier to be lifted. My mother's driving. She ties her hair back.

'Pretend to be asleep,' she says over her shoulder. 'If our papers don't get us through, be ready to run. We're not going back.'

Esther arranges a blanket over us and drops her head on to my shoulder. She holds my hand underneath the rough checked wool.

The truck pulls up at the checkpoint, and there's a wave of cold air as my mother winds down the window. A voice says, 'Documentation.'

'Good evening, officer,' my mother replies.

There's the rustle of papers as she hands things over to the border guard. Then a patch of held breath, silence so tense it feels like a balloon about to burst. Esther squeezes my fingers – my bones creak.

The truck moves again.

We're out.

EPILOGUE

ESTHER

The ship makes its steady way across the horizon. The *Jewel of Innisfree* is a small vessel compared with the *Arcadia*. Just a few hundred passengers aboard. A stream of smoke rises from one of the funnels on top, and I already know that her engine's having trouble. It's OK. We'll go out there in tiny two-person boats and get the people off one by one if we have to.

'Hello, stranger.' A voice comes from behind me.

I turn to find Nik standing a few metres away.

I run to him, and he hugs me, rocking side to side so we almost slip on the damp grass. Everything smells of ocean and early summer. It rained overnight, the drops pinging against the corrugated roof of the temporary house I'm staying in – so loud and for so long I couldn't sleep. At least that's what I blamed for my insomnia.

Nik kisses me. I let my hands go to the back of his neck and submit to the dizzying breathlessness of the moment.

'We weren't expecting you for another hour,' I say close to his mouth, our foreheads still touching, Nik's arms tight round my waist.

Epilogue

'I've been away three months. As soon as we got close enough, I jumped on a little transport boat. Couldn't wait any longer.'

'How's it looking on there?' I ask.

The *Jewel*'s had a longer journey than most of the ships. Rough seas. Broken engine followed by a couple of weeks adrift while Nik tried to fix the thing. It took them a while to make it.

He gives a tiny shrug. 'Same as the rest. Malnourishment. Scurvy. And the lice are a problem.' He pauses and scratches his head. 'Let's just say you've got your work cut out for you when you get people settled and start looking them over. They're hopeful though, and that's not nothing.'

'We're ready. The new houses were finished yesterday. Corp and I spent the day restocking the clinic. They'll be comfortable here until the Maine government finds them somewhere more permanent.'

We start walking along the path that snakes down to the camp, Nik's arm resting over my shoulder. When we arrived, we found the Maine authorities had set aside an old army base. Row upon row of ticky-tacky houses with running water and heating and real furniture. The other ships – the reinforcements that were so hoped for, but never arrived – were already here. While we were dealing with Janek in the camp, the remaining ships had fled the Federated States one after another, finally reaching the safety of Maine.

Nik keeps his arm round me as we leave the path and walk between the houses. They're rough, that's for sure. Built fifty years ago to house the families of enlisted soldiers. But, after the camp, this place is luxury.

Epilogue

The house at the end of the row is mine. The outside is painted a dirty yellow colour. The windows are small and a pain to open. The front door sticks every time.

'Mrs Huang's making dinner for us tonight,' I say. 'Everyone wants to see you.'

Nik stops in his tracks and turns to face me. 'Esther,' he says. He shakes his head, hair falling over his eyes. Even with the neat haircut of a Maine liaison officer, Nik still manages to bring the scruffy ex-ship-kid vibe.

'It's time you buried the hatchet. This vendetta has gone on long enough. And you know it'll be a good feed if his mum's cooking.'

'Doesn't matter how many times you try to make us friends, me and Patrick Huang are never gonna work. Pat's never gonna stop being jealous,' Nik says. 'Neither am I, for that matter.'

I run my thumb over his knuckles. 'You'll both have to get used to it. Neither of you are going anywhere.'

I push the front door of my house open with my shoulder. Even after three months, I'm still surprised to see the two people on the settee. My mum and dad. They look more worn than before. My dad's hair has thinned to almost nothing on top. The bags under my mum's eyes never disappear. They both turn to me, and I know immediately something's happened.

'They've put him on trial,' my mum says.

She turns back to the old-fashioned screen that's attached to the wall opposite the sofa. Dad uses the clicker to turn the sound up.

My chest feels like there's a rope tied tight round it. I can't take a full breath. Me and Nik move so that we're standing behind my parents. I lean on the back of the sofa because I don't think my legs will support me.

A news programme blinks on the screen. Barney King's familiar face takes up most of the picture, and behind him the dark crashing waves of the ocean.

'President Atwal announced today the opening of the Federated States' first nautical exile facility,' he says.

The screen transitions to a clip of Harveen. She's standing on a podium in front of the White House, waving and smiling.

None of us know exactly what happened in the hours that followed Nik's trial. Janek died in Coaly custody within the week – a heart attack, the official reports said. Soon after the announcement that Harveen was the new president-elect, President Walsh was killed in a freak fall from a White House balcony. The kind of accident where everyone seems to shrug and say, 'Well, that was weird,' and then move on to something else without giving it too much thought.

Harveen disappears, and Barney King is on screen again.

I think I'm going to be sick.

'This controversial initiative will see criminals and immigrants detained aboard disused container ships, with minimal supervision from the Federated States,' Barney King says.

The image cuts to a motorboat tied to a dockside. A line of orange-clad prisoners, shackled together by the ankles, climbs carefully aboard. I know him instantly. His head is shaved and the prison uniform sags from thin shoulders, but still I'd be able to spot him in a crowd. Alex inches his way aboard the boat using his tied hands for balance.

Epilogue

Barney continues in voiceover. 'Perhaps the most famous person to be housed aboard the first exile ship is Alex Hudson, ex-ship inhabitant and Federated States agent who went on trial earlier today charged with multiple counts of treason and murder.'

The boat shoves off. Alex looks directly into the camera. Directly at me. He's still fixated on the camera when the boat finally lifts over a wave and disappears from view. In the background, the silhouette of the massive prison ship breaks the horizon.

Mum and Dad turn to me. My mum's eyes are wide with worry. I wipe the tears from my cheeks with the flat of my hand. 'Good riddance,' I say finally. I take the remote out of my dad's hand and turn the screen off.

There's a knock at the front door, then Corp's voice. 'Knock-knock. Good to have you back, Nik.'

'Corp,' Nik replies, giving her a nod. I squeeze Nik's arm. He's trying to forgive her, but I wonder if things will ever be right between them again.

'Esther, they're here,' Corp says.

'I'll see you at dinner,' I say to Nik. 'Non-negotiable.'

'Fine,' he grumbles.

I stretch on tiptoe to drop a kiss on his cheek, then follow Corp outside. The sun's warming up, and the ground is already losing its layer of dew.

Corp hooks her arm into mine as we head to the clinic, a squat white building at the far edge of the camp. 'I got the job in Nova Scotia,' she says.

'Congratulations,' I say. 'When do you leave?'

'Three days.'

Epilogue

'That soon. I'll miss you.'

'I'll miss you too. But it's time for me to go. There's too much to remind me of the ship here. I need a fresh start.'

We stop when the clinic comes into view. The door's open, and it's packed with raggedy people spilling out into the street.

'Do you ever think about moving on?' Corp says.

There's a kid with long matted locks tearing into a protein bar just outside the clinic. I don't get a chance to answer before Corp's striding off to him, warning him to eat slowly or risk being sick.

There's no fence here. We're not surrounded by ocean. I can go anywhere in the world, but the longer I stay the less desire I have to escape. For the first time, I have everything I need.

ACKNOWLEDGEMENTS

Thank you to all the amazing readers who have made my debut year such a rollercoaster. I appreciate every review – good and bad – every copy bought or borrowed, every tweet, post and comment. Thank you for coming to my events when I was terrified no one would, and being interested when I feared my book would sink without trace.

Thank you to Tom Rawlinson for your unwavering support and excitement for the world of *The Stranded*. I'm so grateful for your insight and that you pushed me to take a more challenging route with the book. I'm glad that you made me write the events and relationships that I was intimidated by. I'm a better writer having worked with you.

The Stranded series could not exist without the work of the team at PRH and I'm hugely grateful to Chloe Parkinson, Jannine Saunders and Sarah Connelly, as well as the cover artists and designers, proofreaders and sensitivity readers who all had a hand in bringing this project to fruition. Thanks also to Nina Douglas for looking after me on the Penguin Platform YA Roadtrip.

Acknowledgements

Thank you to my wonderful agent Felicity Blunt, Rosie Pierce and the team at Curtis Brown for your continued support throughout the process.

Over the past year the amazing women of my critique group have supported me through self-doubt and have been there to celebrate my successes. Carly Reagon, Asha Hick, Emma Clark Lam, Joanne Clague – I continue to be thankful to have you in my life. Your creativity and kindness is astounding.

Thank you, family, for putting up with another year of my writing obsession, for ignoring it when I stare into space, and for visiting *The Stranded* in every book shop we come across.